I0819931

Alien Hitman

The Euclidian:

Alien Hitman

Jay Cannon

The Euclidian: Alien Hitman

Copyright © 2018 Jay Cannon (JC) and Morgan Gendel

All rights reserved. Printed in the United States of America. No part of this book may be used, reproduced, distributed or transmitted in any form or by any means whatsoever or stored in a database retrieval system without written permission except in those cases of brief quotations embodied in critical articles and reviews.

This is a work of fiction. Names, characters, places, and incidents either are the product of the author's imagination or are used fictitiously.

First Edit: Joel David Palmer

Second edit: Verlene kelsey

Writing consultant: Rose Ragsdale

Cover art: Illustration © 2017, Milan "Shebushei" Mrdjenovic

Book design and formatting: Cheryl Perez

Final edit: Courtney McDermott

For more information, contact the author at:
EuclidianBook@gmail.com JayCannonAuthor.com
@TheEuclidian

Second edition: May 2018

For my niece Erica Cage and all those grappling with writing their first book. Just do it!

Prologue

As he strode through the portal leading to the sports arena deep in the bowels of the resource extraction vessel, *Andrea*, Captain Chaell Shisal took in the crowds that filled the stands ringing the open space. Seated near the captain's personal box, a bunch of regulars alternately cheered and jeered the combatants battling on the arena floor in contests of skill and aggression. They stood to salute the captain with warm smiles as he passed their seats, and he returned the same.

Tall for a Euclidian, Shisal had the muscular body, tough beige skin and bony skull ridges typical of his race. His rugged features, marred by only a few battle scars, and towering frame drew every eye when he entered a room.

Shisal and his bodyguard, Pheebee, climbed the steps to the booth and slipped effortlessly into a couple of comfortable armchairs. A pair of stewards waited patiently to take their orders for refreshments.

Old habits died hard for Shisal, who ran the *Andrea* like a military vessel. A native of the planet Euclidia, which was the head of the Euclidian alliance of planets, Shisal once led a space fighter squadron for the military. But having to send every major decision up his chain of command to get it validated before being allowed to act pushed him to the limits of his patience. The one time he acted on his own initiative, he was hailed as a hero by the populace. But his senior officers did not sanction Shisal's actions, so they set out to make him pay for his insubordination. He finally resigned his command to take the helm of the *Andrea*, a Euclidian mineral resource extraction vessel.

Though the *Andrea* was a civilian operation, Shisal adhered to military protocol in running the ship, except in the off-duty complex where crewmembers could indulge their needs for entertainment and recreation. The ship's designers placed the arena at the heart of the entertainment venues on the *Andrea*, in close proximity to the most populated areas of the ship.

Wearing a specially designed uniform, Shisal also required the ship's personnel to don uniforms when they reported for duty. Though even his casual jumpsuits bore the distinctive insignia of a ship's captain, Shisal's subordinates only wore patches with the *Andrea*'s logo, embossed with special icons denoting the wearer's occupation and department aboard the vessel when they were off duty.

At the helm of the *Andrea,* Shisal was free to rule the ship as he saw fit, including disciplining and even executing members of his crew. Though he was a tough captain, Shisal had never abused his power; instead, he worked hard to treat everyone equitably, regardless of their race or origin.

Most of the *Andrea*'s crew was Euclidian, like Shisal, but the ship also employed individuals from other planets in the alliance. Two members of Shisal's elite security force, for example, hailed from the Ossuary System and his personal bodyguard came from the Delta quadrant.

As Shisal relaxed after ordering his usual Marnician hinsar juice, one for himself and one for Pheebee, he noticed Adar, his favorite fighter and one of the two Ossies in his crew, engaged in a match across the sand. The captain had watched Adar, a seasoned fighter and wily combatant, overcome his opponents numerous times, both in the arena and in actual combat against space pirates.

While the Ossie could come across as a loose cannon, he also exhibited the loyalty and ruthlessness that Shisal needed in an enforcer.

The arena's sports commentator announced the captain's arrival over a loudspeaker, and Shisal stood to wave to the crowd in a tradition handed down from the captains of ancient sailing vessels that once roamed Euclidia's vast seas.

***

A giant digital roof covered the space, displaying a daytime view of a sun arcing across a wide expanse of sky dotted with scattered clouds that broke up the direct, simulated sunlight.

High wooden walls bordered the arena's large, round space, making it difficult for a combatant to escape an overpowering opponent. Various nonlethal weapons hung on the interior walls of the compound. Combatants used the weapons at their discretion to pummel or maim an opponent into submission.

But no fighter was allowed to kill another, under the ship's rules. Sickbay attendants tended to the arena's casualties, nursing them to recovery as quickly as possible. This allowed both the victors and the vanquished to hone their fighting skills without fear of dire consequences.

To mimic the esthetics of similar ancient venues on the home planet, the arena's floor was covered with a mix of dirt and sand. Lit torches in wall sconces broke up any shadows created by fighters. Most of the spectators watched the contests from wooden benches perched on risers above the walls.

Sweat, blood and urine stained the arena floor, a visual patchwork that matched the stench rising in the air. Though unpleasant, the smells ratcheted up the excitement spectators felt watching the fighting. Hawkers added to the carnival atmosphere, offering all manner of drinks, food and narcotics in the stands.

***

In the middle of the arena three figures engaged in an intense contest drew the attention of the crowd. Two large males pounded away on a smaller one with rigid fists, drawing a cacophony of cheers and jeers from the people packing the stands.

Dust swirled upward from the floor of the arena, sticking to the sweaty bodies of the combatants, filling the air with a gritty closeness that added to the reality of the spectacle. In the stands, the audience ate, drank, placed bets, and interacted with others via an interstellar social media system.

Just when the smaller combatant, Adar, looked to be down for the count, he leapt up, grabbed one of the larger fighters by an arm and flung him against the wall of the arena, knocking him out.

***

In the captain's box, Pheebee sat on the edge of her seat, flexing her muscles in reaction to each blow as it landed. Clearly, she wanted nothing more than to join the fighters in the arena.

Pheebee, a tall, slender, former soldier devoted her free time away from the ship to arena fighting. Still, she exuded a femininity that, along with her striking features, invariably attracted males of several species until they ran head-first into her abrasive attitude. The only times she allowed a male to get close to her was when she brutalized her challengers in an arena.

"I don't see why I can't have time in the arena every once in a while," she complained to Shisal.

"Because you are supposed to be protecting me, which you can't do if you're in the midst of a fight," he patiently explained for the umpteenth time.

"You are well-protected up here away from the crowd, with the ship's security system monitoring your every move.".

"Tell that to my predecessor, may he rest in peace," Shisal said. "Fortune and power are great motivators. You certainly aren't here for your health."

"I earn what I make, and I'm not with you for the power. It's just a job for me," Pheebee insisted, her temper rising at what Shisal implied.

Ironically, base compensation for the *Andrea's* crew was little more than a pittance. However, currency or credits of any kind were unnecessary aboard the ship, as crewmembers had every need met by the mining company as part of their pay. In addition to dining, exercise and sleeping quarters, the ship maintained the entertainment venues, which enabled the crewmembers to relax onboard during downtimes. Still, most of the *Andrea's* vast interior was devoted to the storage of various minerals in the all-important cargo bays.

Off the ship, a worker's base pay didn't stretch far enough to provide even a modest livelihood. But when the *Andrea* successfully delivered large quantities of high-quality minerals to market, every crewmember received a generous share of profits lucrative enough to provide them with a comfortable life, and in some cases, even allow them to retire.

The mining missions, however, were dangerous. It hadn't happened often, but members of the *Andrea*'s crew had been killed in accidents and in skirmishes with pirates seeking to raid the vessel. The entire ship could conceivably be lost in space. Still, individuals from across Euclidian space regularly applied for available berths aboard the *Andrea.* The low wages and inherent dangers of the job failed to deter these eager prospects who considered resource mining in space a promising path to adventure and great wealth.

"But Pheebee, you benefit from your position with me, nonetheless. The contacts you make, the invitations to events and offers of gifts would not happen otherwise." Shisal gave her a knowing wink, hoping to soothe her growing irritation.

"I'd leave tomorrow if something more advantageous came my way," she replied, pouting. She jumped to her feet, almost daring Shisal to object and give her an excuse to quit.

Pheebee presented a defiant front, but inside she was mindful of the debt she owed the captain for saving her life and giving her a job. She wouldn't really leave him unless she was seriously provoked.

Still, the Deltan remained aloof, knowing she eventually would have to leave Shisal to return to her planet to join the resistance fighting against the Alphas who occupied Delta.

"Look at that!" barked Shisal, his attention returning to Adar's fight.

In the arena, his remaining opponent charged the Ossie. Adar quickly launched himself into the air, executing a spinning kick that planted a foot squarely in the oncoming attacker's chest, knocking him to the ground. He then grabbed the larger fighter's foot and wielded his leg like a club to repeatedly slam the fellow's body against the floor of the arena with no more apparent effort than it took to toss a sack of grain.

Before long, he dropped the fellow, leaving him a bloody mess with cuts and abrasions all over his body. The defeated fighter rolled to his knees, gasping for air and tapped out. The crowd gasped in shock, and then erupted in applause and cheers.

"You didn't have to be so brutal with me," the combatant growled, glaring up at Adar.

"If you don't like being banged up, stay out of the arena," the cocky little fighter replied, extending his hand with his thumb downward toward the kneeling figure. "You don't see Goron complaining."

Goron was the fighter Adar took out earlier in the match by slamming him against the arena wall.

"That's because I'm a Euclidian soldier, and he's a communications officer." Goron said, still struggling to recover his breath from his earlier defeat by Adar.

Goron and Adar had opposed each other in several arena fights and fought side by side on past missions. The arena gave them a way to maintain battle readiness, while the third combatant in today's contest was merely fulfilling a fantasy of going toe-to-toe with real soldiers without risking his life. Adar had little respect for such wannabes. He longed for true battle, where life and death hung in the balance.

All three combatants, two of them Euclidian, had served aboard the *Andrea* for years. Adar belonged to a race of warriors with a fierce tradition of fighting among themselves. Still, the Ossies banded together to oppose the Euclidian when the invaders arrived on their planet. Eventually, the Euclidian signed a truce with the Ossies. The little aliens typically exhibited great strength relative to their small body mass. That, along with exceptional fighting abilities, made the Ossuarians formidable foes and nearly invincible in arena fights. For that reason, Adar often chose to fight multiple opponents at one time.

After the match, Adar joined the captain in his booth.

"Good job in the arena, as usual. You have amazing fighting ability, Adar," Shisal praised the Ossie, striking him in the chest with his fist.

"So far, I've been unbeatable." Adar mimicked the gesture by pounding his own chest. "I don't think anyone on this ship can beat me."

"I'd love to get into the arena with you to disprove that boast," interjected Pheebee, thinking back to the time she defeated another Ossie in a battle of honor for the captain. That contest became legend across the mining fleet.

"Why do you have this Delta guarding you and not an Ossie?" Adar asked, his misogynistic upbringing showing.

Adar grew up on a planet where females led lives mostly subservient to their mates. Pheebee's home, however, was a planet where society mimicked the life of spiders. The female was the stronger member of the Delta species and fought to defend her home, while the frailer Deltan male typically stayed home and cared for the young.

"I'm quite up to the challenge, and less violent," Pheebee retorted, itching to prove that her legendary win against an Ossie wasn't a fluke. "Your fighting skills are pretty impressive, Ossie, but I could beat you blindfolded."

That likely was no hollow boast. Deltans, who grew up in the dark conditions on the island of Arubia where Pheebee was born and raised, had uncommonly keen senses, giving them the ability to perceive details of their surroundings with their eyes closed. She often fought blindfolded to ensure that she retained this ability.

Adar turned to face Pheebee. *What is it with these Delta women? They just don't know their place.* Adar considered this silently. *Just because females are the dominant gender on her planet, doesn't give Pheebee the right to challenge me. Does she think she can beat me like she did my other countryman?* Chuckling inwardly, he thought, *She's in for a rude surprise.*

"I've got time right now, if you'd like to jump into the arena," he said, eager to deliver the comeuppance he believed the Deltan female deserved.

"I'd love to, shorty," hissed Pheebee, leaning toward Adar as if straining against an invisible leash.

Shisal watched the exchange between Adar and Pheebee without comment. He liked to let crewmembers settle their own differences, but the feud between these two might have gone too far. If he didn't find both of them extremely beneficial to the mission, he would kick one of them off the ship.

The *Andrea* followed a strict schedule and had more mining stops planned for this mission. The captain also made commitments for contracted deliveries once the *Andrea* returned to port on Euclidia.

Shisal was focused on completing the current mining operation. His mining officers performed their jobs with care and precision, reflecting both long years of experience and an awareness of the significance of only collecting the highest possible quality of minerals and only those in high demand.

***

As the Euclidian expanded their presence across the galaxy, they encountered other sentient beings. Most were fairly primitive, like the humans who lived on the Sol-orbiting planet called Earth, their next mining target, and posed no threat to the invaders. The Euclidian typically mined a planet and then established an outpost on the planet's surface before moving on to their next target.

Some years ago, the Euclidian encountered societies of advanced sentient beings in the Alpha and Delta systems. These alien races had developed space travel, though not to the technical proficiency of the Euclidian. Thanks to exceptional diplomacy, the three races managed to co-exist peacefully for more than two years, until the Alphas launched a surprise attack against the Euclidian in an effort to destroy the invaders and seize control of their technology.

During the short war that ensued, Alphas killed millions of Euclidian while suffering only minimal casualties. Shisal lost several close comrades in his squadron during the war. Eventually, the two sides reached a truce. Years later, Shisal led a surprise attack against the Alphas and destroyed their home planet. The action made him a hero back home, but also a target of surviving Alphas seeking revenge. The Alphas, nonetheless, remained in the alliance to avoid being isolated and to retain access to the Euclidian markets.

Returning his attention to his two antagonistic crewmembers, Shisal wondered whether he should send Adar away on an assignment where he could let off some steam.

"That's not going to happen, you two," the captain said, stepping between the Ossie and the Deltan. "I need Pheebee to keep me secure, and you need to prepare for our next stop, Adar. I want you down on the planet during the handoff of the prisoners."

Adar dreaded boring assignments like that, but still favored the work over being stuck on the ship.

"I guess you got lucky this time, Ossie," said Pheebee, as she moved away from Adar and returned to the captain's side.

"Captain, the mining is completed." The XO's voice came over the captain's communicator, breaking into the tense exchange. "All of the mining vehicles have been stowed, and we are ready to leave orbit."

"Great, set aside 50 kilograms of gold ore to be transferred to the prison and open a portal to the Alpha prison planet. Adar, prepare for departure and meet me on the bridge."

"Aye, aye, Captain," said Adar, stalking away in a huff.

"Pheebee, let's head to the bridge," Shisal said.

"I'm right with you, Captain," the bodyguard responded, falling into step behind Shisal, but her eyes remained locked on Adar as he left the arena.

***

When the *Andrea* reached its next stop, the Alpha prison planet, Shisal gave orders to prepare a shuttle to transport him and his security detail, including Adar, to the planet's surface.

After a short flight, Shisal exited the shuttle and was immediately flanked by Pheebee and Adar.

Ahnbar Tulmolt, director of the prison, rushed forward to meet the captain and his party. They spoke in Euclidian, the language of commerce for all alliance members.

"Greetings, Captain Shisal. Please come this way," Tulmolt said, his wide mouth opening and closing repeatedly in excitement.

The short, pudgy Alpha gestured for Shisal to precede him as they walked toward the director's office, chatting.

Alphas had soft human-like skin, but their small, bright eyes, perched above pronounced snouts in rounded faces, gave their features an ursine quality that brought to mind the look of a child's teddy bear. However, despite their benign appearance, the devious nature of the Alphas made them pariahs across the galaxy.

Tulmolt's appearance did not affect Shisal one way or another. He had come to the prison planet to complete a business transaction, not to make friends.

"Greetings, Director Tulmolt. This is my bodyguard, Pheebee, and security officer, Adar, who will be heading up security for the prison transfer," said the captain, as he joined the Alpha in strolling toward the prison offices.

"An Ossie. I don't suspect you'll lose any prisoners with him around," the director told Shisal, ogling Adar with wide eyes. "I am surprised you would bring a Delta to our planet though. They're pretty hostile to us," he added, throwing an uneasy glance at Pheebee.

"What do you expect? You Alphas took over our planet and enslaved my people." Pheebee fairly spat the comment as she struggled to hide her virulent distaste for the Alpha.

"If your people had stayed out of our war, you wouldn't have been enslaved."

"After you defeated the Euclidian, it would have only been a matter of time before you came after us," Pheebee retorted, taking a single step toward the director, ready to push her verbal sparring match with Tulmolt into a more satisfying physical confrontation.

But Shisal also moved forward, throwing out a hand to bar Pheebee's path.

"Let's not open old wounds," he suggested mildly. Hoping the hostile energy that spilled into the director's office with the little group would dissipate, Shisal changed the subject.

"Do you have our 20,000 prisoners ready, director?" he asked.

"Yes, Captain. They're coded and ready for transfer. Be aware that you will need to increase their dosage of 'Serenity,' or they could become unruly during the voyage. The work here keeps their minds occupied and away from negative thoughts."

"I'll take that into account. We'll use our mining vehicles to transport the prisoners to our ship. Your payment will be brought down in the first vehicle."

"Excellent. I'll have my people meet the craft and transfer the gold to our storage area. Releasing so many prisoners is going to leave us a bit shorthanded down here." Tulmolt pouted in a bid for sympathy.

"Then you should tell your law enforcement officers to start arresting more people." Shisal smirked. "Do you have any entertainment on the premises? I'd like to give my crew some shore leave while we're here."

"We have a few places here to keep our staff happy. But they're not big enough to accommodate your crew. As you can imagine, we don't get many visitors here," Tulmolt explained, his expression regretful.

"No problem. I'll stagger their leave over several periods until everyone on the ship is satiated."

Clapping a hand on the director's shoulder, he added, "Let's grab a drink, Tulmolt, and talk about how we do more business going forward."

"Be happy to, Shisal. Be happy to," Tulmolt murmured, rubbing his hands together as a greedy smile wreathed his chubby face.

***

Four prisoners watched as others trooped onto the shuttles, waiting for the right moment to make their break for freedom.

Rosda, a chemist and leader of the group, was imprisoned after running an illegal mining operation. She designed a drug cocktail in the form of a pill that circumvented the effects of the pacifying Serenity. While they had no inkling of the ship's final destination, the foursome knew they did not want to remain in prison nor become captives of the Euclidian.

"These foolish Euclidian only have a few guards watching us," observed Rosda. "They think we are sheep like the rest of these Alpha weaklings. As soon as they turn away, we make our move without hesitation. Got it?" she instructed the others quietly, but firmly.

Her three companions nodded in agreement, fearful of attempting to escape but craving freedom even more. As the guards shifted their attention to the front of the prisoner line, the four escapees ducked and fled.

Part I

Chicago

Chapter 1

The Cheoili Break into Prison

On the outskirts of Beakar, the capitol city of the Alpha planet of Moorland, on the top floor of a large warehouse, members of the Juban gang–headed by Fosta Juban–tabulated the gang's haul for the week. Several guards protected access to the tabulation room, but for the most part, accountants filled the space.

Moorland was a planet located in the Norma Arm of the Milky Way Galaxy, the same as Euclidia, but several light years away. It became the most populated planet in the Alpha system after the Euclidian military destroyed the Alphas' home planet. A Euclidian shuttle stopped at Moorland several times a day bringing visitors from various points across the Euclidian Alliance of planets. Some came seeking adventure. Others came seeking fortune. A trifling few arrived seeking to make a name for themselves as criminals.

Moorland was lush with animal life, vegetation and plenty of fresh water, and it remained unpolluted by industry. Being newly inhabited, the planet's air was still clean and heavy with the smell of wildflowers and decomposing vegetation. Aware of what can happen to a planet after decades of bad planning and environmental disasters, organizers of Moorland's newly formed government placed strong ecological restrictions on all merchants and manufacturers doing business on Moorland.

A growing population and bustling commerce, however, brought with it crime and those aspiring to rise to the top of the criminal world. Fosta Juban was one such miscreant, a walking and talking parasite who made his living by taking from others.

Juban's accountants sat at sturdy, wooden desks covered in money, loot and receipts. In one corner of the room, appraisers placed prices on jewelry, devices and other goods obtained by gang members through nefarious means. The appraisers and accountants wore nice suits and carried calculators instead of guns, relying on heavily armed guards inside and outside of the room for their safety.

Cameras in the ceiling surveilled all activities in the room. Reinforced panes protected the windows. The guards kept an eye out for possible threats coming from the outside as well as possible pilfering from the inside. For the most part, the guards outside the counting room in the warehouse had pretty boring jobs, considering they hadn't had to act on anything for more than a year.

"Excellent collection of goods we got in today, everyone." The head accountant praised the others, after tallying the day's receipts. "Look at these stacks of money, gold, jewelry, and devices. Whoever said crime doesn't pay was a lousy criminal."

Everyone obligingly laughed at the supervisor's lame attempt at humor.

While the occupants of the room indulged in the light moment, an aerial speeder pulled up to a second-story window of the warehouse. The visitors' approach in the dark went undetected by the guards. Three figures quickly exited the vehicle, removed the window and climbed inside before making their way to an elevator.

Two guards protected the door to the tabulation room. At the opposite end of the wide, well-lit corridor in front of them, elevator doors opened and out walked three individuals. As they moved forward, their boots clumped heavily on the wooden floor, sending echoes ahead of them down the hallway. This should have signaled trouble to the guards. Instead, the duo didn't react until one of the strangers, resembling their boss, greeted them, as did his two associates.

"Gentlemen, how goes it?" asked the Fosta Juban imposter, impeccably dressed in typical mob boss attire–a pink, starched Nehru shirt with a finely woven burgundy suit, complete with lapel pin signifying his credentials as a mob boss. The impostor gave the guards a stern stare, silently communicating that he came to do business and not to exchange pleasantries. Still, his greeting had been civil.

"Great haul this week, boss," ventured the friendlier of the two guards, nervously.

"Open up for me," the fake Juban ordered, dismissing the two with a quick glance. This signaled an end to the small talk.

"Sure thing, boss," said the first guard, turning to unlock the door.

A whiff of a flowery scent reached the nostrils of the other guard, begging him to take a closer look at the three visitors. A quick scan of their eyes and skin texture gave them away as interlopers. But before the guard could retrieve his weapon, two of the imposters covered his mouth to muffle his cries and stabbed him repeatedly. The other guard, meanwhile, disengaged the lock and opened the door. The third intruder pulled the remaining guard back from the doorway and stabbed him to death before he could raise the alarm.

All three imposters, who migrated from the Cheoili System, possessed the chameleon-like ability to change their looks and coloration. This enabled them to fool the guards into thinking their boss made an impromptu visit. The disguise isn't foolproof though. The Cheoili's eyes and odor could give them away. The Alpha guards made a fatal mistake by failing to notice in time.

The three assailants entered the counting room and moved quickly to flank the internal guards before they could suspect deception. The trio drew their weapons and started blasting away. They killed everyone in the room, shot up the place, and dropped a note that left little doubt that the carnage and theft were acts of war by a rival gang. The note read:

What's yours is now mine!

Tinsal

Filling their bags with Juban's loot, the robbers scurried back to the open window where their speeder waited. But the shooting attracted more of Juban's men into the hallway outside the counting room. The Cheoili shot them, too, before speeding away to Rudi Tinsal's place. At Tinsal's they re-enacted the same scenario, except this time they impersonated Tinsal and his associates to gain entrance to his hideout. After killing everyone there and absconding with Tinsal's goods, they left another note. This one read:

What's yours is now mine!

Juban

With the speeder loaded with valuables taken from Juban and Tinsal, the three Cheoili siblings, Daloi, Dholi, and Tatan, headed to their hideout to lay low and weather the tempest created by their actions.

The three kept a modest-looking cabin in the woods several miles from the city. Beneath the cabin, they maintained an enormous basement with a reinforced bunker designed to protect them from an attack. This underground refuge also provided an escape route through tunnels linked to a personal spacecraft. The vehicle would enable them to get off the planet as a last resort if necessary.

"Was that amazing or what?" said Dholi, flopping onto the couch in the cabin's main room. "Look at all those bags of treasure. I am going to live the life I've always wanted." She grinned at the prospect, rubbing her hands together in satisfaction.

"We should tell Moyer the job is done so he knows it's okay to break up the party," said Tatan, their brother. "Not a bad idea to have our gang throw a party in a public place to give us an alibi. I checked our delayed video blog showing us enjoying the party. It went out as scheduled, which puts us in the clear. I'll move the loot into our space vessel, just in case something goes wrong."

"Tatan, you worry too much," said Dholi. "Can't we just enjoy looking at it for a few days?"

"You can go down to the ship any time you like and look at it. Taste it, run your feet through it, and whatever else turns you on," Tatan quipped, grabbing a bag. "Once the heat blows over, I'll distribute the loot, not a moment sooner. Until then, we need to be prepared to abandon this place in an instant. We have been poor too long to risk losing it all by being careless."

"Dholi, Tatan has a point. I don't want to be thrust into a situation that takes me away from you two again," Daloi said, giving her sister a hug. "Turn the vid-screen on so we can see the local news stream. Do a split-screen and filter Juban's and Tinsal's neighborhoods. I'd like to avoid any surprises. While you do that, I'll check in with Moyer," said Daloi, her no-nonsense tone curbing the high spirits of her siblings.

***

"Juban, Tinsal here. I got your message. Now listen to me loud and clear." Juban heard three gunshots go off in his earpiece. "Did you hear that okay, Juban?" Tinsal called from a club that Juban's people frequented. Tinsal had captured three of his rival's henchmen and executed them while Juban listened.

"Yes, I heard it," said Juban, his tone irritated even as dread stole over him. "What's that supposed to mean?"

"That I just whacked three of your guys, and I'm just getting started. This won't be over until your corpse is being devoured by my dogs!"

"What the hell is this about? I thought we had a truce."

Juban and Tinsal had a long history. The two grew up in the same neighborhood in the Flats, a poor suburb of Beakar. As youngsters, they played team sports together in school, until Tinsal's family moved to a wealthier neighborhood when his father earned a big promotion at work. Juban and Tinsal lost touch with each other until they both joined gangs in different parts of Beakar.

As their territories grew, the two gangs skirmished from time to time, leaving people dead on both sides. It wasn't until they ran into each other at a local bar in neutral territory that Juban and Tinsal realized they fought each other. They shared a few drinks that night and decided to collaborate, dividing up the city to squeeze territory from rival gangs.

The latest attacks came as a complete surprise and sparked a burning desire for revenge in both of them.

"We did until you attacked my place and stole my money."

"That never happened," denied Juban, bristling at the accusation that he had double-crossed his old friend.

"I have your note right here, asshole." Tinsal crumpled the paper near his mouthpiece so Juban could hear it rustling.

"Does it look like this one?" asked Juban, displaying the note left for him on the screen of his communicator.

"What the hell!" Tinsal gawked at the note Juban held in disbelief. "I didn't write that. Why the hell would I leave you a note? That's not even my handwriting."

"Exactly! We've been set up," said Juban, relieved that Tinsal now realized he would never break their truce.

"Who would be dumb enough to do that?" Tinsal scratched his head, partly from embarrassment and partly from amazement that anyone would be foolish enough to attack the two largest gangs in the city.

"One of the smaller gangs looking to take over more territory," Juban suggested. "Did you check your recordings?"

"Why would I bother when there's a note that makes things clear as day?" asked Tinsal, irritably.

"Look, you check yours, and I'll check mine. Let's reconnect in an hour," Juban said. His voice then dropped, roughening like it scraped over gravel. "Oh, and I will expect payment for my men that you just executed, after we get these assholes."

"I apologize for the misunderstanding. You'll be properly compensated, and you better believe the perpetrator will pay dearly for this," Tinsal replied quickly. He ended the call, his anger smoldering at being duped into betraying his childhood friend. *I'm going to make whoever did this suffer,* he vowed silently.

***

"Moyer, Daloi here. We're finished on our end. What are you hearing?" Moyer, one of Daloi's lieutenants, helped her set up the alibi. Daloi had confidence in her plan, but liked to verify every step of the way.

"First off, you are totally in the clear," Moyer reported. "Tinsal has already launched an attack against Juban. We suspect Juban will launch a counterattack, and things will escalate from there. My police contact just told me that law enforcement is investigating all the shootings as gang-on-gang violence."

"Good. You can end the party whenever you like. Just make sure everyone is accounted for. I don't want any of us implicated in the shootings."

"I'll take care of everything on my end, boss," Moyer said. "What's next on the agenda?"

"Keep everyone out of trouble," stressed Daloi. "No monkey business. I don't want to draw any undue attention to ourselves over the next few days. We'll be back once the heat dies down."

"Not to worry. See you soon," said Moyer, excited to be bringing down the two rival gangs that had refused to let him join. He could see his star rising in the underworld.

***

"Juban, what did you find out?"

"Someone impersonating me got the jump on my guys," said Juban. "The odd thing about it, the imposters had funny eyes."

"Same here. You know what that means, don't you?"

"The Cheoili twins."

"Yep, the twins. They've always been too greedy for their own good. They should have stayed on their own damn planet."

News about the unusual Cheoili twins spread quickly across the underworld soon after their arrival on Beakar. Natives of planet Cheoili, they have the ability to morph their appearance, a valuable trait for someone looking to become a successful criminal.

Averaging 1.73 meters in height, Cheoili humanoids have the ability to change the color of their skin as well as expand and contract the skin's cellular walls to closely mimic the shape and texture of any other species' skin.

The gangs of Beakar had enlisted the twins eagerly to help carry out their plans. Their brother, Tatan, played a minor role in any negotiations. But the gangs' plans soon went south as they found that the twins and their brother could not be trusted. Daloi, in particular, had too much ambition to settle for being the lackey of a mob boss.

"Since you already owe me one, why don't you take the lead on this, Tinsal?" said Juban, wanting to drive home the point that Tinsal's actions against him warranted some sort of retribution.

"No problem, I've already sent some of my people out looking for the Cheoili." Tinsal felt embarrassed, realizing that taking the lead would only be a down payment on what he owed his old friend.

“We should get law enforcement involved, too. Why use up all of our resources? I’ll call a contact of mine at the precinct.” Juban wanted to acknowledge Tinsal’s apparent remorse by showing his willingness to help, too.

“I’ll also pick up the twin’s lieutenant, Moyer, to see what he knows. I’m sure I can squeeze some info out of him,” Juban added, eager to start inflicting pain on the perpetrators of the attack.

The rival gangs, now working together, investigated the attacks on their offices. Normally not fans of law enforcement, they decided to share their intel with the local police to improve their chances of finding Daloi and Dholi. *It’s never a bad idea to get in the good graces of law enforcement by giving them violent criminals to put away*, Juban thought.

***

Daloi, Dholi, and Tatan relaxed at the cabin, confident investigations into their power play would turn up nothing that implicated them. Sitting in cushioned leather chairs around a large wooden table in the dining area, sharing a pitcher of Tammarian grog, the three began planning their next move when Daloi’s communicator rang.

“Daloi here,” she answered, apprehension making her voice tight.

“This is Tinsal. Do you mind stepping outside? Juban and I would like to discuss a recent irritation with you.”

“Hold on a minute, Tinsal.” Daloi whispered urgently to Dholi and Tatan. “Look outside, and tell me what you see!”

"Juban, Tinsal, and several of their people are outside. What should we do?" Tatan's voice squeaked in panic.

"You two get the ship ready. I'll see if I can reason with them," Daloi told her siblings, though she didn't expect to live long enough to escape.

"We're not leaving without you sis," said Dholi. Tatan nodded in agreement.

"Don't worry you two. No one's going to break us apart," Daloi said firmly. "Now go prepare the ship. I'll be right down once I take care of these clowns."

"Tinsal, what's the problem?" asked Daloi, infusing her voice with a nonchalance she didn't feel as she looked out the window.

"Why don't you step outside, so we can have a quick chat?" the gang leader purred, waving to Daloi with a fake smile on his round face.

"Forgive me, but you don't seem to be in a chatting mood. If this has anything to do with those shootings, just ask Moyer. He can confirm our participation in a blogging event all evening."

"Why don't you ask him yourself?" interjected Tinsal, losing patience and tossing the head taken from Moyer's corpse towards the house.

"That wasn't polite. We could have settled this without more bloodshed," said Daloi, wracking her brain for a way she could get out of the mess she created unscathed.

“Oh, we are way past the ‘shedding blood’ stage, Daloi. You better believe that once this is over, what’s yours will definitely be mine,” Tinsal said, using her own words against her.

“And mine,” chimed in Juban. “You have one minute to step outside with your siblings, or we’re coming in, blasting.”

“Hold on, you two,” said a police officer, stepping into view with several others. “This is a law enforcement matter. You civilians step back across the road. Daloi, this is Chief Barer. Everyone come out of the cabin now with your hands up, or we’ll knock down the door and drag you out.”

Daloi made an obscene gesture toward the police chief and stepped away from the window to join her siblings. Juban, Tinsal, and their people hurriedly retreated across the road to watch from a safe distance.

The chief ordered his officers to join him in front of the cabin. Moving to meet them in a crouch with a two-handed grip on his blaster, Barer paused to scrutinize Moyer’s head, turning to look at Juban and Tinsal who merely shrugged.

“Take down the door!” the chief shouted, returning his focus to the cabin. Seconds later, the building exploded in a giant fireball, incinerating all of the police officers. Within minutes, a small airship rose above the smoke and soared into the sky.

“Look, Juban, those bastards are getting away,” said Tinsal, shaking his fist at the spaceship as it quickly gained altitude and distance from the confrontation.

"They won't get far," said Juban. "I have a pirate ship in space that's on its way here. It should be able to intercept them. I'm just glad we didn't decide go in after them."

***

"Daloi, I'm sure that killing those police officers is not going to help our cause," said Tatan, worry clouding his pale yellow eyes.

"What did you expect me to do, invite the officers in for tea and crumpets while harboring a spaceship full of stolen goods in our basement?" Daloi demanded angrily. "Even if we avoided being arrested by the police without incident, there is no way we would have been able to get rid of Juban and Tinsal. You missed the part when they rolled Moyer's head up to the house."

"Did he have to be that damn obscene," said Dholi, her hand to her mouth as nausea swept over her.

"So what do we do now?" asked Tatan, who calmly checked his seat restraints.

"We go to the next planet in the Alpha quadrant, refuel, check the newsfeeds, and then we head to Euclidia. We can easily get lost there. The long-range sensors are clear. Let's get into hyper-sleep, so we can save our resources. I'll wake you once we arrive," Daloi said, her adrenaline from their narrow escape beginning to recede. Daloi placed her hand on the transparent covers of her siblings' sleep chambers as they closed and gave them each a smile before climbing into hers.

For six months, the ship sailed along in the splendid isolation of deep space. The three fugitives rested undisturbed in their sleep chambers, an automated system feeding them oxygen, water and all necessary nutrients, intravenously. But Juban's pirate ship finally intercepted them.

"What the hell's going on?" shouted Tatan, awakened by a jarring of his sleep chamber and loud beeping alarms.

"Someone's firing on us," said Daloi. "Now they're hailing us. Just be quiet, while I answer this. This is Daloi from the planet Cheoili," Daloi replied to the caller over the ship's communicator. "My siblings and I are taking a leisurely trip through the Alpha quadrant. What is your intention?"

"Cut the crap," said the pirate commander. "Juban told me you murdered several of our people, along with a group of police officers, and to bring you back dead or alive. What's your choice?"

"I suggest you back off before we disable your engines with our weapons," threatened Daloi.

"You are piloting a recreational vehicle. It has no weapons," the commander replied dryly, his tone laced with amusement at the feeble bluff.

"Fine, I choose death then, but you'll have to catch me first," shouted a defiant Daloi, engaging the small ship's gravitational engines. "Bye, bye, asshole."

The ship's sudden acceleration threw Dholi and Tatan against the bulkhead as the big engines kicked in. Caught by surprise, the pirates watched futilely as the Cheoili craft sped away.

"What happened?" asked a dazed Tatan, pulling himself off the floor.

"Sorry about that. I engaged the gravitational drive. We lost them for now, but that cost us a lot of energy. Uh oh, I got another blip on my screen. Damn! It's a military vessel. I don't think we'll be able to outrun them."

"What should we do?" Tatan asked, his muscles going rigid at news of yet another threat.

"It's still several days away. I'll head for an asteroid field and try to buy us some time. Get some rest. I'll wake you, if I need your help."

The bolder twin used every clever trick she knew to lose the pursuers, but nothing worked. The private spaceship had neither the speed nor maneuverability of a military cruiser. Though she reached an asteroid field before the heavily armed vessel caught up, the ploy only bought the trio a few additional days of freedom. Daloi, fearing they would soon be boarded, decided to wake Dholi and Tatan. Configured for long space voyages, the little craft contained an escape pod for use in emergencies where the vessel became inoperable.

"Sorry to wake you." Daloi roused her siblings from hyper-sleep for the second time. "We are probably going to be captured soon, and I need your help getting you two to safety. I can overload one of our engines and jettison it in the path of their ship. During the explosion, the two of you can get away with some of the money in the escape pod. Dholi, you load up the escape pod. Tatan, look for a place to send it. Hold on, I'm being hailed. I'll try to stall them while you prepare to evacuate."

Thumbing on the ship-to-ship communicator, Daloi answered the hail. “This is Daloi from the planet Cheoili. State your business,” she said, infusing her tone with a touch of indifference.

“This is Captain Kraton with the Alpha military police. You are wanted for murder and grand larceny. Shut down your engines and prepare to be boarded.”

“Those are all lies. We’ve been in space for several months and couldn’t possibly be guilty of those crimes,” Daloi cried.

“I’m not here to argue with you. If you are innocent, you will be cleared in court. Stop your vessel or be fired upon,” the Alpha commander countered. His military-grade fighting cruiser came equipped with weapons easily capable of destroying the Cheoili vessel. It also contained plenty of trained soldiers to overwhelm the trio if they had to board the Cheoili craft.

“Don’t fire, I’m slowing down now,” Daloi cried, before muting the ship’s communications. “Tatan! I need those coordinates for the escape pod! Dholi, when you finish loading the pod, bring our weapons up here. I want to be able to defend us, if they board the ship.”

“What guns? There are no guns on this ship,” Dholi shouted from below.

“What do you mean, there’s no guns? How are we supposed to protect ourselves?”

“It’s supposed to be an emergency spaceship, not an armored car,” Dholi retorted sarcastically. “We kept all of our guns in the cabin where we needed them. When we ran for the ship, we grabbed money and food. Things we would need in space.” I can’t believe you are giving me crap about not loading guns as if I had time to go through a packing list.

"Well I've got my gun, so at least I will be able to shoot back if I have to. What are you going to do if law enforcement or bandits are waiting for you when the pod lands?" Daloi asked, annoyed by her sibling's lack of forethought.

"If we survive the pod landing, I don't think we'll be able to walk, let alone engage in a shootout," snorted Dholi. "I'll tell you what. If we survive this stupid trip, the first thing I'm going to buy is a bunch of guns. Cause we don't need fuel, food or water on a long space voyage. We need GUNS!"

"Will you two stop fighting? I think I found something better than squeezing into an escape pod," said Tatan. A devious grin lit his countenance.

"What's that?" asked Daloi, hoping for a worthwhile response.

"There's a small planet near us. We could reach it in nine hours with the gravity drives." Tatan's brows arched in hopeful inquiry.

"If we do that, and there's no fuel on that planet, we'll be stuck there," Daloi argued.

"I'd rather take my chances being stuck there than in prison or dead," Tatan retorted, hoping Daloi would embrace his suggestion.

"Okay, punch in the coordinates. We can use the gravity from that planet to give us an extra boost," Daloi replied, before shouting, "DHOLI, STRAP IN. WE'RE FIRING UP THE GRAV ENGINES AGAIN."

"You have five seconds to bring your vessel to a stop before we fire on you," warned the Alpha commander.

"Relax commander, I'm engaging the reverse thrusters now," Daloi cooed, after momentarily flipping on the communications switch. "Tatan, those coordinates had better be correct because we're going there now. BRACE YOURSELVES. I'M ENGAGING."

Daloi accelerated, using the gravitational engines, keeping them engaged as she drained their energy cells. The small craft zoomed away from the cruiser before its weapons officer could fire the first shot.

Kraton resumed the chase. A few hours later, his vessel again drew within firing range and locked onto the smaller craft.

Daloi quickly jettisoned her gravitational engines and detonated them in the path of the cruiser. She then used her ship's remaining plasma engine to propel the craft to within the gravitational pull of the nearby planet before jettisoning and destroying the drive. This maneuver bought the Cheoili several more hours of freedom, but eventually their little ship again loomed in the targeting grid of the military ship's weapons.

"Daloi, what happened to our engines?" yelled Tatan, his fear mounting as the seconds ticked past. "What about using the escape pod now? I don't want to die out here."

"It's too late for that. They would easily capture the pod at this point. One more shot and our shields could be gone. But we are so close I don't want to give up now. If we go back, you know we are as good as dead."

Another hit flung Daloi forward and completely disabled the ship's shields. Without shields and engines, the tiny craft was incapable of evading the military vessel.

"BRACE YOURSELVES!"

"Now what?" muttered Tatan.

"Shut up, and let her concentrate!" barked Dholi.

"Now that we're entering the planet's atmosphere, I'm putting us in a death spiral and setting the controls to automatically start the landing sequence once the ship nears the ground. Of course, the bad news is the ship may break apart or burn up in the next few seconds, or crash land and kill us all. The good news is we'll all probably be unconscious the whole time. Either way, we should avoid another direct hit. ENGAGING!" Daloi yelled, then pushed herself back into her seat and pulled hard on the restraints.

The trio's ship started to spin in a wide arc as it headed toward the tiny planet, which seemed to grow in size as the craft careened toward the surface.

Above, Kraton let out a grunt as he watched, flabbergasted, as the Cheoili ship spiraled erratically toward the planet's surface. If he did nothing, the ship would more than likely be destroyed, killing everyone aboard. But he wanted to be sure the craft's occupants died.

"Weapons officer, fire on that ship as best you can," he ordered.

"Yes, Commander."

The military cruiser fired numerous shots at the small craft before finally scoring a direct hit, sending sparks and debris streaming from the ship just as it deepened its plunge into the atmosphere.

"Should I continue firing, Commander?" queried the weapons officer.

"No, they are outside our jurisdiction now. If they don't die in the crash, they'll freeze to death, be eaten by wild animals, or the local authorities will drag them to prison for invading their territory. Rest assured, that ship won't be taking off again. Navigator, set a course for home."

"Yes, Commander."

***

The navigation computer aboard the Cheoili ship adjusted its wings to glide to a less than destructive landing. The computer evaded the trees and large rocks, steering the vehicle onto a wide snowfield and bringing it to a somewhat gentle, yet lopsided stop.

"I can't believe we're all still in one piece," said Dholi, unbuckling her restraints and tumbling to the floor. "Are you two still alive?"

"I am, but I'm not sure I want to be," groaned Tatan. "I'm in crazy pain."

"At least we're alive," said Daloi. "Pain is always better than death. Dholi, get the medical kit and look after Tatan. I'll see what I can find out from our instruments."

Daloi checked the ship's vital signs then moved to her twin sister's side, placing a hand on her shoulder.

"Will we survive, sis?" asked Dholi, turning to look up at her sister.

"The ship is intact, but unless we find food somewhere we won't last very long," said Daloi. "We should at least be able to stay warm for a while. Eventually the batteries will give out and we will freeze to death. There is no warm spot on this planet and no life that I can find with our limited sensors, except for a few animals that would love to eat us."

Daloi walked back to the ship's sensor control panel in response to a beep. "Wait, I lied. This is odd. There is someone standing on top of a ridge a way from here, but I can't see any buildings, or a ship, or any other people near him."

"He must have come from somewhere," said Dholi.

"I can't tell with our limited sensors. He's about 50 kilometers from here. Let's suit up, get the speeder from the cargo hold, and see what we can find out."

The three put on their foul weather suits, installed nasal filters, grabbed a bunch of their stolen gold coins and stepped outside their ship. They were greeted with a bright sun and a slight breeze that brought a chill to their bodies. Their feet sank almost a meter into the snow as they worked to position the speeder for mounting. As far as they could see in every direction were snow covered hills and mountains. It was like looking across tall mountains in the dead of winter.

Daloi selected a path toward the solitary figure that she felt would give them adequate cover from detection. As they came to within a few hundred meters, the figure disappeared on the far side of the ridge. They floated to the top of the ridge and parked the speeder. Peering over the ridge, they could see the figure chasing four others across the snow.

"What the hell is that?" asked Tatan, pointing at a large formation of beings.

"Those are Alphas in prison uniforms. The guy with the weapon must be a guard," said Daloi, "though I don't recognize his species."

"Look over there," said Dholi. "A bunch more prisoners are being loaded into a ship. I don't know about you, but I'd rather take my chances mixing in with those prisoners than freezing to death in our ship. If they're getting off this planet, it can't be a bad thing."

"Agreed, sis," said Daloi. "That's a Euclidian ship. Look at the guards near the opening. I'll bet the guard chasing the prisoners has never met a Cheoili before. Let's go see if we can catch him by surprise and replace the prisoners he's chasing."

***

Capt. Shisal sent Adar to the surface of the prison planet to monitor the prisoner exchange. *Getting him off the ship will distance him from Pheebee and give him an opportunity to do something he enjoys*, thought Shisal as he issued the order.

On the ice planet, Adar positioned himself atop a ridge high above where other crewmembers loaded prisoners into mining ships. In the distance, he saw snowy mountain peaks, wisps of clouds and broad fields of snow. Weak rays from the sun reflected brightly on the cold, white landscape around them, but did little to diminish the brutal cold. Adar stood on his perch, unaffected by the cold. Windy gusts of frigid air beat against his exposed skin, making him feel alive.

Adar looked down on the prisoners being loaded, unconcerned about any of them escaping. If any tried to flee, they would have to run in his direction because the prison wall, steep hills and mining ships blocked all other possible escape routes. After a couple of long hours of waiting, Adar finally got the excitement he craved.

At last, four of you have the balls to make a run for it. This is going to be fun, he told himself, laughing out loud.

Adar loped down from his perch at a leisurely pace to recover the four strays. He didn't want to engage them too soon and spoil the fun. This might be his only action for a while.

The prisoners moved quickly, as if they had a destination in mind, not understanding that the giant chunk of ice on which the prison is situated provided very little in the way of shelter and no way off the planet.

Adar laughed to himself, just thinking of the fun awaiting him.

"Argh!" Adar shouted, hoping to strike fear into the fleeing prisoners.

"Someone's chasing us!" yelled the prisoner at the rear.

"So stop him!" shouted Rosda, who led the group. "He's not that big."

Before the prisoner at the rear could react, Adar punched him in the back hard enough to send his body flying forward. As he fell, Adar leapt onto his shoulder using it as a springboard to pounce onto the next prisoner. He grabbed this one by the back of his coat, flipped him in the air, and easily tossed him into the fleeing forms of the two remaining prisoners.

"Okay, line up right here," Adar yelled, a bit groggy from the takedown. "We are going to march back to the loading area where you are going to peacefully get on board one of those ships. If you are not in agreement with that proposal, please raise your hand now, and I will pound your face until you do agree or you need a stretcher to carry your unconscious body onto the ship."

"He stopped to yell something at the prisoners," said Tatan, watching Adar. "Although he is small, I don't think we can take him. He certainly made light work of those four."

"Let's just sneak up on him. I can stun him with my gun if we have to. Once we are close enough, we can use our special talents to force him to do our bidding," Daloi proposed. "I'll lead the way. Just stay behind me. He won't even see us coming."

Daloi removed her gun from its holster and set the weapon to stun. The three Cheoili stealthily approached Adar from the rear as he admonished his captives. When Daloi drew within a few meters of Adar, he suddenly spun around, pulling his blaster and pointing it at her chest.

Startled, Daloi wondered, *What manner of creature is this. He's obviously part of the Euclidian force, but I have never seen one quite like him. He's almost animal-like*.

Like all Ossies, Adar's skin was covered with orange and black stripes similar to those of a tiger. A black band on either side of his nose highlighted the area where one might expect to see eyes. Ossies have a horizontal optical slit across their face instead of separate eyeballs. This unique organ gave them extraordinary peripheral vision and a total visual field of nearly 300 degrees. It enabled Adar to see the Cheoili sneaking up behind him.

"Who are you and what do you want?" he demanded.

"What's he saying?" asked Tatan, cowering in preparation to run.

"It's Euclidian. You took it in school, remember? Just stay put," said Daloi in Cheoili.

Turning back to Adar, she switched to Euclidian. "Forgive the intrusion. I'm Daloi," she said, storing her gun and holding out a hand to Adar, which he ignored. "Our engines gave out, and we crash-landed about 50 klicks from here. We saw you from our landing site and thought you might be able to help us out."

"Is that why you had your gun pointed at me?" Adar growled, studying the strange creatures.

"I misinterpreted your actions as robbery until I got close enough to see that you are one of the good guys," Daloi replied smoothly.

"Get in line with the prisoners," said Adar, waving his rifle to point the way. "I'll take you to our ship. Maybe someone there can help you."

"We're not interested in being treated like prisoners. We are Cheoili, part of the Euclidian Alliance and—"

"I never heard of you," said Adar, cutting Daloi off. "Your Euclidian is good enough, so maybe you are telling the truth."

"I actually spent some time on Euclidia a few—"

"I don't care. Join the prisoners, or I'll kill you and leave your bodies here to rot. Toss me your gun, while you're at it. Nice and slow-like," he demanded.

"You are going to be sorry you treated us like this," said Dholi, feigning indignation to approach Adar, in hopes of helping her sister get close enough to strike.

"I'm not familiar with that emotion. Maybe you can explain it to me on the walk back," replied Adar, turning towards Dholi, disinterest on his face and his finger twitching on the trigger of his photon rifle.

"Don't shoot. I'm going, I'm going," said Tatan, following his sister's lead and throwing his hands up.

Adar believed the strangers did not pose a significant threat and decided to holster his weapon.

This is an odd-looking trio, he thought. *They don't seem to have any pigment in their skin. I can make out the flesh beneath. Ugh!*

"What's that on your neck?" asked Daloi, using her siblings' distractions to move close enough to grab Adar at the back of his neck. The Ossie flinched, struggling to free himself from Daloi's grip.

Daloi was a strong female, several centimeters taller than Adar. She succeeded in overwhelming him, using her strength and special enzymes secreted through her fingertips. "Relax, fellow, and stop resisting," she urged, quietly. "What's your name?"

"Adar," he answered, the stress of trying to resist making his voice waver.

"Adar. That's a nice name. Adar, give your weapon to my sister, Dholi." Adar complied as the four prisoners cheered.

"Kill him, kill him," the Alpha prisoners chanted.

"Oh, we're definitely going to kill someone, gentlemen," said Daloi, wrinkling her nose with smug humor. "Don't damage their uniforms, we'll need to wear them."

Taking her cue, Dholi quickly killed three of the prisoners with shots to their heads. Adar grunted angrily, causing Dholi to hesitate just long enough for Rosda to chime in.

"I can help you survive on the ship," the remaining Alpha begged, hoping to bargain for her life. "I'm a chemist. The food and drink on the ship will be tainted with a chemical that takes away your willpower."

"So why don't I just kill you and take it off your dead body?" asked Dholi, pointing the weapon at Rosda's face.

"Because you don't know what quantity to take or how long it lasts. Unless you want to spend your life as a lemming, I suggest you let me help you," Rosda replied, slowly placing a finger on the tip of the weapon Dholi held and pressing it toward the ground.

"Dholi, we'll take her with us," said Daloi. "Adar, my good friend, I want you to escort us to the loading area and then forget this incident ever happened. Nod to let me know you agree." Adar nodded without resistance. "What is to be done with the prisoners you're loading?"

"They are being taken to our ship, which is orbiting the planet. They will eventually be sold off as laborers."

"Why don't the prisoners try to overpower the guards?" asked Daloi. "There are only a few of them."

"Their food is drugged so they don't resist commands," Adar replied.

"Just as I told you," said Rosda, lifting her hands into the air.

"Okay, so you can earn your keep. Don't get cocky." Daloi eyed Rosda suspiciously.

Returning her attention to Adar, she asked, "How long before the prisoners are sold off, Adar?"

"Probably another month or so. We need to perform a brief reconnaissance visit to another planet we plan to mine. Maybe some other stops. I don't control the schedule."

"Oh, that's right. I heard your government flies around the galaxy mining the life out of planets. You feel you have the moral high ground because you leave the planets habitable," said Daloi, suddenly chatty.

"Says the female who just murdered three innocents," observed Adar, his voice thick with sarcasm.

"At least we're honest about our vices. You're just government sanctioned pirates. As soon as a more powerful alien species comes along to put you in your place, you'll be crying foul. Won't you?"

"No, I won't be crying anything. I'll survive as I always do. And once you release my neck, I'm going to take you out," Adar promised, his strong will surfacing even with the Cheoili's enzymes flooding his bloodstream.

"Even when I'm not gripping your neck, I expect you to do what I say and forget what happened here," Daloi continued. "If asked, simply tell people you captured the fleeing prisoners and escorted them back to the ship. That's it. Understood?" she instructed, shoving him forward.

"Yes, I understand," said Adar, a moan escaping him as he twisted his head.

"Give him his weapon back," ordered Daloi. Dholi complained, but reluctantly handed the firearm to Adar. Adar grabbed the rifle, but didn't attempt to shoot the trio.

"You are a feisty one, aren't you?" said Daloi.

Adar did not respond.

"Let's get dressed and get out of here you two," she told her siblings. "We should drag these dead bodies out of sight, so they are not easily found."

"Daloi, I remember you telling me our enzymes could bend people to our will," said Dholi, "but I didn't realize it worked so well or so quickly."

"To tell you the truth, neither did I. During my visit to Euclidia, I tried it on several people and got surprising results. We can send people into ecstasy or make them our slaves simply by touching them with our fingers and using a well-placed whisper," she boasted.

The three Cheoili changed their features to mimic the Alphas that Dholi killed. While they were taller than most Alphas, they hunched their bodies to blend in with the other prisoners.

"Pretty neat trick," said Rosda, who observed their transformation in awe.

"That's not all we're capable of. So be careful how you behave," said Daloi, hoping to intimidate Rosda.

"You'll need to get rid of your weapon," Rosda observed, pointing at Daloi's blaster. "They scan the prisoners before they board. There's no way you will be able to sneak it on the ship."

Rosda smirked.

Daloi ignored her, but tossed her weapon away.

Daloi, Dholi and Tatan donned the dead prisoners' uniforms and headed back to the loading area with the Alpha chemist, mixing in with the other prisoners. Adar returned to overseeing the transfer process, the incident forgotten.

Eventually, the Cheoili climbed aboard one of the mining ships for the transfer to the *Andrea*. After the loading door closed, only portable lights illuminated the craft's dark interior. The prisoners had to stand for the short trip, propping up each other to keep from falling onto the floor which was covered in water from snow melting off prisoners' boots.

Once aboard the *Andrea*, the Euclidian guards escorted the prisoners into a holding cell. The Cheoili, unlike the other prisoners, viewed their captivity as a gateway to freedom.

Chapter 2

The Cheoili Escape the Andrea

"Here," said Rosda, handing each of them a pill. "This will block the effects for a week and then you will need to take another one."

"This little thing?" said Tatan, eyeing the tiny blue disc in disbelief.

"Yes, sometimes amazing things come in small packages," Rosda chuckled.

"You're not that amazing, and you came in a small package," Dholi quipped, drawing laughs from Daloi and Tatan.

"Enough with the chit chat." Daloi broke up the levity. "Go check this place out. This corner of the room will be ours." Daloi pointed to five beds and a table. "If anyone tries to move in, we'll just throw them out. See what you can find, and we'll meet back here in an hour or so. You, too, Rosda. For now, you are a new member of our gang."

"Thank you, Daloi. I'm honored to be part of the team," Rosda said, bowing.

"Just get to work and stay out of our way," replied Daloi.

***

Daloi eyed the massive holding area. Beds were evenly spaced at different heights with mini partitions to provide a modicum of privacy. Food and beverage stations all along the wall kept people fed and tranquilized. Sanitary booths with curtains gave people some privacy, but not the ability to hide, while expelling waste. *What an enormous and ingeniously designed place this is,* she thought. *Who could ask for more in a temporary prison?*

The Cheoili and their one disciple resumed strolling around the confinement area, looking for flaws and a better understanding of its layout. Before long, the smell of the Alpha prisoners permeated the space, which displeased the Cheoili.

Why can't they smell more like us? Dholi thought. *Or at least take a shower. Too bad the drugged food doesn't make them bathe more often. Ugh!*

On the other hand, the Cheoili's aromatic odor caught the attention of other prisoners as they passed, prompting them to raise their heads and sniff the air. The team ignored this, unconcerned that anyone might alert the authorities to their presence.

"Aren't these ceilings and upper walls interesting?" Dholi commented, walking up to Daloi. "It's like looking out into space. They have even synchronized the movement of the sun to simulate a normal solar cycle. I can only guess it is based on their destroyed home planet of Alpha. Look how they praise the sunset."

"Yeah, they just can't seem to let go," Daloi said, but her attention remained focused on the task at hand. "Keep looking around. I have yet to find a door in this place."

Daloi knew there had to be a way in and out.

Dholi was less optimistic. “They used transporters to deliver us here from the cargo bay,” she said. “Since then, the Euclidian have only communicated with us via the monitors on the wall. Like that repetitive, annoying ‘stay calm and relax’ message. Why would they ever need to have a way to enter here?”

“We’ll have to figure that out,” said Daloi, continuing to study the wall.

When they completed their individual tours, the siblings and Rosda regrouped in the corner they had staked out to compare notes.

“Did either of you find anything worth talking about?” asked Daloi.

“Not me,” said Tatan.

“Other than odd-looking Alphas, no,” said Dholi.

“I think I can use some of the food ingredients to make a fire if we need to,” said Rosda.

“That’ll come in handy if we decide to have a barbecue,” joked Dholi. “So how are we supposed to get out of this place? If we are still in here after reaching Euclidia, our chances of escaping are greatly diminished. They may even discover that we are the Cheoili wanted by the Alphas. Our crashed ship won’t go unnoticed forever.”

“Hopefully, someone will show up in person to indoctrinate us, which will give us an opportunity to interject ourselves into the conversation. If that doesn’t work, we’ll start a riot. Anything that will get people to enter this place. Trust me, we are not going to some work farm or petting zoo," said Daloi, working to reassure everyone. "Until then, let's learn what we can from the people here."

"I know how we can get them to talk. Dholi, let's blow this joint," said Tatan.

"You read my mind," said Dholi. "You take the girls."

"You two aren't really going to do that, are you?" asked Daloi, her expression dubious.

"Hell yes, I am," replied Dholi. "I'm going to start on that wall and work my way across the room."

"Fine, but no compulsion. I don't want you taking advantage of the prisoners."

"I won't have to. Look around. There are plenty of people already ahead of us. I'm thinking about taking on five at once."

"I don't even want to ask how you are going to do that," said Daloi, a look of disgust crossing her face.

"You won't have to. Just sit back and watch me work my magic," said Dholi, smirking and snapping her fingers.

"I don't think I'll be doing that."

"I'm an Alpha, and I don't want to have sex with a bunch of random strangers," said Rosda.

"I'm with Rosda," said Daloi, giving the little prisoner a high five.

"Aren't you just a little curious about those Alphas?" asked Dholi, placing her hands on her hips. "I want to know how they smell under their clothes, how they taste and what noises they make at that special moment. Do they ever fart during sex?"

"Okay, that's going too far," said Tatan, this time grimacing with distaste.

"As if you never slipped one out," Dholi shot back, giggling.

"Not on purpose. Either way, it's too crude to talk about. I could start my investigation on Rosda. At least she's not sedated." Tatan looked at her, a lustful gleam in his dark eyes.

"No thanks, I'd rather keep my clothes on, if you don't mind," said Rosda, hurriedly walking away.

"Try not to make nuisances of yourselves, you two," said Daloi, giving her siblings a stern look. "Remember, we are being monitored."

"The stupid orientation video had instructions on how to behave," countered Dholi. "The instructions said nothing about refraining from sex. Plus, they may have some important information to share."

"Still, don't risk exposure. Our chameleon abilities have limitations. Continue to speak Alphan as well, as long as we're in here."

"Okay, I'll try to be discreet while I screw my way across this giant prison cell." Dholi gave Daloi a huge grin before sauntering off to find her first target.

Dholi and Tatan gravitated toward one corner of the holding area and proceeded to engage its occupants in various sex acts. The more sex they had, the bolder they got with their activities. These endeavors, however, did not go unnoticed by the Euclidian.

***

"What do you two think you are doing?" asked the Euclidian guard, who approached Dholi and Tatan after entering the room through a door hidden in the wall.

"It's called the multi-orifice, double-grip maneuver," Dholi replied matter-of-factly. "If you don't mind waiting a few moments, I'm sure I could fit you in."

"I'm not interested in joining your private orgy. Stop having sex and stick to your personal area," ordered the frowning guard, placing a hand on his weapon holster.

He wore a crewmember's uniform with several stripes, which gave Daloi the impression that he had some power.

"Don't be so angry," she said, approaching the tall guard from behind and gripping his neck. After a moment of resistance, he calmed down.

"Don't fight me. Just relax. What's your name?" Daloi crooned.

"I am Goron, the supervisor for this holding area. Sex is allowed between prisoners, but not to this degree." He looked at Dholi with disgust. "Keep your sexual activities to two people, or I'll have you sedated and restrained in your cot."

Goron was a senior security officer assigned to monitor the confinement of the Alpha prisoners on the ship. He often led security teams during extraterrestrial missions.

"You speak Alphan quite well. Why is that? You are Euclidian, right?" asked Daloi.

"Yes, I'm Euclidian. As officer in charge of containment security, it's important to learn the language of the people we hold here. I wouldn't be effective, otherwise," he replied, twisting his head as if attempting to wake from a dream.

"Why don't you take us out of here to someplace private where we can have more freedom of movement?"

"That is not permitted. You must–"

"Do it for me," requested Daloi, rubbing Goron's chest and tightening her grip on his neck.

"Of course," said the guard. "Follow me. I'll take you to a place where you will be safe."

The three Cheoili walked out with Goron, to the surprise of everyone around them. Rosda stepped in line behind them before being stopped by Daloi.

"Back inside with you," the Cheoili growled, grabbing Rosda around the throat and shoving her back into the room.

Goron led the three Cheoili into a narrow passageway that connected to many other holding areas. The dimly lit hall was so long the Cheoili could not see either end of it. Goron stopped at one point, touched a spot on the wall next to a mauve light, and another hidden door opened.

"What is this place you are taking us to?" asked Tatan nervously.

"It's a mechanical transport," said Goron. "We need to go to the lower decks where they keep the minerals. Those storage rooms are left unlocked and are not monitored."

"Tatan, let him do his job," scolded Daloi. "The longer we are out here, the longer we are susceptible to being discovered."

"You should listen to her," said Goron. "There are roving anomaly monitors on every level. They wander the ship looking for anything that might be out of place. It could be structural, electrical, radiation, or security related. If one spots you, I may not be able to keep it from reporting you."

They stepped inside the small transport room, but before the door could close, Rosda jumped in. The door then closed, whisking them downward several hundred meters.

"How is it you're here?" asked Daloi.

Rosda smiled. "The antidote I created seems to have a nice side effect. It protects me from your compulsion enzymes.".

"I guess you can stay for now. We might find another use for you," said Daloi, before returning her focus to Goron.

When the transport stopped, the guard led the group along another dimly lit corridor and cautiously stepped into a large room with piles of minerals. Goron directed them to a small office in the far corner.

“You won’t be bothered here,” Goron assured them. “You can come and go as you please, but I suggest you stay within this area. There is some food in that cabinet, and I can bring you more later.”

“It’s good of you to find us a safe place to stay,” said Daloi, placing her hand on his face. “Do you know when we will arrive at the next destination?”

“We will be docking with a few cargo vessels over the next few weeks and then head out on an observation mission. We should be back on Euclidia in around five weeks.”

“That sounds promising,” said Daloi. “Before you go, tell us about that striped security guard who was overseeing the prisoner transfer.”

“That was Adar, an Ossie. He has tremendous speed and strength and is able to make himself invisible,” explained Goron. “A pretty neat trick if you ask me.”

“I’ll remember that. You can go now,” said Daloi. “Don’t tell anyone that we are here, and I expect to see you soon with more food.”

“I will return shortly, as you request. Good-bye,” said Goron, leaving the area through yet another invisible door.

The Cheoili watched as Goron left, amazed that their escape from the holding area had gone so well. They made an inventory of their immediate surroundings, anxious to identify anything that might give them away.

“Daloi, why did you let him go?” asked Tatan. “He could warn someone of our presence.”

“His being here might look suspicious. The last thing we need is a bunch of nosy guards coming in here and finding us, and worse yet, discovering that we’re not really Alphas. Why don’t you three make a loop of this area and see what you can find on the other side of that pile of rubble?”

“That could take us hours!” exclaimed Tatan, not eager to take yet another long walk around a big room.

“What else do you have to do?” asked Daloi, shooing him away with her hand.

Dholi pulled his arm. “Come on, Tatan. Let’s go see what we can find. You go around that way Alpha,” Dholi requested, pointing to the other end of the pile.

“My name is Rosda.” The short, chunky Alpha directed a disgusted glare at Dholi before moving away. Seeing her influence in the small group waning, she decided to take the time alone to think of another way she could ingratiate herself with them before they decided to kill her as they did her former colleagues.

As Dholi and Tatan walked off, Daloi gazed out the window from the small office of the enormous storage area. The pile of iron ore nearly touched the high ceiling and stretched for several kilometers. It reminded her of the hills near her home on Cheoili, before her parents migrated to the planet Alpha. She wondered if she would ever see her home again.

Circumstances had thrust her into the criminal lifestyle she now embraced. Finding a decent paying job on Alpha was difficult for the foreign-born Cheoili. After learning a trade, Daloi left her family on Alpha, who were struggling financially, for a lucrative position on the planet Euclidia as a trade liaison for a local manufacturing company. She sent money home and spoke with her family on a daily basis.

While she was away, burglars killed her parents while her siblings were at work. Angered by the loss, Daloi returned home. She took a job with a local gang, hoping to find her parents' murderers. She eventually succeeded, bringing the murderers to justice--her kind of justice. After disposing of their corpses, she and her siblings moved to Moorland to start anew.

While living on Euclidia, Daloi learned to speak the Euclidian language fluently and to understand the Euclidian culture, which reflected their cruel nature. As an outsider, she found herself a target of locals who made fun of her. They played tricks on her, and men took advantage of her naiveté. That is, until she learned the power of her touch.

The enzyme secreted by a Cheoili calmed other beings when it came into contact with their skin. It also made them susceptible to suggestion.

When Daloi discovered this ability, her parents discouraged her from developing it out of fear of attracting unwanted attention from the authorities. The enzymes didn't work on other Cheoili, and Daloi didn't know what would happen if she tried it on an alien species.

Then a Euclidian lover told Daloi in an abrupt manner that he no longer cared to spend time with her. It hurt Daloi deeply to be tossed aside like a piece of rubbish. *It's like every man on Euclidia wants to have his turn with me before dumping me for the next shiny new object*, she thought.

Deciding she had had enough, Daloi stopped her suitor before he could finish explaining all the ways that he had become disinterested in her company. She placed her hands gently around his neck, focused on releasing the enzymes in her fingers and spoke softly to him while gazing into his eyes.

"You look so sad about our breakup," sighed Daloi.

"I am," he replied.

"Then you should show me how sad you are by stripping naked and running through the streets to let everyone know how sad you are."

"I should?" said her erstwhile swain, bewildered by the statement.

"Yes, you should. Do it right now!"

With that, her lover disrobed and ran down the street, professing his sadness to anyone who would listen until the police arrested him for public indecency. Daloi cackled at the delightful surprise that her suggestion had worked so well.

From now on things are going to go differently for me. No longer will I be the ingénue here for everyone's entertainment. I will be the dominatrix, and people will respect me, she vowed.

As time passed, Daloi spent more time discreetly testing her abilities on the Euclidian and individuals of other species. She learned how quickly the enzymes took effect, the limits of what she could demand, and how long the effect lasted. She also learned to fight so she could use her fists to protect herself when her enzymes could not.

On Euclidia, she also learned how well her chameleon abilities worked. Early in the life of her planet, its humanoid species developed chameleon and compulsion abilities to protect themselves from Cheoili's many carnivorous animals. In that way, evolution spared her race from extinction. Over time, the Cheoili no longer needed their unique protections, and since they worked poorly on each other, they rarely used them. Daloi planned to bring them back into use, at least by her siblings and herself.

***

Tatan and Dholi walked into the office after touring the storage space to find their sister having fun with Goron.

"What are you planning to do with him?" asked Tatan, watching Goron as he sat on a couch with his shirt off, massaging her feet.

"You know how my feet hurt after I've been walking on them for a while," said Daloi, with a mischievous grin. "He offered to rub them and I'm too polite to say no. Where's the little one?" she asked, looking around.

"Who knows? Hopefully she got buried in a landslide and died," Dholi laughed.

"Daloi, is there anything else I can do for you?" asked Goron.

"Not for now. Just tell me what you got us," she requested, looking in the bag he brought with him.

"I brought you some better food, water, and a container of Tammarian Grog."

"I have fond memories of that grog. Did you get me any toys?"

"I got you each a photon pistol, a personal transporter and this hologram training program, which will teach you about the planet we are going to. The transporter won't work on the ship, but it will work once you are on the planet."

"Good boy. Any update on when we arrive?" asked Daloi.

Goron shrugged. "We are still several weeks away." "That's a long time, but I guess it gives us time to prepare for our new adventure. Forget what you saw here, but swing by every eight hours or so to check in on us. Now get back to work," said Daloi, patting Goron on the butt.

"Yes, mistress." Goron walked out feeling good about the visit, but unsure why.

"Sis, are you sure you can trust him?" asked Tatan.

"Yes, because I know how long the compulsion lasts."

"So is it the compulsion or your relationship that makes him obedient?"

"Probably a little of both."

"Tell us what you have been planning, sis," prompted Dholi, looking excited.

"We should eat some food first," said Daloi. "Then taste this grog. It will absolutely blow your mind. When you are in the right mood, I'll tell you what I have planned."

"Hello everyone. I'm back," said Rosda, holding up a handful of soil she had dug out of the pile.

"Good for you," said Dholi. "Why are you bringing that mess in here?"

"I believe that I can make crude hand grenades from this material. Once it is compressed into a metal cup and thrown against a hard surface it should cause a small explosion, which could come in handy, don't you think?" Rosda smiled, hoping they would be impressed.

"I like the idea," said Daloi. "Once again, you've earned your keep. Make us a few and then join the training session."

***

Weeks had passed since the *Andrea*'s visit to the prison planet. Seated in his favorite lounge aboard the ship, Adar looked forward to a drink prepared by his favorite bartender, Vikktor.

About 15 tables, scattered here and there in the dimly lit lounge, were occupied by crewmembers looking to imbibe during their downtime. The digital walls allowed patrons to watch an event or play interactive games.

A long, horseshoe-shaped counter dominated the front of the bar where Vikktor crafted his magical elixirs.

"What'll you have, Adar?" Vikktor asked, approaching him with a wide grin bisecting his round face.

"Just get me a Tammarian grog." Adar looked pensive and nodded at Vikktor. "I need to think a bit."

"Coming right up." The bartender retreated and soon returned with the effervescent, turquoise-colored drink and placed it on the polished stone bar in front of Adar.

Adar took a swig, studying the few other customers sitting at tables near him. *Something is not right here. Everything looks normal but it is not,* he thought.

Adar chugged the rest of his drink down and started a rhythmic tapping of his nails on the bar.

Vikktor eyed the empty glass in the front of the Ossie. "How about a fresh drink, Adar?"

"Not now Vikktor. I'm going to go down to the sports arena and see what I can get into. Maybe I'll swing by later."

Before Adar could leave his seat at the bar, in walked Raina and Rhana, twins well-acquainted with the Ossie.

"Hello, ladies. I didn't expect to see you tonight," said Adar, smiling as the sight of the two exotic women lifted his mood.

"But you're happy we're here, right?" asked Raina, pursing her lips.

"Of course I am. Why don't we head to my stateroom and play some bondage games?"

Females of another alien race, Raina and Rhana differed dramatically from Euclidian women. They had tougher constitutions, higher libidos, and they welcomed interludes with foreigners.

"Let's go. I can't wait to feel you pressing me against a wall," Raina gushed.

"And I'll be right next to you, baby," said Rhana.

"Adar, we need you in operations," said a voice from his communications device.

"Damn it! Sorry, ladies. I'd better go see what they want. I'll catch up with you later."

"You'd better." Both women pouted.

***

"Adar, why such a long face?" said an operations officer looking up from his monitor. "No one around to kill?" The others in the office laughed, knowing Adar's frustration with assignments that lacked violence.

"Not quite," said Adar. "You interrupted my plans to entertain a couple of twins. Tell me what you want so I can get back to them."

"While you monitored the prisoners being brought aboard our ship did you notice that someone killed three of the prisoners, dragged them away, put on their uniforms and took their place with the other prisoners?"

Adar searched his thoughts, an uneasy feeling welling up inside of him. "Of course not. I would have seen it and done something about it."

"The captain got word from Central Control about it. According to the Alpha authorities, prison guards discovered three dead

Alpha prisoners several meters away from the prison entrance, unclothed and covered in snow. It is believed that the perpetrators mixed in with the Alpha prisoners somewhere on this ship. For now, Captain Shisal wants this to be your No. 1 priority."

"How could that have happened?!" asked Adar in disbelief. "I was there the entire time. Those bodies must have been placed there before we landed."

"The prison passed on to Central Control that all of their prisoners were accounted for before the transfer began," said the officer, who sympathized with Adar, knowing how much pride he took in his work.

"I'll contact Central Control and start working the case," Adar said, troubled by his thoughts.

Central Control's oversight helped to ensure that the planet's ships complied with the law. The government agency also approved trade deals for the resources the ships brought back to Euclidia.

***

Adar sat at a desk in his cabin, waiting for his connection to go through. He wondered what Central Control knew about the escapees.

"Adar, this is what we know right now," said the officer, who came online. "Three gang leaders from Cheoili, living on Moorland, killed members of two rival gangs during a couple of heists. Soon after, the Alpha Police surrounded the Cheoili hideout. An explosion killed them while the Cheoili sped away in a spaceship. Their ship was tracked to the Alpha prison planet where the Alpha military shot it down. But the ship obviously survived the crash. It appears the Cheoili killed three prisoners and took their place on your ship."

"How is that possible? Wouldn't we notice if Cheoili tried to take the place of Alphas?" Adar was experiencing his worst fears about the case. Had he been duped somehow into helping the Cheoili stow away aboard the *Andrea*?

"Not necessarily. They are able to take on the looks of other species. I suggest you check your recordings and figure out what happened."

"Okay, I will check with security here and get back to you." Adar ended the communication, angry and confused. He was afraid of what the security recordings would reveal, not only to himself, but to others about his clumsiness. *I know there are gaps in my memory from the planet, but how could that much have happened without my knowledge, without my fighting back?*

***

Adar walked into the security office, angered by what he learned from Central Control and his follow-up investigation.

"I want every monitor on the ship programmed to detect Cheoili DNA right away!" he shouted at the security director. He paced back and forth, thinking of what else he could do to track down the stowaways.

"Adar, what makes you think they are on our ship?" demanded the security chief, annoyed by Adar barking orders at him. Though

Adar was considered part of the ship's security team, he reported directly to the captain and not to the head of security. The chief needed to balance maintaining his authority in front of his team with placating Adar, who could pummel him without worry of retribution.

"Because I personally worked with Dr. Valera to check the mining vessels used to transfer the prisoners to our ship." Adar paused to glare at the chief. "Once we found traces of their DNA, I searched every one of our holding areas until I found the one where they were housed."

"So why do you need my help?" asked the chief.

"Because they were no longer there!" shouted Adar, leaning over the chief's desk. "No one has departed the ship since we left orbit, which means a security officer helped them to escape and hide somewhere on our ship. So get off your butt and help me find them." Adar pounded his fist on the chief's desk to reinforce the urgency of his request.

"Fine, I'll have the monitors reprogrammed and check with my officers right away," the chief said in a conciliatory tone.

"Good, you let me know as soon as you find something." Adar stormed out, unsure of whether he should direct his anger at himself or at the chief. *What if someone asked how the Cheoili got on the ship in the first place? How would I respond?*

***

In a cargo bay in the bowels of the ship, the three Cheoili and their Alpha companion spent their time studying Earth culture and learning about the operation of the *Andrea* from Goron, who visited every eight hours like clockwork.

As the four fugitives reviewed the lessons, the Earth training hologram periodically changed its age, gender, dialect, and ethnicity to familiarize them with the diversity of human life forms. At the end of each lesson, they swallowed a shot of grog to celebrate and unwind.

Artificial intelligence in the program enabled it to have simple conversations in Earth languages with them and to correct their mistakes. The Cheoili, like many sentient species in the Euclidian alliance, had higher brain functions than Earth's humans, giving them nearly perfect recall.

A few days after finishing their training sessions, the moment the Cheoili had been waiting and studying for finally arrived. Goron came in and told them that the *Andrea* was positioned behind the moon orbiting the planet called Earth. He described to them the means by which they could reach the planet's surface.

"Our shuttle bays have several small vehicles of different sizes capable of transporting anywhere from two to a few dozen people through space to the surface of a planet," Goron reported. "However, it is unlikely that you would be able to get a vehicle off the ship without being detected. In operations, we have transporter rooms that can send you to the planet in an instant. You would be detected leaving the ship, but at least you'd have a chance to disappear before someone came after you."

"Are we possibly going to another planet soon?" asked Tatan.

"As far as I know this is the last stop before heading back to Euclidia. You should know that they discovered that you killed the Alpha prisoners and are on the ship somewhere," warned Goron.

"We'll transport down now," said Daloi, making the decision for the group. "Give us a few moments to gather our things, and we will follow you to operations."

"Wait here for a while. I'll come back in an hour with some nose filters and other things you will need to survive on the planet," Goron suggested before walking out.

"Luckily, Earthlings' looks seem easy enough for us to imitate, except for poor Rosda there," said Dholi, eyeing the little Alpha. "I'm sure we can find some way to hide that strange face of yours."

Rosda only grimaced in response to Dholi's taunts.

It was the middle of June on Earth, which meant summer in America. Daloi wanted a large city on the northern side of the country and settled on Chicago. It had lots of summer activities that attracted throngs of people from different regions, a thriving crime culture, and not much of a military presence.

But the decision to seek refuge on Earth didn't come without trepidation. Several concerns crossed Daloi's mind. Could they blend in with Earth's culture? Would they be able to survive on the food? How long before the Alphas or Euclidian came after them? Would the breathing filters that Goron pilfered work?

"Daloi, are you sure you want to be marooned on a primitive planet with little possibility of ever making it home again?" asked Tatan.

"I agree there are a lot of unknowns about this Earth. But we don't have any less risky alternatives. If we stay here, sooner or later we will be discovered," she said. "Then the Euclidian will turn us over to the Alphas. The Alphas will surely stick us in that icy prison for all eternity or just turn us over to the mob, who will torture us for weeks before executing us."

"What is your hesitation, Tatan?" asked Dholi.

"I'm afraid of what we might find on that planet. We could get sick, imprisoned, or just be miserable for the rest of our lives," Tatan lamented.

"So you think we should stay on the ship and take our chances?" Dholi asked.

"Oh hell, no. Now that they know we're on the ship somewhere, we can't stay here," cried Tatan, who suddenly envisioned the walls closing in on him.

"Then we are in agreement?" asked Daloi, looking at each of them for confirmation.

"We're with you, sis," said Dholi, nodding with approval.

"I'm coming too, right?" Rosda asked, revealing her anxiety about being left behind.

"Of course," Daloi replied. "Did you finish making the grenades?"

“Yes, I made six of them,” said Rosda, handing them to Daloi.

“Here you two. Grab these for me.” Daloi handed metallic lumps about the size of ostrich eggs over to Dholi and Tatan.

“This is for you,” she said, turning to Rosda and stabbing her several times in the chest with a small knife she had concealed in her prison clothes.

“Thanks for your services. We won’t be needing you anymore,” Daloi sneered, looking down at Rosda’s slumped form. She then walked towards the office door. “Let’s go, everyone,” she ordered.

“Don’t you think we could have kept her around a little longer?” Tatan whined. “What if someone discovers her?”

“Our presence is not going to be a surprise once we force their operations department to transport us to the planet.” Daloi scoffed at her brother’s continued worrying. “I would have brought Little Miss Sarcasm along, but I don’t think she would have blended in well with her looks.”

“As usual, you thought this through, big sis.” Tatan sighed, his shoulders slumping in resignation.

“And as usual, you worry too damn much,” Daloi snapped, annoyed by his timid criticism. “Let’s get away from this body. I don’t know what effect it might have on Goron if he sees it.”

The three Cheoili moved to the main door of the storage room to wait for Goron, while Rosda lay bleeding to death on the floor.

***

"Here is the bag of items I promised you." Goron handed a bag about the length of his forearm and just as wide to Daloi. "It should help you survive for a few days until you find a way to fend for yourselves. We can head to operations whenever you are ready."

"We're ready," said Daloi. "We want to get off this ship as soon as we can."

As they entered the operations area, the technician on duty confronted Goron. Daloi quickly grabbed the Euclidian's face with her hand and cooed to him, influencing him to do her bidding. Moments later, the Cheoili stood in the middle of Chicago's Millennium Park, examining their surroundings and embracing their newfound freedom.

***

Adar met with security officer Rangel to go over what her office had uncovered. A Euclidian taller than Adar, she had no interest in starting a fight with him. She knew she had to respect the volatile little Ossie's position, while standing firm against any outbursts from him.

"Our team tracked the Cheoili to the point where they overpowered an operations officer and transported down to Earth. Upon checking the recordings, working our way back from the operations center, we determined that the Cheoili hid in one of the storage areas where Goron took care of them after freeing them from containment."

"Why the hell would he do that?" growled Adar.

“The same reason you helped them board the ship,” said Rangel, matter-of-factly.

“I did no such thing,” denied Adar, afraid of being seen as a collaborator.

“Do you remember going after four escaped prisoners?”

“Of course I do,” he replied, suspicious of the question.

“So what happened during the recovery?” Rangel looked at him with accusing eyes. Now that she had Adar back on his heels, she didn’t want to back down. “We have evidence that the Cheoili replaced three of the prisoners.”

“I don’t know!” said Adar, hesitant to go on. “I captured the four of them and told them they had to go back to the ship or I would beat the crap out of them. The only other thing I remember is returning them and watching them board one of the mining vessels. I don’t recall running into any Cheoili. How could I have missed that?” cried Adar, suddenly feeling very vulnerable. He grabbed his head, realizing that his worst fear might be real.

“For the same reason that Goron agreed to help them break out of our holding area and hide in a storage room for serval weeks. The Cheoili are able to compel people to do whatever they want by touching them and then making them forget it ever happened,” Rangel explained.

Seeing the anguish in Adar’s face, she wanted to console him, but kept her distance, aware of the Ossie’s volatile temper.

Adar stood motionless for a moment, digesting the evidence, knowing it had to be true. “I need to tell the captain right away.” He took a deep breath before heading to the bridge.

***

After a short briefing from Adar, Capt. Shisal’s normally pale face darkened to a dull maroon as his features contorted with fury. “Why am I just now hearing about this?” he demanded.

“I’m just now finding out myself, Captain,” Adar replied, keeping his focus on what should come next. “Central Control wants us to return these Cheoili to Alpha immediately.”

“Communications, connect me with Central Control,” Shisal ordered.

“Aye, aye, captain. I have Burrtha on the forward monitor for you.”

“Burrtha, we have evidence that the three Cheoili you are looking for fled our ship for one of the planets we are monitoring. I can have the coordinates sent to you so your team can follow up.”

“I don’t need coordinates, I need the Cheoili,” barked Burrtha, a deep frown visible on her broad, pale face even on the bridge’s video screen.

“This is a law enforcement issue. The crime happened off my ship, by aliens moreover,” Shisal countered.

“Don’t give me that legalese deflection. YOUR crew brought them aboard YOUR ship and then helped them escape. YOU are responsible for your crew. Moreover, YOU know the logistics of that planet, since YOU'VE been monitoring it. Stop trying to pass your failure on to me and go find those Cheoili!" Burrtha shouted, pounding her fist on her desk. "Their being on that planet could jeopardize your mission. Remember the radiation fallout from the Boltazar mission due to an alien exposure that forced us to abort the mission?"

Burrtha paused to wipe her mouth and compose her features before continuing. "Your predecessor, in his arrogance, thought he could just burst on the scene with weapons ablaze and force the planet into submission. But what happens when you corner an animal?" she asked.

"It fights back," Shisal said.

"You're damn right it does, and so did they, filling the air with toxic radiation and other putrid chemicals," said Burrtha, waving her hands about. "That's probably what led to the mutiny and his downfall. You do remember that?"

"Yes, Burrtha, I remember, which means your team should be looking after this. If you disagree, we should take this up with the director. My time is far too valuable to be playing cop for you."

"You are absolutely right. My investigators tell me that the Cheoili are capable of making themselves look like Euclidian or any other species. I'm thinking they are probably still on your ship posing as some other crewmembers," said Burrtha, pointing her finger at the screen.

"That's preposterous. We are certain that the Cheoili fled my ship for Earth," Shisal objected.

"Just to be sure I want your entire crew to report here for inspection early tomorrow."

"It would take several days to check my entire crew," Shisal said, now visibly angry.

"I'm thinking it will take several weeks. I'll have a security team come onboard to sweep your ship for any stowaways, while your crew is here with us," she countered, pushing her face closer to the camera until it filled the monitor on the bridge. The bridge crew stared at the screen in shock.

"Burrtha, I would hate to put you and your team to all that trouble," said Shisal, hoping to soothe the Central Control officer's ire. "Why don't you let my crew track down these murderers for you and bring them to your office with a nice bow around them?"

Leaning back from the camera, Burrtha's face lit with satisfaction. "Lovely idea, Shisal. But don't plan to go on any missions until those Cheoili are brought to justice."

"I wouldn't think of it, Burrtha, and I'll put my best person on it." Shisal's smile didn't reach his eyes.

"You'd better. Burrtha out!" The Control officer's image winked off the monitor.

Capt. Shisal and his crew breathed a collective sigh of relief.

"Adar, get prepped. You're going to Earth. I'm taking the ship home to offload its resources. I'll return in about an Earth year to start mining this planet. Have this taken care of before we return. Wylyy will pilot an attack ship to assist you."

"Aye, aye, captain," said Adar, acquiescing to the captain's request. He realized now was not the time to debate the captain's orders. Typically not susceptible to melancholy, the Ossie fell into a funk that threatened to overwhelm him.

As Adar departed the bridge, headed for his quarters to prep for the pursuit, his thoughts roiled with the sick feeling in his stomach. *Damn it! Here we go again. Another boring assignment on a backward planet. At least this isn't just an outpost. I can't believe I let those Cheoili get the jump on me.*

He swung at the air as if punching at some invisible enemy. *I had planned on another interlude with those twins tonight. Instead I have to chase down some murderous new species I never heard of. Who knows how many people they've already killed on that planet? If they expose our mission, there will be hell to pay.*

Making another fist, he punched at the wall to activate the inter-level transporter so he could descend to the section with the crew's quarters.

***

As the *Andrea* emerged from dimensional space just behind the moon, it partially obscured the stars being viewed from powerful telescopes stationed at one of Earth's observatories.

"Dr. Egorin, I need you to look at some data just in from our lunar telescopes," said Leslie Golden, one of the science fellows monitoring the output from the lunar telescope array at NASA's Meteoroid Environment Office.

"The instruments show that the stars around the background of the moon disappeared from view for a moment. What's more disturbing is we seem to be getting flashes from the dark side of the moon, but above its surface. The effect might be caused by one large object or several small ones hovering in space above the moon. We believe this to be the case because we are able to observe the anomaly from both sides of the moon, though I don't understand how something could have gotten there without being noticed."

"It's too bad we can't send a probe to see what's going on up there. I don't understand why we can't have a satellite permanently orbiting the moon," said Dr. Melanie Egorin, disturbed by the amount of bureaucracy she had to wade through to get anything done.

The lab where the two scientists worked had several screens that provided different views of the sky captured by their telescopes. The screens provided the only light in the otherwise dark room. Scientists in white coats darted back and forth across the linoleum floor, gathering data and making reports. All of them hoped to make an important discovery that would catapult them to the forefront of their fields, making years of staring at the sky worthwhile.

"The lack of an international agreement is the biggest roadblock to placing a satellite in orbit around the moon," Golden said, trying to sound well-informed. "I can contact one of our partners if you want to see what they know," she offered, eager to show her value as a new team member.

"Which contacts do you have?" Egorin asked, surprised that someone still in college would already have significant contacts.

"I know of two offhand. Amy Hall manages the NEOSSat telescope and Sarah Levin manages the Spitzer telescope, although I don't know if either will be able to position their telescopes to help us. What should I say to them?"

"Tell them we are recording flashes on the surface of the moon where they should not exist. We should contact the Defense Department as well," Egorin replied.

"Do you think it might be an alien ship?" Golden asked eagerly, while bouncing up and down on her toes. She could already see herself standing next to Dr. Egorin and accepting an award for outstanding achievement as a rookie scientist.

"I don't want to speculate at this point. Let's just stick to what we know. It's an anomaly that blocks light and does not seem to be affected by asteroid strikes."

***

"Welcome back. I'm Joe Scarborough along with my cohost Mika Brzezinski on MSNBC's Morning Joe. We have been speaking with Dr. Egorin at NASA, who has confirmed that there is some sort of object on the dark side of the moon. No word on what it might be, but people are speculating that it might be an alien object of some sort. What can you tell us, Dr. Egorin?"

"Please, just call me Melanie. We don't know much more than you just mentioned. We certainly have not received any communications from the moon. We are receiving higher than normal energy readings though."

"Do you think some aliens saw *2001: A Space Odyssey* and planted a giant monolith there as a joke?" quipped Scarborough.

"No, not at all. But if they did, I don't think we would like what they did next. I spoke with Admiral Orth from NORAD, and she mentioned that the Chinese sent a probe up to the moon last night."

"I didn't know the Chinese scientists had been actively engaged in a moon mission."

"No one did," said Egorin. "They just sprang it on us. I guess with everyone focused on what's up there, they figured no one would complain about their plans." *What I can't tell the public is that the Chinese observed an object that appeared to be a vehicle leaving the moon and heading to Earth*, she thought.

***

"Dr. Egorin, do you think the Chinese are telling us all they know?" asked Golden, worried that politics would interfere with information-sharing between the scientific communities of both countries.

"Yes, because they are just as fearful as we are about what could be going on up there and what came to Earth," Egorin replied emphatically. "Plus, they want our help, which is evident in how they engaged us. The Chinese gave us more info about the object that came toward Earth than they presented to the press. According to their telemetry, it appears to be some sort of manned craft. NORAD picked it up as well and tracked it into the Atlantic Ocean off the coast of Nova Scotia."

“Couldn’t it have been an asteroid or some other space rock?” Golden asked, searching for a more palatable alternative.

“No, not at all. According to NORAD, the object changed direction and then decelerated before entering the water.”

Dr. Egorin reviewed her notes. “Leslie, could you ask Kerry to come in?”

Golden’s brow furrowed in confusion. “Carrie’s on vacation this week. She’s in Charleston at a blues festival.”

“No, Kerry with a ‘K’. And ask him to bring in his binders. I want to document all the images of the lunar anomaly for future reference.” The section chief turned away and began poring over the images on a screen in front of her.

***

“This is Megyn Kelly in my new role at NBC News. I have breaking news this hour on the lunar mystery. The Chinese have reported that their rocket just released a satellite over the moon, and it is now in a stable orbit. After the completion of three orbits it found no unexpected objects or debris anywhere on either side of the moon. Their satellite detected high levels of energy and radiation on the far side, which is out of the ordinary for that area of the moon–or anywhere on the moon for that matter. I hate to disappoint the conspiracy theorists listening, but the lunar landing vehicles are there as expected.” Kelly laughed before taking a pause.

“Okay, let’s get back to reality here,” said Kelly, scrawling on the papers in front of her, then looking directly into the camera.

"We have Amy Hall from the NEOSSat observatory, Sarah Levin from the Spitzer observatory and Melanie Egorin from NASA– excuse me, that's Dr. Melanie Egorin of NASA– who have all been involved in watching the skies over Earth. Thank you for joining the show."

"Happy to be here," the three scientists chorused.

"Dr. Egorin, I believe your team first spotted the anomaly."

"Please, call me Melanie. Yes, my science fellow, Leslie Golden, alerted me to the finding during a review of the previous night's logs. It showed that something had momentarily blocked out the stars from one of our telescopes that monitor the moon. Judging from our calculations, it had to be a pretty large object."

"We saw something similar," Hall chimed in. "We have telescopes at a slightly different elevation, and we detected a large object moving into position on the far side of the moon where it remained for several days."

"I can concur on the sighting, as well," interjected Levin. "We also monitored the Chinese satellite as they placed it into orbit. However, we never saw any object traveling from the moon towards Earth."

"If you consider that the event occurred during daylight hours in North America," Hall said, "we had no ability to see anything from our land-based telescopes. Our space-based telescopes are designed to observe narrow areas of space. We had them pointed at both edges of the moon at the time they spotted the object, well out of the area of visibility to see what type of object came towards Earth. However, according to the trajectory given to us by the Chinese scientists, the alleged object started its journey from the southern tip of the moon."

"I don't want to discount your findings, Amy, but we are beyond allegations at this point. A craft of some sort did travel to Earth from the moon, and it had to be of alien origin," Levin insisted, eyeing Hall as she gave a little nervous laugh.

"So you're saying there are some aliens possibly walking around on our planet right now?" Kelly asked, arching her eyebrows.

"We don't have any evidence that there are aliens on the ground," said Egorin. "But Admiral Orth, our contact at NORAD, informed us that she tracked a vehicle entering our atmosphere that later submerged below the waters off the coast of Canada."

"It could have just been a rock falling from space, right?" Kelly posited, throwing her hands up in disbelief.

"No, not really," replied Egorin, annoyance pinching her features. *I do this for a living and this 'journalist' thinks she knows more than me because she reads Wikipedia.*

"Number one, an object, which we believe to be around the size of a greyhound bus, would have created a huge tidal wave upon entering the water, but it barely made a splash. Number two, after entering the water, the UFO, if I may call it that, changed course, dodging a whale and dived out of SONAR range. Number three, working with the Woods Hole Oceanographic Institution (WHOI) using one of their HROV vehicles, we tracked the UFO to a location off the coast of Puerto Rico at a depth of about 5,000 meters before the tracker was destroyed."

“The UFO destroyed the HROV? It didn’t crash into something or just run out of fuel?” Kelly asked.

“Not according to their logs,” replied Egorin, leaning into the camera.

“Sort of odd that their acronym is WHOI, not pronounced hooey, I’m sure. Well, you heard it here first on the Kelly File. Aliens visiting Earth. At least the part covered with water. After this commercial break, we will be back to get an update on the Big Foot sighting out of Saskatchewan.”

Chapter 3

Adar Goes to Earth

Adar stood motionless against a wall in a Chicago alley, hiding in the shadows. He pushed his head against the wall behind him, attempting to force calm into his mind. Interplanetary jumps always left his brain jittery, with sparks flying like a live electrical cable scraping along a metal wall. His chaotic thoughts flashed back to the transporter room, where a medical officer fussed over him during last minute preparations before his deployment.

"Adar, try to keep still. I did what I could for your face and head," said Doctor Valera, giving him a final scan. "I can't do much about your eyes."

"There's nothing wrong with my eyes," snapped Adar. "It's the rest of you that have the problem." He had no eyelids or eyelashes above the centimeter-wide optical slits that wrapped around his skull from the bridge of his pointed nose to just in front of his ears on both sides of his face. Tear ducts kept his eyes clear. Millions of tiny optical receptors gave him a thin, but wide field of view with an astonishing degree of both near- and farsighted vision. Adar also could see quite clearly in very low-light.

"Maybe so, but your unique eyes will be noticeable to the people on the planet you are visiting unless you do something about them," said Valera, frustrated by Adar's cavalier arrogance.

The doctor, a small, wizened female of indeterminate years, worked in the indoctrination department of the *Andrea*. She helped to ensure the health of new crewmembers who reported to the ship and prepared them for new environments when leaving the ship.

“I’ll figure it out,” replied Adar, eager to start the mission. “Just place me in an alley near the location where the escapees landed, and make sure it’s dark out.”

“I can take care of that,” said Krystyy, an operations officer waiting at the controls of the transporter to handle Adar’s descent to the Earth’s surface. “Now is a good time to go, if it’s okay with you, Valera.”

“Just give me a minute. Here are some gloves to cover your hands. Keep your collar up to hide the strong contours of your neck. I dyed your hair black and fashioned it like their faux-hawk style to cover your pointed head. The gene therapy I used to fade your facial and neck stripes should last you for a good while. Your skin now has a beige tone, which should allow you to move about unremarked among any of the racial groups on their planet. I could have done your entire body, but you would be more likely to suffer from negative side effects.”

Adar gave her a sideways look as he put on the gloves and snarled at her. “Just back away, and let me get on with it.”

“You can’t go down there and expose the fact that you’re from another planet. The captain doesn’t want the population to know they’re being monitored by aliens. You’re just supposed to kill or retrieve the escapees and get back without being discovered.”

"Don't worry yourself, Valera," said Adar, climbing onto the transporter platform. "If anyone discovers me, I'll just kill them."

"You can't just kill everyone," Valera snapped.

"Oooh, but I can, kill a lot," said Adar, twisting his head to meet Valera's eyes and bare his sharp teeth. "Doctor, just back away so Krystyy can send me there. I don't need you to floss my teeth for me. The food there is a snack for later. Krystyy, let's do this."

Valera stepped away from Adar and signaled Krystyy to proceed. The operations officer called up coordinates for an alley in the West Loop area of downtown Chicago, near the location where the Cheoili disappeared, and engaged the tech that dematerialized Adar and enabled him to travel to Earth in mere seconds.

"That guy is so creepy," said Krystyy, frowning in distaste. "You see the way he snarled at you when you tried to help him?"

"Yeah, but if I needed help in a fight, he is definitely the one person I would want by my side."

***

On the darkened streets of Chicago, around the corner from where Adar materialized, two members of a local gang approached a teenager, intent on relieving the youth of his valuables.

"Hey, kid, where you going?" asked one of the men.

The scrawny teen walked along with his head down, sticking close to the buildings and away from the street lights that cast shadows across the litter-strewn sidewalk. A model student who focused on his books and avoided socializing with the miscreants who infested his neighborhood, Malcolm Stewart headed home a half-hour earlier from his job washing dishes at the hamburger joint near his school. Malcolm knew that hanging around dishonest people likely would lead to being involved in dishonest acts, and he wanted none of it.

"I'm on my way home," Malcolm told the husky gangbanger as he hurried along, not bothering to look back. "My mother's waiting for me."

"You got anything for me?" asked the man, quickening his pace to catch Malcolm.

"I don't do drugs," the teen retorted, walking even faster without actually running.

"I know you don't have drugs. I want your money." The guy snorted, then made a grab for Malcolm. The youngster dodged the outstretched hand and broke into a sprint. Seeing his path ahead blocked by another gang member, Malcolm darted to the left down an alley in hopes of finding a door left open or some other hiding place. But after a few paces, he tripped on a discarded bottle and fell on his face. When he heard footsteps approach his sprawled body, fear crawled up the boy's spine.

I hate my life. I do all the right things, and bad things still happen to me. I hope they don't hurt me this time.

Honoring his mother's guidance, Malcolm always played by the rules. He went to church every Sunday and treated strangers with respect. Still, he found himself the target of bullies at school and on the street. He believed, perhaps naively, that good behavior would be rewarded.

***

Adar inhaled deeply through his nostrils to let the implanted filters do their job. He could smell the garbage in the alley and the stench of urine and animal excrement. As his eyes adjusted to his new surroundings, he could see small creatures, which his training enabled him to identify as rats, scurrying along the far wall. Bugs flittered in a florescent light over a doorway across the alley. Muggy heat that day exacerbated odors in the alley, a nauseating cocktail of reeking runoff from a nearby dumpster and oily drippings from cars that traversed the alley.

Adar double-checked his appearance, ensuring that the long, black, microfiber coat he wore covered the handle of his spear and his rifle grip sufficiently. His black and grey patterned, long-sleeved shirt fit tightly across a muscular abdomen. Loose-fitting, black microfiber pants covered his lower limbs and the tops of his black boots. A black, metallic belt at his waist held his spear and photon rifle in place and provided an anchor for his personal shield, which would keep him safe from weapons fire. He kept his universal connection device, or UCD, in his right pants pocket. It provided him with several capabilities, including the ability to contact his colleague, Wylyy, aboard the attack ship.

Adar removed his gloves and placed his hands on the wall behind him so he could feel the texture of the bricks used to cover the façade of the building's back wall. *Crude building materials*, he thought. He scraped at the bricks with his dense fingernails and examined the red dust collected there. *I can't imagine these buildings last very long*. The odd distraction helped relieve Adar of his brain jitters, and he noticed the mugging in progress a few meters away.

Adar looked down the alley where he heard sounds of a struggle. *Two big guys beating up on one little guy. That does not seem reasonable,* he thought. *Hmm, I think a fight is the very thing I need to get my head straight*. With that, Adar replaced his gloves and headed down the alley to investigate the disturbance.

"Please don't rob me," begged Malcolm, still lying on the dirty alley floor. "I need my money to help pay for our rent. I worked all week for it."

"I don't give a damn how long you worked for it or if you pay your rent or not," said the bullying gang member, clearly accustomed to getting his way. "Cough up the dough, or I'm going to punch you again."

"Stop whining, bitch, and give us the cash," said the other gangbanger, kicking Malcolm in his thigh with his beige Timberland boots.

"So, in this place, it is okay to terrorize the weak?" Adar slowed as he approached the altercation.

"Who the fuck are you, little man? Back away, before me and my boy tear you a new one," said the husky assailant, a bit shocked to see Adar.

"I am not sure what you are saying, but where I come from, one does not take advantage of the weak. However, if you decided to attack ME, I would happily take advantage of you."

"Shoot the punk," said one of the assailants. The other guy went for the gun at his waist. Adar grabbed the talkative one by the arm and slung him against the far wall of the alley. He then spun and shoved his short spear into the chest of the other man before he could fire his weapon. The man grabbed at his chest, then aimed a look of disbelief at Adar. A gurgling sound came from his throat as Adar removed his spear, leaving him to fall to the ground, dead.

Adar stiffened slightly, noticing the blood dripping from his spear. This was the first human he had killed. The metallic smell and bright red color of the liquid spewing from the body was unfamiliar. He tasted it, letting the salty flavor swirl around his tongue.

"You killed them!" said the small human, attempting to rise from the ground.

"No, the one by the wall is still moving," said Adar, pointing to the man attempting to pull himself across the alley floor. "Hold on." Adar walked over to the gang member writhing in pain, ignored his pleas for mercy and shoved the spear into his skull.

"He is pretty much dead now," said Adar, wiping his spear on the man's pants. He then walked back toward the teenager.

"Please don't kill me," begged Malcolm, backing away from Adar.

"I am not going to kill you. I am Adar," he said, holding out his hand to Malcolm.

"I'm Malcolm," the teenager said, shaking Adar's hand nervously. "What's wrong with your eyes?"

"I am squinting." Adar looked over the two dead bodies. He took the shades off of one of them and placed them on his face. "That is better, huh?"

"You still look a little weird."

"So do you. I need a place to stay. Do you know where either of these reside?" Adar asked, pointing a gloved finger at the bodies lying in the alley. "I am sure they will not need their place anymore."

"No, but I'm sure they have driver's licenses with their addresses in their pocket. You should probably take their wallets and move out of the alley before someone sees us here."

"You go ahead and get them, while I keep watch," suggested Adar, turning toward the alley entrance.

"Okay, give me a second." *What the hell am I doing here rifling through the clothes of two dead guys?* Malcolm looked up at Adar. He wondered if he would be the next to die. Still, he followed the funny-looking guy's directions and retrieved the wallets.

"Hey, what did you do to them?" asked a third gang member who had been watching the alley. He wore the same gang colors as the duo who had accosted Adar and Malcolm. Walking towards them, he reached for a gun. Before he could aim, Adar buried his spear into the man's chest, driving him to the ground with the force of his thrust.

"We should definitely go now," Adar grunted, pulling his spear out of the latest corpse before striding out of the alley.

"You go ahead," said Malcolm. "I'm going to go this way."

"Are you my friend or my enemy?" asked Adar, tightening his grip on his spear and moving towards Malcolm.

"Friend, friend," said Malcolm, frantically waving his hands in front of Adar.

"Then help me find a place to stay," insisted Adar, grimacing.

"Okay, let's go to the corner where there's more light."

At the corner, Malcolm pulled the licenses from the wallets. "It looks like they are brothers. They have the same last name and live at the same address, which means they probably live with their parents."

Adar was confused by the statement. "So what are you telling me?"

"You're not from around here, are you?" asked Malcolm, beginning to toy with idea that the person in front of him probably wasn't born on Earth. But he'd always heard that aliens were "little green men." This Adar was little, but he wasn't green. And he wasn't thin and spindly like aliens in the movies.

Adar just cocked his head as if to study Malcolm. "Okay, don't get angry. I just mean that there are probably other people living at their house," the boy explained hastily.

"So what do you suggest?" Adar asked, attempting to analyze Malcolm's statement.

"The people you just killed work for the pimp EZ Smooth, who has a house a few blocks from here. I'm sure he lives there by himself, except for maybe some of his hoes."

"Hoes, what does that mean?" Adar looked confused. From his English lessons, he could only come up with garden utensils, which didn't make sense to him.

"Prostitutes, women of the night." Malcolm was surprised that someone who spoke English so well would not know that term.

"Why would someone live with prostitutes? Just take me to his place. I assume that he is a bad guy, if those people worked for him."

"Yes, he's very bad."

"Good, no one will miss him." Malcolm noticed a sneer cross Adar's face, and suspected another person would die tonight.

***

A few minutes later, Malcolm and Adar arrived at the pimp's house. Along the way, Malcolm looked for opportunities to get away from Adar. Adar's talent at hurling his spear at adversaries made the teen doubt he could escape.

"That's his place right there," said Malcolm, pointing to the pimp's house as they approached. EZ Smooth lived in a modest two-story brick house with wide cement stairs leading to the front door. A brightly lit doorbell glowed in the dark.

"How do we get inside?" asked Adar, unsure of how to get the attention of the occupants.

"You knock on the door or ring the doorbell and wait for someone to come to the door," said Malcolm, giving him an odd look. The evidence against Adar being from Earth was adding up.

"That is an odd way to announce oneself," Adar replied, wondering at the low-tech approach. "You go ahead and do it. When someone responds, I will do the rest."

A man opened the door to EZ Smooth's house, and Adar shoved his spear into the man's chest, pushing him back and motioning for Malcolm to follow him.

"Billy, who is it?" inquired a well-dressed man with a light coffee complexion and luxurious ringlets of black hair that touched muscular shoulders clad in an ivory silk suit. The man reclined on the deep-cushioned, white couch as Adar stalked into the large room.

"You can call me Adar, as if it matters," Adar said, before propelling the bloody spear in his hand into the fellow's chest before he could react. EZ Smooth grabbed at the spear before falling sideways. A long, glass coffee table in front of the couch held money, drugs and an unfinished tumbler of Morgan and Coke.

"Oh my God, you killed them!" gasped Malcolm. "You just killed two people for no reason."

"You said they were bad guys," Adar retorted, confused by Malcolm's distress.

"Yes, but they're supposed to be arrested and get a trial." Killing the attackers in the alley could be justified as self-defense, but these two hadn't threatened them in any way.

"Why bother?" Adar regarded Malcolm calmly.

"What are you going to do with the bodies?" asked the teen, his panic rising. He was now an accomplice to five murders, and the night wasn't over. *How do I get away from this madman?*

Adar remained calm. "Is there someone we can call to pick them up?"

"No! Not unless you want to have a bunch of police here to arrest you." Malcolm looked side to side, as if he expected an answer to his dilemma or a way out of this nightmare to magically appear out of thin air.

"Hold on," said Adar, turning away slightly. "Wylyy, are you there?" he asked, speaking into his UCD in Euclidian.

"Yeah, Adar. What's up?" answered Wylyy, from his perch in the attack ship, which now rested on the Atlantic Ocean floor.

"I got a couple of dead bodies here I need to dispose of. Just send them somewhere out of the way. They are a few meters away from me."

"What did you say and what kind of cell phone is that?" cried Malcolm, staring at Adar. "Oh my god, his body just disappeared," the teen gaped, pointing at the spot where EZ Smooth's body lay on the couch seconds earlier. He turned towards Adar, his dark eyes wide and frightened. He saw anger suffuse Adar's face.

“Friend, friend!” Malcolm shouted, waving his hands back and forth in front of Adar. “I need to go home now. My mother will be worried.” Malcolm’s legs shook and he feared he would pee his pants.

“I do not care if your mother is worried about you. Do I need to worry about you discussing what you have seen tonight?”

“No, it’s just that I am usually home by now, and my mother is probably wondering where I am.”

“Fine. Take some of this currency with you. I will need to see you later to help me figure some things out.”

“Okay, I’ll come back tomorrow before school,” Malcolm assured him, grabbing a stack of money from the coffee table and stowing it in his backpack before hurrying to leave the room. “I’ll put a sign on your door, so no one bothers you. The body out here is gone! Never mind. I’m okay. Bye!” he shouted, breaking into a sprint to the door.

Malcolm rushed home to the one-bedroom apartment he shared with his mother, his only real family. His father left years earlier, and of his two older brothers, one was serving a 20-year jail sentence, while the other had been killed two years ago by gang members. His mother, Raleesha, saw Malcolm as her last hope of being rewarded for all her years of struggling to keep a roof over her family’s head and be a good mother. She worked as a cashier in a grocery store during the day and a cleaner of office buildings at night. Malcolm wished he could do more to supplement her income.

Arriving home, he skipped dinner, went to his room and hid under his bedcovers, trying to make sense of the evening's events. *What I thought I saw can't be real. Maybe getting hit in the alley gave me hallucinations; or maybe the stress of dodging the gangs is making me crazy; or, maybe someone is playing a nasty trick on me. That's it. That guy can't be no alien. He just comes from some far off place I've never heard of. I'll just see that guy at the pimp's house tomorrow and prove it.* His next step in mind, Malcolm turned over and willed himself to sleep.

***

Adar slowly surveyed the dwelling's interior. The house seemed unremarkable outside, which camouflaged its opulence inside. The pimp had spared no expense, upgrading the kitchen with high-end stainless appliances and adding a man-cave in the basement with the latest gadgets in an elaborate entertainment center. But the house paled in comparison to Adar's typical living quarters. *This is primitive and poorly designed,* he thought. *I've been in escape pods better equipped than this place. It will have to suffice for now, but I'd better make sure no one else is here and then look around the neighborhood.*

After his reconnaissance, Adar strolled toward Adler Planetarium at the south end of Monroe Harbor. He stood for a time, watching boats as they sailed or motored by. He found the crescent moon interesting, too. The scents wafting his way from Lake Michigan captivated Adar. *No matter where I go in the universe, the water always smells different,* he thought. *I do not like being in the water, but I like watching it, listening to its sounds, and most of all, I love the smells. It constantly changes and brings life to a planet.*

Adar attached a small sensor to the railing that would detect Cheoili DNA if one of the fugitives happened to pass by. As he walked along the waterfront toward Navy Pier, Adar placed more sensors in inconspicuous places. He eventually stopped at the edge of Navy Pier to enjoy the water.

“Excuse me, mister, do you have a dollar?” a beggar asked Adar, interrupting his concentration.

“Yes, I do,” said Adar, annoyed by the intrusion.

“Can I have it to get some food?” the man asked, hunching his shoulders and holding his hand out to Adar.

Adar found the request disturbing. “This city provides free food. I have been given the location of such places. Even if they did not exist, why should I give you my money?”

“I’m broke and need the money. I’m sure you can spare a dollar.” The beggar had a beseeching look in his eyes.

“If you want money, work for it or fight for it.”

“Fuck you, asshole,” growled the fellow, before straightening his spine and turning away.

Adar reached out, grabbed the man and flung him from the pier into the water. “Now you can catch all the food you want!”

Turning to leave the pier, Adar only took a few steps before three men threw garbage at him.

“Do you not see the trash can over there?” yelled Adar, indignantly.

"Piss off, runt," one of the men retorted. "You pick up my trash."

Adar rushed toward the mouthy litterer, grabbed him by the back of his collar and slammed him against a post on the pier. The man's companions watched as Adar wrapped his gloved hand around the offender's neck and yanked him to his knees. He then placed his spear tip in the man's crotch and sliced upward through his head, cleaving him vertically, before letting the two halves of his body fall into the water.

Witnessing this brutality, the other two men tried to run but failed to get very far. Adar pulled out his photon rifle and depressed its trigger, enveloping them in an energy beam that instantly disintegrated their bodies. *These humans are such weak, self-absorbed excuses for intelligent life. I'm surprised they survived this long without being taken over,* he thought dispassionately.

The alien then walked away from the pier, dismissing the killings from his thoughts. He turned down Michigan Avenue and headed to his new lodgings to get some sleep. *Tomorrow, I go after the Cheoili*, he vowed.

***

Upon arriving in the city of Chicago, the Cheoili immediately mingled with the crowds at Millennium Park to avoid discovery. Their study of the English language had prepared them for the trip, but their looks could still give them away. From experience, they knew that when you wore a hat and glasses and covered the rest of your face with your hand, people tended to just ignore you.

"Each of you find a human and mimic the person," Daloi instructed. "Monitor how they talk and express themselves. Luckily, we learned this English language aboard the *Andrea*, and now we need to learn how to speak with the proper intonation. Let's meet over by the Peanut, as they call it, in a couple of hours."

"Shouldn't we change our clothes as well?" asked Tatan.

"Yes, we should probably get out of this prison clothing. If you like, there are plenty of places across the street to obtain clothing," replied Daloi. "It shouldn't matter what we pick out. Look around you. It's festival season here, and people are wearing all sorts of clothing. That's one of the reasons I picked this spot."

"What's the other reason?" asked Dholi.

"There are people here from all over the planet, so our differences won't be as noticeable. Let's keep moving. I suspect the Euclidian will be sending someone to this area soon to try to find us," Daloi explained, as she strolled among the festival-goers.

The trio spent considerable time mingling with visitors to the park, observing how they interacted. Daloi also contemplated their next steps. *How do we survive in this crazy place? I need a way to convert our gold and find a place to stay. In a few years, the Euclidian should forget about us.*

***

"Hey, you two," said Daloi, as Dholi and Tatan approached her. "Nice garments. Let's go find a wealthy benefactor and lay low for a while. Are you with me?"

“I’m ready,” said Dholi. “What does a benefactor look like on this planet?”

“I’m sure it’s the same as always. Nice clothes, nice accessories, and a big ego. We should be able to find someone at the Art Institute.”

“Sister, let’s find out what the most adorable look is for women here and change into that,” suggested Dholi. “It’ll make it easier to catch the right fella. We should see if this planet likes twins, as well.”

“Agreed, Dholi. You certainly have your head on right when it comes to attracting males,” said Daloi, smiling at her sister and giving her shoulder a squeeze.

“I’ll just be the cute brother hanging out with his sisters,” said Tatan, poking out his lips. The two females tittered.

***

Early the next morning, Adar opened the door to his house, annoyed by the banging on it. “What the hell do you people want?” yelled Adar at a group of men assembled on his stairs.

“Who are you, and where’s EZ Smooth?” asked the man standing in front of Adar.

“None of your business who I am,” said Adar, kicking him in the chest and over the heads of the group. “I do not know or care where EZ Smooth is. Get away from my door before I kill all of you, and do not return,” said Adar, waving his hand at them in irritation.

"Excuse me," said Malcolm, pushing his way to the front of the group and standing on the top of the stairs. "What Adar means to say is, EZ Smooth took his money and moved to Miami because he prefers the weather down there, and he liked the offer of a bigger piece of the pie from a local mob boss. His second-in-command is supposed to take over his territory here."

"That works for me," said Philly, the second-in-command, speaking up. "Who gets the house?"

"I do, unless one of you wants to fight me for it," said Adar.

"I'll fight you for it, punk," said Jimmy, a six-foot-four boxer standing behind Philly. Adar leapt from the stairs and knocked Jimmy out with one cracking blow to his face. The others stood in shock as he fell to the ground.

"Anybody else want to challenge me?" Adar asked, looking around the group.

One man reached for a gun, but Adar put the tip of his spear to the guy's chest before he could retrieve his weapon.

"I think we're good here, Adar," said Philly, slowly moving Adar's spear away from the man's chest.

"Do not come back," said Adar, walking back into the house.

Malcolm entered the house after Adar and closed the door behind them. "Here, I got you some wraparound shades so you will look more normal." *I guess I wasn't going crazy yesterday. At least I remembered to get some glasses.*

“Do I not look normal?” Adar asked, with a puzzled look on his face.

“No, and you talk funny,” said Malcolm, twisting his face expecting some backlash.

“What do you mean, I talk funny? I speak perfect English.”

“Yes, but you are speaking too proper, without contractions. No one speaks like that around here. Where are you from?”

“A long way from here.”

“Did you call there with that device last night?” Malcolm asked, hoping Adar would clear up some of his suspicions.

“No, I spoke to a colleague named Wylyy. He’s the commander of a ship not too far away.”

“Does Wylyy look like you?” Malcolm wanted to know more. He sat on the edge of the couch and listened intently to Adar’s every word.

“No, he is a Euclidian guard that is here to help me find the Cheoili that escaped from our ship. He’s assigned to the *Andrea*, just like I am. His specialty is piloting space vehicles. Mine is killing people.” The alien thought he might be telling Malcolm too much, but it felt good to share.

“What’s a Euclidian? Were you trained to be good at your jobs?” asked the teen, eagerly. He wanted to learn as much as he could about this strange person who had saved him from being beaten and robbed the night before.

"The Euclidian are a species from the planet Euclidia. They are generally much taller than I am, have beige skin, with sharp ridges on their face. Their eyes are more like human eyes, but they don't have hair on their heads like humans. The Euclidian developed the technology to transport us to different planets as well as transport us around this planet. One day they came to our planet, and my people joined their alliance. I was a warrior on our planet, and I was asked if I wanted to be paid to kill people. How could I say no? Wylyy was trained to be a good pilot."

I knew it, I knew it, I knew it. Malcolm tapped the toes of his tennis shoes up and down on the wooden floor with excitement, startling Adar. *Now what do I ask him?* "Which species are you?"

"I am an Ossie from the Ossuary System. I get the impression you are enjoying our little session here," Adar said, smiling at Malcolm and shaking his head.

"Yes, this is the best time I've ever had in my entire life. Before you change your mind, I want to know more. The Cheoili, I guess they are another species. Do they look human? Are there humans on other planets?" Malcolm thought back to the time that he watched all six of the Star Wars movies back to back. He looked at the movies with wonder. The magic of cinema filled his mind with ideas of what alien life could be like, but he never dreamed he would experience such moments in real life. But here he was. *Wow*.

"No, just Earth as far as I know. The Cheoili are able to change their appearance to look like humans. Enough talk," said Adar, a little perturbed by Malcolm's barrage of questions. "The more you know, the more likely I may need to kill you later."

"No problem, I don't want to die. Just tell me what can I do for you? I need to leave soon to go to summer school."

"Let us go. We can talk on the way," Adar suggested, moving towards the foyer.

"You should say 'let's go' instead of 'let us go'. We can go whenever you're ready."

"I am ready. Let's go," Adar replied, trying out the contraction.

"I'm ready," said Malcolm, continuing to give him grammar tips.

"I'm ready," said Adar, a bit embarrassed at the corrections but happy to be improving his English so he could blend in better.

Malcolm headed to the door. "We should hurry up, I need to meet my friends so we're safe getting to class."

"What do you mean, so you are safe?"

"Gang members hang out near the school and will hassle us if we walk alone."

"You should fight them," said Adar, shoving his fist at Malcolm. "Fighters earn respect and can become heroes."

Adar thought about growing up on his planet of Ossuary. Kids were taught from a young age how to fight and take care of themselves. Adults were often killed in battle or by animals. One was expected to be self-sufficient at an early age. Those that failed to meet the challenges of life did not last long. No one was coddled.

“I’m not a fighter or a hero. I wish I could be,” Malcolm said, his youthful face suddenly sad.

“Should not the police help?” Adar asked.

“Shouldn’t the police help? Sure, but they have too much to do to escort us to school every day. They don’t come around until after someone is hurt.”

“Don’t, hmmm. I will escort you to school to keep you safe.” That settled, Adar changed the subject. “Can you tell me where people mostly hang out in this city?”

“Most people stroll along Millennium Park, Navy Pier, or the Miracle Mile,” the teen replied.

“I have been to those places already and haven’t detected the people I am looking for.” Adar sniffed the morning air as they walked along the busy street, catching whiffs of cooking human food, ammonia and carcinogenic smoke intermingled with exhaust fumes from combustion engines.

“There are the museums, the baseball park, and the beaches up north,” Malcolm ventured.

“Okay, I will check those places,” said Adar.

“See those bus stops there?” Malcolm pointed ahead of them. “That’s where most of the kids get off of the city buses for school, which is a block away. There’s another big bus stop on the other side of the school. We usually walk around the block together, pick up our friends along the way, and head to school in a large group. That helps keep us from being attacked.”

"Hi, guys, this is my friend, Adar," Malcolm said, as he approached several teens standing on the sidewalk. Adar grunted. "He doesn't talk much," he added, falling into step with his friends as they moved forward.

Adar followed the students to school, listening to them chatter along the way, trying to pick up their speech. The group soon arrived at the school's front doors, and Adar turned to Malcolm. "I'm going to go visit those places you mentioned. Where would I go to convert this gold coin to local money?" asked Adar, showing Malcolm a coin of the kind that would have been stolen by the Cheoili.

"A gold shop or coin shop. There are several around the Washington Metro Station. Do you know where that is?"

"I can find it. I have been briefed on the area."

"Please don't attack or kill people in public. Even if you are in the right, the police might arrest you anyway, that could be a problem for you."

"I will keep that in mind. When will you be available to talk some more?" Adar asked.

"At 3:00. Listen for bells from that church over there chiming three times in a row. I'll meet you right here," said Malcolm, pointing at his feet.

"Okay. I may have a solution to your problem," said Adar, before turning and walking away.

***

"Michael, this is my sister, Daloi, and our brother, Tatan," said Dholi, walking up to her siblings in the park. "Everyone, this is Michael O'Leary. He is visiting from Dublin, Ireland and says he would like us to join him in his penthouse overlooking Lake Michigan. He's renting it for the summer so he can enjoy all of the crazy activities here."

Michael, a tall, rangy man in his mid-30s, wore his beet-red hair in a longish crew cut that complemented his muddy green eyes and pale, freckled complexion. A venture capitalist who worked on funding for startups, he looked into expanding his company's reach into the United States and found that Chicago appeared to be an overlooked market for nurturing startups. Being single and looking for an adventure, he decided to spend the summer in Chicago to broaden his portfolio and take advantage of the festival season.

"Please call me Mike. I don't know anyone in this town, and I would love to have you lovely ladies, and of course Tatan, join me if you like. Dholi hinted that you can be quite accommodating with the right stimulus."

"Oh, we can be more than accommodating, Mike," said Daloi. "We can be downright generous. Isn't that right, Tatan?"

"You bet," said Tatan. "I'm willing to do whatever I can to make this trip memorable for you."

"I don't usually swing that way, but I'm willing to try anything once." They all laughed and headed to Mike's place.

***

"Has anyone been in here with a coin similar to this?" asked Adar at the counter of a coin store.

"No, I've never seen a coin like that," said the clerk behind the counter. "Is it gold?"

Adar left without responding. *That's eight places so far and no luck. I need to find some paint*. Adar purchased two cans of gold paint, some brushes, and headed to Malcolm's school.

"What's the paint for?" asked Malcolm, walking up to Adar who waited for him outside his school.

"It's for placing a protective shield around the school."

"Right. How does that work?" asked Malcolm, thinking Adar was confused about how paint works on Earth.

"You paint the edge of the curb around the block with this paint. If anyone attempts to harm someone who is inside the protective shield they will be dealt with by an invisible force."

"Ha, ha, ha," Malcolm laughed, holding his belly.

"Why are you laughing?" asked Adar, his expression bewildered with a hint of annoyance.

"Because it sounds ridiculous. I mean, I'm not sure how it would work," said the teen, his chuckles subsiding.

"Take the paint and start painting the curb. If someone bothers you just point at the person and say 'go to sleep'."

Malcolm erupted in another fit of laughter. "You are killing me with this."

"Just do it!" shouted Adar.

"I want to be a hero, but this seems like a dangerous way to become one. The first gang member that comes along is going to beat me up if I tell him what I'm doing."

"Heroes are built out of conflict, not calm," said Adar, seeking to enlighten Malcolm.

"Fine, I'll do it." Malcolm shrugged his shoulders and opened a paint can. Adar cloaked himself and stayed close to the youth.

Where'd he go? Now I'm certain to die, Malcolm thought.

Being an Ossie, Adar could use a type of mental energy field to cloak, or make himself invisible, for as long as 15 minutes before suffering brain fatigue. A person could stand right in front of a cloaked Ossie and even touch one without registering his or her presence. Ossies also could distort light reflecting from their bodies to make them appear as grey blurs to any monitoring devices. The randomness of the distortion also made it difficult to target the beings during combat.

"Malcolm, what are you doing? Aren't you going to walk with us to the bus stop?" asked Lauren, one of his classmates. Lauren was the rebel to Malcolm's conformist. She wore a short afro with one side of her head shaved. Her left ear had five piercings, while her right ear had none. She loved wearing Betsy Johnson fashions, while most students wore more demure clothes.

"No, I need to paint a protective coating on the curb so we'll be safe from people hassling us."

"That is the dumbest thing I ever heard. But I guess we'll get a chance to see if it works," said Lauren, noticing a menacing character approaching them.

"What are you doing kid?" asked a gang member, walking up to Malcolm.

"I'm putting this protective coating on the curb so students will be safe from bullies attacking them," said Malcolm, hoping the hulking fellow would just walk away.

"I don't know what they teach you in that school, but crap like that don't work. What's going to stop me from kicking you in the face?"

"Go to sleep," Malcolm said, pointing at the gang member, who promptly fell to the ground. Everyone gasped, even Malcolm. "I guess it works," said Malcolm, who continued painting.

"Let me help," offered Lauren. Placing her Gucci backpack on the ground, she took a brush from the bag and dipped it into the can Malcolm held.

"Will it work if I say it?" Lauren asked, hoping to get a turn at using the phrase.

"I guess. Only one way to find out," said Malcolm.

"What did you do to my friend?" demanded another man, who approached the two.

"Go to sleep," said Lauren, pointing at the man, who immediately crumpled to the ground.

Other kids began to cheer.

"Let me do it, let me do it," begged Justin, a fellow student, walking up.

"This is not a game. You can't just knock people out for no reason," said Malcolm, hoping not to start a ruckus.

"Okay," said Justin. "Can I at least carry the extra paint can for you?"

While the kids focused on painting the curb, news of their exploits spread across the block like wildfire. Gang members heard about the strange episodes and worried that their street cred might be damaged if they didn't confront the kids. To regain control of the situation, the gangbangers decided to investigate in person.

"You kids need to get up out of here, now!" shouted a gang member, as he drew near. "And if any of you point at me, trying to put me to sleep, you dead. You feel me?" He patted the gun in his waistband to make his point.

Lauren and Malcolm stopped painting and looked at each other. "What do you think Malcolm?" asked Lauren. "I don't want any of our friends to die because of what we are doing."

"They need to choose for themselves," he replied. "I'm not backing down."

Turning to the bystanders, he shouted, "All of you need to go home. Lauren, Justin and I will finish this. If we don't make it, hopefully our deaths will force the police to help the rest of you."

"We're not leaving!" their friends declared, defiantly gathering around Lauren, Justin and Malcolm.

"Then you're all dead," sneered the gang member. "Let's blast them."

Two of his compatriots pulled guns from their pants, and Lauren and Malcolm pointed fingers at them. This prompted a third person to go for his gun.

Just like in the movies, everything seemed to move in slow motion. The teens' friends threw themselves on top of the three painters to try and block the barrage of bullets about to stream their way.

Startled by their friends' actions, Lauren and Malcolm covered their heads and looked away from the attackers. One of the gang members used his gun to fire at the pile of children in front of him. The mere squeezing of the trigger sent shockwaves through the crowd before the bullet even left the gun's chamber. Following the shot, a loud *whoosh* of a concussion from an unknown blast pushed the crowd back on its heels. Two gang members standing next to each other glowed a bright blue and vanished in a cloud of ash. The third gang member got off a shot, but then suffered the same fate.

The crowd stood stunned by the apparent vaporization of the three men into thin air. They looked at the children, the target of the gun shots, and found they had come to no harm. Two mangled slugs lay motionless on the ground in front of the teens. Lauren picked one up with trembling fingers, realizing that this moment empowered her to confront the gang members.

"We are not afraid of you," she shouted, standing and pushing kids away from her as she emerged from the crowd. Dropping the slug, she continued her verbal assault on the miscreants who remained. "You now see that not only can we put you to sleep, but we can cause you to burn. I considered sharing the block with you, but no more. Leave now or be burned!" she warned, pointing at the remaining gang members.

Silently, they retreated into the shadows as the crowd cheered. Malcolm suddenly had a lot of people wanting to help finish painting the curb.

"Thanks, Adar," he whispered, looking up at the sky. In his ear he heard the words, "You're welcome."

***

Lauren and Malcolm finished painting the block with help from their fellow students and some neighbors. Nearby residents also brought cake and punch to celebrate the project's completion.

"Here they come!" someone shouted, pointing at a car slowly rolling toward them. The car steadily cruised closer to the festivities. Eyes peered at the crowd from the dark interior of the car as it passed. Fingers could be seen pointing their way from the open window. Malcolm rushed to the curb and waved his finger back at the car in defiance. The car sped off down the street and around the corner. As everyone feared, it returned from the other direction. Lauren took her place at Malcolm's side.

"Malcolm, I'm not sure how this is going to turn out, but I'm with you to the end," said Lauren, grabbing his hand.

The two kids pointed their fingers at the car as the occupants opened fire on the two youths with automatic weapons. The crowd moved away from the kids hoping to avoid getting shot.

"Get down," came shouts from the crowd, but the two refused to move. Slugs from the gun shots merely fell at Malcolm and Lauren's feet. As the car continued down the street an invisible force smashed the back window of the car window and the attackers could be heard screaming loudly as the car slowed and rolled to a stop against the curb several meters from the teens.

"Oh, my God! There's nothing in that car but a pile of bloody flesh," screamed a woman, who looked in the car window as she scampered by.

***

Shortly after the shooting ended, the Chicago Police arrived to investigate.

"Captain, you are not going to believe what I'm looking at here," a patrol officer spoke into his radio mouthpiece. "It looks like a giant blender went off in the car. There's blood and body parts all over the place. I don't think I'm going to be able to eat for a week. The witnesses I've been able to interview are telling the most fantastical stories. I don't know if we will ever know what really transpired here."

Lauren and Malcolm walked toward home, after giving a statement to the police. They left out the part about putting people to sleep.

"Lauren, I'm not sure what happened here today. One thing's for certain though, we won't have trouble getting to school anymore." Malcolm gave her a fist bump.

"You are so right, Malcolm. Gimme five!" she exclaimed, high-fiving her friend before he pulled her close for a hug.

***

Mike and the three Cheoili ambled around Millennium Park enjoying the various activities and trying the variety of food they ran across. The Cheoili did what they could to learn about life on Earth during their stroll, asking Mike many questions, while taking care not to reveal anything about their origins.

"Mike, we didn't bring a lot of cash with us, and we're running low," said Daloi. "Is there anywhere we could convert coins like this to dollars?"

"What is this, gold?" Mike asked, flipping one over in his hand.

"Yes," said Daloi, wondering if telling him was a mistake.

"It's certainly a big one. This coin alone must be worth over $5,000."

"Is that a lot?" she asked, projecting wide-eyed innocence.

"You obviously don't get off the farm much. You can't buy a nice car with it, but it's a lot to be carrying around on you. There are people who would kill you if they knew you had this coin."

Good thing they don't know we have lots of these coins. "So you think we can convert them to cash?" Daloi persisted.

"Sure. There's a place a few blocks from the condo I'm renting. It has some French name," said Mike, scratching his head in an attempt to remember the name.

"Let's go by there on the way to your place. We could use some cash to buy some booze and food for this evening's festivities," Daloi suggested.

Mike smile broadly. “So should I be excited or afraid?”

“You should be afraid, very afraid.” Daloi grinned up at him, showing her teeth. “We are going to do things to you that will make you wish you had a bodyguard to get us off of you.”

Mike clapped his hands together loudly as he laughed. “I cannot wait to see what you have planned.”

***

After walking Lauren home, Malcolm ran to Adar’s place.

“Adar, are you there?” he yelled, banging on his door. Adar opened the door, and Malcolm wrapped the little alien in a bear hug. “It was you, wasn’t it? You saved us.”

“I killed some bad guys. That is all,” replied Adar, disinterestedly. “Now stop embracing me.”

“Thanks for doing that.” Malcolm hugged Adar again.

“You don’t need to thank me. I did what I did because I don’t like cowards, especially when they are attacking someone I care about. It is like they are attacking me, and I won’t tolerate that. Why are there so many violent people walking around?” asked Adar, hoping to gain additional insight into Earth culture.

“It’s not like this everywhere,” Malcolm started. “Areas where there are fewer jobs can make people feel desperate enough to commit crimes. Chicago Mayor Rahm Emanuel was supposed to fix things when he took office, but crime in the city is just as bad as ever,” Malcolm said, thinking of friends from his neighborhood who had been shot recently.

"On the Euclidian home planet, it is rare for anyone to ever get shot. When it does happen, it tends to be a visiting alien carrying illegal weapons that causes the shooting." Adar made a face as if he remembered a personal incident.

"When are you going to tell me how you are able to do what you did to those gangbangers?" Malcolm asked, sitting up in his seat, eyeing the alien intently.

"It would be safer for you not to know," replied Adar, turning away from Malcolm and walking into the house.

"I've never felt safer in all my life than since I met you. I'm usually afraid going to school, afraid going home, and afraid to go to sleep at night. Now I have real confidence. I won't let those people bully me anymore."

"You should never be afraid. It is better to die than to live in fear. What is wrong with your eyes?" Adar asked, stopping to stare at Malcolm's face.

"It's nothing. I'm crying, but it's because I'm just so happy that I got to know you."

"That is sickening. I need you to give me more info on how to find people new to this planet. If a person just arrived in this city, how would that person survive?"

"Well, the person could get a job, use public services, or become a criminal," Malcolm theorized.

"Getting a regular job is not practical for them. What is public services?"

"There are places in the city where you can get free food and a place to stay, but you have to sleep with a bunch of smelly strangers."

"They wouldn't do that. How does one become a criminal and survive here?"

"You can steal things, sell drugs, become a prostitute, and if you are good enough you can have your own gang that does it for you. It's like those people who harass us on the way to school and the guy that used to live here," Malcolm said sadly.

"I don't see them being on the street, but they might finagle their way into a place like this."

"Tell me more about who you're looking for and maybe I can help you find them."

Adar turned his head for a moment, as if lost in thought. "Okay, but I need you to keep this to yourself."

"I will," said Malcolm, sitting on the edge of an ottoman and listening intently as Adar began his story.

"I work in the security department on a spaceship that is many light years from here."

"Why do you look so normal? Except for your eyes of course."

"There are people on the ship that specialize in helping us to adapt to new environments. They modified my face pigment, they gave me nostril filters to wear, and they refashioned my pointed head to look like your fauxhawk hairstyle. They couldn't do anything about my eyes though."

"How'd you learn English and how to get around?"

"The same way you did, I studied. I'm just better at it," Adar said proudly. "We are given logistics on every place to which we are being dispatched before we transport down. I read maps, understand commerce, and know how to operate all sorts of vehicles. Those things are similar on all planets."

"Will I ever get to go with you to see what life is like on other planets?" Malcolm asked, his eyes widening.

"Probably not. While visiting other planets might sound thrilling, being alone in a sea of aliens can wear on you. Three aliens from the planet Alpha killed a lot of people and got away with a bunch of loot, including gold coins that look like this one." Adar showed a coin to Malcolm. "They escaped from our ship and came here."

"You said they look like humans, so how will you recognize them?"

"By their smell or their blood, and I have sensors that can detect their DNA," Adar said, pulling one from his coat pocket.

"It would take forever to sniff and cut everyone in this town," said Malcolm, shaking his head in disbelief.

"I understand that. There are other things I can do. I'll start off by investigating some gang leaders, which would be a way for them to get some money and find a place to stay. Maybe that will give me some clues. Where do gangs usually hang out?"

"I would guess places where there's crime. The south side has the most crime. I would suggest going over closer to State Street."

"Okay, I'll see what I can find," said Adar, walking out the door and leaving Malcolm alone in the house.

Chapter 4

The Cheoili Settle In

Back at Mike's rented condo, he and the three Cheoili were getting better acquainted. Mike lay on top of Daloi, Tatan lay on top of Mike, and Dholi stood at the foot of the bed and whipped Mike's feet with a belt.

"Oh my god, stop, I can't take anymore," gasped Mike, totally exhausted. "Where's a bodyguard when I need one?" They all laughed, remembering Daloi's earlier witticism.

Dholi used some cucumber towelettes to cool Mike down and wipe the sweat and bodily fluids from his skin.

"Does that feel better?" cooed Dholi.

"You bet it does," said Mike, basking in the extra attention. "Where did you learn to do that?"

"We used to do a little rolling in the hay back on the farm in Iowa. Not much to do on the farm at night, especially in winter. Election season is always fun, though."

Dholi enjoyed spinning stories, one of her great talents. Not as extraordinary as her ability to seduce others, regardless of gender. Unlike their sister, Dholi and Tatan had a hard time learning the culture and language on Alpha. Finding a decent job had taken them even longer. They finally settled on being spa technicians. The enzymes secreted by their touch helped people relax, and their talents as masseurs kept them flush with clientele.

Clients found their talents to be literally orgasmic, though the pay was still lousy.

The three Cheoili played off of each other's talents: Dholi, the amorous one; Daloi, the ambitious one; and Tatan, the cautious one. This worked to help keep them safe. After struggling through numerous low-paying jobs, Daloi decided that a life of crime provided the best means of making money and stuck with it.

"You could be professional prostitutes with your talents," squealed Mike.

"What does that really mean?" asked Tatan. "I know what the words mean, but what do they really do and how do they make money at it? What does one even look like?"

"If you want to see a few in person, there's a little action at State and Illinois. You need to walk west on Madison Street, starting at Michigan Avenue, if you want to see where they mainly hang out. Why don't we just go by there and have a look for ourselves?"

The three nodded, and Mike headed into the bathroom to shower. The four of them left the condo a short time later and grabbed a cab to West Madison Street, where they planned to take a stroll in the evening air. Tatan stepped from the vehicle first, only to be greeted by a woman of the night.

"Hey, sugar, looking for some company?" asked the woman, stepping out of the shadows and sliding her hand down Tatan's arm.

"I have company," Tatan stammered, surprised by the scantily clad brunette who seemed to appear out of nowhere. Though he had participated in escapades with Daloi and Dholi, the Cheoili male was a bit shy on his own. He found humans mysterious and feared engaging one without his sisters at his side. *What are their mannerisms? Do they bite? Do they exchange strange bodily fluids that might make me sick?* Tatan, though eager to learn about this new species, preferred to move at his own pace.

"I'll bet your friends won't do what I'm willing to do for you," said the curvy female, rubbing Tatan's chest and scratching at his nipple. "I'll even let them watch."

"Tatan, I see you already found someone to keep you company," said Mike, chuckling.

"I'm happy to make it a party," the lady said with a smile. "My friends would be delighted to join us and make it one big party if you like. What do you think?" she leaned forward and exposed her breasts under her loose-fitting top. Three other women in heavy makeup and tight, skimpy clothing approached and posed seductively around her.

"We're just out for a stroll," said Mike. "Though I must admit, I find your offer quite titillating."

"Come on, Mike," ordered Daloi, pulling him away. Dholi grabbed his other arm. "Why do you need them when you have us?"

"How much do they charge for their company?" asked Dholi, fascinated by the exotic-looking women.

"Depends on what you want them to do, how many are involved, and how long you want them to stay. It can cost a hundred dollars for a simple hand job or several thousand to have the four of them spend the night and do all sorts of strange things to you."

"If it's so lucrative, why aren't there lots of people out here doing it?" asked Dholi, looking around.

"The biggest reason is because it's illegal. Performing sex acts for strangers can be a brutal profession. You never know how a client is going to treat you. Plus, the pimp keeps most of the money. It's not easy for the pimp either. He has to keep his women safe and happy, pay off law enforcement, and possibly split his profits with a mob boss just to do business out here in public."

"Who does the mob boss report to?" Daloi asked, eager to learn the mechanics of crime on Earth.

"Normally, no one. Major cities usually have a group of mob bosses that split the city up into territories. They typically cooperate with each other to avoid turf wars that might scare away clientele and draw the attention of the police."

"So we should become mob bosses," said Daloi.

"Easier said than done," said Mike, wondering how serious Daloi might be.

"Okay, but I find the idea interesting," she persisted.

"I'm going to head back, you three," said Mike, angling his thumb in the direction of his condo.

"Okay, you mind if we don't join you? We want to stay out and play for a while," said Daloi, her eyes full of mischief.

"Sure, but you need to be careful. It can get dangerous out here."

"We can be pretty dangerous, ourselves." Daloi grinned and cast a sly glance at her siblings.

Mike ordered an Uber on his phone and headed home.

"Why don't we find a mob boss to hang out with until we learn the system, and then take over his territory?" suggested Daloi. "If we have to stay in this hell-hole of a planet, we might as well enjoy ourselves."

"Why don't we just find a rich guy and live off of him?" countered Tatan."

"Because I like to run things," Daloi snapped. "We'll stay at Mike's place for now, but let's find out who the main mob boss is around here and get an introduction."

***

Adar took Malcolm's advice and headed to Chicago's south side, looking for evidence of the Cheoili.

Here I am on the south side, but where's the crime? Doesn't look like a place the Cheoili would hang out. I hear they're too prissy for this type of area. What's that over there? Looks like a street fight. Maybe I can join in.

Adar saw four men attacking a woman in a grassy area behind a high school. As he approached them, one of the attackers knocked the woman to the ground while the other three lunged at her.

"Why would you take on four people you obviously can't beat?" Adar asked the woman lying on the ground.

"They attacked me, asshole," the woman retorted.

"You can have her when we're done, buddy," said one of the attackers. "She's one of those cage fighters who thinks she's too good for us."

"I *am* too good for you. You're broke and illiterate, and you smell like an ashtray. Quick, give him a math problem and watch him stutter for five minutes."

"See what I mean?" The talkative assailant grabbed the woman's wrist and slapped her. "She doesn't know when to shut the hell up."

"Do you want me to help you, lady?" asked Adar.

"Yes, please give this guy a breath mint."

"Bitch, I'm going to knock you out and you're going to wake up with my baby inside you," the thug warned, his voice a throaty growl.

"If I do, I'll dig it out with a spoon." The man pulled his arm back to punch the woman in the face, but Adar grabbed him before he could let fly and pulled him away.

"What the hell's your problem, buddy?" the man asked angrily, sizing up Adar as being easy to crush.

"How far do you think it is to that trash receptacle?" Adar asked the guy conversationally.

"You mean the dumpster? Are you stupid?"

"I told you math problems make his head hurt," the woman interjected, laughing.

Adar leaned forward, grabbed the man by his crotch and tossed him into the air. The assailant landed on the edge of the dumpster, loudly cracking his neck and falling to the ground.

"Damn it, I missed," cursed Adar. "I'll try to do better with the three of you," he added, turning to the other men.

The three remaining attackers had been watching the action, dumbstruck.

"The hell you will," said one of them, before Adar grabbed him by the crotch and tossed him towards the dumpster.

Adar made quick work of two attackers, planting them in the nearby dumpster like gangly shrubs, while the woman punched the remaining one into oblivion. Adar snatched him up and then flung him towards the dumpster, just missing getting both of his legs inside.

"I need to practice that more. By the way, I did not need your help. I enjoy fighting," Adar said, looking back at the woman as he walked away.

"Phenomenal work," gushed the woman, stopping Adar with a hand on his shoulder. "How are you able to throw a person that far?"

"I grab the person by the crotch and twist my body real fast," explained Adar, demonstrating the move. "What is the cage fighting they talked about?"

"I'm an MMA fighter. You know, mixed martial arts," the woman said, taking a fighting stance.

"I never heard of it. Sounds interesting though. I would like to see one of your fights."

"Of course. By the way, thanks for saving me. I'm Yolanda." She held out a hand. "Want to come by my place for a drink? I'd like to thank you, properly."

Yolanda was a statuesque, muscular beauty with curly, dark hair fashioned in a short afro, deep brown eyes, full lips and hips to match. She wasn't much for conversation or waxing poetic with intellectual guys. She didn't like dumb men without ambition, either. She liked getting raw and physical with a man who knew what he wanted and wasn't afraid to go after it. Someone like Adar appeared to be. *Yummy!*

Though she had a degree in political science, Yolanda spent most of her time perfecting her MMA skills, her bigger passion, to the extent that she had quit her job at a lobbying firm to pursue fighting full-time. Of course, the coworker's finger that she broke for patting her ass had something to do with her change in careers as well.

Fighting didn't pay much, at least for now. So all she could afford was a small one-bedroom apartment near State Street and South Lowe on the south side of Chicago. The area was crime-ridden, but cheap.

Yolanda didn't like to sleep around, but she did have needs. She avoided men in the neighborhood and ones at the gym. Adar, however, had possibilities. *He could probably teach me a thing or two about fighting. And why not get me some, while I'm at it? I bet he could take me hard!*

"I am Adar," he said, shaking her hand. "I'm not sure what you mean, but I would like to find out."

"Don't worry, I'll explain as we go," she assured him, grabbing his arm and leading him toward her place.

***

Seamus Duggan became a Chicago mob boss early in life. He ran criminal operations in North Chicago, including the coveted Gold Coast, where tall luxury condominium buildings lined the western shore of Lake Michigan. Business leaders, senior politicians, and even celebrities such as Oprah, John Cusack and Vince Vaughn lived there. Seamus kept the rich satiated with prostitutes and drugs, and they paid him handsomely and kept the police off his back.

Seamus was a short bowling ball of a man who enjoyed punching an opponent's face in. He used his fists, in fact, to batter his way up through the ranks to become a mob boss in Chicago. When the previous boss unexpectedly died, Seamus fought the other lieutenants for the top spot, leaving them broken and bloody. His short stature made him difficult to hit and made it impossible for opponents to duck his punches. The best a person could hope to achieve was to outrun him and keep running. Seamus had too much class to shoot a person in the back.

Seamus ran his operation like a corporation and owned legitimate businesses. His people had healthcare, retirement plans, and even gym memberships. His one blind spot was trust. He counted on his men to manage the collection of funds from the street, believing paying his people well kept them from wanting to skim from him. However, his team, being greedy, could not resist taking extra money. His lieutenants figured they would eventually cash out or run like hell if he caught them.

Daloi, Dholi, and Tatan walked into Seamus's office at the top of a building in Lincoln Park where he ran his drug operation. Daloi had convinced Alegra, a hooker she met during their outing, to get them a meeting with the mob boss.

"Hello, Seamus," said Daloi, shaking his hand. "Thanks for meeting with us."

"How could I say no to Alegra's passionate plea for an introduction," Seamus said, eyeing his visitors with keen interest. "You made quite an impression on her."

"We can be quite persuasive when we need to be. We thought a man like you could use our talents to help make sure your operation runs smoothly." Daloi smiled with satisfaction.

"Forgive me. You are quite attractive, which may entice people to do your bidding. However, you don't seem like enforcer types to me," Seamus said, his voice condescending.

"I can understand why you might be a little hesitant to trust strangers. Why don't we give you a sample of our skills? I hear Ronny over there has been skimming from you. Let's find out what he does with the money," Daloi suggested, walking over to a man sitting in an armchair to Seamus's right.

"Seamus, the bitch is crazy!" cried the guy named Ronny. "You know I wouldn't steal from you."

"Just relax, Ronny," Dholi said, grabbing the man's hand and rubbing his neck.

"Yes, take it easy, Ronny," said Daloi, grabbing his other hand. "It's just the three of us here. Don't you want us to make you happy?" she said, rubbing his chest.

"Yes, I do." Ronny was panting.

"Is it easy to hide money from Seamus?" Daloi inquired in a soft voice.

"Yeah, he's so busy kissing politicians' asses he doesn't have time to monitor what we're doing." Ronny snickered, his true feelings surfacing as toxins from the Cheoili's hands overwhelmed him.

"So where do you keep the extra money?" Daloi asked.

"I ship most of it to the Bahamas where I run some gambling rackets. Once my casino opens there, I'm leaving this dump. I hate the winters here."

"Who else knows about this?" whispered Daloi.

"My boy, Giorgio. He helps me run the operation," Ronny said, hooking thumbs in his lapels and grinning widely.

Daloi looked back at Seamus to see his reaction.

Seamus nodded once, and Dholi covered Ronny's mouth while Tatan held his legs. Daloi then dug her fingers into Ronny's chest and ripped out his heart.

Daloi held Ronny's heart out to Seamus as if offering him a trophy before she licked it, all the while studying the mob boss for his reaction.

"What do you think, Seamus?" Daloi asked. "Do we have a job?"

"Yes. For now, you certainly do. Your first task will be to take control of those gambling operations and get me my money back." He pounded his desk for emphasis.

"I will be delighted to." Daloi tossed the heart into the trash and wiped her hands on Ronny's pants. "Tatan, I need you to memorize this guy's looks for me."

"I can do that," Tatan replied, studying Ronny's face.

"Do you want me to check the rest of your staff to see what they're hiding?" Daloi asked Seamus.

Stan, another of Seamus's lieutenants, stood abruptly. "Boss, this ain't right."

Seamus glanced at him briefly, before telling Daloi, "That'll do for now. But I do need you to clean up that mess."

Daloi, who began watching Stan after his outburst, slinked over to the mobster, grabbed his face with both hands and kissed him on the lips. "Stan, you don't mind taking care of this mess for us, do you?"

"No, not at all," he replied, confusion contorting his swarthy features.

"Good boy." Daloi patted Stan on the head. She then crossed her arms and shot Seamus a smirk over her shoulder.

"You three are going to work out just fine, Daloi." Seamus laughed, thinking that Daloi's antics were delightful.

***

Adar followed Yolanda into her apartment and took a look around while she visited the ladies room. She clearly lived a Spartan lifestyle. No pictures hung on the walls, and a few pieces of rickety furniture filled her tiny living room, along with a small TV for entertainment.

"Adar, have a seat on the couch, and I'll grab you a beer." Yolanda returned to the room, wearing a red t-shirt and matching jogging pants. "You okay with Bud Light? That's about all I can afford."

"Sure, that sounds fine," replied Adar. He had no idea what she meant, but thought he would at least give it a try.

"Here you go." Yolanda handed him a can, after popping the top, and then plopped down on the worn, tweed couch next to him. "I have to tell you that men who can fight and respect women just turn me on, tremendously. Cheers!" She sighed, clinking Adar's beer with her own can.

Adar said, "Cheers," and took a swig. "This is fizzy. Does it contain alcohol?"

"Yes. Haven't you had beer before?" Yolanda smiled and nudged Adar. Her eyes sparkled, though one had been blackened in the fight. She didn't care–the pain of the altercation was already behind her. She wondered when Adar would tear off her clothes.

"No, and I can probably do without any more," Adar said, grimacing after his first taste of the brew.

"That's okay. I can think of something else we can do to pass the time," Yolanda cooed, before setting her beer on the scarred coffee table her mother gave her. She leaned toward the alien to kiss his neck.

"Do I detect cinnamon cologne? You smell just like a cookie, and right now all I want to do is eat you," she said, nibbling his neck. "Come on into my bedroom."

Yolanda took Adar by the hand and led him into her darkened bedroom where she started to take off her clothes.

Adar watched her disrobe, using his acute eyesight to view her every curve and muscle. She was fit, but didn't have tough skin like female Ossies.

Not what I had hoped for. But any port in space, he thought.

Adar undressed and pushed Yolanda against the wall. He then wrapped his hands around her thighs, lifting her until her lips met his.

Now that is a man with vim and vigor, the woman thought, screeching with delight and digging her nails into the alien's shoulders. Adar used his long, soft tongue to ensure she was thoroughly moist. He then lowered her into place and began thrusting into her.

That's what I like, a strong man who knows what he wants and takes it. Yolanda moaned as pleasure filled her core. Then she noticed that Adar was losing his balance.

"What's wrong, are you getting weak in the knees?" she asked.

The tiny amount of alcohol he imbibed in the mouthful of beer had taken its toll on the alien's equilibrium, making him teeter with the wriggling woman in his arms. "Don't worry, baby. I'll take care of you," Yolanda crooned, easing herself off of him.

Yolanda pushed Adar onto the bed behind him, straddled his waist and proceeded to take charge. She grabbed his wrists, pinning him to the bed, and drove herself against him, until ecstasy hit her like strong waves crashing into a rocky shore. "Oh, that is so good." She groaned and squirmed enthusiastically.

The entire time that Yolanda had her way with Adar, the alien emitted growly whimpers as he tried to regain his strength. Resigning himself to being taken, Adar was enthralled by the multiple peaks and lulls of sensations coursing through him.

Yolanda exhausted herself with the energetic workout and rested her head on Adar's chest. Minutes later, she rolled off of him and lit a candle.

"What's with the funky tattoo and black mask? Are you part of some strange gang?" she asked. Her arms akimbo and hands gripping her sides, she gave Adar a stern look.

Adar stared at her blankly. Confused by the questions and drained by the sex and alcohol, he just threw up his hands.

"And where the hell are your balls?" she asked. "Okay, you're just a bit too strange for me. Thanks for helping me out and the sex" –she paused to snicker–"but you gotta go. Go on, get out of my apartment. If I get in the mood to have sex with a man with tiger stripes all over his body again, I'll give you a call."

Adar grabbed his clothes and his glasses and walked out, frustrated. *First time I've ever gotten that reaction from a woman. I guess I should have kept my glasses on. Why can't I find a Raina or Rhana down here*?

***

Daloi and Tatan met with Ronny's boy, Giorgio, at his Wicker Park apartment to learn more about the money Ronny had skimmed from Seamus with Giorgio's help.

"Hi, Giorgio. This is my new woman, Daloi," said Tatan, posing as Ronny. "Forgive me for dropping over here out of the blue, but the boss is on to us. Where are the books?"

"You know where the books are," said Giorgio. "Why are you asking me?"

"Humor me," said Tatan, grabbing Giorgio behind the neck and giving him a gentle stare.

"Sure. They're in the safe. Let's go get them." Giorgio handed the books to Tatan, who began poring over them.

"Thanks. I'll get these back to you. Why don't you get everyone together so I can explain how we are going to be operating going forward?"

"I should be able to set something up for tonight. I'll ping you once that happens."

"Great. I look forward to seeing you all tonight," said Tatan, walking out with Daloi.

"Once we get an understanding of who the players are, we will exterminate Giorgio and you'll take his place," said Daloi. "Slowly but surely, we will make Seamus' empire our own."

Chapter 5

Cage Fighting

Malcolm sat up in bed contemplating his life as he listened to his mother leave the apartment, headed to her next job. *What can I do to make a difference? All my life I've been afraid. Afraid of being beat up, afraid of going hungry, afraid my mother would disappear, leaving me alone. I want to stop being afraid of bad things happening and step up and defeat them when they appear.*

In answer to my prayers, the Almighty sent me this amazing gift of Adar. He's short, doesn't know our culture, and is trying to find other aliens who act like chameleons in Chi Town, which has nearly 3 million residents. But he charges head-on at a problem, taking down anybody who gets in his way. I need to go help him. I need to go learn from him. Maybe I'm worried that if he leaves I'll go back to being afraid again. Maybe I will, but for now, I choose to face my fears.

With new resolve, Malcolm leapt out of bed, pulled on a polo shirt in his school colors, slid into a pair of G-Star jeans, laced up his new pair of Skechers and headed to Adar's place.

***

"What are you still doing here?" Adar asked, walking into his house. Malcolm was perched on the edge of the couch watching an episode of *The Walking Dead*. In it, he noticed how the good guys stayed ahead of the zombies. He perked up at the sight of Adar.

"I thought about what you told me, and I want to help you find those bad guys." Malcolm grinned ruefully. "You did help me get rid of my bad guys."

Though Malcolm returned to Adar's house to face his fears, he also envisioned embarking on a space adventure. *How cool would it be to stand on the bridge of the Starship Enterprise, helping Captain Kirk kill the Klingons? Now, here I am in the middle of my own sci-fi thriller, and I don't want to pass it up because I'm too afraid.*

"If you want to help, tell me about MMA," Adar prodded.

"You mean mixed martial arts?"

"Yes, that."

"It's where two people go into a boxing ring, arena, or cage and fight each other. The fighters can use their hands, feet, or other parts of their body to attack their opponent. It's much more interesting than boxing, but more dangerous for the fighters. There are matches at different places across town. There should be one at the UIC Forum tomorrow night, if you want to see one."

"Good. I want to go see it," said Adar, punching his fist into the palm of his hand.

Malcolm became excited, realizing he could do something for Adar. He had never seen him in such a good mood before. "I can go with you, right? I can help explain everything about the fighting to you."

"Sure. Just stay out of the way," said Adar, uneasy about having to rely on a juvenile human.

"Do you fight in arenas where you come from?" asked Malcolm, eager to learn more about Adar's life in space.

"Yes, I do some of that from time to time," Adar bragged.

"I'll bet you're pretty good. Do you fight different-looking aliens like in *Star Wars*? Do you have any pictures?"

"I do not know your *Star Wars* so I can't tell you if our aliens are similar to the ones you've seen or not. There are a variety of aliens that I have fought on my ship. Here, let me show you." Adar sat next to Malcolm on the couch and pulled out his UCD.

Malcolm watched attentively as Adar showed him stills and videos from a few of his matches. The scenes astonished the teen, many of them showing the different forms of humanoid creatures. "What's that in the background?" Malcolm pointed to an area on the screen behind the fighters.

"That is a group of entertainers they use to help fill the quiet moments between matches. The promoters like to keep people in their seats, so they have bizarre acts perform magic tricks, shoot fire out of their mouths or do other things that will attract the attention of the crowd," explained Adar, gesturing wildly with his arms.

"That person looks a bit outlandish, sort of like the performer on our planet named Madonna. Is she flying?" Malcolm pointed to movement across the screen.

"She is probably just wearing an antigravity belt or using an antigravity pad. The Euclidian discovered a way to control gravity some time ago. However, there is a species that can control gravity mentally and kind of fly without technology. They almost destroyed our ship."

"How did your ship survive?" Malcolm asked, hoping to hear a Star Wars-like story.

"We killed them all. At least most of them. We have one confined in a holding cell back on my ship," Adar said, without embellishment.

That revelation shocked Malcolm, and he wondered if Adar's presence heralded a prelude to a full invasion. "So is that our fate? Are you going to kill all of us?"

"I am just here to find three escapees and then I'm headed back to my ship," said Adar, avoiding a direct answer to Malcolm's question.

"I'd love to see it someday. I always wanted to be part of a great galactic adventure. We have lots of science fiction movies that pretend they know what life is like on other populated planets. You really know. You really live on a spaceship," Malcolm said, his eyes large as saucers.

"It is not practical for you to visit my ship. And you do not have to go light years away to be part of an adventure. You can have your own adventure right here, like taking me to the fights tomorrow."

Malcolm laughed. "I'm sure that will be a great adventure for you. But I want one of my own."

"Stick around me long enough, and you will have one," said Adar, shoving Malcolm's shoulder playfully.

“So how old are you and how long before you had your first space adventure?” Malcolm asked.

“It’s hard to express my age in your terms. If 365 days is a year, then I’m about 59 years old. I was 51 when I left my planet in a spaceship and headed for Euclidia where I live now.”

“Wow, you look great for 59. Why did you take so long to leave?” Malcolm asked, admiring Adar’s great shape.

“I stay active, eat right, and Euclidia has amazing medical treatments,” Adar explained. “Before the Euclidian arrived, our planet didn’t have a means of space travel. I was around 49 when they first visited our planet. Why don’t we go for a walk, and you can tell me about your planet.” Adar rose from the couch.

“Sure, let’s go,” Malcolm said, eager to continue hanging out with Adar. “You have to show me some more fight moves though.”

“No problem. I’m sure we will find someone to practice on.” Adar punched his fists together.

***

Daloi, Dholi, and Tatan walked into Seamus’ office carrying a duffle bag full of money. Daloi wrestled the big bag onto his desk.

“Ronny told the truth about his gambling efforts in the Bahamas,” Daloi reported, taking a seat in front of Seamus’ desk. “He and Giorgio had amassed quite an operation with people, machines and a thriving numbers racket. The casino he is building is quite impressive as well. I felt you would be happier if we left everything intact, providing you with an additional revenue stream and an expanded empire."

"Daloi, I appreciate the way your crew took care of Ronny's betrayal," said Seamus. "Here is a token of my appreciation."

He handed her a large envelope full of hundred-dollar bills.

"Thanks, Seamus. We enjoyed taking care of that little issue for you. We're just hoping we can do more for you," said Daloi, handing the envelope off to Dholi and Tatan to look through.

Seamus thought for a bit and then offered them a challenge. "There is some craziness happening over near the West Loop that you could look into. There's rumors of some teenager at a school there who took over an area from one of my gangs, and got them talking some superstitious nonsense about how stepping into his territory causes them to pass out or be disintegrated into a cloud of ash. I want that unrest put to rest so my profits from that area can start flowing again."

Daloi, Dholi, and Tatan looked at each other, collectively suspecting that the Euclidian might be responsible for the odd occurrences.

But why would the Euclidian help these Earthlings and risk being detected? "Don't worry, Seamus," said Daloi, a look of unease crossing her face. "We'll look into the issue first thing tomorrow and get the money flowing again."

"Speak to a guy named Philly. You can find him at the Checkers at 115th and Halstead. He should have a video of the kid and the school hours so you'll know when to look for him. I don't need you to interrogate the kid. Just kill him."

"No problem, Seamus. Let's go, guys," said Daloi, getting up to leave.

"It sounds like someone could be helping that kid. Someone from the Euclidian ship," whispered Dholi.

"I know," said Daloi. "We need to be careful and decisive. We don't want to expose ourselves here. If things get out of hand, be prepared to ditch this place and find another city to hang out in."

"Aren't we getting ahead of ourselves?" asked Tatan, who for once wasn't worried about getting caught. "It could be something completely innocent. Either way, I'm not going to let it disrupt my plans to go to the MMA fights tonight," he said, tugging on the lapels of his coat. "They probably aren't as good as the ones on Beakar, but I hear they are entertaining."

"Fine. Just stay alert and try not to stand out." Daloi was worried that Tatan would risk going out in public when a Euclidian might be walking around looking for them.

"It would be great if you monitored me with the personal transporter in case something comes up. I don't know why we didn't get three of them," Tatan mused.

"Sneaking a transport device off of that closely guarded ship is hard to do. Goron said they monitor the inventory closely. At least we retrieved weapons before we left. Go enjoy yourself. We'll be sure to monitor you with the personal transporter. Right now, let's go find that Philly person."

***

Strolling into Checkers, the three Cheoili found all the TV screens fascinating. “It’s odd that these humans love their visual entertainment so much that they can’t eat without surrounding themselves with it,” observed Daloi.

“I’d rather be the entertainment than watch it on some stupid screen,” said Dholi.

“I know you would.” Tatan smiled at his sister and grabbed her arm.

“Can I help you?” The restaurant’s hostess approached the trio.

“Yes, we’re here to see Philly,” said Daloi.

“Oh, certainly. He’s the gentleman in the white three-piece suit in the corner booth,” she said, pointing their way.

“Thanks. He’s expecting us.”

“Come on, I’ll walk you over. Would you like menus or a drink?”

“No, we just came for a quick conversation, and then we’ll be on our way.” Daloi smiled at the friendly human.

“Philly, I’m Daloi,” she said when they reached his booth. “This is Dholi and Tatan. Seamus said you had problems with some kid casting spells on your people.”

“Hey, whassup Daloi? Yeah, there’s a kid at the school named Malcolm, who appears to be casting some sort of voodoo spell on anyone who gets near him. I'm not sure if it's voodoo, magic or some high-tech gear he's using, but something is affecting my people. Check this out," he said, pulling up a video on his iPhone. "I didn't catch the whole thing, but you can see the kid pointing at this one guy and he falls over. Later, these guys decide to shoot the kid and boom, they're vaporized," he said, mimicking an explosion with his hands.

"That's pretty scary," said Tatan, making a gulping sound.

"Calm down, Tatan," said Daloi, placing her hand on his shoulder. "Philly, I think we have what we need. Tomorrow, when the school lets out, I need you to have some of your people attack the kids. No weapons, though. Just rough them up. We'll be there to neutralize Malcolm and his so-called voodoo."

"The school's closed on Sunday. I can have everything ready by 3:00 on Monday," Philly proposed.

"That works for me," Daloi said, nodding her head before retracing her steps to leave with Tatan and Dholi.

***

"Did you get a good look at that video?" Daloi asked her siblings when they reached the sidewalk outside Checkers. "Based on what we learned from the training program on the *Andrea*, they don't have that type of technology on this planet. So that had to be caused by someone from the ship."

"So what do we do?" asked Tatan.

"We're going to set a trap for those fuckers and kill them if we can. Otherwise, we'll have to find another city to call home."

***

Adar walked into the UIC Forum Saturday night, feeling the anticipation of a fan attending his first Super Bowl game. The large, covered arena had bright lights across its huge dome. A giant four-sided jumbotron hovered over the central space. Odors hit Adar's nose that caught his interest.

"What is that they're eating?" he asked, pointing to a couple eating white morsels from a bucket.

"That's popcorn," said Malcolm, surprised by the question. "You never heard of popcorn?"

"I know what it is. Heated corn kernels. I just never saw or smelled it before." Adar looked on with bewilderment. "It can't be very filling. What is that thing that woman is eating?" Adar pointed to a woman shoving food in her mouth.

"That's a hot dog," Malcolm said, chuckling. "It's in a hot dog bun and looks like she has catsup and mustard on it."

"I know what those things are. A hot dog is also known as a wiener, made from pork or beef, but no dog. Catsup is made from tomatoes, no cat. And mustard is made from a mustard plant," Adar said, with a note of sarcasm. "Odd terminology. A hot dog goes in a hot dog bun. But if you place a hamburger in it, one does not call it a hamburger bun, does one?" Adar asked, looking solemnly at Malcolm for an answer.

"No, and I can't explain why they name food the way they do. You learned about food without ever seeing it?" Malcolm asked, puzzled.

"I learned vocabulary and pictures, which is not enough to understand the texture, smells and variations one might run into."

"Your English is so good. It's odd you don't know what anything is." Malcolm gave Adar a questioning look, to which the alien responded by frowning.

"Let's just find our seats," Adar suggested, moving toward the seating area. The two grabbed seats and watched the first match.

"What did you think?" asked Malcolm, excited about seeing his first MMA match in person.

"I found it interesting. I'll be right back," Adar said, standing and walking down the long set of stairs near where they were sitting.

"Where did you go, Adar?" asked Malcolm when his new friend returned. The tattooed crazies around him made the teen nervous. He tried to be brave like Adar, but he wasn't there yet.

"I signed up for the open-fighting session, which happens at the end of the regular matches," said Adar. "Watching these men fight makes me want to fight, too. You should spend more time learning to fight. It will help you be the hero you want to become one day."

"I'm not ready for that yet, but I will pay close attention to what you do in the ring. I'm worried about you going down there. Don't you think it will be risky to get into the ring with other fighters? Someone might realize that you're not from around here. Even if they let you fight with your glasses on, they won't stay on long. And you can't take your devices with you."

“Ugh! I will take that risk. I will need you to hold my UCD and electronic shield while I am in the ring. Monitor the UCD screen and let me know if you get a flashing message with a map pinpointing a location. It will be one of the escapees I am looking for,” Adar explained, handing over his devices.

“You might want to take it easy on your opponent while you’re in the ring. They’re not used to people with your strength on our planet,” suggested Malcolm.

“I’ll consider it, but I won’t promise you anything. I tend to get carried away when I’m fighting.”

“Look on the jumbotron,” pointed Malcolm, bouncing in his seat. “It’s Jennifer Hudson and Common. They’re both famous singers from Chicago, but I’ve never seen them before in person.”

“I don’t understand,” Adar said, confused by Malcolm’s statement. “Are you saying Jennifer Hudson has something in common with someone?”

“No, she’s sitting next to Common. Maybe they’re dating,” Malcolm said, laughing at Adar’s inability to understand.

“Common what? Common person, common singer? I don’t understand,” Adar said, shaking his head in frustration.

“The man sitting next to Jennifer Hudson is named ‘Common’. Well, his nickname is Common. I don’t know his real name.”

“Why would someone want to be called ‘Common’? Why not ‘Special’ or ‘Unique’?”

"Adar, I thought that was you," said Yolanda, walking over to where Adar and Malcolm were sitting. "Is that your son? I can take him down to meet them if you like. I went to school with Jennifer."

"I know you! You're Yolanda Yates, the fighter," Malcolm yelled, jumping up from his seat. "Why didn't you tell me you knew her?" Malcolm demanded, punching Adar's arm. "Please, can I go meet Jennifer Hudson and Common?"

"See, your son wants to go meet them," Yolanda interjected, before Adar could respond. "Sorry about being a bit bitchy the other night. After being attacked by gangbangers, I wasn't happy about being in bed with one."

"You slept with Yolanda Yates?" Malcolm shouted, eyeing Adar with awe and incredulity. The noise he made drew the attention of the spectators around him.

"Sit and calm down, Malcolm. You too, Yolanda," ordered Adar. "So saving you from three attackers doesn't make me a hero, but sleeping with a famous fighter does? That is just dumb. Yolanda, this is not my son. He is a kid I found in an alley. Malcolm, I met Yolanda briefly the other night. I didn't know she was a famous fighter, as if that matters."

"You found this kid in an alley and now you are hanging out with him. You are strange," Yolanda said, raising her eyebrows at Adar.

"It's not like that," said Malcolm. "He's like my uncle. He's teaching me to fight. Can I go meet them before the next fight starts?"

"You two go. You are drawing too much attention to me," Adar said, shooing them away.

Malcolm and Yolanda hurried off in the direction of Jennifer's and Common's seats. A few minutes later, Malcolm returned, overjoyed with his experience. "Yolanda says she wants to see you again," he reported, laughing.

"Just sit down and enjoy the matches. I don't want you telling people about me." Adar grabbed Malcolm's arm and pulled him into his seat. *I can't believe she wants to see me again after the way our evening ended. Maybe I will go by and see Yolanda after the fights tonight.* Adar liked that idea a lot.

The two watched the evening's scheduled matches with great interest. Malcolm felt excitement, fear and pride all stirring in his gut as he tried to absorb every aspect of the experience of attending an MMA match in person. While he enjoyed watching from a distance, Malcolm couldn't imagine going toe-to-toe with a fighter in the ring. As the evening drew to a close, Malcolm slipped away and soon returned with a gift for Adar.

"Here, Adar, this will help you in the ring," said Malcolm, handing him a pair of tinted fighting goggles.

"This gift is unnecessary," said Adar.

"You're supposed to say 'thank you'." Malcolm smiled at his new friend. "It's the least I could do, considering what you have done for me."

Adar just grunted.

"All those looking to participate in the open fight night come down ringside, now," said the arena announcer.

"I'm going down. Remember to monitor the screen for me while I'm in the ring," Adar reminded Malcolm.

"Sure. You remember not to kill anyone in the ring," the boy countered, smiling.

***

Tatan left Mike O'Leary's condo, while Daloi and Dholi prepared for another romp with Mike.

"Dholi, expand the personal transporter and place it on the dresser, so we can watch it in case Tatan gets into trouble," Daloi instructed.

"How are you expanding the screen like that?" asked Mike.

"Don't worry about that, Mike. It's a prototype screen we picked up from a friend of ours," Daloi explained hastily.

"Look, it's just a boring image of Tatan, watching a boring couple of guys beating up on each other," said Dholi. "Mike, take your clothes off. We're going to do something that's a lot more exciting than what Tatan is watching and definitely more intense."

***

"Tonight, we have an extraordinary opportunity," said the announcer, standing in the center of the ring at the MMA arena. "This tiny gladiator will take on all comers and will give $1,000 to anyone who can put him on the ground." An eruption of jeers and shouts came from the contestants and the crowd not believing what they just heard. Adar stood in the middle of the ring swinging his fists in the air impatiently.

One by one, fighters entered the ring only to be quickly taken out by Adar. His speed and strength quickly overwhelmed each challenger. He fought two at a time, and then three at a time. At this point, his opponents appeared to get the better of him. Two held him against the side of the ring while a third pounded on his abdomen.

“Are you two seeing this?” Tatan said out loud to himself, hoping Daloi and Dholi kept their promise to watch over him. However, engrossed in pleasuring Mike, they didn’t notice.

“Adar, one of them is here!” shouted Malcolm, running down to the ring. Adar just gave him a sideways glance then focused on taking out his opponents. He threw the one on his left arm across the ring, knocking him out against the chain-link wall. He swung the one on his right arm around in a circle, using him to subdue the person pounding on him, and then smashed the remaining person into the ground.

The referee declared Adar the winner before he rushed out to meet with Malcolm. “Give me the device! One of the Cheoili has definitely been here. Let’s go by the exits before everyone leaves.” They circled the walkway around the arena, until Adar detected something.

“Here’s the DNA trail again. I can even smell that disgusting scent they have,” Adar said, crinkling his nose.

“What scent?” asked Malcolm.

"It's like flowers."

"Why is that disgusting?"

"Just follow me. There are too many people here." Adar left the arena and headed to where he detected Cheoili DNA. "I'm losing the scent. I'm not picking up anything on this side of the street. Let's cross to the other side."

"Shouldn't we be able to recognize the person?" Malcolm asked.

"No. Remember, the Cheoili can change their looks."

"You mean they're shapeshifters?" Malcolm queried, trying to understand what to look for.

"No, nothing like that. More like chameleons. They can't change their shape or size, or add limbs, but they can look like Earthlings. I'm picking up the DNA again. The person is in front of us. I want you to cross over and watch the crowd as I run by. Let me know if you see anyone reacting to what I'm saying."

Malcolm crossed the street and watched while Adar ran alongside the crowd shouting in Euclidian, "CHEOILI, I KNOW YOU'RE HERE. I CAN SMELL YOU. WHEN I CATCH YOU, I'M GOING TO RIP YOU TO PIECES." Adar continued to shout while monitoring Malcolm for a signal.

Finally, Malcolm ran up to him. "Back there, a guy looked at you real scared like. He turned the corner and started walking away real fast. He went down that street along the river."

"That's him right there in the blue jacket. You stay here, while I go get him," said Adar, placing a restraining hand on Malcolm's chest.

"How can you tell who that is and what color jacket he's wearing way over there? I can barely see him at all from here," said Malcolm, astonished at Adar's confidence. "Do you have some sort of high-tech vision?"

"I see things the same way you do, just better. I can make out things that are far away even in the dark. Now stay back in case there is trouble."

Adar raced around the corner, caught up with Tatan and threw him through the air against a parked car.

"Daloi, Dholi—where the hell are you?" Tatan pleaded to the air, hoping they would see him. "This guy is going to kill me."

"Hello, Cheoili," said Adar. "You must be Tatan, the male one. Where are your friends?"

"I don't know what you're talking about, buddy," Tatan stated, hoping to fool Adar.

"You know what I'm talking about," said Adar in Euclidian, grabbing Tatan by the front of his shirt. Tatan grabbed for Adar's face with his hands. "No, you don't, Cheoili," said Adar, throwing him against the railing by the river. "You try to touch me again with those magic fingers of yours, and I'll rip your hands off."

Adar walked over to Tatan, who cowered on the sidewalk against the railing. Malcolm caught up with Adar, but kept his distance.

"Tell me where your friends are, or I'll throw you into the water piece by piece."

"You'll kill me anyway."

"No, no, I promise I will send you back to the ship alive and whole," said Adar, leaning into Tatan and using a soft voice. "But don't try my patience."

Blam, blam came the sound of blasts striking Adar, pushing him against the railing and away from Tatan.

"I'M WEARING MY PERSONAL SHIELD, YOU IDIOTS!" shouted Adar, standing up and looking for the source of the blast. "YOUR BLASTER WON'T HURT ME."

"This will!" said Daloi, hitting Adar in the chest with a baseball bat, sending him over the railing and into the water.

"Let's go," said Dholi, rushing up and activating the personal transporter. Malcolm stood transfixed as the three Cheoili disappeared in front of him.

***

Malcolm ran down the riverbank to check on Adar.

"Are you feeling okay, Adar?" he asked, helping the alien climb out of the water.

"I feel fine," Adar hissed at Malcolm. "I just don't like being wet. Especially when it's the result of being knocked off a bridge. If I had my weapons that confrontation would have turned out differently."

"If you had your weapons, you would not have made it into the arena." Adar only grunted, then took a moment to look out over the Chicago River. It didn't have the clean smell of Lake Michigan, but still he enjoyed the sound of the waves as they lapped against the cement banks. Small boats cruised by, some silent, some with small parties of revelers enjoying their drinks in the night air.

"What is it?" Malcolm asked, seeing Adar lost in thought.

"As much as I dislike being in the water, I do like looking out at it. Wylyy, can you tell where the Cheoili transported?" asked Adar, speaking Euclidian into his UCD.

"It'll take a few seconds," Wylyy replied, checking his monitors.

"Why is it taking so long?" prodded Adar.

"Because we don't have legal access to that data. Krystyy added a hack, but it takes time to get the data. Okay, they landed in front of a building not far from you. I'll send you there now."

Adar vanished from his spot next to Malcolm and arrived at the location to see a line of people at the entrance of a hotel getting into cabs, with no evidence of the Cheoili. He cursed the sky, then rejoined Malcolm by the river.

"What happened to you? You could at least tell me where you're going and if you are coming back. I didn't know if I should wait here for you or not," said Malcolm, sounding frustrated and more than a bit frightened.

“I went to find those people that attacked me, but I lost them,” Adar explained apologetically. “Then I decided to come back and look out at the water again.”

“It’s just a smelly river,” Malcolm said, crinkling up his nose.

“You are describing a solitary, collective scent without breaking down its parts. I smell fuel, fish, fiberglass, different types of wood, chemicals, tobacco smoke and the food people are eating. They are not all pleasant, but they are each interesting in their own right. You make a binary judgment, while I seek to unravel the intertwined, disparate aromas.” Adar punctuated his lengthy explanation by waving his hand toward his pointed nose as if to pull the river’s bouquet into his nostrils.

“Why would an assassin care about how the river smells?” asked Malcolm, with genuine curiosity.

Adar looked at the teen, perplexed at why he would view him as a one-dimensional figure. “Because it helps keep me calm and focused. Embracing one’s environment accentuates one’s talents. Open up your senses. Don’t just see something, smell it, hear it and feel it. You should find something that helps you relax and open up your senses to it.”

“Being around my friends relaxes me.”

“Friends don’t last. You should find something more permanent and readily available.”

“I’ll work on that,” said Malcolm, wondering what Adar was like growing up. “What does getting beamed around feel like?”

“The short-range transfers don’t feel like much of anything. It’s the interstellar transfers that shake me up,” Adar replied, shivering.

“Your transporter can send you to distant stars?”

“Yes, in an instant,” said Adar, looking up at the night sky.

“I would love to do that one day,” Malcolm said, lifting his gaze upward at the few stars he could see through Chicago’s light pollution.

“That’s probably not going to happen. At least not in your lifetime.”

Maybe I’m wrong, Adar thought. *I grew up in a more primitive environment, and here I am*.

“Let’s get moving,” he urged. “I want to put on dry clothing. You did a good deed tonight, but I am no closer to capturing my prey.” Adar walked away from the river and back toward the house he had acquired.

“You are pretty wet. I can even hear your boots squishing.” Malcolm laughed. “See, I’m opening up my senses.”

Adar just ignored him and kept walking. *Tonight is a good night to visit Yolanda,* he thought.

***

The Cheoili sat in Mike’s condo thinking about the attack by Adar. “I did not risk my life stealing that loot and getting to this planet to be killed by an Ossie,” said Daloi, pacing the floor.

“We all risked our lives to get here,” said Dholi.

“I am the only one here who has been beaten by that Ossie,” said Tatan. “I’m sure the human talking to him in the arena is the same one that caused the problems at that school.”

“At least there only appears to be one person after us. Tomorrow, we kill the Ossie,” said Daloi. “Then we’ll assume new human identities and avoid the Euclidian as best we can. If they harvest this planet, we’ll lay low until they’re gone and run what’s left of it. The most important thing for us is to not forget what we mean to each other. We’re family, and together we can conquer any foe.”

“Sounds like a plan to me,” said Dholi, grabbing her sister’s hand. “I’m with you all the way.”

“Me too,” Tatan said, hugging his two sisters.

“Tatan, tomorrow you cash in some coins. We should find another place to stay on the other side of town. Now let’s talk about how we kill that Ossie,” Daloi said, pounding her fist into her hand.

***

On the way home with Malcolm, Adar placed more sensors along the area around the Gold Coast and near coin shops on the north side of Chicago. Adar waited at the sidewalk near the front door to Malcolm’s apartment building to make sure he got inside safely.

“Malcolm, the aliens I’m after have seen you, which may place you in danger. Try to be more careful when you are walking around. If anyone bothers you, just chop them in the throat. That will take them down no matter what planet they're from," Adar said, placing a hand on his chest.

"Thanks Adar. I had a great evening. The fights, meeting Jennifer and Common, and most of all being part of a real alien battle," Malcolm said, making fighting noises and punching his fists in the air as he had seen Adar do.

Interesting kid, thought Adar. *Makes me want to have a kid someday. Speaking of which, I wonder how Yolanda is doing.*

"Just go inside and get some rest," insisted Adar. "I'll see you tomorrow." He waved to Malcolm, picked up a bag at his place, and walked to Yolanda's.

***

Who the hell is that at the door? Yolanda heard a knock and opened her door.

"Adar, I was hoping you would show up." She greeted him with a big smile and a hug. "You really should call before dropping by. What if I was entertaining someone else tonight?"

"Then I would toss the unfortunate jerk into a dumpster," Adar said, demonstrating his throwing technique with his arms.

"I prefer you save that strength for lifting me up against the wall again," she said, taking a deep breath and sighing. "A girl never gets tired of that. And no beer this time. I want you to finish me against the wall."

“I have one request before we get started,” Adar said, giving her a sentimental look. “Could you teach Malcolm to become an MMA fighter? In return, I would like to give you this briefcase full of cash, which you can use to find a safer place to stay and to have the time you need to focus on your fighting. Are you okay with that?”

“Hell yeah, I am.” Yolanda beamed. “That Malcolm is a special kid. I’m going to enjoy working with him. Now how about you pin me to the wall like you promised?”

“I would be delighted to.” Adar grinned. “You’d be surprised at what I can do when I’m at full strength.”

“Oh, surprise me, baby. Surprise me.” Yolanda grabbed Adar’s hand and led him into the bedroom, where they spent the rest of the evening roughhousing.

***

Around noon the next day Adar received an alert from one of the sensors. *Aha, it’s near a coin shop. I knew they would be looking to change money eventually*. Adar went to the shop, cloaked, and walked to the window to see a man exchanging Alpha coins.

Tatan walked out of the shop where Adar waited to attack him. Adar threw Tatan against a nearby wall, and the impact forced the Cheoili to struggle to remain upright. “Changing your looks doesn’t change your smell, Tatan,” Adar cried angrily.

“You know my name. You’re Adar the Ossie right?” Tatan asked, working to buy some time.

"Yes, why is that important to you?"

"I just want to know what to call you when I kill you and your friend, Malcolm."

"What?" yelled Adar, turning quickly to look behind him to see who had just thrown a brick at his back. Though his shield protected him from being hurt, the projectile still stunned him. Seeing no one, Adar spun the other way with his spear in his hand just in time to see Tatan had been joined by Dholi, who stood next to him.

"Bye, Adar," said Tatan, as he and his sister disappeared.

"Wylyy, can you tell me where the Cheoili went?" asked Adar.

"Somewhere near your friend's school," Wylyy answered promptly.

So that's what Tatan meant about Malcolm. "Wylyy, place me there, on top of the school." Adar materialized at the elevated location and cloaked before surveying the area. *No Cheoili, but why are there so many gang members just hanging out across the street? I bet the Cheoili have something to do with this*. Adar waited for the children to leave the building at 3:00, hoping to assess the danger before anyone could get hurt.

The bell rang and students poured out of the school. En masse, the gang members crossed the street and started attacking the students. One by one, Adar stunned the gang members, but didn't kill them since the students weren't in mortal danger.

There's Malcolm. "Malcolm, go back in the school!" shouted Adar from the roof, realizing that he actually cared what happened to the young Earthling. Malcolm never heard Adar. Instead, he felt searing pain when Daloi scored a direct hit to his chest with her blaster. The teen fell to the ground, and the gang members cheered. Adar stood up, screaming. He also uncloaked, which gave Tatan the opportunity to grab Adar using the personal transporter and shift him to a spot high above the Earth.

"Die, Adar," said Tatan, releasing him in atmosphere too cold for most living beings to survive.

Adar turned towards Tatan and fired his weapon, but the blast hit empty space. "Wylyy, send me to the ship now."

"Wait a minute," said Wylyy.

"I don't have a minute!" Adar's voice wobbled as his body began shivering violently.

"Take a deep breath."

"What!" From one moment to the next, Adar went from extreme cold to extreme wet, as he found himself under water and out of air. No sooner than he began to drown, he felt the deck of Wylyy's ship beneath him as he gasped for life-sustaining oxygen.

"Have you–lost your–damn mind?" Adar demanded, coughing up water. "You know I hate being in water."

"At your downward velocity you would have been crushed if I brought you straight to the ship," Wylyy explained calmly. "Putting you in the water slowed your descent enough to transport you safely to the ship. You should expect that if it happens again."

"I don't ever expect to be hurtling through space like that again," Adar growled, wiping the water from his face.

"Should I send you to Tatan's last location?"

"No, I'm sure he's long gone by now. What happened to that kid I've been working with?" Adar asked, concern in his voice.

"He had been burned pretty badly so I sent him to Valera. We told her he is a friend of yours."

***

Adar had Wylyy transport him to the *Andrea* where he watched Valera finish up with Malcolm.

"Looks like you got that trip you wanted, after all," said Adar, watching Malcolm move his fingers over Valera's face.

"We can't keep him here long, Adar," said Valera in Euclidian. "The captain won't be happy about bringing someone from a planet we may be mining aboard the *Andrea*."

"What'd she say to you? Tell her I like the way her face feels." Malcolm continued to touch surfaces around him, as he tried to take in the textures, rigidity and smells of everything near him. He also stared at things beyond his touch, marveling at the array of devices he'd never seen before. *I wonder why that light looks so funny.*

"She said I need to get you back. I think she knows you like feeling her face," Adar replied, uncharacteristically patient with the youth.

"Can I see other aliens before I go? And what it looks like outside the ship?"

"Let me check. Valera, how is he doing? Is he well enough to take back?" Adar asked, switching to Euclidian.

"He's fine. He suffered some bad burns on his chest. I fixed that and gave him a shirt to wear. Just don't over exert him."

"She said you can go home now, Malcolm."

"Please let me see something before I go."

Adar decided to indulge the youngster just this once. "We'll take a short walk to where you can see some more people and look outside the ship."

Coming aboard the ship felt like visiting heaven to Malcolm. It was a dream come true for him to be in an alien ship on the far side of the galaxy, communicating with aliens. Adar led Malcolm to a nearby lounge. Along the way, he described the different species and devices they encountered. In the lounge, they took seats near a viewing screen.

"What is that planet?" asked Malcolm, pointing at the screen.

"It's our home planet of Euclidia. It's just outside the ship. You can zoom in and see some of the cities if you like."

"How do I do that?"

"Just make gestures in front of the screen like this to zoom in and out and move around," Adar explained, giving Malcolm a few examples.

"Wow, everyone is moving. Is this a live feed?"

"Yes, you can call it that. Two Tammarian grogs, Vikktor." Adar ordered drinks from his favorite bartender in Euclidian.

"Coming right up, Adar," Vikktor replied, smirking at Adar's nurturing moment.

"What is this?" asked Malcolm, when the drinks arrived.

"It's one of my favorite drinks. Try it. It will help you relax."

"Wow, this is amazing. My skin is tingling."

"Yeah, it has that effect on me, too," said Adar, smiling.

Malcolm got up and walked around the lounge, touching everything he encountered, including the clientele.

"Adar, I think your friend needs to take it easy. He's being a bit disruptive," Vikktor murmured.

"Okay, I'll take care of it. Malcolm, let me show you another part of the ship," Adar called as he headed toward the exit.

"Oh boy, I can't wait," Malcolm said, skipping towards Adar.

"Finish your drink and we'll go."

Malcolm chugged his drink and walked out the door with Adar, who led him to the transporter room. "Krystyy, could you send my guest and me to Wylyy's ship?"

"Wow, that person is big," said Malcolm, pointing at Krystyy. "What is she doing? Whoa, how did I get here?" Malcolm asked, looking around the attack ship.

"Wylyy, could you give him a sedative and put him in his bed?" Adar said, in Euclidian. "Then send me to my house."

"Right away, Adar," said Wylyy. "Looks like he's had a few."

At home Malcolm stirred from his sleep when his mother's hand touched his shoulder. "Malcolm, when did you get home?" she asked, surprised that she didn't see him come in.

"I'm not sure. I was playing with some friends after school and just lost track of time. I felt so tired that I just collapsed in the bed. I don't remember looking at the clock when I came home. Oh my goodness, mother, I had the strangest dream. You won't believe what happened."

"I'm sure I won't. It will have to wait, though. I'm on my way to work. Food's on the stove. Bye, dear," his mother said, kissing him on the forehead.

"Bye, Mom." Malcolm looked down at his shirt and squealed with excitement. *It wasn't a dream!*

Chapter 6

Tatan Takes Out Adar

Adar came awake and for a moment felt disoriented by his surroundings. This wasn't his compact berth aboard the *Andrea*. Instead, soft, dark linens tangled his limbs as he lay on a flat surface broad enough to support six of him comfortably. The young human called this structure a king bed. Adar wondered what king had once slept here. But the question failed to occupy his thoughts for long. Instead, his mind returned to his difficulties tracking down the Cheoili, making him angry and impatient.

Adar hated being angry. He perceived anger as nothing but a distraction, like so many things he had experienced on this mission. He had been beaten by opponents before, though rarely. Still, he accepted defeat as a learning experience. But the Cheoili's actions went beyond the pale. They didn't just want to beat him, they wanted to kill him.

As Adar shed the last cobwebs of sleep from his head, he took stock of his situation. *I need to finish this job, so I can enjoy the rest of my time on this curious planet. The captain is going to be checking in with me soon, and I don't want to tell him I let these fugitives slip through my grasp, again. If they are still in this city, I will find them. As a matter of fact, I'm going to find them now.*

Hopping up from the bed, he spoke into his UCD. "Wylyy, I'm going to walk up to the northern part of the city. I'm sure they are holed up there. I need you to stay alert in case I need you."

"You mean, like if you're falling through the sky again," replied Wylyy, laughter erupting in the background.

"Just do it!" growled Adar. *I know this will work. I just need to find where they hang out*. Adar walked two dozen blocks and sure enough, he finally detected Cheoili DNA. *I knew I would find you. Now tell me where you're hiding*.

Adar circled the block looking for more clues. *I can't believe those amateurs got the drop on me three times. I've been wasting too much time being nice to them. It's this building. I'm sure of it*. Adar stood in front of a tall condo building looking up as if searching for signs of his foe. *This had to be it. Their DNA is everywhere*. "Wylyy, I'm going in. Keep an eye on me."

"I'm right with you, Adar."

Adar walked into the condo building and went floor by floor until he came across a door with an overwhelming amount of evidence. *I can smell their flowery scent. I've never been so happy to inhale that horrible smell*.

"Wylyy, scan the apartment in front of me and tell me what you see," whispered Adar.

"There is one male human inside and no one else."

"So should we transport him to the ship for interrogation or should you place me inside to interrogate him or should I just kill him and wait for the Cheoili to show up?"

"Why not just knock on the door and ask him where everyone is?" Wylyy giggled.

Adar grimaced and knocked on the door.

“Hello, can I help you?” Mike inquired politely, after answering the door.

“I am looking for Tatan, Daloi, and Dholi. We used to work together.” Adar tried to sound friendly.

“I’m looking for them myself. They moved out a couple of days ago, and I haven’t heard from them since.”

“Do you have any idea where I can find them?” Adar persisted.

“Unfortunately not,” Mike replied, shrugging his shoulders.

“Okay, goodbye.” Adar turned and walked away. *Now I have to start over*. He grumbled under his breath.

“Wylyy, keep an eye on this place, in case they come back. I’ll keep searching.”

“Will do, Adar.”

***

“Daloi, Mike here,” said Mike, calling Daloi with his mobile phone. “Some guy just came by looking for you.”

“Did he give you his name?” Daloi asked, sounding worried, since no one was supposed to know to look for her there.

“No, but he’s a short, wiry looking guy. He wore some weird wrap-around shades.”

“Did he have a fauxhawk and a long coat?”

“Yes, that’s him. He said you used to work together.”

"Yes, but he's not our friend. Thanks for letting me know." Mentally, Daloi was going through the reverse of five stages of grief, lamenting the fact that Adar still lived.

"So when am I going to see you again?" Mike whimpered.

"Soon, baby. Soon," cooed Daloi, in her most soothing tone. She knew it was a lie, but she needed him to trust her in case he had further news for her.

I can't believe he is still alive, thought Daloi. *It's to the point where we need to make a concerted effort to kill this guy, or leave.*

***

Daloi decided to go by Checkers to see if Philly or his people might have any new information on Adar's whereabouts.

Locating the gangster a short time later, Daloi approached him. "Philly, forgive the interruption, but I need you to help me find a guy," said Daloi. "He's a short guy, wears dark glasses, and used to hang around that voodoo kid."

"You mean Adar?" asked Philly. "He took over EZ Smooth's place. As a matter of fact, that's how I got to be over all this new territory."

"You know him? Why didn't you tell me?" Daloi cried, startled by the coincidence.

"You never asked. Do you think he had something to do with that weirdness at the school?"

"Just tell me where he lives." Daloi took down the address and hurried away to confer with Dholi and Tatan about her new plan to get rid of Adar.

***

Adar was still out for his stroll around northern Chicago when he got a call from Wylyy.

"Adar, we just got a transport alert at Millennium Park," said Wylyy.

"So send me there," Adar requested anxiously.

"Daloi, Adar just showed up here," Tatan said, calling Daloi on his mobile phone as he watched Adar from a bench in the park.

"Good. Stay out of sight, and do what you can to keep him there," Daloi ordered.

"Don't worry. I'll throw the explosive devices about that Rosda made for us to keep him occupied." As Tatan launched the grenades, Adar ran to investigate the explosions, suspecting the Cheoili might be involved. Unfortunately, he arrived too late to detect Tatan.

"Tatan, we're done here," said Daloi. "Come join us and watch the fireworks when he shows up.

"I'm on my way," replied Tatan, who took a cab to join Daloi and Dholi, who had hidden across the street from Adar's place.

"Look, there he is." Dholi pointed at Adar as he walked through the front door of his house.

“Great, but we have to wait for him to go upstairs,” said Daloi. “There he goes. Now! Set it off now!” A series of explosions engulfed the house in flames. “Let’s see the Ossie survive that.” Daloi smirked.

“Wylyy, transport me to the ship now!” Adar screamed in a panicked voice.

Seeing Adar’s condition, Wylyy shouted, “Oh, my goodness! Krystyy, I need you to transport Adar to sickbay now! Let Valera know he’s badly burned.”

***

Once he was aboard the *Andrea*, Dr. Valera treated Adar’s burns.

“Adar, you need to relax,” Valera said, trying to calm Adar when he awoke following the surgery. “I had to apply a lot of cellular rejuvenation to replace your burned skin. It’s going to take a while for the new growth to stabilize.”

The nerves in Adar’s brain danced in a fiery undulation. He could see himself falling, Tatan laughing at him, being knocked into the water, and the house exploding over and over again. “Get away from me!” said Adar, shoving at Valera.

“Adar, I need to administer some medicine.”

“Fine. Get it over with then. I keep having these head flashes,” Adar complained, grabbing the sides of his head with his hands.

“Lay back and let me look at you.” Valera pushed gently on his chest hoping to force him to remain stationary.

Adar tried to keep still, but his body kept twitching. “Here, this will help you relax and diminish those flashes in your head,” said the doctor, administering an inhalant.

“As soon as you repair the damage to my skin, I’m going to kill those bastards,” Adar wheezed, between deep breaths.

“You know who did this to you?”

“Those damn Cheoili caused this, who else? They have tried to kill me a couple of times already and failed. I’m not tolerating these attacks from that weak species!” Adar pounded on his bed with tight fists. “They would not dare to challenge me to my face. Get me my UCD so I can get out of here.”

“Captain, Adar’s awake and he’s agitated. You need to get down here before he tears the place apart,” Valera said quietly into her communicator.

Shisal materialized a moment later in sickbay. “Adar, you need to stay and rest so you can heal,” he said firmly.

“I need to get back so I can kill those Cheoili,” Adar argued, gritting his teeth against the pain as he tried to stand.

“You can relax and follow Valera’s orders, or you can be further sedated and restrained. And I’ll hold your UCD until Valera tells me you’re ready to return to duty. Until then, shut up and do as you’re told. By the way, kill them if you must, but if you do, I will need evidence I can turn over to Central Control.”

“Aye, aye, captain.” Adar saluted, before allowing a med assistant to help him lie down again. Valera gave him a strong sedative, which caused him to slip into an amorous dream about Yolanda.

***

"Adar, welcome back to the land of the living," said Wylyy when the enforcer materialized a few days later on the attack ship.

"You are not going to believe what is happening right now. Take a look." Wylyy grinned and pointed at the scene unfolding on one of the ship's viewing screens, where the tiny craft's three crewmembers had focused their attention.

"Is that Tatan with the human I met the other day?" Adar asked, his voice rising with incredulity.

"Yes, it is." Wylyy smiled. "He walked into the apartment several minutes ago. I heard you were heading back here and decided to save this moment for you."

"Wait until he is just at the moment of climax, then transport him here," Adar directed.

"I think he's ready. Stand back." Wylyy transported Tatan to the ship, face down upon the deck.

"Argh, what the hell?" yelled Tatan, startled by the change in his surroundings. He then growled, "Did you have to bring me here so I'm slamming my penis into the deck?"

"Do you think we wanted you spewing ejaculate all over us?" Adar asked, sounding both sarcastic and menacing.

"Adar? You're alive!" shouted Tatan, scooting away from the Ossie in shock.

"Why wouldn't I be? Because your friends shot at me with their blaster, or you dropped me from space, or you blew up my house with me in it?"

Tatan smirked. "We like to have fun. We knew you would survive those pranks. Nothing personal."

"Glad you feel that way. So tell me. Where are those fun-loving friends of yours?" Adar asked, a playful look hiding much darker emotions.

"I'm not sure where my SISTERS are. I saw them wandering around the park earlier today." Tatan sounded vague and evasive.

"How about telling me where you live now?" Adar asked, his anger growing.

Tatan shrugged nervously. "I can't really say."

"Oh, you're going to tell me. And there's no way they'll be saving you from here," Adar said, leaning forward menacingly.

"Okay, we live at the place you transported me from," said Tatan, holding his hand to Adar's chest and daring to push him back.

"He's lying," said Wylyy. "He's the only person that's been there since you left."

"We've been traveling. They'll be back in a couple of days," Tatan insisted.

"You mean from the park?" asked Adar in disbelief. "You know how it feels to be burned alive, Tatan?" Adar pulled out his blaster and disintegrated one of the Cheoili's feet.

"Ahhh, what are you doing? You didn't even give me a chance to answer." Tatan grabbed his smoking leg and shrieked with pain.

"I'm just going to keep blasting you until you tell me what I want to hear," Adar said, pressing a button on the weapon and watching Tatan's other foot turn to ash.

Tatan screamed again and cradled his legs in his arms.

"Adar, remember we have to have evidence that we killed them," said Wylyy.

"Don't worry, I'll leave one of his hands," said Adar, blasting off one of Tatan's arms.

Tatan let out a loud yell, partly from pain and partly from fear of dying. "Don't kill me. I'll tell you what you want to know, just don't kill me."

"We're listening," said Adar, pausing to give Tatan a chance to gather his composure.

Tatan whimpered for a moment and then began to speak. "We took over an apartment on the west side. I'll give you the coordinates," Tatan blurted between bursts of unintelligible noises.

***

Daloi, worried about Tatan's absence, called Mike on a cell phone she had acquired. "Mike, is Tatan with you?"

"No. I don't know where he is. One moment we were in a strong embrace, and a moment later, he vanished."

"What do you mean he vanished?" asked Daloi, afraid to hear the answer.

"I felt him on top of me and then I didn't. I don't know how to explain it," Mike said, sounding confused.

"Did you hear that, Dholi? You have the personal transporter, right?"

"Yes, it's right here," responded Dholi.

"The Euclidian must have him. We need to get out of here now. Thanks for the warning, Mike," said Daloi, hanging up.

***

Daloi and Dholi fled the new apartment before Adar could catch them. This put Tatan in an awkward predicament.

"Adar, that apartment looks like it could be the place. There's no one there, though. Hold on. I just got another transport alert. Guess where it originated from?" Wylyy asked, rhetorically.

"That apartment! Tatan, you warned them somehow," accused Adar.

"No, I swear I didn't."

“Bye, Tatan,” Adar said, grimly blasting away the remainder of the Cheoili’s body, except for one hand. “Make sure the captain gets this hand. Now send me to the coordinates of the transport alert,” Adar instructed.

When Adar materialized, he identified his location as just outside Chicago’s Union Station, but he saw no sign of the Cheoili. *Great! Another dead end. At least I got one of them*, he thought.

Part II

New York

Chapter 7

One Down, Two to Go

Back aboard the attack vessel, Adar worked with Wylyy and the other crewmembers to plan his next steps. The four sat at a table in the area behind the cockpit to discuss options.

The attack vessel was the size of two Greyhound buses side by side. The cockpit was a roomy space that fit three people comfortably: the pilot, co-pilot navigator and technical officer who managed weapons, communications and ship-to-shore transport.

A multi-use area behind the cockpit contained a shower, commode, transporter, kitchen and dispensary. The area could sleep eight and seat 20, as needed. The rest of the ship housed the engines and weapons systems.

The ship's skin appeared dull grey when inactive, though the special metal alloy of which it was made could change to any color or pattern to blend in with its surroundings and avoid detection by the Euclidean's enemies. Equipped with both plasma and gravitational engines, the vessel needed to dock with the larger resource ship when interstellar travel was required. This meant Wylyy and his entire crew were stuck on Earth until the *Andrea* returned to retrieve them.

Wylyy commanded and piloted the craft, while Kulick served as copilot and Rookelyy filled the technical slot. Their sole mission was to support Adar in his quest to capture or kill the escaped Cheoili. For the most part, they stayed onboard, except to occasionally raid a grocery store at night to obtain food. The crew used the ship's scanning technology to explore different areas of Earth and sometimes to spy on its inhabitants. So far, their surveillance had provided little assistance in finding the Cheoili.

"Rookelyy, have you received any transport alerts from the Cheoili?" Adar asked, not bothering to hide his exasperation.

"No, not a one." Rookelyy shared Adar's disappointment. "I searched the area and didn't notice them anywhere. Of course, they probably took on entirely new forms to evade us."

"I had our computer programmed to search new broadcasts for keywords about alien activity," Wylyy stated. "Nothing new beyond the sighting of the *Andrea* and other so-called UFOs."

"Okay, patch me through to Commander Cobalt," instructed Adar. "Maybe he can provide us with some suggestions."

Cobalt served as a planetary interrogation officer. An inhabitant of the planet Majorelle, he had humanoid features and blue reptilian-like skin. His species had a keen ability to learn new languages and perceive a person's emotions regardless of their species. He had been placed in charge of logistics for the possible mining of Earth's resources. He became familiar with Earth's cultures, languages and cities. He also cultivated several operatives on the planet using various forms of incentives.

"Cobalt, I don't know if you have been tracking my mission here, but I have been working on hunting down three Cheoili who killed several people in the Alpha system and then escaped to Earth." Cobalt was able to detect the anxiety Adar felt in his voice.

"Yes, Adar, but only tangentially. How can I help you?" Cobalt asked, his tone calm and comforting.

"I tracked them to Chicago and killed one of them, and I believe the other two escaped by train. What do you think their destination might be?"

"Considering the distance to similar cities, I would suggest that they might go to Baltimore, Detroit, Philadelphia, or New York, with New York being my first choice."

"Okay, I will go to New York. Any other tips?" Adar asked, hoping to improve his chances of finding the escapees.

"New York is an enormous city, much like our own Occum. I propose that you focus on Manhattan initially. I have an operative there who can set you up with an apartment. Meanwhile, you should check all the trains headed east to see if they boarded any of them. You could get lucky," Cobalt said, trying to sound upbeat.

"Good idea. Cobalt, I have one more bit of business I need you to take care of, if you are agreeable. It has to do with the house where I lived before it was blown up."

Adar explained what he needed done to Cobalt, who found the request completely out of character for Adar, and even touching.

"I'm sure with my connections I will be able to execute your request," Cobalt said, smiling.

"Great. That is all I need for now," said Adar, ending the communications with Cobalt. "Wylyy, let's go down the list of trains headed east. I want you to place me on each one, starting with the last one that left the station for New York."

Adar and Wylyy worked together to search more than a dozen trains, but came up with nothing. Not one trace of Cheoili DNA could be found anywhere outside of the station itself. Adar eventually gave up and had Wylyy transport him to Chicago to deal with one piece of unfinished business.

"Adar!" Malcolm cried when he answered the door. He flung his arms around the alien's shoulders in a hug before inviting him into the apartment. "I saw your house blown up and I was worried you had been killed."

"Malcolm, I'm not one for pleasantries, but because of you, I'm learning," Adar said, patting Malcolm on the back. "I have to leave for New York to continue my search for the escapees. That means I probably won't see you again. I set up a couple of things for you though. First, Yolanda will train you to be a fighter, so you will no longer have to be afraid. Pay attention to her lessons. You could learn a lot from her."

"Yes, yes, yes," Malcolm broke in, hugging Adar again.

"Try to be less emotional," Adar said, pushing Malcolm away though he looked pleased.

"Sorry, Adar," Malcolm said, stepping back and trying unsuccessfully to rein in his smile.

"Second, I am having the house I lived in rebuilt. Ownership of the house will be signed over to your mother." Hearing this,

Malcolm gave up fighting his grin and started to do a little dance around Adar.

"A colleague will be dropping off the paperwork. Don't let his appearance scare you," Adar added.

"I won't. I promise. I won't," Malcolm squealed, while he bounced on the balls of feet and clenched and unclenched his fists at his sides.

"Goodbye, Malcolm. Thank you for helping me find my way around Chicago and improving my English." Adar extended his hand towards Malcolm, which the teen ignored.

Instead, Malcolm grabbed Adar with both hands to his upper back and pulled the alien into a rib-bruising hug, which he held for a full minute.

"Oh my goodness, you said 'thank you'. I'm never going to forget you or our adventures," Malcolm said, finally releasing Adar from a surprisingly strong grip and swiping a hand negligently at the moisture gleaming in his eyes.

"I won't forget you either, Malcolm." Adar paused to stare at the youth before turning away.

Adar looked back once as he walked out of the apartment, giving Malcolm a little wave. Moments later, he stepped into the shadows of an alley and had Wylyy transport him to Manhattan.

***

Daloi and Dholi arrived in Times Square on a bus from Montreal with new disguises after a long day of travel.

Mesmerized by all the lights and video billboards, they stood for a moment, taking it all in.

"We selected a bus that took us on a roundabout path to get here, but I feel we chose the safest approach," said Daloi. "Now I can do what I've been waiting to do since I got on that damn bus." Daloi clinched her fists and let out a blood-curdling scream. "Arghh, that bastard is going to pay for whatever he did to Tatan!" Daloi let out a small whimper and fell to a knee as Dholi hugged her.

"I'm okay, Dholi. No more sadness. What do you think of these crazy lights and billboards?" Daloi asked, standing and wiping her eyes. She turned around slowly on the sidewalk, trying to see everything at once.

"They're pretty exhilarating," said Dholi, fighting to regain her composure as well. "Look at all the damn people. I thought Chicago was big. This place is crazy. You see the people dressed in costumes? You know, I'd enjoy all this more if Tatan were here with us. We should have left sooner. Tatan might still be around. We underestimated Adar's support system. The Euclidian have been infiltrating planets like this for decades. There's no way that we could take them on. Even if we kill Adar, they'll send someone else, maybe even a dozen people."

"Right you are, sister. Let's take what we learned in Chicago and build a life for ourselves here." Daloi's dark eyes shone as she relished the challenges that lay ahead.

***

Wylyy dropped Adar off in the heart of Manhattan. Night had already fallen, but bright lights shining down from buildings and street lamps gave Adar a clear view of his surroundings. He found the bright lights and tall buildings odd. *If you like your surroundings well lit, why block the natural light from the sun with tall buildings? What a crazy planet.*

What is permissible depends on the city, state, or country you are in. Of course, skin color and income determine how harshly a law will be applied to a person. Then there is me. I am an alien. Their laws don't apply to me unless they catch me, and I will not make that easy for them, he vowed.

Adar walked the streets of Manhattan to familiarize himself with the city and install the few sensors he had left. He also continued his internal musings.

Finding the Cheoili in this city would be like finding a needle in a very large haystack, blindfolded. This city reminds me of the Gut in Occum, without the alien life. People here are always up doing something, and a lot of it illegal. In every city, though, there is that person who has a finger on the pulse of everything that is happening. If I could find that person, it would make my job a lot easier.

"Wylyy, I need to recharge my synapses. Did Cobalt find me a home to inhabit?"

Wylyy was alarmed by the weariness he heard in Adar's voice. "You do sound exhausted. I'll contact Cobalt and get back to you."

Adar walked to the waterfront and watched the boats going by. The water calmed him and helped him focus, though some things still annoyed him. *This place is smelly. Look at all the rats. These people only care about their space, as if what happens outside that space doesn't impact them. They spend many resources on constructing tall buildings but nothing on cleaning up the areas around them. It doesn't matter if a pleasure craft has gold-plated suites, a rotten hull will still sink the ship.*

"Adar, I spoke with Cobalt. You are to meet with his contact, Li Xiao, at the west entrance to the United Nations building tomorrow at 10:00 a.m. local time."

"What does local time mean?" Adar asked, not up on colloquialisms.

"Get a chronometer or timepiece or ask someone. Most humans carry one," Wylyy suggested.

"Okay. How do I recognize Cobalt's contact?"

"She'll be wearing a red scarf."

"Got it." *I know where I can get a timepiece. I just need to find an alley.* Adar walked down a few alleys until someone approached him.

"Hey, buddy, what are you looking for?" a strange human approached him, stepping out of the shadows.

"I need a timepiece," replied Adar.

"You're not from around here, are you?"

"No, I just came in from Chicago," Adar responded, unaware that the stranger was sizing him up.

"Chi-town. You got any money?"

"Sure," said Adar, pulling out a wad of cash from his coat pocket. "How much is it?"

"Great, we'll take all that off your hands." Two men now stood behind Adar carrying nightsticks.

"Do I get the timepiece?" Adar asked, even as he realized the trio wanted to mug him.

"No, but you get to watch us beat the crap out of you, if you don't hand over the money." The stranger nodded at his two friends, who immediately began beating on Adar with their nightsticks.

Adar's face crinkled into a wicked smile as he started to snicker. *This is fun. I will have to make this part of my nightly routine,* he thought. The alien then punched one assailant in the chest hard enough to knock him into the wall behind him. He grabbed the other one and threw him over the head of the dark stranger and into the opposite alley wall. "I'll take that timepiece now, unless you would like me to rip your arm off and take it myself."

The stranger rubbed his chin, sizing Adar up and wondering if he could take him. In the end, he decided to give Adar his wristwatch.

"Another thing, if I wanted to find the mobsters that run this city, where would I go?"

"Talk to Luigi over at Max's in Tribeca." The guy began sidling away, eager to get far away from Adar as soon as possible.

Pausing in his stealthy departure, he peered at Adar's dark glasses. "Say, where can I learn those awesome skills you have?"

"I was born this way," said Adar, walking away. He had barely reached the end of the alley when the stranger caught up with him.

"Hey, I can show you where Max's is and give you an introduction, if you like. You can call me Ahmed," he said, holding out his hand, which Adar ignored.

"Why are you trying to help me, Ed?" the alien asked, suspicious.

"No, my name is AHmed," he said, annoyed that Americans kept making that mistake. "Those two back there have been getting me into trouble since I got here. I only met them since moving here a few weeks ago."

Adar merely eyed the strange human, wondering if he made a mistake letting him live. "Look, I can introduce you to Luigi and other bosses here. I'm a runner for them."

"I'm Adar," the alien said, grabbing Ahmed's hand and shaking it. "Lead the way." Ahmed nodded and the two began to walk across Tribeca.

"Ahmed, you help me get what I need, and I will take care of you. You cross me, and I will kill you in a painful way," Adar informed the human, his voice matter-of-fact.

"You won't have to worry about that," Ahmed assured him. "Max's is in the next block."

"Won't, is that 'would not'?"

"No, it means 'will not'. 'Wouldn't' is would not."

Adar snorted. "What a stupid language."

The two continued their walk across Tribeca in silence. This southern part of Manhattan was darker and devoid of the giant skyscrapers one would find in other parts of the city. Few people were on the street, but Adar noticed the odd rat here and there.

"Here it is, but it looks like they're closed. Meet me here tomorrow around 5:00 in the evening, and I'll show you around." Ahmed waited for Adar's nod before sauntering off in a different direction.

Adar continued his stroll around Manhattan, taking in all he could. He noticed that the foot and car traffic led him towards midtown and Times Square. *What is with these food trucks everywhere selling old meat? Why would they take perfectly good meat and cook the flavor out of it or mix it with grain? Too many lights, too many people here. I need to see water.* Adar walked to the East River and looked across the water to more lights, those of Jersey City. He noticed the disparity between the two waterfronts. *Why is it cleaner and better groomed over there, but people come here to enjoy themselves? Is it indicative of their nature, preferring more ignoble surroundings as a reflection of their inner selves? Time to move on.*

Adar eventually found a quiet spot to sit and nap while he waited for the sun to come up.

***

Dholi looked around the apartment that she and Daloi had just scored. They had reverted back to the twin disguises that they used in Chicago in hopes of leveraging the work they did there with a new boss. *We are so lucky to be on a planet where the people value looks so much, and the males harbor a lust for twins. I'm willing to forget trying to take over the crime world and just enjoy being pampered here. It's just hard getting used to this primitive lifestyle.*

"Dholi, what do you think of this place that Sonny put us up in?" Daloi asked, placing her hands on her hips and taking a slow turn around the expansive living room, which included a commanding view of Manhattan's upper west side.

"I love it. It's even nicer than the penthouse in Chicago," Dholi stated, walking out to the balcony, which extended across the entire width of the building.

"It's funny that he calls himself a businessman and politician with family values, but is happy to share a bed with us. Why does he have to pretend at all? It seems this is only the land of the free and home of the brave as long as you follow their rules," Daloi said, perplexed at the duplicity of the situation.

"I enjoy promiscuity, fine clothes, and jewelry," said Dholi, twisting a strand of lustrous, black, Tahitian pearls between her thumb and forefinger. "I wonder if he has a sailboat. I would love to be out on the water feeling the breeze in my face. Even if the water is salty. Could you live here forever?" asked Dholi, with a positive ring in her voice, hoping to get Daloi to consider a permanent move to Earth.

“I know it might be safer to stay here and remain hidden, I just don’t know if I can live without all the conveniences we had back home. But I also don’t want to wind up captured like Tatan. I’m sure whatever they did to him, it wasn’t pleasant.” Daloi grabbed her face and looked at Dholi with an air of sadness. But then, she looked up with confidence, knowing what she had to do.

“Let’s just be careful. We can lay low for a while and enjoy ourselves. If things get dicey, we can look for a way out of this place,” said Dholi, trying to sound hopeful.

“I want to be careful, but I am not interested in laying low. We are highly evolved compared to these humans, and we should show it!” Daloi said.

Chapter 8

Moving Into the Big Apple

Adar arrived at the United Nations building at the appointed time, and scanned the area for Cobalt's contact. He approached the west entrance where he saw a woman wearing a red scarf. *That must be her. She looks pensive. I wonder if she understands who Cobalt really is?*

"Hello, I believe you are Cobalt's contact," said Adar, walking up to the woman.

"Yes, I am Li Xiao," she said, extending a hand and looking Adar up and down.

"I am Adar." He shook her hand. "I believe you have something for me."

"Yes, here are the keys to an apartment in Gramercy Park. This note explains where the building is and how to get into the apartment." Xiao handed him the items. She wondered why the man wore gloves and a long coat in such warm weather.

"Got it," said Adar, taking the items and walking off without another word.

He's a strange one, thought Li Xiao. *He does not look or act normal at all. Another strange incident that Cobalt will have to explain if he wants me to keep working with him.*

***

Adar arrived at the apartment building, which sat across the street from a large park in the middle of the Gramercy Park Historic District. He noticed that the area was cleaner and better maintained than other areas he had walked through. When he entered the apartment, he took time to acquaint himself with the layout of the two-bedroom place. He liked the view of the park but wished he could see the water. Wylyy helped him obtain additional supplies to keep him fed and help him get around. *New location, same lack of inspiration. How do these people get anything done or connect efficiently with such outdated technology?*

No digital wall, no voice activated system to control the apartment, and I'll bet the stove doesn't create food for you. Devices here get power from a cord that is plugged into the wall. Adar laughed at his antiquated surroundings.

A knock at the door stirred him from his thoughts. "What do you want?" Adar asked, after opening the door. Two men stood before him dressed in shabby grey suits. One was tall and slender, while the other was medium height with a stocky body.

"We're the welcoming committee. We want to welcome you to the building," said the stocky gentleman, holding his hands out to him in a convivial manner, while the tall man watched Adar with a stoic look on his face.

"Beat it!" said Adar, attempting to slam the door on them.

"Wait a minute, buddy." The tall man stuck his foot in the door to block it from closing. "We also want to give you an opportunity to buy some renter's insurance."

“I do not need insurance, but I do need you to move your foot before I break it off and shove it up your butt.”

“Without insurance, something unfortunate could occur to you or your apartment. I would hate to see that happen, my friend.” The tall man sneered.

“I’m not your friend,” said Adar, shoving the man back into the hall. “Move away from my door, or I’m going to give you flying lessons, right out that window at the end of the hall.”

The man grabbed Adar by his shirt and reached for the gun he wore in a holster in his jacket. Before the poser could say another word or extract his weapon, Adar picked him up and threw him down the corridor and out the six-foot-tall window beside the stairwell.

“How is it possible that you threw him that far?” the other man asked in wonder.

“Let me show you,” Adar said, before grabbing the back of the man’s neck and tossing him out the same window after his companion.

“Oh, my god, I can’t believe you did that,” cried a woman in a robe and slippers, who emerged just then from the apartment across the hall.

“You want to see if you can fly, too?” asked Adar, eyeing the woman.

“Oh mercy, no. Where are my manners? I’m Abigale, your neighbor.” She smiled at Adar and shook his hand vigorously.

"Those two have been terrorizing us for over two years now. I am so glad you got rid of them."

Abigale had tufts of grey hair showing from under a scarf she had wrapped around her head. Her light brown eyes sparkled as she gazed at the alien. Her wide smile revealed yellowed teeth that she didn't bother to brush much anymore.

"Whatever, lady," said Adar, turning to walk back into his apartment.

"You know, I haven't been in here since my good friend, Ethel, passed away," said Abigale, pushing her way past Adar, her unbound breasts swaying under her clothing. "I like what you've done with the place. I guess it wasn't you, though, since you just got here." She covered her mouth and chuckled as if she were hiding a secret.

"Look, lady—"

"Abigale, please call me Abigale."

"Abigale, please leave. I want to get some rest." Adar's request fell on deaf ears.

"Did they repaint the bedroom? There used to be an awful stain on the wall that she tried to cover with a mirror instead of just painting over it. Oh look. This is just lovely," said Abigale, ignoring Adar and moving into the bedroom.

"Abigale—"

"You never did tell me your name," she said, lowering her voice and pressing her hand against Adar's chest.

"It's Adar." Her hand felt warm through his shirt. The scents of her hair conditioner, deodorant, mouthwash and perfume filled his nostrils in a miasma of odors.

"Adar? Is that Persian? I never had a Persian before. A man who can throw a man out a window the way you did could probably have his way with me." Abigale fell back onto Adar's bed, opened her robe and started to rub her thin body through her sheer, pink nightie. She kicked her big fluffy blue slippers past him onto the floor.

Adar was perplexed. "Abigale, what are you doing?"

"I can barely breathe. Could you massage my chest?" she asked, panting as she cupped her breasts with her hands.

What the hell is wrong with this woman? I don't know if I should kill her or have sex with her. "I'm going to close the shades. If you're still here after that, I'm going to close the door and do sexy things to you."

"Don't you dare rip my clothes off and thrust yourself deep into me! Do you have lube?" Abigale asked, looking around at Adar.

"What's lube?"

"Never mind, we'll figure something out. Now get over here and spank me hard. That'll make me wet for you."

How is it these people built a modern civilization? Adar laughed silently. *As much as I would just like to toss her out the window, I think I'm going to follow her suggestion to rip off her clothes and spank her hard.*

***

Later that evening, after finally expelling the sex-starved Abigale and taking a nap, Adar received an urgent call from Wylyy.

"Adar, I need to patch the captain in to your UCD.".

"Put him through," said Adar, fearing it would not be good news.

"Adar, Captain Shisal here. What's going on down there?" Shisal demanded.

"I had a crazy moment with a neighbor, but I'm okay now." Adar was embarrassed to be caught off guard and wasn't sure how to respond.

"I really want to know how your search for the Cheoili is going," Shisal said impatiently.

"Oh, that. One dead, two to go. The twins escaped to another city, but I'm sure they are hiding out with local crime bosses."

"I need you to find them, Adar. Try to keep at least one of them alive so we keep the government happy."

"I'll do what I can Captain," Adar said, ending the transmission. *What does he think I am doing down here, randomly killing people? It's a planet with more than seven billion humans, and I am supposed to find two Cheoili that can change their appearance at will.*

Later, Adar walked down Lafayette Street and across Duane Street, headed to his rendezvous with Ahmed at Max's. Along the way, he took note of the various eateries, attempting to match the look and smell of these food items with the ones he had learned about during his training. *The variety of foodstuffs in this city appears to be so much broader than what I found in Chicago*, he thought. Before long he arrived at Max's.

Nestled between two parks on opposite corners from each other, the small restaurant was on the bottom floor of a narrow nine-story building. Adar took a moment to stroll through the parks. He was astonished by the smell of a woman who wore a concentrated perfume, sitting on a bench next to a person who apparently had not bathed in days.

Adar arrived at Max's just after 5 p.m. He walked into the dimly lit restaurant and looked around. With his acute eyesight, he quickly spotted Ahmed sitting in a booth just beyond the end of the bar. He surveyed the room for dangers, using his wide peripheral vision. Most of the tables and other booths were empty. Red and white checked plastic tablecloths covered eating surfaces, and the aroma of pasta, garlic and tomato sauce filled the air. Though he was unable to match the aromas to the words he had learned, Adar did not find the fragrances repulsive. Still, he longed for the smell of raw meat.

"Can I help you?" asked a short, round, dark-haired man, walking up to Adar.

Adar pointed towards the booth where Ahmed was seated. "I'm here to see Ahmed."

"You may go ahead and seat yourself. Here is a menu," the man said, offering him a plastic-bound volume.

Adar waved away the menu and walked towards Ahmed who was sitting in a booth across from a balding, dark-haired man with a large gut that prevented him from buttoning his coat. As the alien approached, Ahmed eyed him and gave him a quick head nod before standing up.

"Adar, I'm glad you could make it." Ahmed waved a hand toward his dinner companion. "This is Luigi. He runs things here."

"Hello, Luigi. I'm Adar." He held out his hand to Luigi, though the gesture felt awkward.

Luigi looked at Adar above shiny, half-rim glasses as he devoured a plate of lasagna. Sauce from the pasta had dribbled down his chin and the front of his starched white shirt. Luigi grimaced, displeased by Adar's unusual looks.

"You some kind of hippy freak or skinhead? I don't want to deal with your kind. I don't care how badass you are," Luigi said, waving Adar away angrily.

"I'm none of that. I'm someone who knows how to kill people." *Why would this stupid human call me that before even talking to me? Considering this small bar is his office, this is probably the wrong person for me to be meeting. The smell of dirt and mold in here tells me this is an old, poorly kept establishment, which is probably indicative of how he runs his business.*

"Either way, I don't trust you. Skinheads have been trying to make inroads on my territory for years. You think I'm going to bring one of them into the fold? Not going to happen." Luigi returned to eating his food and ignored Adar.

"Maybe I should join them and see if they could use my services to get rid of you and your people," said Adar, flipping on his personal, protective shield, expecting an outbreak of violence at any moment, violence that he would initiate.

“Maybe we should fill you full of lead and throw you in the East River. Boys, take out this trash,” Luigi snarled without even looking up from his plate.

Someone punched Adar in the back. Shaking off the blow, he turned and stabbed the attacker in the chest with his spear. Two other men drew their guns and began shooting at Adar, who responded by leaping toward them and slicing off the arm of one and the head of the other.

“What kind of demon are you?” screamed Luigi, jumping to his feet and knocking the food to the floor.

“The kind who does not like to be threatened,” Adar replied, stabbing Luigi in the chest.

This action precipitated more gunfire from the other end of the bar. Adar pulled out his photon rifle and quickly took out the shooters who had scattered across the restaurant to find cover. When it was all over, seven men lay dead on the floor, and one man stood shaking in the middle of the bar, his pants wet with urine. Tossing his gun to the floor, he made a show of raising his hands before the attacking alien.

“Please don’t kill me, I’m unarmed,” the man pleaded, falling to his knees.

The attack by Luigi angered Adar. This group of people tried to kill him. But his personal code wouldn’t let him kill an unarmed man who wasn’t threatening him. It wasn’t enough to be stuck on this backward, low-tech planet full of weaklings. He also had to hide his identity. *Out of the billions of galaxies in space these people think they are the only intelligent life that exists. And I use that term loosely. Maybe I should just go to other gang areas and take turns fighting for different sides. I'd have some fun and help clean up the gene pool in this place while waiting for the Cheoili to show up again.*

"You can go, but keep this incident to yourself," said Adar, wiping his spear on the pants leg of one of the men he had just slain. "I'm not interested in a discussion with the authorities."

Bang! A shot rang out coming from the gun Ahmed held, killing the man on his knees.

"We can't leave witnesses that might seek retribution or call the cops. Let's get out of here," Ahmed said, before he beckoned for Adar to follow him out a rear door. The pair then walked quickly down the alley away from Max's.

"If what you said back there is true, why should I let you live?" Adar stopped as they neared the end of the alley to confront Ahmed.

"Because I'm on your side," said Ahmed, grinning.

"Since when? Since you led me into that ambush?" Adar placed his hand on the spear under his coat.

"I got you the meeting with Luigi like you requested. Why did you pick a fight with him?" Ahmed felt cold fingers of dread climbing his spine as he stared at Adar's strange face. Was death closing in on him, he wondered, as a wave of panic shook him. He knew he couldn't stop this madman from killing him.

“He picked the fight with me!” Adar countered, bristling at the accusation.

“Same thing in the end. They’re all dead. Why didn’t those bullets hurt you, and where did you get your laser rifle?” Ahmed peppered the alien with questions, hoping to distract him and learn more about the odd person standing before him.

Adar stopped and scrutinized Ahmed. *I really should kill this one. He knows too much.*

“From your looks and behavior, you need someone to help you navigate the territory here,” Ahmed added quickly.

“I can get around just fine. I have a digital map.” Adar raised his UCD in the air as if Ahmed would understand it.

“That’s what I mean, your English is a bit rusty. You may know the physical landscape of New York, but you don’t know the political landscape.” Ahmed slapped the back of his hand into the palm of the other one as if the alien would understand the gesture.

Though he didn’t follow some of what this Ahmed said, Adar heard the man’s heartbeat speed up. He also saw beads of sweat emerge on the human’s brow and smelled fear emanating from the man when he panicked.

“Fine, but if you cross me, I will kill you,” he warned, moving his hand away from the shaft of his spear and resuming his march down the alley.

Heaving a deep sigh of relief, Ahmed hurried his steps to keep up. “I think we already covered that. By the way, I know another guy you should meet. He will be happy to hear you took out Luigi."

Placing a hand on Adar's shoulder only to have it shrugged off, Ahmed turned right when they reached the sidewalk, leading Adar towards Chelsea.

"Since you know a lot of people around here, I'm trying to find two women. They are probably hanging out with mobsters."

"I know Sharon and Sheila who are part of Charlie's crew."

"They would have arrived here a few days ago."

"It's not them, then. They've been around for a while. I don't know anyone else like you described." Ahmed relaxed, knowing he had dodged a bullet and maybe made a new friend.

"Okay, let's go meet this other guy you know." Adar scanned his surroundings for danger as he walked, checking whether anyone had followed them from the restaurant. He was still uncomfortable with Ahmed, but finding a new contact might take longer alone and increase his chances of being exposed.

"Wow, a contraction. Your English is improving." Ahmed laughed, hoping to get Adar to relax.

Adar shook his head and moved down the street, not understanding Ahmed's attempt at humor.

Chapter 9

One Woman in a Man's World

At Harry Moran's offices in Manhattan, crime bosses from across the borough sat around the long mahogany table, discussing how to split up the territory vacated by a newly deceased boss.

Harry puffed on a cigar after tapping ashes delicately into a bulky, crystal ashtray. Diamond cufflinks sparkled in the light as he adjusted the sleeves of his Armani suit. His short, round body filled the comfy leather armchair at the head of the table. Harry rubbed his chubby, red face in exasperation as he looked around the table at the other bosses, who came to the meeting dressed to the nines in their custom-tailored suits and wing-tip shoes. His gaze lingered on the person seated directly opposite him at the other end of the table, who was making demands of him.

All of the bosses who reported to Harry were men, except for this woman, who now rose from her chair and slapped both hands loudly on the table's surface, yelling at Harry about the lack of equitable treatment from him and the other bosses.

"WHAT DO YOU MEAN THAT TERRITORY IS NOT MINE?" shouted Toni, her eyes fixed on Harry's. "I ran the books, I handled the transfer of goods and I kept the bitches in line, most of them men."

Toni Stapleton belonged to the mob family run by Harry Moran. For the most part, the family ran organized crime across

Manhattan, its main rackets being drugs, prostitution, stolen goods, and identity theft. Recently the Moran family moved into hacking businesses and selling the intellectual property they stole on the Dark Web.

"I don't mean to imply that you didn't work hard," said Harry, calmly. "But when a boss dies, his territory passes to one of his lieutenants. You'll still be part of the family, though." Harry added that last assurance, hoping to assuage Toni's concerns.

She pounded her fist on the table. "That boss was my husband!"

"And he died screwing my wife!" Harry said, slapping his hand on the table and looking at Toni as if to place some of the blame on her.

"No one ever accused him of being a saint, but that territory should still pass to me." Toni jabbed her finger in her chest to accentuate her point, then took her seat.

Toni had a brilliant business mind, along with strong ambitions. She thumbed her nose at the crumbs Harry offered her. Serving for years as her husband's enforcer, she had struck fear into the lower ranks of the organization, all the way down to the people on the street. Toni had a slender body, long, well-groomed blond hair, perfectly manicured nails and disarming big blue eyes.

With her stylish wardrobe and fit body, Toni could easily be mistaken for a Cosmo cover girl. However, anyone who treated her like one soon felt her wrath. She would eagerly punch a person in the face or cut up anyone who crossed her. She also used her looks to control men, not just to attract them.

"Look, I'm going to split your husband's territory equally between Samuel, Lee, and Jackson, and that's the end of it." Harry abruptly waved his hands across the table, indicating that the discussion was over.

"Oh, the snakes-on-a-plane brothers. You know what happened to the snakes in the end, don't you?" Toni tapped her fingernails on the tabletop and showed her displeasure by contorting her face and narrowing her eyes.

"We're not brothers, and that attitude is not going to get you any closer to what you want," snarled Lee Jones, a robust, dapper man with dark hair and hazel eyes in his late 30s. Lee had long coveted Toni from afar. He always clocked Toni's movements when they occupied the same room. "I'd be willing to share operation of my territory, if you'd be willing to give up something."

"I'm no whore, Lee!" Toni protested, leaning forward to cross and re-cross her long legs.

"I never used that word. You're not listening to me. Can't we just have a discussion without all the acrimony?" Lee implored as he extended a meaty hand toward the woman, palm upward. He gazed at Toni with open admiration on his sweaty, florid face.

"Sure, but I hope you understand that I have a certain antipathy toward men that treat me like a piece of meat." Her eyes flashed fire for a second, before a weary sigh escaped her. Holding Lee's gaze, she added, "Come by the club tonight. We can talk after the show."

Toni then grabbed her coat and stalked out of the conference room, her thoughts churning. *I would love nothing more than to carve those three morons up and feed them to rats. This deal is far from over, fellas, far from over.*

Lee watched Toni leave the room, lust in his eyes. He hoped he could mend things with Toni once they connected at her club. *Gosh, I would love to have Toni as my woman*, he thought.

Toni managed a club in Greenwich Village called the Blue Note. Though she sang there on occasion, she mostly used it as a front to run the mob's business. Likewise, the ladies that hit the stage at her place weren't there just to sing. Toni, being quite the looker, got offers all the time, but she never mixed business with pleasure. She stayed focused on her mission, which didn't include romance. She didn't just want to take over her husband's territory, she wanted Harry's job, too.

Growing up an only child of parents who both taught classes at a college in Ithaca, NY, Toni learned early that knowledge is power. Thus, she set out to learn as much as she possibly could to quench her burning thirst for power. Because her name was Toni Titus, she suffered the nickname "Titty" from teasing boys all through school. This experience spawned in her a deep disdain for members of the opposite sex. She eventually shed the hated moniker after college, but she retained her distrust of men. When she married, she took her husband's name of Stapleton to distance herself from her unpleasant youth.

Toni earned a political science degree from Princeton and an MBA from Harvard. Afterward, Toni undertook a lucrative career on Wall Street, investing in high-tech startups. She quickly climbed to the executive ranks of her firm, but felt blocked from attaining a position in upper management because she was a woman. Her husband taught her she could earn substantially more money pursuing illegal business activities. This led to her changing careers, but she never lost her drive to be on top.

Toni walked the few blocks from Harry's Chelsea penthouse office towards her club in Greenwich Village. *They are not going to take what's mine*. She pounded her fist into her other hand, deep in thought. *I ran that territory, not my husband, and they know it. And Lee has the audacity to think he can just pick up where my dead husband left off. What do they take me for? A flaming idiot? Or just another dumb broad? Well, we'll just see about that.* Toni ducked into an alley to smoke a cigarette and think about her next move. As she leaned against a wall and slowly exhaled a cloud of smoke, a figure approached her.

"Hey, lady, what you doin' in an alley?" asked a husky man in jeans and a hoodie when he drew close. "Don't you know it's dangerous to be wandering around an alley by yourself?"

After getting a closer look at her, the would-be mugger pulled back his hoodie to expose his curly black hair and flashed his bright brown eyes at her, hoping to ease her suspicions and catch her off guard.

"Don't worry. Stick close to me, I'll keep you safe." Toni smirked as she tossed away her spent cigarette, unimpressed by his size or his looks.

"Oh, you got jokes. Why don't you give me that Chanel bag and I'll let you walk away unharmed," the guy growled, flexing the defined muscles in his arms in a show of intimidation.

"I got something you'll enjoy a lot more than walking around with my bag over your shoulder," Toni said, propping her right foot up on a paint can nearby and sliding her skirt higher to expose most of her thigh. She took a deep breath and sighed to feign interest in the fellow.

"Now you talkin'. Let me see what you got," the man said, eagerly rubbing his hands together.

"Come closer. I want you to feel me," Toni said, reaching her arms out toward him.

The mugger moved in close, enjoying the vapors of expensive perfume that wafted from her neck. He found the scent intoxicating as he nuzzled the area behind Toni's ear. But when Toni pulled a dagger from a sheath on her thigh and thrust it into the mugger's abdomen several times, his hands clenched around her arms.

"You feel me now, big boy?" Her whisper was rough and feral as he slid down her body onto the alley floor.

Toni stared at the crumpled body at her feet, her normally sultry eyes cold and dispassionate. She snatched up her knife as if she were pulling a straw from a glass of water to toss in the trash. Wiping the blood on the mugger's shirt, she returned the blade to her thigh sheath.

She noticed a blood stain on her cashmere coat. "Now look at what you've done to my nice suit. If you weren't already dying, I'd kill you for this," she said.

Toni removed the garment, turning it inside out to cover the blood and strode off down the alley, pulling out another cigarette as she walked.

Oddly enough, that moron back there gave me a good idea. Momma always told me to never give up on my dreams.

Sometime later, Lee walked into the Blue Note club and dropped into a seat at a table near the stage. Toni's singing and her looks captivated the big guy. He once offered to take out her husband so they could rule his territory as equal partners.

She turned me down, now she has nothing. Finally, I've got her just where I want her – at my mercy. He chuckled to himself.

Toni smiled at Lee as she finished her song:

A tale as old as time, boy you got what you deserved
And now you want somebody to cure those lonely nights
You wish you had somebody that could come and make it right.
But boy I ain't somebody with a lot of sympathy
You'll see I thought I told ya,
What goes around, comes back around.

"You singing Justin Timberlake songs now?" asked Lee, sliding a chair up for Toni as she arrived, so she could sit across from him.

"It just seemed apropos to our situation." Toni smiled, momentarily placing her right hand on his.

"Is that directed at me or Harry?" Lee asked, beginning to worry about retribution from Toni.

"Just the situation. Grab your drink. We should talk where we can have some privacy," Toni said, looking to reassure him. She stood and motioned for him to follow her.

Lee heaved a relieved sigh. "You took the words right out of my mouth."

Toni led the mobster backstage and up a flight of stairs to her private office and boudoir.

"Nice office you got here, Toni. Even has a view of the park," said Lee, looking around and checking out the view of Washington Square Park out her window.

"Let's move into the next room. It has a bed and some champagne. We can get more comfortable. Be a doll and grab a bottle of Veuve out of the fridge and open it for me," said Toni, pointing at the small fridge on the other side of the room.

"I'd love to. You certainly know how to treat your guests. Does this mean we can be business partners?" asked Lee hopefully. He plopped on the love seat next to the bed, unwrapping the cork and opening the bottle of champagne with a pop.

Toni stepped behind a screen, meanwhile, to remove her dress and don a red silk robe. "I'm not sure I want to share with you a portion of what is supposed to be all mine. As a matter of fact, we should squeeze Harry for more territory, period."

"That's going to be difficult to do. He's careful not give too much power to one individual."

"He must have a weakness. Something he wants enough to make a trade," Toni prodded, hoping Lee would open up.

“Well, since the oil revenues have dropped off, the Russians in Jersey City are being pressured by Putin to send more cash home. That has forced them to start making inroads into Harry’s territory.”

“You know that Bobby’s crew in Newark is looking to take over Jersey City,” Toni offered.

“If we could get them fighting, it could weaken them enough for us to move in,” said Lee, hyped to be included in a planning discussion with Toni. He poured some champagne into two glasses he found on a nearby shelf.

“Lovely idea, Lee.” Toni took one of the flutes from Lee. “Let’s toast our future together and then maybe I’ll let you consummate our new partnership.”

The two touched glasses and took a sip of the bubbly. Toni slid a finger down her robe, loosening the belt and letting it fall open to reveal pink lace underwear.

“Why do you still have your clothes on? You like to keep a lady waiting?” Toni said in a sultry voice, batting her eyelashes at him.

She turned toward the bed and let her robe fall to the floor past her firm ass and long, well-toned legs. “You don’t mind if I prepare the room, do you? And you better have a condom. I just hate getting all messy before going out. It would be nice, if we could have dinner later.” Toni looked back at Lee, smiling.

Lee felt like a kid out on a first date with the school’s homecoming queen. “Of course I have a condom somewhere. I probably have a couple, so let’s not be in a hurry to go out. Go ahead and get things ready. I'll undress and wait for you in this comfy loveseat," he said, patting the right arm nervously.

Toni lit some candles, turned off the lights, put on some mood music, and pulled the covers back on the bed. She turned toward Lee and slowly peeled off her lingerie. "I hope you don't mind if I leave my stilettos on."

"Not a problem. Not a problem at all," Lee replied, finding it harder to breathe.

"Good. Now put that condom on and get over here and take care of me," she ordered, her lush, red lips parting in a wicked grin. Sitting on the edge of her king-size bed, she studied the middle-aged man hurriedly undressing before her. Lee grabbed at his clothes with all thumbs, almost falling in his eagerness to remove his pants.

I can't believe this is happening. Lee Talmadge is about to have sex with Toni Stapleton. Yes! Should I take off my socks? I hope she doesn't laugh at my penis. That would just ruin it for me. My goodness, she looks sexy.

Toni widened her smile as Lee moved toward the bed while fumbling with a condom. He watched Toni as she scooted back toward the center before reclining on her elbows, her baby blue eyes narrowed to a mischievous glance.

Lee slowly climbed onto the bed and crawled to Toni, inhaling deeply as the odor of her fragrant perfume mixed with the natural scent of her womanhood hit his nostrils.

"I can't wait to watch you cum with me inside you," he growled, his eyes roving over her smooth tanned flesh, panting in anticipation of what was to come. "I've been wanting to be inside you for a while," Lee whispered.

"What a coincidence. I've been wanting to stick something inside you as well," said Toni, pulling a shiny, double-edged stiletto from under a pillow and jabbing it into Lee's hairy beer belly. He tussled with Toni on the bed, and they toppled onto the floor with the woman ending up on top of the mobster. She grabbed his throat and stabbed him three more times in the chest for good measure.

As Lee gasped his last breath, Toni leaned in and stared into his eyes. "You won't get to watch me cum, but I'll get to watch you go, motherfucker."

Wiping her hands on his dress shirt, Toni grabbed her cell phone and made a quick call. "Johnny, cleanup on aisle five. Don't bother me with the details. I'll be in the shower."

Chapter 10

Havoc in New York

Given his involvement in taking out Luigi, Ahmed thought the timing good to present Adar to Harry. Luigi had been a mob boss before Harry came to power and usurped his claim to the position of *capo dei capi,* or boss of bosses, in Manhattan. Luigi had frowned on this new world order, and boldly expressed his disapproval to Harry every chance he got. He constantly chided the mob boss, and his payments were always late and deficient.

Harry had connections and guns. The bosses he didn't kill he had thrown in jail. The only higher authority he reported to was the Syndicate, and only for administrative purposes. They were like the Pope, anointing the new *capo* for each area. They kept the peace among the families. So long as Harry stayed within his territory, he could do as he pleased.

Ahmed felt that a position with Harry would give Adar a view of any major activities across the different crime families, which hopefully would lead him to his quarry. Ahmed also envisioned the new collaboration leading to an elevated status for himself.

Ahmed led Adar to Harry's offices at the top of a building at 10th Avenue and West 28th Street, which had a view overlooking High Line Park and the Hudson River. The two stepped off the elevator and admired the spacious, open foyer with its high ceiling. A large, elegant painting of Mayor Fiorello H. La Guardia hung over a fireplace. Harry felt a special connection to the legendary mayor because they shared similar physiques and successes in the city.

Tall potted plants dotted the perimeter of the room, and an extravagant flower arrangement sat atop a wrought iron table that graced the center of the space, adding a sweet aroma to the air that Adar found repugnant.

The pair walked across white marble flooring onto an enormous, silk Persian rug, where a couple of Harry's guards met them. They frisked Ahmed and took his gun. When they reached to frisk Adar, he kicked one of the men against the wall with the heel of his boot, knocking him out and placed his spear against the other man's neck, while grabbing him by the shirt.

"Adar, what are you doing?" screeched Ahmed. "You trying to get us killed?"

"I don't like people rubbing their hands on me," Adar said unapologetically. "Let's go see Harry," he said to the guard, shaking him by his grip on his shirt.

Ahmed picked up his gun and followed Adar.

"Right this way," said the guard, holding his chin away from Adar's spear and walking down the hall sideways towards a closed set of double doors.

Ahmed opened the door to see Harry seated in the middle of a long conference table. Several men around the table went for their weapons as they entered. Ahmed rushed to defuse the situation, hoping to avoid another gun fight.

"Harry, take it easy. We just came to talk." Ahmed inhaled sharply, puffing out his thin chest as he glanced nervously at three henchmen who drew closer as he and Adar approached the mob boss. Ahmed also slowly placed his gun on the table and raised his hands into the air.

"You have an odd way of showing it! Let my man go, and I'll listen to what you have to say!" barked Harry, anger reddening his face.

Ahmed nodded at Adar, who pushed the man he was holding to the side, put away his spear, and switched on his personal shield, just to be safe.

"I would like to introduce you to Adar, an amazing assassin," said Ahmed, speaking slowly with his arms still raised. "He just took out Luigi and his crew, with a little help from me," he bragged. "He's looking to be the muscle for a local boss. I thought that might interest you."

"That interests me a lot." Harry gave Adar an assessing stare. His heavy jowls split in a broad grin as he leaned back to capture Ahmed's gaze, his plush leather chair creaking under his 250-pound frame.

"But how do I know I can trust him?" said Harry, rising from his seat and slipping past Ahmed to study Adar with a thoughtful stare.

"I'm Adar. You can trust me," Adar said, offering his hand to Harry.

"Then why did you have that spear at my man's throat?" asked Harry, ignoring Adar's hand.

"I don't like men rubbing on my body or taking my weapons. It makes me feel disrespected. I'm a dangerous person. That can work for you or against you." Adar turned his head to the side as if waiting for an answer from Harry, which would trigger one of two responses he had planned.

"Okay, I could use a dangerous addition to my team," Harry said, grabbing Adar's hand to shake it. "Have a seat and let's chat a bit. You get the hell out and close the door behind you!" Harry yelled at the guard that came in with Adar.

Ahmed and Adar took seats at the end of the table while Harry's personal guard closed the door. The mob boss sat next to his visitors, ignoring the other men at the table.

"I've been looking for a way to push Luigi to the side without starting a turf war. I appreciate you managing that irritant for me. So where are you from, and why should I trust you not to try to take me out?"

"I am not interested in taking over any territory," Adar said quickly. "Luigi attacked me so I defended myself. I just came in from Chicago to settle some business. I'm here looking for a couple of female snitches. They are gorgeous twins with an uncanny ability to get people to do what they want. It would be great if you would have your network inform me of any new women with those particular attributes. Until I find them, I am looking to stay busy and I would love to help you gain more territory and take out any of your enemies along the way."

"Interesting story. It's too early to believe I can totally trust you, but I'm glad to have you on my team," said Harry, smiling from ear to ear.

Adar didn't care about Harry or his territory. He wanted to find the Cheoili. Meanwhile, if he got to kill a few people, so much the better.

"Do you have anything that we can take care of for you?" Ahmed asked, eager to establish himself as an essential member of Team Adar.

"I assure you that you will be pleased with our results," he added, eyeing Harry happily.

"Yeah, I got something for you. Luigi has a partner in Little Italy named Vinnie Romano. If you could take him and his crew out, that would give me an opportunity to take over his territory and put two hundred grand in your pocket."

"Each?" Ahmed raised his eyebrows, figuring he had nothing to lose by asking.

"Sure. Now go get it done, and be careful that this isn't traced back to me." Harry wagged his forefinger at them as he rose from his seat and walked back to join the men at the other end of the table.

***

Dholi stood in the kitchen of Sonny's condo, drinking a beer as she waited for her all-beef hot dog to heat up on the stove. She paced back and forth, a bit upset about the video she just saw on a local TV news program. It depicted a shootout at a local bar.

Though the security footage was grainy, Dholi could clearly make out Adar killing a man with his photon rifle.

"Daloi, you saw that news report about the attack at the bar, right?" she asked her sister, who nodded in response. "You know who that was, don't you?"

"Yes, I know," Daloi said, a worried look on her face.

"What are we going to do about that Ossie?" Dholi asked, raising her hands in frustration.

"We need to get help. Let's see if we can get the human police force to help us out."

***

Daloi and Dholi walked into Manhattan's 17th precinct police station, this time disguised as two very young women new to the city. After explaining their issue briefly to the desk sergeant, they found themselves seated in stiff, plastic chairs in Captain Ron McKee's office.

"Captain McKee, I'm Daloi and this is my sister, Dholi," she said, shaking the captain's hand.

Daloi pleaded with Captain McKee for his help. She batted long-lashed brown eyes at him, while Dholi watched quietly. It had taken Daloi the better part of an hour to gain this audience with the perspiring human before her. Apparently, he was in charge of the Homicide Unit of this police force. Daloi felt it was imperative that she get him to go after Adar.

"This guy killed our friend, and he's after us," she whined. "I swear to you he's an alien. Look at his eyes!" She showed him a video of Adar attacking Tatan in Chicago.

McKee sat in his creaky, reclining desk chair rubbing his day-old whiskers as he rocked back and forth, listening to the young woman before him. His middle-aged, bulging waistline tugged at the buttons of a wrinkled, coffee-stained dress shirt as he leaned forward over his desk to give the two ladies sitting across from him a long, assessing look. Ordinarily, the captain would chalk this up as another couple of loonies who hadn't taken their meds in a while. But the face on the video looked familiar. *That looks like the guy they want for the slaughter at Max's,* he thought.

"Hold on a minute," the captain said, as he strode to his door. "Calvin, could you come in here a minute. I want you to listen to this. It has to do with the shooting at Max's. Ladies, this is Sgt. Calvin Peters. He's working on the case involving a shooting that may have involved the same perpetrator."

"Can you tell me the location of your friend when the 'alien' attacked him?" McKee asked, using air quotes.

Daloi seemed genuinely distressed as she recounted her story, but her companion Dholi kept crossing and uncrossing her legs, causing the tiny pink mini-skirt to drift upwards, flashing him tantalizing glimpses of her inner thighs, all the while grinning at him like a sly Cheshire cat.

"It was somewhere in Chicago," said Daloi, working to look as distressed as possible. "We visited there for a while and decided to move to New York. Now he's here," Daloi said with emphasis to show she was serious.

"Do you think he's following you?" McKee asked, looking for a connection.

Daloi worked to muster a look of fear onto her face. "We don't know. We can only imagine he wants to get rid of any witnesses to the crime. After seeing the video on the news, we decided to come to the police."

"Play your video again, so Sgt. Peters can see it," said McKee.

"That is definitely the person from Max's attacking your friend," said Peters, after watching the screen for a few seconds.

"We need to keep that recording," McKee said, reaching to take it from Daloi.

"This is my only way to communicate with my sister," Daloi cried, pulling her communicator away from his grasp. "Could you possibly make a copy?"

"Sure, let me grab one of my body cams." McKee recorded the scene from Daloi's screen and then handed her one of his cards. "You call me if you have any other information."

"We will, Captain," Daloi purred, as both ladies grinned widely at McKee, their unique teeth hidden behind bright, glossy lips that gleamed under the garish fluorescent lights of the police station. The two curtsied before leaving McKee's office.

***

The case perturbed McKee and it showed. He bounced a tennis ball against the wall in front of his desk, thinking. *I don't want to believe that we have an alien in our midst. That video from Max's place with apparent waves of energy emanating from that perp's weapon is hard to explain. And the victims' wounds suggest some sort of energy weapon was used*. The captain stepped to the door of his office and yelled into the squad room. "Johnson, any progress on picking up Ahmed?"

"Not yet, captain. We have a detail watching his apartment though, and I spread the word to our patrols. It's only a matter of time before we apprehend him," said an older detective, shaking his bald head as he sat hunched over his desk.

"Stay on it. We need to catch this guy," McKee said, spurred by a nagging sense of urgency. He returned to his own desk to rock in his chair and stew on what he had just seen and heard.

***

"Adar, you have to tell me where you learned those amazing fighting moves and where you got that laser weapon of yours," Ahmed begged, excitement gleaming in his dark eyes as the duo left Vinnie's offices, located at the back of a pool hall on 21st Street.

Adar and Ahmed had killed Vinnie and all of his people. Adar took the lead, using his spear except for a couple of instances when he fired the photon rifle. Ahmed assisted in the rampage, using a silencer on his 9mm Glock. The sounds of their attack were muffled by the music playing on the intercom throughout the building and by sounds of the patrons shooting pool in the front part of the building. Once done, the two sneaked out the back of the building and down the alley.

"The less you know, the safer you will be," said Adar, who was reluctant to share anything with Ahmed. Adar studied the young human. Thus far, he had been most helpful, but like the other beings he had encountered on this backwater planet, his curiosity was becoming tedious.

"I'm hungry and need to eat," Adar said, looking to change the subject. "Why don't we meet in the morning and go over to Harry's"

"That works for me. I'll come by around 10:30," said Ahmed, turning to walk towards his place.

Adar went home and ate a couple of raw steaks that he chased with a glass of Tammarian grog. He was halfway through his shower when he heard a knock on the door. Wrapping his dripping body in a robe, he opened the door to find Abigale standing there with a sugar bowl in her hands.

"Forgive me, Mr. Adar. I was making some tea and seemed to run out of sugar. Could you help an old lady out?" Abigale smiled innocently.

"No problem, Abigale. I keep the sugar on the nightstand next to my bed. If you follow me in I'll let you have some. Does that work for you?" Adar asked, escorting her towards his bedroom.

"Why Mr. Adar, I do believe you are making me blush," Abigale gushed, eagerly trailing behind him.

Chapter 11

A Mission to Syria

Ahmed arrived at Adar's place just after 10:30 the next morning. Upon entering the apartment, he noticed a sugar bowl on the floor by the door.

Ahmed held the bowl up in the air. "Adar, you want me to put this in the kitchen for you?"

"No, leave it there. My neighbor will come by looking for it later." Adar thought warmly of the previous evening's excitement.

"Let's give Harry an update and see what else he has for us," Adar suggested, hoping for another chance to kill some bad guys as he pulled on his coat. "I also hope he has news about any new women joining the mob," he added.

"I'm just going to be happy to get that money. I need it to get my family back," said Ahmed, sounding worried.

"What do you mean, get your family back?" Adar asked, cocking his head to the side in puzzlement.

Ahmed sighed, momentarily overwhelmed by the fear and worry he rarely let others see. "Being part of a religious group back home, I was responsible for carrying out certain tasks. One of those tasks required me to travel to America to set off a device that would kill a bunch of people. After I arrived here, I couldn't get myself to do it. Americans aren't the evil people my leaders led us to believe they are. People have been pretty hospitable to me, considering I'm Muslim and come from Syria."

Making a visible effort to shove inside the emotions clouding his features, Ahmed continued, "Anyway, our leader back home became unhappy with my lack of resolve and decided to kidnap my wife and two kids. He said I had to carry out the attack, or pay him $150,000 to get my family back."

"Screw that. Let's go get your family back. Where are they being held?" Adar demanded, his voice rising with excitement at the prospect of undertaking a new violent mission.

"In a small village just east of Hamrat, Syria. Do you even know where Syria is?" Ahmed wondered if he was wasting his time.

"I know where every country is on this planet. You'll have to point out the city to me though. Just point to it on here." Adar held his UCD up to Ahmed and stretched it out to make the screen easier to view.

"How'd you do that?" Ahmed asked, startled by the ease with which Adar was able to display a map of the world on the unfamiliar high-tech device.

"Focus on where you think they are," Adar said, pointing to the screen.

"There's the village." Ahmed pointed to a spot with his forefinger. "Can you zoom in?"

"Sure, how's this?" Adar moved his hand over the screen to magnify the view of the village.

"Great, there's the building that serves as their remote headquarters. It's also where they hold their meetings and keep beds for their people. I believe the small building to the left is where they keep prisoners."

"Let's see if they're in there," said Adar, doing something else to the screen to view the interior of the building.

"What the hell! Are you using some sort of advanced satellite technology?" Ahmed looked at Adar with incredulity after seeing the view on the screen go right through the wall to what appeared to be a live shot of the interior.

"Something like that. Do you see your family?" Adar asked, motioning for Ahmed to look back at the screen.

"Yes, that's them in the cell right there. There's only two guards on the door and one inside. We can catch a plane to Turkey, cross the border into Syria, take the guards out and free my family with little or no effort," Ahmed suggested, looking at Adar eagerly.

"Screw that. Let's kill everyone at that site so you won't have to worry about any of them bothering you again." The alien threw an amused glance at Ahmed. "As far as getting there, I don't take airplanes," Adar said, grimacing.

Adar felt a rush of adrenalin at the thought of going into battle. *The odds will be stacked against these feeble humans, but that's the chance you take when you initiate aggressive behavior against those weaker than you*. Adar started to pant, thinking about the people he was about to kill.

"Adar, are you okay?" Ahmed asked, watching the changes come over Adar.

"Yes, I just need to contact my ship to get us to the site." Adar spoke to Wylyy in Euclidian on his UCD. "Transport me and my partner here to the field outside this building," Adar requested, after transmitting the coordinates to Wylyy.

"What is that language you are speaking?"

"Ahmed, lay down on the ground and whatever you do, don't scream," Adar instructed, ignoring the question.

"Why would I scream? Uhmmf!" Ahmed fought to muffle his fear as he stumbled and fell to the ground. One moment he was standing in Adar's apartment and the next, he was lying in the sparse grass of the Syrian countryside.

"That's why." Adar laughed, watching Ahmed try to figure out what had transpired.

"What the hell just happened?" whispered Ahmed. They lay in a field of bushes outside the building he had just seen on Adar's screen.

"That's their headquarters, right?" Adar pointed through the bushes towards a dirty beige one-story building a hundred yards away.

"Yes, but how the hell did we get here? You're freaking me out, man," Ahmed said, patting his body to see if he was still in one piece.

"You've seen *Star Trek*?" asked Adar, remembering one of the training sessions he went through on the *Andrea*.

Ahmed tried to get his head around the question. “Yeah. So you’re Captain Kirk?”

“No, I’m one of the people he might visit. Now, let’s focus on getting your family back. There are three people in front of the main building and two in front of the smaller building. I will take them out. Then we can go inside and take care of the rest.” Adar looked for Ahmed’s consent, but the former terrorist still looked dazed.

“I guess that explains why bullets don’t hurt you, and that laser rifle,” Ahmed mumbled, talking to himself as he tried to understand how he suddenly wound up in Syria.

Adar ignored Ahmed’s ramblings. “I’ll go down first and use my spear so I don’t create a lot of noise. You might want to take out your gun in case a patrol comes up here.” Adar slapped Ahmed’s shoulder in an attempt to get him to focus.

“You think that’s a possibility?” asked Ahmed, still a bit confused. He pulled out his Glock from a waist holster, noted a bullet in the chamber and took the safety off before screwing in the silencer. He also felt for the extra magazine in the left-hand pocket of his short leather jacket before looking back at Adar.

“Yes, I do. Now try to pay attention,” Adar said sternly.

Ahmed shook his head in amazement, understanding now why his benefactor had such poor English skills.

“Ahmed, I’m going to cloak so those people don’t see me coming. Follow me into the building once I have taken out the exterior guards and gone inside."

"How am I supposed to see you go inside if you're cloaked?"

"Good point." Adar grabbed Ahmed's arm and bit him, sending Ossie enzymes into his blood stream.

"What the hell did you do that for?" Ahmed screeched, looking at the bite mark on his arm.

"Stop whining! I barely broke the skin. I just needed to give you my enzymes so you can see me and not shoot me or run into me. Can you see me now?" Adar prodded, looking at Ahmed.

"No, you disappeared. Pretty good technology," Ahmed said, reaching towards the spot where he last saw Adar.

"It's not technology. It's part of my natural ability," Adar said, dodging Ahmed's attempt to touch his face.

"Wait, I can see you again," said Ahmed, mouth agape.

"Good, but they won't," said Adar, getting up to walk away.

Adar ran right up to the guards in front of the building and decapitated them using his spear, then wiping the blood off on their clothing.

Holy shit, that guy is brutal. Ahmed watched Adar finish up his handiwork and creep into the building. *Okay, here we go. Try not to get your ass killed saving your family, you James Bond wannabe.*

Leaving his hiding place, Ahmed followed Adar inside. They walked along a dimly lit hallway that stretched down the left side of the building. Devoid of pictures or furniture, it looked abandoned. The floor of rough cement was covered in dust and cobwebs. They approached a set of double doors on the right that led to a large room with about 15 people sitting around a long conference table. Adar entered and started killing people with his blaster. Ahmed dashed into the room after him, firing away.

Two remaining soldiers threw up their hands.

“Ahmed, tell them I’m going to beat them to death unless they fight me. If they beat me, they can go free,” said Adar uncloaking, putting down his blaster and spear.

Ahmed translated Adar’s challenge, and in response, the two large men laughed.

“Looks like we got ourselves a fight,” said Adar, leaping at them.

The fighters dodged Adar’s fists and shoved him to the ground. The two men took turns kicking Adar across the floor. The alien attempted to roll under the table, but one of the soldiers grabbed him by his foot and slung him against the wall. The other soldier grabbed an AK-47 and started spraying the room. Both Adar and Ahmed ducked under the table. From his lower vantage point, Adar reached out and grabbed the gunman by the leg and broke it into two pieces like a rotten tree limb. Leaping to his feet, he then crushed the screaming assailant’s throat with his boot.

The other soldier charged the little alien with his double-edged bayonet knife, but Adar stuck out his elbow and using the Arab’s forward momentum, broke his forearm with an audible snap. Adar then shoved the blade into the screaming man’s chest.

"Why didn't you just shoot them?" Ahmed asked, his eyes bulging with a mixture of fear and wonder.

"What would be the fun in that?" Adar replied, smirking. Retrieving his spear and gun he strode out of the room to clear the rest of the building of potential threats. Three men lay in a basement room, asleep in their bunks. Adar slapped them awake. One man attacked Adar with a knife. Adar quickly twisted the man's head, breaking his neck.

A second pulled a pistol attempting to shoot the alien, who quickly grabbed the man's wrist and squeezed it until he dropped the gun. The third man punched Adar in the face knocking him to the ground. Together, the two Arabs pummeled Adar with their fists as he lay on the floor. But the alien managed to brush one of the men to the side, before hopping astride the other one, twisting his head and breaking his neck. The remaining man kicked Adar across the floor, just before Ahmed walked in and shot the man in the head in with his Glock.

"Good job, Ahmed. I am happy to see you join the fray and not just sit this one out," Adar commented wryly.

"It looked like you were having way too much fun for me to jump in, but then at the end, it looked like you needed my help." Ahmed returned the gun to its holster at his back, not knowing what to think of Adar's proclivities towards violence. "Let's go get my family."

Adar and Ahmed swiftly and silently killed the two guards in front of the holding area, breaking their necks in near simultaneous motions. They then strolled inside the prison where the alien finished off the remaining guard with one quick thrust of his spear.

Ahmed hurried to free his family. They sat up from a pallet of blankets against the wall where they had been sleeping, startled to see Ahmed walk in. Ahmed's wife and two children ran to him, crying and hugging him with joy.

Moments later he asked, "Is it okay if we release the other prisoners?"

"Of course. Just don't give them any details on how we freed them," said Adar.

"Agreed." Ahmed held a fist up to Adar.

"Let's get out of here. I'll have Wylyy transport us back from a closet in the other building. If your family asks how they arrived in New York so quickly, just tell them that it is a top secret government closet-to-closet transfer mechanism that they can never mention," Adar said, a serious look on his face.

"Sure, that will make as much sense to them as anything else," Ahmed said, shrugging his shoulders. "You certainly seemed to enjoy killing those guys back there."

"I don't kill for the fun of it," Adar said, anxious to clear up the misunderstanding. "I kill out of necessity and only bad guys. I was raised from birth to be a warrior and protect the weak, not kill aimlessly. If you are ready, I'll contact Wylyy."

"Who is this Wylyy guy you keep mentioning, and why do we never see him?" Ahmed asked.

"Wylyy is the commander of the attack ship that assists me with getting around. He's a Euclidian from the planet Euclidia, the government that sponsored my mission to find the escaped alien prisoners. We don't see him because we don't need to. He pilots the ship as needed. When it's not needed, he hides it on the bottom of the ocean with two other crewmembers. They spend their time studying this planet, playing war games, and they probably walk around isolated areas on occasion."

"That's all very strange," Ahmed said, astonished. "So that whole thing about aliens visiting us for years has been true."

"No, we've only been here for a few months. Humans just made that stuff up, the way they made up Santa Claus and vampires," Adar said, snickering.

"Laugh if you want, I'm sure your planet has some strange beliefs. Oops, sorry honey, we're leaving now," Ahmed said, responding to his wife's impatient plea. "Adar, we should get out of here. My family is getting restless."

"Good, I'm ready to go as well," Adar said, cautiously walking into the main building.

The five of them squeezed into a closet, which totally annoyed Ahmed's wife. "This is the silliest thing I ever heard of Ahmed, father of my children. You break us out of a tiny cell and place us all in an even tinier place with a strange-looking man I've never seen before. This is just nuts," she scolded him in Arabic.

"Trust me, darling wife. You have not seen nuts. Hold on to our children. Something even stranger is about to happen," said Ahmed, hoping his wife wouldn't ask too many questions.

Chapter 12

Moving in with Adar

The instantaneous trip to New York startled Ahmed's wife, but she quickly adjusted to the sudden change in scenery. She had long since learned not to ask questions when her family was safe and unthreatened. Ahmed's children enjoyed the ride and immediately asked if they could do it again. They later went into the closet and pretended it took them to exotic places around the globe.

"Adar, can we stay at your place for now?" asked Ahmed. "I'm afraid that if I put my family in my apartment, it will raise suspicions. I've been sneaking up the fire escape to get in and out."

"Yes, but you will all have to share the second bedroom," Adar said, unhappy about his loss of privacy.

"Not a problem," Ahmed said, just happy and relieved to have his family back safe and sound. "I'm going to go by my place and get a few things for my family," he added, before explaining everything to his wife.

"I will go with you, in case you run into trouble," said Adar, not wanting to remain in the apartment with Ahmed's family.

"Of course, because there is no way I would be able to make it home and back without your assistance," Ahmed said sarcastically. "You know I survived just fine before you showed up."

“How about I am not interested in being cornered in this apartment alone with your wife and two kids,” Adar said quietly but angrily into Ahmed’s ear. “I would rather fight a cave full of Gorman creatures barehanded,” he added, with a growl.

“Ah, maybe you have a point,” said Ahmed, his thoughts already turning to the things he needed to collect from his place. “Let’s get out of here.”

Ahmed waved goodbye to his family and the two walked out the door.

***

Ahmed and Adar arrived at Ahmed’s apartment without incident. As Ahmed began to open the door, shouts from police officers coming out of the apartment across the hall halted his progress.

“Hands above your heads, gentlemen, and move real slow-like,” said one of the uniformed cops. Adar shoved Ahmed into the apartment and turned to engage the officer right behind him. The alien grabbed him by the front of his shirt and tossed him down the long hallway. As another officer rushed out of the apartment, Adar grabbed him by the crotch and flung him down the hallway.

Yelling, “Stop, you’re under arrest,” more officers rushed into the hallway from a stairwell, drew their weapons and began shooting at Adar, who ignored them and calmly walked into Ahmed’s apartment and closed the door behind him. Having turned on his personal shield, he was protected from the officers’ barrage of bullets.

"Sergeant, did you see that?" asked one of the officers. "The bullets had no effect on him."

"He's probably wearing body armor. Break down the door!" ordered the sergeant. "Let's gas them."

Inside the apartment, Ahmed asked, "What's going on?"

"I was attacked by the police," Adar replied, confused by their presence. "They must have come for you. I'll have Wylyy transport us out of here."

Suddenly the door flew open and two canisters spewing tear gas rolled into the room. Adar and Ahmed ran into a nearby bedroom to take cover, slamming the door behind them. Bullets followed them, riddling the door full of holes before the police cracked it open to toss in another canister of tear gas.

"My eyes are burning," said Ahmed.

"I cannot wait for Wylyy," said Adar, throwing Ahmed over his shoulder in a fireman's carry. "Hold on. I'm going through the window."

"What? We're three floors uuuuuupppppp!" Ahmed screamed.

Adar landed in the alley below, with Ahmed none the worse for wear.

"What the hell did you do that for?" yelled Ahmed. Ahmed continued to grumble, trying to shake off the shock of falling three stories and landing safely without a parachute or a safety net.

"We made it, didn't we?" Adar's calm was almost as disconcerting as his precipitous actions. "Can you walk now?"

"Yes, put me down. You might have cracked some of my ribs, though. Let's keep moving, before they start shooting at us. Did you really need to do that?" Ahmed grimaced, more put out than hurt by Adar's actions.

"I did not have much choice. We had no time to contact Wylyy. Plus someone might have seen us getting transported out of the room."

"So you jump out of a third-floor window?" Ahmed's voice rose, hysteria edging his tone.

Adar was surprised by Ahmed's reaction. "Is that not normal?"

"When we get back, you have got to tell me more about what's going on with you," Ahmed pleaded, tired of being left in the dark. "I'm starting to think you might be Superman or something."

"I've already told you too much. The less you know, the safer you will be." Adar looked at Ahmed and hoped he wouldn't ask any more questions.

"Man, you keep saying that, but I'm beginning to the think that ignorance around you is just downright dangerous, Adar," an exasperated Ahmed groused.

Adar stared at the young man for a long moment, his oddly shaped eyes unblinking, before he looked away as if recalling his purpose.

“I should probably start wearing a hat and glasses. It appears people are looking for me or us,” Ahmed said, recalling the police ambush with some uneasiness.

As Adar and Ahmed arrived at the door of their apartment, Abigale popped out of her door and touched Adar on the shoulder. “Forgive me Mister Adar. I left my sugar bowl in your apartment. When you come back with it, can you check something for me?” Abigale asked, her expression fearful. “I think someone sneaked into my apartment and is hiding under my bed,” she said, wringing her hands.

“Sure Abigale,” Adar replied, frowning. “Ahmed, this could take a while. Once I return, we should go pick up the payment from Harry.”

“Whatever you say, player. Let me get that sugar bowl for you. I’ll be ready once you finish investigating the break in.” Ahmed smiled and crooked his fingers in air quotes with his final words.

Chapter 13

Toni Takes More Territory

Toni took a car to Jackson's place, intending to get him out of the picture. She pressed the buzzer to his apartment and waited for him to respond.

"Can I help you?" asked Jackson, over the intercom.

"Jackson, it's Toni. Can I come up? I have a proposition for you," she said, attempting to sound seductive.

"Sure, come on up." Jackson pressed the buzzer. "I'm in 2211. I'll pour you a drink." He rubbed his hands together, hoping this was his chance to connect with Toni and squeeze out Lee and Sam.

"I'll take a scotch, neat," Toni said, a bit more confidence in her voice.

"I'll have it ready when you get here."

Toni sauntered through Jackson's front door, wearing a long, clingy white silk dress, pearls, and pumps.

Jackson smiled, eyeing Toni's lithe figure appreciatively as he closed the door. "You are looking lovely tonight, Toni. To what do I owe the honor?"

"I thought we could talk some business. Who's the thug?" Toni flashed a grin at Jackson, before casting a sideways glance at his bodyguard.

"That's Arthur. He helps keep me safe and ensures that people pay me on time."

"I'm glad I don't owe you any money. Hello, Arthur. You're a pretty big guy," Toni said, trying to wrap her fingers around the girth of his bicep through his suit.

"Hi, Toni. I've seen you around. I like your singing," he said, grabbing one of her hands and kissing it.

"Thanks. Maybe I can give you a private show some time," Toni said, running a fingernail down his shirt. *Wasn't expecting to have to kill two men. Especially one this big.*

"I thought you came to see me. Why you giving him all the attention?"

"Don't get jealous Jackson," said Toni. "I'm just making friends with the big guy."

"Please call me Jackie, like Jackie Robinson or Jackie Wilson," Jackson said, pulling on his coat lapel and puffing out his chest.

"Okay Jackie, where's that drink?" Toni said, eyebrows raised. *Pretty soon you'll be meeting both of them.*

"Here you go," said Jackson, handing her a scotch in a cut-crystal tumbler. "Let's drink to success."

"Yes, our mutual success." She took a sip. "That is good. Glad you're not serving me the cheap stuff. Look, Lee offered me a lame deal. In general, he just wants to screw me. Literally and figuratively. I'm looking to partner with someone who wants to expand and give me an equal share that I can run on my own," she said sternly, locking glances with Jackson.

"I'm your guy, Toni," said Jackson, raising his glass to Toni and taking another sip.

"Maybe you heard, Luigi and Vinnie lost their places. Harry is willing to let me manage their territory in return for a share in my club. I thought you and I could pool resources and expand our operations," Toni said, bending the truth a bit.

"You guys go ahead and do your thing. I'm going to hit the john," said Arthur.

"Go ahead, Arthur. Look, Toni, I'm willing to do business with you, but only if we are going to be partners in every sense of the word," Jackson said, leaning in towards her.

"I'm still grieving from the loss of my husband, dirty shit that he was. Give me some time to work through it. I'll come around for you. As a sign of good faith, I'll let you have a look, if you like." She pulled up the side of her dress.

"I certainly wouldn't turn down a look from a lady."

"We do have a deal, though, right?" Toni cooed.

"Of course. I'll let my boys know you're joining our little group. Now come over here and let me take a whiff," Jackson said, his nostrils flaring.

"I thought you'd never ask, Jackie. I like a man who knows what he wants," Toni purred, raising her leg. Jackson leaned toward Toni's crotch, and she promptly whipped out her stiletto and slashed his throat. She then stabbed him several times in the gut.

"Did you get a good whiff, Jackie?" She sneered, straightening and smoothing the wrinkles from her dress.

"Everything okay?" asked Arthur, his face creasing with concern as he emerged from the bathroom.

"Just peachy," said Toni as she grabbed the scotch bottle and cracked it over Arthur's head. Next, she tried to stab him in his stomach with her knife, but Arthur grabbed her wrist and punched her in the chest, knocking her to the floor and forcing her to drop the knife. Wiping blood from his face, he followed after her. But Toni shoved her heel into his groin before shoving her foot into the side of his knee. A loud cracking noise ensued, sending the big man crashing to the floor screaming in pain. She rolled away from his grasp, jumped on his back, and started choking him with his necktie. Putting her knee in the middle of his back, she pulled hard on the tie, until Arthur stopped moving.

Damn, you were hard to kill, thought Toni. *One more and I get my territory back. Might as well call Samuel now.*

After straightening her mussed hairdo, she checked her dress for blood spatter in a full-length mirror on the door of the bathroom, finding none. She then pulled out her cell phone and punched in a number.

"Sammy, it's Toni. What do your plans look like for tonight? Then how about lunch at my place tomorrow? Now that isn't very trusting. Okay, I'll see you at your bar tomorrow around 6:00."

He is not going to be as easy to get rid of, but he will go down, she vowed silently.

Toni jumped when she heard a knock at the door. "Jackson, it's Roger. Is everything okay in there? The neighbors complained about some noise coming from up here."

Damn it. This isn't going to look good, thought Toni, slipping out the back door and taking the emergency exit to leave the building.

***

Adar and Ahmed reached Harry's place and sat in two armchairs in front of his wide desk.

"Harry, we took care of Vinnie and his crew and came to get paid," Ahmed reported.

"Great work, you two," said Harry, who had already heard that the hit went well. Digging out two large envelopes from a drawer in his desk, he tossed them to Ahmed. "Now I have a very special mission for Adar. I need you to take out my associate, Toni. One of my lieutenants died from multiple knife wounds and another one has gone missing. I'm sure it's Toni, looking to take their territory. Sammy is probably the next one on the hit list. Here's the address for Toni's place. I need this to be taken care of quickly and quietly."

"I will take care of it now," Adar replied.

"I'll wait here for you," said Ahmed. "I have something I want to talk to Harry about."

"Be careful. Toni is cunning and ruthless," Harry said, waving his finger at Adar.

Good. I look forward to a worthy adversary, thought Adar as he left the room.

***

Toni received a call from Sammy canceling their meeting and threatening to take revenge on her for Jackson's death. She denied having anything to do with it, but he ignored her pleas.

In response, Toni hunkered down in her apartment, preparing for an attack.

"Look, you two," she told her lieutenants, Bobby and Stan. "I expect to see Sammy and his boys here any minute. I know you two are tempted to jump ship, but I promise I will take better care of you than Sammy ever will."

"What about Harry?" asked Bobby.

"Once Sammy is out of the way, I will make peace with Harry. He just wants assurances that his operation will run smoothly and the money will keep flowing in. I will make sure that happens and make you two wealthy in the process."

"Toni, there's something wrong with one of your cameras," said Stan. "I'm getting some sort of interference on the one over the stairs."

***

Adar cloaked when he entered the back door of Toni's club. Finding the stairs to her upstairs apartment, he ran up them and rammed her front door open with his head. Uncloaking, he chopped Bobby across the neck with a stiff hand, sending the man to the floor gasping for breath. Stan pulled out a gun and pointed it at Adar. The alien swiftly twisted the weapon out of the henchman's hand and flung him across the room where he crashed into the wall.

Bobby stumbled as he attempted to rise, but Adar quickly snapped his neck. He walked over to Stan and twisted his head, silencing his moans. On the monitor Toni could see Sammy coming up the stairs with three of his men in front of him.

Adar looked over at Toni. "Which one of these men is Toni?"

"Neither one," replied Toni, thinking quickly. "I brought them here to protect me from Toni. Look, he's coming up the stairs now with his crew," said Toni, pointing at her monitor.

Adar ran out the door and stood at the top of the stairs looking down. *How the hell do I kill four people quietly?* Adar lunged at the four men, sending them to the bottom of the stairs. He pulled out his spear and quickly stabbed two of them in the chest. Sammy shoved the third man at Adar, knocking the spear from his hand and pinning him under the heavy man. Adar pushed the man to the side and with a quick motion snapped his neck. Sammy got to his knees and pulled out his gun but Adar kicked it away before he could get a shot off.

Adar looked at the hulking figure of Sammy sideways as he stood up from the floor to tower over him.

Let's see how tough this Toni fellow really is. I don't care how tough you are, buddy. You are still going down, Adar thought.

He ran at Sammy and took a swing at his chest. Sammy slipped the blow and punched Adar in the chest, sending him rolling across the floor.

Sammy grabbed Adar's ankle and started slinging him against nearby walls, dazing him. He used one of his large hands to pin Adar to a wall by his throat as his feet dangled off the ground, taking away his leverage. Adar swung at him with his right fist, to no avail. Sammy grabbed his wrist and prevented him from making contact. Adar tried swinging his left fist, but Sammy easily deflected it with his elbow. A trained wrestler, Sammy knew how to immobilize his opponent. Adar kicked and squirmed, but could not loosen Sammy's grip. He could feel himself blacking out. *I can't believe I'm dying at the hands of a human*.

Without warning, Sammy loosened his grip on Adar's throat and fell to his knees. Adar rubbed his throat, happy to be free from certain death. He looked on as the woman he met earlier flipped Sammy onto his back.

"You should have taken the deal Sammy," said Toni, kneeling on Sammy's chest. "Now you have to lay there on your back, taking your last breath as you watch me take your life," she said, as she stabbed her knife into him several times. Sammy made a weak attempt to push Toni away. Toni used one hand to brush away his attempts, while using the other one to twist her knife in his side. "Poor baby," she whispered into his face as she puckered her lips.

Toni finally looked up to see Adar looking down at her, astonishment plain on his face.

“I hope you don’t mind me stepping in. It looked like you could use some assistance. I guess you owe me your life now.”

“One could say that,” replied Adar, rubbing his neck, still confused at what just happened.

“So you wouldn’t mind killing someone for me,” said Toni, smiling and wiping her knife off on Sammy’s clothes as she stood up.

“I guess I owe you that much,” said Adar, wanting to ask Toni a couple of questions.

“Good. I want you to kill Harry. And none of that hand-to-hand combat bullshit. I just want him dead.” Her face hardened with focused hatred.

“Why do you want him dead?”

“I guess I should introduce myself. I’m Toni,” she said, holding out her hand.

“Adar.” He smirked. “You certainly lived up to your reputation. I have one condition.”

“What’s that?” asked Toni, lighting a cigarette.

“You make Ahmed one of your lieutenants.”

“I don’t know him, but if you vouch for him, I’ll give him a try,” Toni said, tilting her head to the side.

“What about the bodies?” asked Adar, pointing around the small space at the bottom of the stairs.

"Don't worry about them. I have a cleaning crew that will take care of this mess." As Adar walked away, he heard Toni speaking into her phone. "Johnny, cleanup on aisles five and six. You're going to need some help with this one."

***

Adar went back to Harry's and made short work of killing the mob boss and all his men.

"Adar, what the hell did you do that for?" asked Ahmed, having just finalized a deal with Harry and still sitting across from him.

Adar turned towards Ahmed, anger distorting his features.

"Wait, don't kill me! I wasn't fond of Harry, either," Ahmed interjected.

"I am not going to kill you. I got you a new job. You are going to be one of Toni's lieutenants," Adar replied, his face resuming its customary blandness.

"How did you pull that off? You didn't kill her?" asked a shocked Ahmed.

"It is a long story. It suffices to say that she is cunning and ruthless, just like Harry warned," said Adar, turning at a sound behind him.

"Did I hear my praises being sung?" said Toni, walking up to Adar and Ahmed with two large men at her side. Visibly anxious at her sudden appearance in the room, Ahmed placed his hand on his gun and cast a steady gaze her way. "Stay calm," Toni said, raising a hand towards Ahmed. “I believe we’re all friends here. I take it that you are Ahmed.”

“Yes, I am,” said Ahmed, taking his hand off of his gun and walking over to greet her.

“Am I going to have to worry about your loyalty to me or your ability to help me consolidate my territory?” Toni challenged, storm clouds moving in her sky blue eyes.

“Not at all, Toni,” Ahmed replied, shaking his head vigorously and pursing his lips.

“Adar, I have to ask. What’s with the bulky dark glasses all the time? You look like some old guy after cataract surgery,” Toni said, shooting him a look of slight disgust.

“My eyes are sensitive to the light, but I assure you I can see quite well, Toni. You might want to fix that tag on the back of your Armani dress. Seems it was made in China,” Adar retorted with a mocking smile.

Toni gave Adar a look, half annoyed, half curious. “Check my tag,” she demanded, turning her back to the muscular man closest to her.

“It says Armani, made in China.” The man snickered.

“And tuck it in you idiot!” Toni ordered, glaring at Adar. “I guess you do have decent eyesight.”

Prowling to the other end of Harry’s office, Toni looked out the window as she punched a number into her phone. “Johnny, when you finish with my place, get your people and come over to

Harry's. I have some trash here that needs to be disposed of. Bring a moving van, too. I want to get rid of his dated furniture."

"Toni, we're going to go out and celebrate a bit while you do your thing," said Ahmed.

"Fine, but don't you two get too drunk. I want you here when I address the family in the morning. Nine o'clock sharp!" Toni pointed a long finger at them, a stern pout wrinkling her bow-shaped lips.

"We'll be here. Adar, let's bounce. I need to check in on my family and then we can go to a bar that I think you'll like."

"Okay, but I need to take it easy on the alcohol," Adar said, forcing a half frown.

"Don't worry, I'll be there to get you home safe. Ciao, Toni," Ahmed said, looking back at her.

"Ciao, Ahmed."

Chapter 14

Aundria

Ahmed and Adar walked towards the Whiskey Tavern, Ahmed's favorite drinking hole. It was located in the heart of Chinatown, just south of Little Italy. Adar could smell various aromas wafting from the Asian kitchens, which he didn't care much for unless they accompanied the strong smell of raw beef.

They took Bayard Street to get to the tavern, which led them by Columbus Park. Here, the more pleasant scents of grass, insects, birds and other vegetation assailed him. He found he didn't enjoy the smell of unbathed humans and their garbage so much.

A park with no water is such a waste, Adar thought, before turning away and heading to the tavern with Ahmed.

The Whiskey Tavern was housed in a five-story brick building in the middle of the block on Baxter Street. The two entered the tavern and paused to look around. To their right, a formal dining room had tables laid with white linen and stainless cutlery. On the left, a wide bar took up half the space. A row of barstools with vinyl-covered cushions stood in front of the bar and a scattering of cocktail tables surrounded by comfy easy chairs and low-backed couches filled the rest of room. Wooden beams covered the rustic, aging ceiling.

"I don't smell steak," Adar complained, holding his nose in the air. "I smell hamburger, but it's not the same."

"How can you tell all of that with your nose?" Ahmed frowned at Adar. "We're not here for the food anyway. We're here for the drinks and the ambiance."

"Ambiance. Is that French for bad taste?" Adar let out a chortle.

"Are you actually making a joke?" Ahmed laughed, while Adar shrugged. "Let's take a seat at the bar and get this party started."

The Tavern, a dark, quiet bar frequented by locals, drew Ahmed like a magnet. Patrons often went there for quiet conversations away from the crowds and bustle of more trendy establishments. Ahmed also liked hanging out with the staff.

"Hey, Steve," Ahmed greeted the bartender, who stood a few feet down from him behind the bar. "A couple of scotches neat and two IPAs for me and my friend."

"Coming right up, Ahmed." The bartender smiled, eyeing the pair as he vigorously polished a glass with a soft white cloth. "Haven't seen you around lately."

Ahmed returned his smile. "Been busy trying to make money."

"I'm glad you decided to spend it at my place. Here you go, gentlemen." Steve placed their drinks in front of them on the heavily varnished bar top.

"Adar, here's to our new adventure," said Ahmed, raising his shot glass in a toast.

Adar watched Ahmed drink the liquid down and did the same. *I hope I won't regret this later*, he thought. *This bar seems calm enough. I should be able to get in and out without any trouble. I do like the sting of this Earth alcohol.*

Ahmed took a swig of his beer and built up some courage to ask Adar about himself. “Adar, since I sort of live with you, and we’re going to be working more closely together, I thought you could tell me more about who you are.”

“I came from a planet many light years from here. I’m hunting down a couple of criminals that escaped from our planet and are hiding out on Earth. It’s the two women I asked you about earlier. They are hard to find, but I believe they are in New York.”

“Wow, that’s deep. So you wear those glasses to cover up your freaky alien eyes?” Ahmed ventured, hesitantly.

“Something like that,” Adar said, briefly taking off his wrap-around shades so Ahmed could have a quick look.

“Whoa, that’s different,” blurted Ahmed, spitting his mouthful of beer on his clothes. “Sorry about that, I’m just not used to seeing aliens every day.” He tried to brush the splatter from his clothes with a couple of cocktail napkins.

“You have seen me every day for a week now.” Adar took another swig of his beer, hoping it would quell his urge to abandon Ahmed.

“You’ve never taken your glasses off around me before,” Ahmed said, trying to regain his composure. “What do you do when you are not trying to kill people?”

“I participate in arena fighting to stay in shape,” replied Adar. “I also exercise, learn about new weapons and train security personnel. After work, I grab a drink with the few friends I know. On occasion, I'll visit other planets."

"So what's it like on other planets?" Ahmed asked, eager to hear his answer.

"A lot like here, just better technology. There are good and bad places and people all over the galaxy." Having seen life on many planets, Adar had a jaded view of intelligent life.

"Give me an example," Ahmed urged, putting down his glass and gazing intently at the alien.

"Take this bar, for example. I could sit at a table in the corner, order whatever I wanted from my device here," Adar said, holding his UCD up for Ahmed to see. "The order would arrive on my table right away and the establishment would be paid from my account. If I want to show you something on my UCD, I can just grab the corners and pull on it to make it as large as I want. If I place it edge-wise on the bar, legs automatically will appear to keep it stable."

"Oh my goodness, I've got to have one of those," Ahmed exclaimed, slapping Adar on the shoulder, causing him to flinch.

Meanwhile, a woman attempted to walk behind them. "Nice ass," said a guy seated farther down at the bar, slapping the woman's bottom.

The waitress grimaced. *Most days working in this bar to earn money for school is a decent gig*, she thought, and scowled at the drunk. Like most servers in bars, she had found that dealing with patrons who drank too much and acted obnoxiously came with the territory. But some days, it could be a real drag.

Aundria turned and walked back to confront the man. “If you’re going to get that personal, we should at least get to know each other. I’m Aundria,” she said, extending her hand to the grabby customer.

“I’m Bob, and I’d love to get to know you better,” the drunk said, shaking Aundria’s hand and looking deeply into her eyes.

“I’m glad to hear that, Bob,” said Aundria, squeezing his hand and pulling him down from the barstool and onto his knees.

“What are you doing? That hurts.” Bob grimaced at the pain.

“That’s my Kung Fu grip. And here’s my nuclear knee,” Aundria snapped, bringing her knee up into the man’s stomach, releasing his hand and letting him crash to the floor, where he lay gasping.

“Let me know if you’d like to know more about me,” she whispered loudly, leaning over him. “I have a little trick I learned that’ll make your balls pop. I’ll bet you’d like that one.”

“I’ll pass.” The man groaned.

“I thought so.” She sighed, eyeing the crumpled figure with distaste as she walked off. *Why do these assholes think that waitresses are part-time whores?* Aundria worked at the Tavern in the evening and pursued her MBA during the day. Formerly an Ironman competitor, she had even made it past the first stage of the American Ninja Warrior competition.

A redhead of medium height with a muscular build, she had curves that men loved to ogle. Aundria, on the other hand, loved competitive sports, but had to give them up to pursue her education so she could engage in activities that brought in money instead of leaching it all away. Nowadays, the drunk men she served in bars were her only competitors.

Adar smiled at Aundria as she walked by. “You like her, don’t you?” said Ahmed, nudging the alien with his arm.

“I like people who are willing to fight to gain the respect of others. Earth women have given me a different view of females.” Adar turned to watch Aundria walk off. *I wonder if she is a cage fighter. I wonder if Yolanda would be interested in coming here on holiday. Earth women are starting to look more attractive to me,* thought Adar as the alcohol began to make his mind drift.

“I wouldn’t call what she did fighting,” said the man who had accosted Aundria, as he picked himself up off the floor and returned to his barstool.

“I wouldn’t call what you did brave or appropriate,” replied Adar.

“If you were bigger I would punch you in the face,” Bob said, pointing at Adar.

“If you were a man, I would punch you in yours,” Adar said, hopping from his barstool.

“Adar, we don’t want to start a fight in here,” warned Ahmed.

Adar, however, had already grabbed Bob by the shirt and dragged him off his barstool. The drunk stood over Adar, who was rocking on his feet unsteadily. Bob body-slammed Adar and started punching him in the face.

"Enough, you two!" shouted Aundria, bringing her elbow down hard on Bob's back. Bob groaned and collapsed on top of Adar. Aundria grabbed Bob by the ear and tossed him out of the bar. "You okay, buddy?" she said, helping Adar up off the floor.

"I'm not hurt. I just can't handle this Earthling alcohol." Adar stumbled as he attempted to balance himself on his two legs.

"So you prefer alcohol from other planets?" Aundria arched one eyebrow as the corners of her mouth lifted in amusement.

"I have beaten creatures twice his size from planets across the galaxy. He just caught me at a bad moment," Adar said, swinging one arm wildly in the air.

"I'm sure he did. Maybe you should lay off the sauce. I would hate for you to be late for an intergalactic meeting in the morning." Aundria laughed, her lips curving in wry good humor.

"Good idea. Don't bother getting up, Ahmed," Adar said sarcastically, as he struggled to climb back onto his barstool.

Ahmed's brows rose in query. "I thought you had him. I've never seen you get beaten like that."

"There is something about the liquor here that leaves me incapacitated. I am going to head back. You stay and enjoy yourself." Adar patted Ahmed on the shoulder and slowly climbed off of the barstool again and headed for the door.

"Okay, I'll see you at home." Ahmed shook his head, surprised to see his strange new friend in such a state.

Adar, meanwhile, left the Tavern, feeling a little bewildered that humans had taken him out twice. *What's next, a woman beats me up? I need to finish this mission and get back to normal society. Maybe I'll give Yolanda a call when I get back to the house*. "What the—" An SUV roared out of an alley and struck Adar, sending him flying through the air to land on the sidewalk on the other side of the street.

"Don't start fights you can't finish, you little bitch," yelled Bob, as he sped away in the bulky, dark vehicle.

"Hey, buddy, are you okay?" asked Aundria, running from the tavern and up to where Adar lay on the sidewalk.

"Yes, I am fine, just annoyed that I keep getting blindsided here." Adar held his head, which was still spinning from the alcohol. He concentrated for a few seconds, checking to ensure that no part of his body was injured, internally or externally.

"I saw him coming at you from the bar. I just couldn't get outside in time to warn you. Let me call an ambulance," suggested Aundria, pulling out a small cell phone from her back pocket.

"No, that is not a good idea. I just need to get home." Adar attempted to push Aundria away, but missed and fell back to the sidewalk.

Shaking her head, Aundria reached out and grabbed Adar's arm to help him stand. "No, I can't let you go home like that. You must be injured, considering how far that SUV knocked you."

"I will be fine. Just let me be," Adar insisted, getting his feet under him, only to fall back to his knees.

"We're having a slow night. Let me tell Steve I'm taking off, and I'll be right back. Just sit here on the curb, please, and don't move." Aundria steadied Adar on the curb and then hurried back into the bar, while Adar pondered the edge of the curb between his feet.

After updating Steve, Aundria flagged down a cab, helped Adar climb in and directed the taxi driver to her home. Adar had passed out by the time they arrived.

Aundria carried Adar up to her second-floor, one-bedroom apartment where she put him down on a small couch upholstered in bright, yellow fabric, which also served as her guest bed. Tossing her keys on her battered Ikea coffee table, she removed Adar's coat and boots, placing them bedside him on the couch. Noticing his weapons, she gingerly placed them on the couch, too.

Aundria then walked Adar's half-conscious, slightly-built body into her small bedroom and lowered him onto her bed. Stripping him down to his shorts, she carefully examined his body for injuries.

"What are you doing?" cried Adar, coming to and finding Aundria hovering over him.

"I'm just checking you to make sure you're okay. You have some very unusual markings." Aundria gently pushed on Adar's chest, until he again reclined on the bed.

"What did you do with my weapons?" Adar asked, looking around the bedroom.

"They're in the living room on the couch. You in some sort of special forces?" Aundria asked, looking intently at Adar.

“Something like that. Now step aside, so I can get my clothes on and get out of here.” Adar sat up in the bed, staring blankly at the dresser in front of him. There were pictures of kids in colorful frames alongside some stuffed animals. He twisted his head sideways as he tried to figure them out. On the wall to the right of the dresser was a poster of the American Ninja Warrior TV show.

“You’re not well enough to go yet,” said Aundria, pushing him back onto the bed and pinning him by his wrists. “I’ll tell you what. If you can push me off of you then I’ll let you go.”

“You know I cannot because of all the alcohol I drank,” Adar complained.

“Really? So you can lift a person twice your size unless you’ve been drinking?” Aundria asked in disbelief.

“Something like that,” Adar said, wishing he had his UCD close by so he could have Wylyy extricate him from this uncomfortable situation.

“Why are you squinting?” Aundria asked, taking a closer look at his eyes.

“I should have my glasses on.” Adar spied his glasses on the end table next to the bed, but didn’t have the strength to move Aundria to get them. “Could you hand those to me?” Adar asked, reaching out towards the table.

“There, I turned the light off so you don’t need them. Do you have sensitive eyes?” Aundria asked, examining both sides of Adar’s face in the light coming from the living room.

"No, I had a few birth defects, resulting from my parent's response to experimental radiation drugs." *This Earthling is asking way too many questions. I need to find a way to exit without killing her.*

"How do you explain the markings all over your body and why your skin feels so rough and strange? Are they a result of the radiation drugs, too? Oh my goodness. I'm feeling faint." *Something is definitely not right with this guy. His skin, his eyes, his ears and fingernails. This isn't normal and it can't be the result of radiation.* Aundria placed a hand on her forehead, hoping she wouldn't pass out.

"Look—" Adar paused, searching for the woman's name.

"Aundria. My name is Aundria."

"I'm Adar, Aundria. I should probably leave." Adar pushed Aundria to the side and climbed out of the bed. He felt the matted, short pile carpet beneath his feet and noticed his socks were gone, exposing his thin toes with their pointed toenails.

"Why don't you have any wounds on you anywhere? Any normal person who was hit by an SUV like that would be unable to walk. They would certainly be covered with bruises and abrasions," Aundria said, starting to sound frantic.

Adar looked up from his feet, focusing on Aundria. "If I told you, I would have to kill you, and I would rather you live."

"Are you here to take over our planet?" Aundria asked, trying to calm the panicky feeling in her gut as she stood to face the alien.

"It is better that I leave," said Adar, bracing himself on the edge of the bed.

"Lie down!" shouted Aundria, punching Adar in the chest and knocking him back onto the bed.

I can't believe this is happening again, Adar thought. *Is there some sort of cosmic karma thing that I triggered somehow coming to this planet?* "Why did you hit me?" Adar growled.

"I can't hurt you, can I? Are you like Superman?" She thought back to how the large SUV plowed into Adar, who came out of the accident unscathed.

"I am just a guy who likes to work out." Adar stood up from the bed and tried to step around Aundria, who kept blocking his way forward.

"It looks like you have an erection. Do you want me? Can you get me pregnant?" Aundria shoved Adar back onto the bed, climbed onto his chest and held him down.

Adar decided to drop the pretense, recognizing that this Aundria was too astute to believe his lies.

"I cannot hide the fact that you excite me. I like strong women. We are different species so I can't get you pregnant, though I think it is better that we not have sex." Adar wondered if he was trying to convince her or himself.

"You going to stop me? Looks like you're all ready to go," she observed.

“Can I take a look at it?” she asked, her breath coming in short gasps.

“At this point, I do not think I could stop you,” Adar quipped, his own breathing coming faster.

Aundria quickly slipped from the bed, stripped naked, and tried to climb back on top of Adar.

The alien pushed her off and headed for the door. But Aundria blocked his path and punched him hard in the chest. Her aggression whipped him into a sexual frenzy. Grabbing her upper arms, he flipped the woman onto the bed and mounted her eagerly. Excitement and trepidation warred inside Aundria. Adar rode her passionately, and as she climaxed, Aundria began to choke him.

Adar gave a hoarse shout and collapsed on top of her.

I guess it’s the same on every planet. First orgasm, then sleep, Aundria thought, shrugging her shoulders.

She left the bed to take a shower. When she returned, Adar had gone.

Really? Now I’m an intergalactic one night stand?

***

The next morning, Toni held her meeting with all the family’s bosses in the refurbished offices that she’d commandeered after having Harry taken out. As everyone entered the conference room, they noticed the improvement in the décor that seemed to highlight the change in leadership. Toni scanned the faces of the men seated before her in new plush leather chairs, looking for Adar and Ahmed.

"Hello, everyone," she said, smiling. "I appreciate you all showing up here on short notice."

"Where the hell is Harry?" asked Carl, a gruff, loud-talking chieftain.

"Harry fell victim to a sudden and serious medical condition and decided to retire. He subsequently put me in charge," Toni replied smoothly, without so much as an eyelash flicker. She looked around the room to gauge their reaction to that explanation.

"I want to hear that from him. This is bullshit!" Carl groused, banging his fist on the table. A murmur started that slowly grew louder as many of the bosses stirred in their seats, their worry about the recent rash of deaths and disappearances plain on their faces.

"There have been several retirements over the past couple of days, which opens up opportunities for many of you," Toni continued, ignoring the outburst.

"I've also entered into a new agreement that is going to bring a lot more money to our family," Toni said, attempting to put an appealing spin on the news.

"That doesn't mean you get to run things. I challenge your authority," Carl said, shaking his finger at Toni. "I'm going to take this up with the Syndicate!"

"We're meeting with them soon. You can voice your grievances with Mac then." Toni leaned to one side and whispered to Ahmed, who had just sat down next to her, "Where the hell is Adar?"

"He's here. Just point to someone you want out and say 'you're out'. He will do the rest," Ahmed murmured, covering his mouth with his hand to hide his words from the lip readers in the room.

Toni was confused by Ahmed's advice, but decided to give it a whirl anyway.

"Stop ignoring me, Toni! I'm not waiting. I want this resolved now!" shouted Carl.

"Sit down and shut up, Carl, or you're out," said Toni.

"I will not sit down—" the disgruntled mobster began.

"Then you're out," said Toni, cutting him off and pointing at him. Carl clutched his chest and fell to the floor dead.

"Oops, looks like some new territory just opened up. Anybody else want to challenge my authority?" Toni said, aiming a threatening look around the room before sliding a pair of reading glasses onto the bridge of her nose and shuffling papers on the table in front of her.

Gasps and muffled stutters could be heard around the table, but nothing more. Elders in the group gave each other nervous glances, but no one dared challenge Toni. At least not now.

"Good, now let's get down to business. Ahmed, have that body taken away," she added quietly, flicking the back of her hand in the direction of Carl's body.

The onlookers around the room stilled, frozen in disbelief. While several of the attendees objected to Toni taking over Harry's territory, no one else felt brave enough to protest. Toni had some disturbing new power that frightened them.

Maybe she has magical powers. But witch or not, she has to go, they thought.

Harry's former lieutenants didn't like the idea of working for a woman, especially one like Toni. They perceived correctly that she was the kind of woman who didn't like to settle for what she had. She always wanted more.

***

Later that evening, on her way to work, Aundria passed an accident scene with an ambulance, fire truck, and police car surrounding a smoldering black SUV. The firemen endeavored to remove the driver's head from the windshield. The man continued to hold on to life, but barely.

I wonder if that's the crazy Bob character that ran over Adar yesterday? I hope I get to see Adar again. I found him interesting. She entered the tavern where she saw Adar sitting at the end of the bar, nursing a club soda.

"You came back," said Aundria. "I didn't think I would see you again."

“I thought I should at least come by and say hello,” Adar said shyly.

“Why don’t you sit in a booth so I can take care of you?” Aundria suggested. “Steve, could you move his tab under me?”

“There you go, taking my tips again.” Steve laughed. “No problem, Aundria.”

Adar grabbed a booth away from the window. Aundria followed him over and leaned close to him as he sat down. “So was that your handiwork back there on the corner?”

“It’s hard to say. I can honestly say I do not feel bad about what happened,” said Adar, shrugging his shoulders and looking away.

“I need to punch in and make sure my section is taken care of. Promise you won’t disappear on me again.” Aundria smiled brightly.

“I will try to stay around, if I can,” Adar said, knowing that leaving was the furthest thing from his mind.

“Good. I’ll bring you something non-alcoholic that I think you will like.” Aundria kissed him on the cheek before walking off, and then gave him a quick look over her shoulder as she disappeared into the back room.

***

“Sonny, this boat is just exhilarating,” said Dholi. “I didn’t know they could go this fast.” Sonny had taken Dholi and her sister Daloi for a ride down the Hudson River on his new yacht, past Ellis Island and the Statue of Liberty.

"It's a yacht, young lady. Everything I own is fast and powerful," said the businessman, as he narrowed his eyelids against the brightness of the sun on the horizon. He rubbed his hand through his salt and pepper hair, fighting against the heavy breeze coming over the bow. "It's big, too. Fifty feet long with two giant Volvo engines under the hood. A lot like me," he bragged, grabbing his crotch.

"You are certainly powerful, Sonny. I love the way you overpower us in the bedroom," Daloi cooed.

"Next weekend, I'll take you somewhere in my jet. I'll show you the power of being in the mile-high club. Now you two go get some sun. I have some calls to make." Sonny took a seat near the railing, motioning for one of his crew to pilot his yacht.

"Let's go, sister," said Dholi. "We need to get our rest for later." She smiled back at Sonny.

The sisters walked toward the bow in their matching thong bikinis. *How did I get so lucky?* Sonny thought, looking at the two statuesque beauties walking along the railing of his boat. *Oh yeah, I made my luck along with my fortune. I'll have my fun with them and then get two more who are even nicer. Oh, it's great being me.*

"Daloi, if we plan to stay on this planet, we have to go somewhere where we can be safe. I'm not that comfortable hanging out in New York."

"It's hard to think of leaving when we're having so much fun. When we get back tomorrow, we can work on a plan to secure our safety. We should consider connecting with a mob boss the way we did in Chicago."

"The plan will include getting rid of the Ossie, right?"

"Eventually. We need to find more allies first. I'm not sure if the police will be effective in this situation, but we should consider that option. Tomorrow we'll plan this thing out. For now, let's take off our tops and give the old man a show. Come here and give me a kiss, sis."

***

"Bye, Steve, see you tomorrow," said Aundria, as she prepared to leave the Tavern for the evening.

"No, see you next Monday," replied Steve. "I'm headed to the Finger Lakes to do some wine tasting with my honey, Mary. Daçia will be taking my place for the rest of the week."

Daçia flashed her warm smile, waving from the other end of the bar.

"Monday it is, then. Enjoy your trip," said Aundria, grabbing Adar by the arm and heading out the door. "You don't talk much, do you?"

"I'm not much for chitchat," Adar replied. "Especially in a crowded bar."

"How long have you been on our planet?" Aundria asked, not sure she was ready to hear the response.

"Just a few weeks," said Adar, still reluctant to talk about himself.

"You like it here?" She really wanted to know more about Adar and the possibility of other visitors to Earth, but she didn't want to treat him like a specimen the way people did in science fiction movies.

"Not so much. It's pretty primitive." Adar looked at Aundria, wondering how much he should trust her.

"But you like me?" she asked, curious about how he viewed humans.

"I find your fighting abilities interesting," Adar said, nodding in respect.

"I guess that's a compliment. Why did you get so excited when I punched you last night?" she asked, hoping to get Adar to open up and stop being so reserved.

"That's the way women on my planet show their interest. We are an aggressive society. We enjoy lovemaking that forces engagement of both parties," Adar said, wondering how he could express his confusion about male-female relationships on Earth.

"Earthlings, specifically men, look to conquer the female, with little interest in fulfilling the female's desires," he observed. "Lovemaking should be more like tag team wrestling where both partners work together for mutual enjoyment."

"So if I punched you now, you would want to take me right here against the wall?" Aundria asked, pointing to a nearby wall in the parking garage. Merely asking the question made her areolas swell. *What should I do? I can't believe I am getting this worked up over an alien. Is it hot in here or is it just me?*

"Yes, but let's not do that. I don't want to attract attention," Adar suggested, contorting his mouth.

Aundria took his advice and decided to not risk a sexual encounter in the garage. Instead, she drove him home, all the while in awe of the person sitting next to her. Aundria took the Manhattan Bridge to reach her apartment building in Brooklyn Heights. Adar looked out the window, examining the buildings and pedestrians they passed.

Upon entering her apartment, Aundria set out to get Adar to relax.

"I'm not going to steal your coat or fancy weapons," she said, grabbing his lapels from behind. "Just let me place them over here on the chair."

Adar relented and sat on the couch where Aundria dropped to her knees and started taking off his boots.

"This is an interesting locking mechanism on your boots. It's almost like miniature magnets or something," Aundria said, rubbing the material between her fingers.

"It's a pliable, breathable metal," Adar explained, bragging about their design. "It's a durable material that also protects my feet and ankles during battles."

"You say we are a primitive people. What kind of technology do you have that might excite me?" the young woman asked, her eyes opening wide in anticipation of his response.

"This is my universal connection device," said Adar, pulling out his UCD from his belt. "I can talk to anyone in the galaxy who has one of these just like I'm talking to you now, no matter what language they speak. I also can use it to see any spot on this planet. Let me expand this for you."

"Wow, how did you do that?" Aundria asked, intrigued by what she saw.

"The device has the ability to expand by using free atoms in the air. Now here is a live image of New York. Go ahead and find a house or building you would like to look at. Just move your finger toward any point and the image will expand at that point as long as I am pressing the navigation button."

"Okay, I'm going to find my sister's place in Brooklyn. I assume I just swipe the screen to get there?" Adar nodded. "Now I move my finger toward her building and the image expands– Oh, my god. I can see inside the building. How are you doing that?"

"We have dimensional monitors that can move through space unimpeded," Adar explained, pleased by her interest. "They are able to view anyplace on this planet and send the video to my UCD."

"Look, the Millers are having an argument. How do I control the focus of the image?" Aundria asked, biting her lip.

"Hold your hand over the image like a ball and turn it the way you want the image to turn." Adar showed her with his hand.

"And then moving my hand forward—OMG! I am just moving through walls. Now I want to go down. There's my sister and her baby. It's almost as if I could touch her."

"You can't touch her, but you could go where she is or bring her here with the assistance of technology from our ship."

"Get outta here," Aundria exclaimed, looking at Adar in wonder.

"Excuse me?" asked a puzzled Adar.

"It's just an expression," Aundria replied. *This is so freaky. I always wanted an out-of-this-world experience, and here it is. Now what do I do?* She looked at Adar. "Now that you are completely sober, let me see some of that super strength you keep talking about."

"Sure. Sit in that chair by the table." Adar placed his right hand under the chair and lifted her up in the air.

"Okay, this is cool. Now put me down and tell me about your weapons." Aundria was like a little girl going to the science museum for the first time. She just wanted to know more and more about this alien who smelled like cinnamon buns.

Adar lowered the woman, still sitting in the chair, to the floor, and picked up his spear. "This is my favorite weapon. It is lightweight, sturdy, and the blade is extremely sharp."

"And that?" said Aundria, pointing at his rifle.

"This is a photon rifle. It can shoot a blast of energy up to a couple of kilometers away."

"How can you even see that far?"

"My eyes are different from yours. Let me show you." Adar took off his glasses, stepped out onto her balcony, and looked down the street for a target. "See the man over there with the blue cap, eating the hot dog?"

"Barely," Aundria said, squinting to see that far.

"Well, he just threw the wrapper from the hotdog on the ground. That annoys me. Let's teach him a lesson," Adar said, a frown appearing across his face.

"You're not going to kill him, are you?" Aundria squeaked in alarm.

"No, I'm just going to stun him. Watch closely and you will see a faint beam leave the tip of my weapon."

"My goodness, I certainly felt the energy. And there he goes, falling to the ground. Are you sure he's not dead?" Aundria asked, holding her chest. "Okay, he's shaking it off. Let's go inside before someone sees us."

"Good, because I want you to try one more thing." Adar smiled.

"What is it? I can't believe you are actually sounding giddy." Aundria chuckled. "I guess shooting people turns you on."

"No, I've just never shared this much with an alien I've met during my travels. I mean, I have never had a conversation with an alien outside of the Alliance that wasn't about business or killing the person." Adar let out a short sigh, loneliness welling up in him.

"So what is this thing you want me to try?" Aundria asked eagerly.

"Well, there's an elixir that is highly coveted on my planet. It's called Tammarian Grog. Its effect makes you feel like you are a magical unicorn named Lydia with a rainbow coming out of your butt." Adar winced, thinking his attempt at humor was lame.

But Aundria laughed hysterically.

"That is the funniest way I have ever heard a drink described, and I can't believe YOU said it. Are you growing a sense of humor?" She chuckled. "Okay, so let me try it." Aundria bounced on the couch cushion.

Adar pulled a flask from his coat and passed it to her.

Aundria eagerly took a sip.

"Wow! This is a strange flavor." Aundria gasped. "It tastes like a combination of pomegranate, oyster sauce and kerosene with a bit of effervescence. Oh my goodness, I'm feeling waves flow through my body."

Aundria closed her eyes and took a deep breath. *I can't believe I am feeling so horny. I should be scared shitless, but I want this strange-looking fellow to take me in the worst way.*

"Are you okay?" Adar asked, cocking his head to the side.

"Yes, I need help with something in my bedroom," Aundria said, biting her lower lip.

Adar put his things down on the coffee table and followed Aundria into her bedroom. "What is it?" *Humans act so strangely,* he thought.

"My pussy is on fire, and I need you to hose it down for me," she purred, slipping her fingers between her legs.

"Excuse me? Oh!" Aundria punched Adar in the chest as hard as she could, knocking him back out of the bedroom.

Adar got up and ran back into the bedroom, chasing her. Aundria ducked beneath him and flipped him against the bathroom doorframe and onto the bathtub.

"You want to do it in there?" asked Aundria.

"You'll do it where I make you do it," Adar replied, again rushing at her. He lifted her into the air, slammed her onto the bed, and ripped her shirt off. He stared at her breasts for a moment and bit into one. Blood sprayed everywhere.

"Ahhh! What are you doing, you idiot?" Aundria screamed.

"I didn't know you would tear so easily. You seemed so tough," stuttered Adar, clearly shaken. He mumbled something in an alien language and then ran into the living room.

"Wylyy, transport me and the Earthling to the ship, quickly," Adar spoke quietly into his UCD after retrieving it from the coffee table. "She's been hurt and needs medical attention."

Startled by the sudden transition, Aundria screamed again. The crew, meanwhile, laughed heartily in the background. "What did you do this time?" Wylyy shouted between chuckles.

Alarmed, Aundria sat up from the cot where they placed her. "How did I get here? Who are those aliens? Are you going to eat me now?" she asked, clearly confused and frightened.

"Calm down. Why does everyone think I'm going to eat them?" Adar grumbled.

"You did take a big bite out of my breast," she accused him, angrily, pressing on the spot to stop the blood flow.

"I told you I didn't mean to do it. These are my fellow crewmembers. They used the ship's transporter to bring you here to repair your skin. Just relax while they fix you," Adar said soothingly, pushing her down on her back.

Wylyy retrieved the medical kit and rubbed an ointment on her wound that stopped the bleeding. He then cleaned the area and used a light emitting wand to accelerate the healing of the tear until it was sealed. Afterward, he paused to examine her.

"I can't believe I'm all healed. Is it okay if I touch his face?" asked Aundria, amazement shining in her eyes as she looked at Adar for permission.

Adar nodded and Aundria rubbed Wylyy's face, examining the differences in texture between Wylyy's and Adar's skin.

An amused Wylyy decided to join in the fun and pretended to bite her.

"Ahhh, that's not funny!" screeched Aundria, snatching back her hand.

Wylyy and the crew laughed again. "They think you're funny," Adar explained unnecessarily.

"I guess pranksters are the same everywhere," said Aundria, her cheerful, curious demeanor reasserting itself.

Catching Adar's gaze, she asked, "Where are we?"

"We are on a Euclidian battleship several kilometers beneath your Atlantic Ocean. As a spacecraft, it is designed to withstand low and high pressure environments. It has shields, several types of engines, and weapons." Adar searched his mind for what else he could tell her.

"Can I see anything down here?" Aundria asked, looking around the ship at the various screens and blinking lights.

Adar made a request to Wylyy in Euclidian and a nearby screen lit with a view of the ocean outside the craft.

"Oh, my goodness, look at all those animals moving so melodically through the water. Animals I've never seen before," said Aundria, standing close to the screen, enthused by what she saw. Wylyy moved the ship around at Adar's direction, so Aundria could see more of the ocean floor.

Adar touched her on the shoulder tenderly and she fell back into his arms. "I hope you're okay," he whispered. "I didn't mean to harm you."

"I know you didn't," she responded, kissing him on the cheek.

"It's odd that they spend a lot of time trying to explore the universe, and they don't even know that much about their own planet," remarked Wylyy in Euclidian. "They are a funny species, full of contradictions."

"What did he say?" asked Aundria, pointing at Wylyy.

"He said you have nice tits," Adar said solemnly.

“He did not,” said Aundria, punching Adar in the arm.

“Are you ready to get back?”

“Sure. You need to finish what you started, and this time no biting!” she said, poking Adar in the chest with her finger.

Wylyy sent the pair back to Aundria’s apartment where they spent the rest of the evening engaged in a very passionate interlude. While Adar still got physical at times, he resisted biting her again.

Chapter 15

Connecting with the New York Mob

"Sonny, do you know any mob bosses in New York?" asked Daloi, relaxing next to the businessman on a large semicircular couch covered in beige leather in his hi-rise apartment.

"I know everybody who is anybody in New York," he boasted. "There's Harry Moran in Manhattan. Luigi Loren and Vinnie Romano used to share some of it, but some crazy guy took them out a few days ago. Some are calling the guy an alien with a ray gun. People can be so stupid."

Daloi and Dholi exchanged nervous glances, but didn't interrupt Sonny. "In the Bronx there's Charlie Butters. You got Tim Jones in Brooklyn and Jerome Johnson in Harlem. I'm from the Bronx, so I favor Charlie. What's your interest?" Sonny asked, raising his eyebrows.

"Dholi and I did some work for a guy named Seamus in Chicago, and we're looking to connect with someone similar here to make some extra cash," Daloi said, smiling shyly.

"What? I'm not taking good enough care of you?" Sonny asked, feeling his ego bruised. "You got the big screen TV, the pool table, a panoramic view of the New York skyline. You know I can get you a masseuse up here anytime you want. And they give you a COMPLETE massage if you know what I mean."

“Of course, baby,” Daloi said, rubbing the back of his neck, “but we want our own money. Can you give us an introduction?”

“Sure. I’ll have my office contact him in the morning and get back to you.” Sonny nodded, proud of his ability to make the connections people needed.

“Thanks, Sonny. We’re going to enjoy the view,” said Daloi, walking out onto the balcony with Dholi.

“It seems like the police haven’t found Adar yet,” whispered Dholi.

“That’s what it sounds like. We need to stay safe. Aligning ourselves with a mob boss certainly can’t hurt.” Daloi gave Dholi a sideways glance before looking at the view of the Chrysler building while she pondered what to do next.

***

“Did you two celebrate again last night?” asked Toni, typing away on her laptop at her new desk in Harry’s old office as she watched Ahmed and Adar drag in.

“We hung out a bit,” said Ahmed, smiling and nudging Adar.

“Good. Now I want you to help me expand things,” Toni said, planting her hands on top of the desk. “There’s a young chemist named Rohita that makes the most amazing synthetic drugs. The catch is, she has been distributing her wares via a guy named Jesse, who works for Charlie in the Bronx. Jesse is amazing at marketing, otherwise I would kill him and go directly to Rohita.”

“So you want us to kidnap him and bring him to our side?” Ahmed asked, excited to execute a mission for Toni.

"No, Charlie would just have him whacked," Toni said, holding her hand up to the two. "Convince him to do business with us. We'll increase his sales, Rohita will make more money, and we'll get to create a new market in the City," she said, feeding them ideas they could use when meeting with Jesse.

"Can I hurt him a little bit?" asked Adar, twisting his head to the side.

"Yes, but I don't want you to put him in the hospital. He needs to be able to continue working."

"Fine. Where can we find him?" asked Ahmed, shaking his head at Adar.

"He hangs out at the Rambling House in the Bronx. Go take care of it, gentlemen," Toni said, dismissing them and turning her focus back to her laptop.

***

"Hey, bartender, where can I find Jesse?" asked Ahmed, walking into the Rambling House.

"He's up there in the back." The guy behind the bar tipped his head upward as he spoke.

Approaching the man the bartender indicated, Ahmed spoke in a quiet voice. "Excuse me, Jesse. Can I have a moment alone to discuss a business deal? Here's ten grand to show I'm serious."

"Hard to turn down cold hard cash," said the man called Jesse, picking up the money and pinning Ahmed with an assessing glare.

Ahmed's answering stare snagged on the numerous gold rings that adorned Jesse's slender fingers. Except for his thumbs, the guy had at least two rings on each digit, jammed close to each of his knuckles. *Who is this walking jewelry store?* Ahmed wondered.

Rising from his seat, the thin man moved in an uncanny bouncing gait down the stairs and to the end of a hallway. "Let's go talk in my office," he said, waving Ahmed forward. He followed Jesse into a small room, and two of Jesse's bodyguards crowded in after them.

"So what's this business deal you have for me?" Jesse sat at his desk rubbing his hands together, eager to hear what a man who handed him 10 grand for a conversation would have to offer.

"You don't mind if I join you, do you?" Adar said, appearing seemingly out of nowhere.

"What the f—" shouted one of Jesse's bodyguards just before Adar chopped off his arm with his spear and stabbed him in the chest with the same weapon.

"Why'd you do that, Adar?" shouted Ahmed.

"Toni said not to kill Jesse. She didn't say anything about these guys. No you don't," said Adar, using the long blade of his spear to cut off the arm of the other bodyguard as he pulled out his gun.

"Again, Adar?"

"Why are you complaining? I didn't kill him."

"Yeah, but he's bleeding all over the carpet and he's probably going to die anyway."

“Fine!” said Adar, decapitating the guy. “Is that better?”

“Who are you two?” shouted Jesse.

“I’m Ahmed and that’s Adar. He’s a little crazy. You don’t want to piss him off. Toni Stapleton sent us here to see if you want to expand your synthetic drug business.”

“I don’t know what you’re talking about. Tell Toni I only do business with Charlie.” Jesse stuttered as he spoke, then loosened his tie, hoping that somehow he would survive this encounter.

“Fine. I’ll leave you here with Adar,” said Ahmed mildly. Adar snarled, showing his pointed teeth.

“Wait, um, don’t leave me with him. Maybe we can do a deal. I want to be assured that this doesn’t get out. Charlie would kill me if he heard about me doing business with someone else. Who is Toni Stapleton, anyway?”

“Don’t worry, this will be our little secret, Jesse. Toni is the lady that took over for Harry Moran when he retired. She sings at the Blue Note sometimes.”

“Yeah, I know her. She moved up pretty fast. I don’t believe that story about Harry retiring, though. I’ll bet your friend had something to do with that.” Adar snarled again.

“Jesse, we just want to help you reach your financial goals and keep you out of trouble,” Ahmed said quickly.

“How is that supposed to work?” asked Jesse, his voice trembling with fear.

"Our guy, Leon, is going to come over tomorrow around 2:00 in the afternoon to pick up the first shipment from you. You teach him what's what and we'll make sure you get 20 percent off the top. Are you cool with that?"

"Yeah, that's cool," said Jesse, resignation in his voice.

"Here's another five grand for the mess on your carpet. Nice doing business with you." Ahmed walked out of Jesse's office and exited the bar with Adar.

If anyone noticed the ruckus coming from Jesse's office, no one commented on it or the odd strangers that hurried past them.

***

True to his word, Sonny set up a meeting for Daloi and Dholi with Charlie Butters. Exiting the elevator on the floor of his office suite, they encountered Caroline, a short, bubbly woman of Eastern European descent, who flashed an amazing smile when she greeted them. Her bright, blue eyes sparkling with good humor, she ushered the pair into Charlie's office where he anxiously waited to meet with them.

"Hello, Charlie, thanks for taking this meeting," said Daloi.

"Excited to meet you ladies," said Charlie, extending his hand to shake theirs. "Sonny had wonderful things to say about you."

"Thanks, Charlie. Dholi and I just came in from Chicago where we did some work for Seamus, and we'd like to do similar work for you." Daloi held the mobster's hand a little too long while leaning across his glass and stainless steel desk.

Charlie, unlike Seamus, had inherited his position from his father. People didn't view Charlie as a tough guy, but more a man of finesse and ruthlessness. He didn't mind shooting a man in the back or killing members of his family, though he tended to let others do the killing for him. He did like the idea of pitting bosses against each other and swooping in to pick up the scraps once the dust cleared. This is how he earned the nickname of the Vulture.

"He doesn't need any cute bitches to do his dirty work. He has us," said a woman's voice from the back corner of Charlie's office.

"Ladies, that's Sharon and her cousin, Sheila," said Charlie, hooking a thumb in the direction of two slender women in their late 20s sitting on a couch showing off their deep auburn tresses styled in the curly layered hairdos of 40 years earlier. "They do cleanup work for me."

"We're not here to get in the way," said Daloi. "But we have a special set of skills that I think you will appreciate."

"What kind of work did you do for Seamus, exactly?"

"We have a way of getting the truth from people and ensuring that they're not robbing you blind."

"You'd be surprised how willing a person is to spill his guts when he has a gun pressed to his temple," said Sharon, smoothing her fuchsia sheath dress with her long manicured fingers.

"We have a subtler way of getting a person to talk that results in a lot less bloodshed. Maybe I could demonstrate for you." Daloi walked over to Sharon, gazed into her eyes, and grabbed her cheek. "Raise your skirt for me. I'd love to see your panties."

Sharon stood up and started to comply. Sheila, garbed in a similar teal-colored sheath, jumped up from her seat on the sofa, shoved Daloi away and pointed her gun at the alien's chest.

"Maybe you'd like to see how I can subtly space bullets out across your chest. Sharon, are you okay?" Sheila grabbed her partner's arm and shook her.

"Bitch, you touch me like that again," said Sharon, regaining her composure, "and I'll cut your heart out."

"Relax. I did not hurt you. Don't tell me you are afraid of a little hypnosis," Daloi crooned, easing back a step.

"I don't give a flying fuck what you call it. Keep your damn hands off of me," said Sharon, waving her arms and hands in front of her in a warding gesture.

"Cut it out," Charlie ordered. "Aren't you two supposed to be taking care of that problem for me down at city hall?"

"We're already on it," said Sharon.

"It doesn't look like it. Go take care of it now." Sharon and Sheila begrudgingly walked out, while shooting figurative darts at Daloi with their bright, gray eyes.

"So, Charlie, do we have a job?" asked Daloi, straightening her dress with long, thin fingers.

"Maybe. You don't mind if I call Seamus to verify who you are? I don't want to inadvertently do business with snitches trying to put one over on me. Billy, make sure they don't go anywhere, while I get Seamus on the phone." Billy pulled out his gun and pointed it at Daloi and Dholi, while Charlie made the phone call.

"Seamus, Charlie here. What can you tell me about the Daloi and Dholi ladies? Yeah, you're right about that. Really? Good to hear. Talk to you soon. Bye," Charlie ended the call, hanging up. "You can put your gun away, Billy. Seamus said you two are as dangerous as you are beautiful, and I'd be a fool not to use you. So I'm in."

"Good to hear. What can we start on?" Daloi asked, sitting on the edge of Charlie's desk and giving him a seductive smile.

"Something simple so I can see what you're capable of. There's a guy who runs our drug operation on the south side named Jesse. I hear he's running a side business using some synthetic drugs he had developed. I want it to be clear that I get a share of all activity in the Bronx! He doesn't get to do side deals and no one works with Jesse without coming to me first. If you can clarify what's going on with him, you get five G's and 10 percent of whatever action comes out of it. Like the deal?"

"Oh, we love that deal. Just show us what he looks like and where we can find him and we'll take care of this right away," said Daloi.

"He's easy to find. He hangs out at the Rambling House on Katonah. Just tell him I sent you to check on things." Charlie tapped his manicured fingers on the desk.

"Can we kill him?" asked Dholi.

"No, not unless you have to. I don't want to disrupt things down there. Turmoil always impacts profits, and he makes me a lot of profit. I want you to focus on clearing away any obstacles that might impact the profits."

"Got it, boss," said Daloi. "We'll have an update for you by morning."

"Billy, get them the info on Jesse and show them out," Charlie said, dismissing them.

"I'll take care of it, boss," said Billy. "This way, ladies."

Chapter 16

Adar Gets Caught by the Police

Daloi and Dholi walked into Rambling House and made their way to Jesse. They were looking their gorgeous selves, dressed in matching tight jeans and halter tops. Jesse was more than excited to see them.

"Jesse, I'm Daloi and this is my sister, Dholi. Charlie sent us to check on things. Can we talk somewhere?" Dholi was flashing her eyes at Jesse overtime as she ran her index finger across her halter top.

"Sure, ladies. Let's talk in my office," said Jesse. "Why haven't I heard of you before? Not that I'm complaining," said Jesse, fighting hard not to drool.

"We just came in from Chicago. Charlie wants us to validate the effectiveness of his business and asked us to start with you," said Daloi, taking a serious tone.

"So what's to validate here?" asked Jesse, closing the door to his office and signaling his guards to wait outside. "I collect the money from the dealers, keep my cut, and send the rest to Charlie," said Jesse, hoping to switch to less serious topics.

"Don't be obtuse, Jesse," said Dholi, putting her hand around his neck and forcing him against the wall. "You got any side deals going on?"

Jesse had a strong constitution and normally did not rattle easily. After seeing his bodyguards killed in front of him, having two beautiful women trying to shake him down should have been laughable. However, he found himself being mentally disarmed in a way that made him lose bladder control.

"Jesse, should we kill these bitches?" One of his bodyguards queried, opening the door to his office.

"No, leave me alone," said Jesse. "I can handle these ladies. They just like it rough. Go on, get out!"

The bodyguard left the room leaving Jesse alone with the two Cheoili women. Jesse felt afraid and aroused at the same time. Either way, he wanted to see where these ladies wanted to take him.

"So tell us, Jesse," said Dholi, "what deals are you doing on the side?" She was stroking his face and rubbing her leg between his thighs.

Jesse wanted to resist, but the harder he tried the more his resistance faded. "I'm not cheating Charlie on the deals we set up. I cultivated a completely new business on my own. Why should I share that with Charlie?"

"What are you talking about, Jesse?" Daloi asked, taking over the questioning.

"I met an amazing chemist. She's a grad student who likes to mess around with psychedelics. She made a series of chemicals that has taken off in the Bronx. I mentioned it to Charlie, but he showed no interest so I did it on my own," said Jesse, hoping the two women would side with him.

"You know that Charlie owns all the action in the Bronx," said Daloi sternly. "Every bit of it."

"I know, but I couldn't turn this down."

"We understand, Jesse. Now where's the money you made from the deals?" Daloi demanded.

Jesse pointed to a closet. "I've got some here and some at the house."

"Okay, give us what you have here, and we'll let you keep the rest. Any other money that comes in from the new business you share with Charlie under the original agreement. Understood?" asked Daloi, slapping the short man on the face.

"All right, but I wasn't trying to rip him off. You gotta believe me," Jesse said, grabbing Daloi's arm and hoping he wouldn't have to suffer any indignities.

Dholi patted his face. "We do. Does anyone else know about these new drugs?"

"Of course not. My guys sell it for me, but that's it," said Jesse, with a little hesitation. Jesse subconsciously tapped his finger against the wall, which did not go unnoticed by Daloi. She grabbed his hand and started kissing it.

"Jesse, don't hold back on me. Who else knows about these amazing new drugs of yours?" Daloi asked gingerly, her sparkling green eyes shooting him a piercing look.

"I spoke with a couple of guys yesterday about creating a batch for them. But you don't want to mess with these guys.

They're crazy. One had some sort of sword that he used to chop up my guards." He made a chopping motion with his hand.

"What did he look like?" asked Daloi, with a nervous look on her face.

"Short guy. Wore these dark shades around his face. And he had scary looking teeth. It's like he wasn't human," Jesse said forcefully, scrunching his face and balling his hands up into a fist.

"I believe you, baby. So when are they coming back?" Daloi persisted in the questioning.

"They aren't. Some guy named Leon will be picking up the drugs."

"To hell with that. We have a new plan," Daloi insisted. "I'll explain it to you while you're inside me and my sister's fingers are inside you." Daloi grabbed Jesse's hair, pulled his head back and ran her sharp fingernail down his neck. "Dholi, rip off his clothes. We're about to have ourselves some fun."

Jesse was more afraid than he had been watching his bodyguards get butchered, but he couldn't wait for the sisters to get started on him.

***

What a night, thought Aundria. *This is the most exhilarating, terrifying experience I've ever had*. She looked down at Adar and stroked his bare chest, admiring the texture of his skin and noticing that he had no nipples. *Feels like suede. Soft and tough at the same time*.

Aundria slowly turned the alien over and rubbed his butt. "Where's your asshole?" Aundria exclaimed, playing in his crack.

"I don't have one," Adar grunted. "Everything I eat is digested, except for a thick liquid that I urinate away or eventually evaporates via perspiration."

"Lord what I would give to have that capability. And you have no balls for someone to kick," she said, as she continued to rub his body.

"You like touching me, don't you?" asked Adar, sitting up on his elbows and cocking his head to the side to look at her straight on.

"Yes, I find you fascinating. Do I need to be afraid of you?" Aundria asked quietly, her face serious.

"Only if you cross me," Adar replied, hoping not to sound threatening.

"If I stay with you, will you protect me?" Aundria felt insecure because Adar was elusive about his feelings.

Adar twisted his head and looked at the ceiling as if to ponder the question more deeply. *What an odd question. How do I respond to that?* "Protect you from what?"

"From the people you are after. From other aliens. Can I travel with you?" Aundria propped her arm up on one elbow to hold her head, while she studied Adar and rubbed her free hand over his chest.

“I’ll do what I can to protect you, but I don’t think that it is practical for you to travel with me. You are better off here on your planet,” Adar said, sitting up in Aundria’s bed and pushing past her.

“If that’s all you have to say on the subject, I need to eat some breakfast and get ready for school. You can join me for breakfast, if you like.” Aundria watched Adar getting dressed without turning her way.

“No, I have to meet up with Ahmed. Toni is having a problem with people accepting her authority,” Adar said, moving into the living room to put on his coat and attach his weapons to his belt.

Aundria peeked through the door into the living room. “Okay, baby. Be safe. I’ll see you later.”

“Do you need to say emasculating things like that to me?” Adar said, making grumbling noises under his breath.

“Oh, excuse me. ADAR, GO KICK ASS!” Aundria shouted, throwing a fist into the air.

Adar smiled. “Much better.”

***

Daloi and Dholi strode into Charlie’s office to give him an update on their meeting with Jesse. Sharon and Sheila were camped out in their usual spot on the couch in the corner.

“Charlie, Dholi and I had a chat with Jesse. He’s dealing synthetic drugs and making a lot of money at it, so we suggest you let him continue. Which means more money for you. Here’s an example," said Daloi, tossing a duffle bag full of money at Charlie's feet.

"And he's not working with anyone else?" Charlie asked, with a suspicious facial expression.

"Just the dealers, that's all," Daloi lied, with the intention of capitalizing on the info herself.

"How are we supposed to trust these two when they show up out of nowhere?" warned Sharon, sitting forward on the couch.

"Why are you jumping in the middle of something you know nothing about?" Daloi gave Sharon an angry look. "Aren't you supposed to be taking care of something at city hall?"

"We already hammered that problem out." Sharon laughed, bumping fists with Sheila.

"You left a pretty bloody mess, ladies," said Charlie with a broad smile. "Thanks for taking care of that so quickly and effectively, though. Sends the right message that you don't go back on your deals with me just because the heat is too much for you. So how much is in the bag, Daloi?"

"Should be about $700,000," she said, shrugging her shoulders.

"He's been dealing this stuff on the side for weeks, and this is all the money you have?" said Sheila. "This is bullshit, Charlie. I don't like it," she said, scooching to the edge of the couch.

"Maybe I should come over there, and shove your face between my legs. Would you like that?" asked Daloi.

“You come near me, and I’ll put a bullet in your head,” Sheila said, placing a hand in her purse.

“Trust me, you’ll be dead before you pull the trigger.”

“Ladies, calm the hell down,” demanded Charlie. “No more attacking each other. Let’s focus on making money. Sharon and Sheila, maybe you should find out what Bobby is doing in Jersey City,” he said, shooing them with his hand.

Sharon and Sheila stood up with irritated looks on their faces and left the office.

“Sheila, let’s go check on Jesse ourselves,” said Sharon, walking down the corridor out of earshot.

***

Adar and Ahmed made the rounds for Toni, ensuring everyone paid up on time. They chased one bookie late on a payment up to a rooftop.

“Adar, come on. We gotta get some money and bounce,” said Ahmed.

“Where are we bouncing to now?” replied Adar, annoyed that Ahmed interrupted him, while he held the bookie off the side of a building by his throat.

“Leon called. Jesse changed the deal on us. He wants us to pay him in advance and in a public place so we don’t try to kill him. And please don’t drop that man off the side of the building,” Ahmed said, irritated by Adar’s obsession with violence.

Adar cocked his head to the side. “Why not?”

"Because dead men can't pay us."

"Okay," said Adar, throwing the man down on the rooftop. "Where are we headed?"

"Times Square. By the way, you really need to work on your anger management. You are having way too much fun hurting people," Ahmed said, looking back at Adar in disgust.

***

Daloi and Dholi left Charlie's place and took a seat on the balcony of Sonny's condo to enjoy a view of the city while eating an Irish stew his cook had whipped up.

"Is this the life or what?" asked Daloi, walking to the railing with a glass of wine in her hand.

"Yes, it's pretty amazing, Daloi. Did you pick a spot to have Jesse meet Leon yet?" asked Dholi, eating the last bit of stew.

"Yes, we are going to meet in Times Square. The place is full of people so we will be able to more easily hide in the crowd. Once Jesse leaves his place, I'll call Captain McKee and let him know that Adar is planning a big drug deal there. Adar will eventually show up looking for Jesse and hopefully get captured," Daloi said, uncertain about the success of her plan.

"Sounds like a plan, sister. Once he is out of the way we can stop looking over our shoulders, at least for a little while."

"Don't worry your pretty little head, sister," Daloi said, hugging Dholi. "We'll be safely free of the Euclidian soon. We just need to get Adar out of the way."

Dholi gave her sister a fierce grin. “I’m ready when you are.”
“Grab Sonny’s phone and let’s get out of here. Time to get rid of that Ossie.”

Before walking out the door, the pair reverted to the previous disguises they used when they first met Captain McKee, to ensure he recognized them and minimize the risk of recognition by Adar.

***

As Jesse sat on a bench just off Broadway, Daloi stood next to McKee outside the M&Ms store in Times Square. McKee had several of his men scattered around the area, waiting for Adar to show up.

“Just be patient, captain,” said Daloi. “He’ll be here soon enough. Your other men can watch for him on the periphery, but you want to keep the officers near you in reserve close to Jesse to take Adar out, once he arrives.”

“I had my men arm themselves with Tasers, in hopes that they are more effective against the alien. When they ran into him at Ahmed’s place, the guns had no effect on him.”

“I’m sure you’re right, captain. He’s probably using a shield of some sort to protect himself. Captain, look! There he is, over there,” said Daloi. “The little guy with the long coat and dark glasses. I will wait here while you do your thing.”

“Okay, men, let’s approach him from the rear. Two on each side. I’ll position myself directly behind him. We each fire our Tasers on my command.”

***

Where the hell is that damn Jesse? thought Adar, staring at all of the tourists wandering around Times Square. *Why are these idiots taking pictures with clowns? What purpose does that serve, exactly? There he is.*

"Jesse, why did you change our deal?" asked Adar, grabbing him by the arm.

"Where's Ahmed?" asked Jesse. "I feel more comfortable talking to him."

"He's across the plaza looking for you." Adar released Jesse's arm. "I suggest you start talking, if you want to avoid any bloodshed."

Adar paused his conversation as he saw police officers walking his way. *Uh oh, the police found me*. Adar made a run for it through the crowd.

Dholi pulled out her blaster and stunned the people in the area around Adar, who fell to the ground and caused him to stumble. The remaining people in the vicinity of the blast screamed and ran off in a panic.

Adar straightened and reached for his UCD in an attempt to contact Wylyy, but not before the police engaged him. Five police officers activated their Tasers, stunning Adar and sending him to the ground, convulsing.

"Cuff him!" shouted McKee. "Hands and feet. And cover his head with a bag. I don't want to take any chances with this one."

"Look, Dholi," said Daloi. "They got that Ossie bastard. Now we just need to set our other plan in motion to truly be free."

***

Two other people had watched the scene in Times Square unfold.

"Sheila, do you recognize that guy Jesse's talking to?" asked Sharon.

"Isn't that the guy from the video who killed Luigi?" Sheila queried her cousin, squinting. "So Jesse was telling the truth. He must be pretty badass if all those cops had to tase him like that. It looks like that problem is taken care of now."

"Let's get out of here, cousin. We don't want to get caught up in this." Sheila grabbed Sharon by the arm and pulled her away to avoid being spotted by the police.

***

When the bag came off of Adar's head, he found himself bound to a bed in an interrogation room guarded by two officers and naked except for his underpants. Bright lights shone overhead and a large mirror covered one of the walls. McKee and Peters stood over him. *I could probably pop loose from these straps and take out these clowns, but I better play this cool.* "Hello, officers. You want to explain why you have me in custody?"

"Why don't we start with names? I'm Captain Ron McKee. This is Sergeant Calvin Peters. And you are–"

"Just call me Adar."

"Where are you from, Adar?" asked McKee, in a stoic voice.

"I'm from Chicago, and I'm here on business," Adar responded calmly.

"I'd like to believe you, but you don't look like anybody I ever met from Chicago."

"So you arrested me because you are uncomfortable with my birth defects?"

"Roll the video, guys," McKee yelled at the mirror, behind which a roomful of officers crowded together looking at the alien. "We got this from Luigi's place. You are doing some pretty incredible things here, for a businessman from Chicago. You want to explain what this weapon does?" McKee lifted Adar's photon rifle up for him to see.

"That looks like a toy to me. I wouldn't mind buying one for my son to play with." Adar smirked.

"This toy, as you call it, took out a couple of Luigi's guys, as you can see in the video." The Captain attempted to direct the alien's attention toward the TV using his index finger.

"It's amazing what people can do with video these days. That is not me. I do not recall even being in that place." Adar repeated responses he had learned in lessons about evading authorities.

"So you are telling me that there is another alien wandering around Manhattan wearing dark shades, gloves, and a long black coat?" McKee asked, incredulity making his voice rise.

"What is this device?" McKee continued, showing Adar his UCD.

"Just a mobile phone with built-in GPS. It is easy to get lost in this big city, and I need to keep in constant contact with my family," Adar said, with obvious sarcasm.

"So there are other aliens here? Is Ahmed an alien, too?" McKee thought that if he kept the alien talking, he would eventually slip up.

"Who is Ahmed?" Adar asked, turning away from the captain and looking at the mirror, wondering who was behind it.

"The person in the video with you who shot the man at point-blank range. By the way, he's in the room next door. Calvin, bring him in here. We have federal agents coming to pick you up soon. They will probably do more than just interrogate you."

McKee leaned in close to Adar, so he could speak directly into his ear. "They will probably dissect you to see what makes you tick."

"I do not tick. I am just an innocent man being falsely profiled due to the unfortunate circumstances of my birth," Adar declared, turning to look directly at the captain.

"Oh, that's just precious. You seem to know a lot about our culture for an alien. Oh look, there's Ahmed now. Welcome, Ahmed. Would you like to shed some light on what we are looking at here?" McKee said, pointing at Adar.

"Looks like a guy with a far-out body tattoo," said Ahmed.

"When did you meet him?" the captain asked, his expression intense.

Ahmed looked confused. “Just now when you opened the door.”

“Would it be possible to go to the bathroom at all?” asked Adar.

“I would like to go, myself,” said Ahmed.

“Tell me something meaningful, and I’ll give you two a bathroom break.”

“I come from a planet far, far away, where people do not smell nearly as bad as you do,” said Adar.

Laughter could be heard from the other side of the mirror. “Shut up in there. This is not a comedy show. Calvin, take them to the restroom. I want two men on each of them and their hands and feet cuffed at all times.” The captain stood to the side and crossed his arms as his men escorted the alien and Ahmed out of the interrogation room.

“How are we supposed to wipe our butts?” Adar asked.

“Get creative. I want them right back here as soon as they are finished,” McKee ordered.

The cops shuffled Adar and Ahmed into two separate stalls and then stood just outside, waiting for them to finish their business. Adar sat on top of the toilet with his feet off the floor shaking his fist at the ceiling as if cursing at someone. Moments later he and Ahmed sat comfortably aboard Wylyy’s attack ship.

“Adar, watching you strapped to that bed just doesn’t get old.”

“Shut up and get my stuff back from them as well as those recordings!” Adar said angrily in Euclidian.

“What took you so long?” Ahmed shouted at Wylyy, who didn’t understand a word he said.

“Ahmed, we could not just disappear in front of everyone,” said Adar. “For now, they just have a crazy story about some strange-looking guy with a striped tattoo all over his body, who just disappeared from a bathroom.”

“What about the recordings?” Ahmed asked Adar.

“Wylyy, did you get the recordings?” asked Adar in Euclidian. Wylyy nodded affirmatively.

“That has been taken care of, Ahmed. Wait here for a while. I need to go back and check on something.” Adar stepped on to the transporter platform and turned to Wylyy to give him instructions before being interrupted by Ahmed.

“Is it okay if they just transport me to your place?” Ahmed asked. “Your friends look like they might eat me.” Ahmed cast a dubious glance at the attack ship’s crew.

“What is it with you humans? We do not eat people,” Adar said, shaking his head. “Wylyy, send him to my apartment, then transport me to the captain’s office in the police station.”

***

Back at the police station, McKee fumed, wondering who was responsible for the disappearance of Adar and Ahmed.

"What do you mean, they're gone?" he shouted, when the cops checked the bathroom and found it empty.

"We put them in separate stalls," said one of the officers. "We stood outside for a while. They made a little noise, then we heard this popping sound coming from the stalls and then silence. We forced open the stall doors and found them empty. The perps had completely disappeared," said the cop, eyeing the floor, embarrassed.

"So what do we tell the feds when they show up? We lost them in the bathroom? At least we have the tapes."

"Captain?" asked a voice coming from the control room.

"Yes."

"We don't have the tapes. I mean, the DVDs," said the officer in the control room.

"The DVDs are missing?"

"Well, the recording equipment is gone, too," said the officer, sounding confused.

"What do you mean, it's gone? Did someone knock you out and take it?" shouted McKee.

"No, we watched you interrogate the alien through the mirror. When they were escorted to the bathroom, Sandra and I stayed here in the control room. I heard a slight buzzing, turned around, and the whole rack of equipment had vanished," the officer explained.

"Great. Now we're going to look like bumbling idiots to the feds. Sanjiv, call them back and cancel the meeting," McKee told an officer headed his way. "And I don't want any talk of aliens leaving this precinct, you hear?"

"That's what I came to tell you, sir," said Sanjiv. "The feds are waiting for you in your office."

"Marvelous! This day has certainly gone to hell in a handbasket. No one leaves until you have all filled out your reports and we've gone over them," said McKee, storming away.

***

Back in his office, McKee regarded the FBI agents.

"It's unfortunate you two came all this way for nothing," he said apologetically. "My officers misunderstood my orders. Please accept my full apologies, and grab some donuts on the way out."

"You guys should eat fewer donuts and focus on doing better police work," Agent Caitlin Johnson sniped.

"You are absolutely right, Agent Johnson," mumbled McKee, grim-faced and embarrassed.

"Captain, we are part of a task force that has been tracking an alien ship that we believe flew here from the far side of the moon and is hiding out under the Atlantic Ocean." Caitlin started her speech by placing both her hands on McKee's desk and staring at him in full 'glare' mode.

"My partner, Alaina Johnson and I have been getting updates from Admiral Lydia Orth at NORAD, where they have spotted the ship leaving the ocean at speeds that no aircraft could possibly match. That person that you lost, that you 'let disappear' as you say, is an existential threat to this planet, and you treat his disappearance as if you LOST YOUR CAR KEYS." Agent Johnson ended her speech with her hands on her hips and continued to glare at McKee.

After a pregnant pause the captain responded to the agent's verbal attack.

"Agent Johnson, I assure you that this matter is of the utmost importance to me and my team. We are just not equipped to handle a threat of this nature. We would certainly welcome a collaboration between our bureaus," McKee concluded, holding his hand out to the agent as if offering a truce.

Agent Johnson stood motionless and silent for a moment, letting the tension in the room build and enjoying it. *This reminds me of how I used to torment my father's friend with silence in response to his greetings. I love this power.*

She eventually broke her silence. "We're too busy to babysit you and your team. Agent Johnson and I are going back to our office, and we want to hear from you as soon as you have anything— anything—new to share with us. Is that understood?" Caitlin turned to walk out before Capt. McKee could respond, leaving him with his mouth open.

"I certainly will, Agent Johnson," he said, hurrying after the agents. "You and – and Agent Johnson have a safe trip back." *Assholes*, Captain McKee mumbled under his breath as he closed the door.

"Tough break, Captain," said Adar, swiveling around in McKee's chair. "Do you have time to talk?"

"Nice vanishing trick you pulled back there, Adar," said McKee, trying to calm his racing heart after being angered by the FBI and then startled by the alien.

"I traveled thousands of light years to get here, and you think I cannot free myself from a bathroom?" Adar smirked. "I'm here looking for two escaped prisoners who are very dangerous. One of them disguised herself to look like me and shot up Luigi's place. Naturally, when I showed up you mistook me for her."

"Maybe that's true, but why would they imitate Ahmed?" asked the captain, who marveled at himself for attempting to have a rational conversation with an alien.

"They didn't. They have the ability to force humans to do their bidding."

"Let's say I believe all of your mumbo jumbo." McKee leaned over his own desk at Adar. "The woman who fingered you said you are responsible for killing her friend in Chicago. She even had a video of you attacking him."

"That man, along with the lady and her sister, are escaped prisoners from our planet. They are the ones I've been looking for since I landed on this god-forsaken Earth. Now I'm asking you to help me find them," the alien said, leaning toward the captain.

"She didn't look like an alien at all. Not like you," said McKee, unconvinced by Adar's story.

"Tell me, did she have flawless skin and sparkling eyes?"

"Yes, I have to say she did. Recently we filmed two women we thought were Sharon and Sheila, from Charlie Butters' crew, beating one of our assistant district attorneys to death with hammers. At the same time we filmed those identical women at a restaurant having dinner. How does that happen?" McKee asked, seeing a possible connection to Adar's story.

"They are aliens with chameleon-like abilities. They can make themselves look like any human they want. I am sure they contacted you so that you could capture me and get me out of their way," Adar theorized, thinking he was making headway with the police captain. "They stunned all those people in Times Square, but they could have just as easily killed them all. They are obviously planning something else. You need to help me find them before they kill more of your people."

"Really? Chameleons? Well, even if I wanted to help you, I couldn't. I don't have the authority to help an alien capture another alien, if that's what she is or they are."

"This is not a joke!" said Adar, pounding on the police officer's desk.

"Why don't you come back into the interrogation room and explain this to my officers and maybe we can help you out," suggested McKee, motioning his hand towards the door.

"Why don't you fly up your own ass," replied Adar, spinning back around in the chair and disappearing.

How the hell does he do that? Do I believe him or not? I can't believe I'm considering working with what appears to be an alien creature, McKee thought.

He opened the door to his office and walked over to Peters' desk. "Calvin, put a trace on this number. It's the one that lady used to warn me about Adar. I can't believe we are discussing what could be an alien, by name."

"Captain, if you don't mind me saying so," said Peters, "that guy is definitely an alien. I don't know if he was trying to do a drug deal in Times Square, but he definitely killed Luigi and his crew."

"Still, I want to know who that woman is, and track where she goes," McKee persisted, staring into the distance.

"What's the probable cause for the warrant?" asked Calvin, knowing he needed to do things by the book.

"Person of interest in the murder of the assistant DA."

"The judge is going to laugh at this one, Captain," said Calvin, shaking his head.

"I don't care, just make it happen," said McKee, running his fingers through his thinning hair.

Chapter 17

Drawing Out Adar

At precinct headquarters, Sgt. Peters rushed into Captain McKee's office.

"Captain, I got the info you wanted," he said excitedly. "The phone number is registered to one Sonny Foster."

McKee lifted an eyebrow. "The Wall Street guy?"

"The same. The phone itself is located in one of his apartment buildings. I can only assume the woman is in his apartment. GPS can't tell us what floor it's on. Funny, people complain about the lack of privacy, but leave their GPS on all the time, making them easy to track," Peters said, shaking his head.

"So, do you think this Foster guy is involved, dead, or is he just screwing this gal?" asked McKee, leaning back in his chair.

"He's not dead. I saw him yesterday doing some interview on Fox News. But we can't go after him just because he's having an affair with someone," mused Peters, trying to come up with a legitimate excuse to investigate Foster.

"But we can ask him what he knows. Go to his apartment and ask him a few questions. Don't lean on him too hard—he has too many friends in the department that could cause problems for us. While you are there, see if you can detect any traces of that woman or her sister. And do it discreetly, Calvin." McKee went back to doing research on his computer terminal as Peters turned and walked away.

***

The afternoon after the Times Square incident, the two alien fugitives lounged on the large couch in Sonny's penthouse on the 23rd floor of the high-rise he owned in the city. The tycoon's decorator had gone all out. The room oozed opulence, done in ivory suede and velvet with whitewashed wood furniture and gold metallic accents. The gold silk drapes covering the floor-to-ceiling windows cost over $50,000, as Sonny often told them.

The two wore black microfiber miniskirts that clung to their hips like a second skin and snug ivory Chanel tops, which Sonny picked out for them. They didn't particularly appreciate his taste, but they liked the fact that he bought them lots of nice clothes.

Daloi noticed Sharon and Sheila sneaking around while she was in Times Square with Dholi. She wondered if they had figured out the Cheoili's disguises and decided to put a tracker on the cousins. She could follow it with the personal transporter she appropriated from the *Andrea* and hopefully figure out what Sharon and Sheila were doing. Sitting on the couch next to Dholi, she saw something on the personal transporter screen that startled her.

"Dholi, I figured out how those cousins are literally getting away with murder. Take a look at the screen here." Daloi showed Dholi an image on the personal transporter of Sharon and Sheila with two other women. "Those bitches! I'm going to go down the street to catch a cab and confront them."

Dholi, who had been reclining on the couch across from Daloi, leaned back in her seat briefly before flicking a bored glance at her sister. She saw little sense in exerting oneself unnecessarily. "Why not use the transporter?" asked Dholi, concerned that her sibling wouldn't reach the pair before they moved on.

"I don't dare do that. I'm sure those damn Euclidian are still tracking us. You stay here with the device in case they try to attack me. Monitor me from the transporter and come to my aid if you feel you need to." Daloi handed the device to Dholi and gave her a quick nod.

"Okay, sis, but be careful," Dholi said, placing an arm on her sister's shoulder.

"Will do. See you soon." Daloi walked out of the penthouse apartment and headed to the street to hail a cab.

***

Following his captain's orders, Peters drove to Foster's condo, determined to get answers about the two women with whom the billionaire had fraternized.

If I remind him of the possible risks to his business and potential to lose billions of dollars while he wastes away in a jail cell, he might be willing to talk. Of course, I have to do that in a way that doesn't offend him and risk my job, he thought. By the time Peters knocked on Foster's door, the detective was clammy with sweat and eager to get the interview behind him.

“Can I help you?” asked Dholi, answering the door in the disguise she had been using around Charlie, which was unfamiliar to Peters.

“Yes, I’m Sergeant Peters with the NYPD. Is Mr. Foster in?” Peters asked, showing Dholi his badge.

“No, he is usually only here on the weekends,” said Dholi, giving Peters a seductive look.

“And who might you be?” Peters asked, smiling.

“I’m Barbara,” Dholi said, shaking Peters’ hand.

“Do you know where I can find Mr. Foster, Barbara?”

“No, I don’t.” Dholi responded with a pout.

“Is Daloi or her sister around? We spoke briefly at the police station this morning.”

“No, they’re out shopping.” Dholi laughed.

“Let them know I dropped by and let us know if they have any more news about Adar.” Peters handed her a card and tipped his hat to Dholi.

“Certainly, Sergeant Peters.” Dholi smiled again, as she closed the door.

***

Adar walked into his apartment where he found Ahmed anxiously waiting for him.

“I’m glad you’re back. Toni wants us to join her at a meeting with the Syndicate, the guys that run all of New York and New Jersey,” said Ahmed, standing up from the couch, where he was watching a sports program.

“I can go now. Where is the place?” said Adar, always eager for another confrontation.

“It’s at the Syndicate’s offices, a few blocks from here. Remember, we walked by there a couple of days ago on the way to the Tavern.”

“Yes, I remember. Let’s go,” said Adar, heading for the door.

“You don’t need anything before we go? Change your socks or something?” Ahmed asked, a hint of amusement in his voice. He hadn’t seen Adar since the day before.

“Nope, I’m good,” Adar grinned, baring his numerous sharp teeth.

“Okay, let’s go then,” Ahmed said, shivers running up his spine at the sight of Adar’s toothy smile.

***

Ahmed and Adar arrived at the Syndicate’s offices on Hester Street in Little Italy a few moments after the meeting started. Toni approached them, anger darkening her long, thin face.

“Where have you guys been? If you’re going to be on my team, you need to be more accessible. Let’s go inside. They’re waiting on me. I’ll do all the talking. Just stay behind me and watch my back.”

"Did the two women working with Charlie show up?" asked Adar.

"How would I know?" Toni retorted, still clearly miffed. "I've been out here waiting on you two. Let's go in and see."

The trio entered the heavily guarded low-rise building used by the Syndicate to conduct business. Toni slowly strode into the crowded conference room where leaders of the area's different families had seated themselves around a long, wooden table, all of them men. Bright sunshine from the window at the end of the conference room filled the area with light. Small bottles of water graced the middle of the table. Toni took a spot at the table, while Adar and Ahmed took seats behind her along the wall.

"Toni, I'm glad you could make it," said Sherman MacDonald, whom everyone called Mac. "I assume those are your associates." Mac lifted his chin in the direction of Adar and Ahmed.

Mac ran the Syndicate and worked to keep the families in line to prevent all-out war, which could bring undesirable attention to mob activities in New York City and surrounding areas. He acted as more of a mediator than an enforcer. He didn't much care who ran Harry Moran's territory as long as it didn't start a war.

"Yes, Ahmed is my lieutenant, and Adar is my muscle," Toni replied, pointing to each of them in turn.

"A little small for muscle, isn't he?" someone shouted from the other end of the table, sending a ripple of laughter across the room.

"Laugh if you want, but that's the guy who singlehandedly took out Luigi and his guys. Probably Harry's as well," another voice cautioned. This quieted the room.

"If you guys are finished jabbering, let's get down to business," Toni said soberly. "My husband ran the south side of Manhattan until his untimely death, at which time his territory should have gone to me. Harry felt differently, but when his new lieutenants fell prey to their own calamities, Harry made a deal with me." She looked around the table.

"You mean when you had them killed!" shouted another boss at the table.

"That is unsubstantiated," said Toni, continuing to describe her version of the facts. "Later, Harry decided he wanted me out of the picture, but he lost that battle. According to the rules, what was once his is now mine."

"I don't belong to you!" said Jerome, leaping to his feet and pointing his finger downward to emphasize his point.

"You worked for Harry, now you work for me. Am I wrong here, Mac?" asked Toni, raising her hands above the table for emphasis.

"Jerome, you know the rules," Mac replied.

"I'm not working for no skirt and that's that," replied Jerome, smacking the table.

"Jerome, you don't run enough territory to be a boss, which means you have to report to a boss," insisted Mac.

“I’ll take him,” said Carlos Quitoni, the boss of Queens, holding a hand up.

Toni gave Carlos a stare. “That’s not the way it works.”

“To keep the peace, I will allow it,” said Mac, putting a hand out to calm Toni.

“We can’t just have people jumping ship anytime they don’t like their boss,” Toni insisted, scowling at Mac.

“This is an unusual circumstance, Toni. Why don’t you get settled into your new position, and we can discuss other opportunities later?” Mac requested, looking to placate Toni.

“Which means shut up and do what you’re told, little lady. Just because I don’t have a penis don’t think I’m weak,” said Toni, standing up and leaning over the table. “Carlos, you want to take what’s mine, let’s you and me go into a closet together and whoever comes out alive gets everything,” an indignant Toni offered, staring Carlos down.

“There’s no fighting here, Toni, and this deal is done!” Mac shouted, slamming a hand on the table.

“The deal is done when I say it’s done. Let’s go, boys,” said Toni, storming out. Facing Adar and Ahmed on the sidewalk, she said, “I want this fixed, you two. Whatever you need to do, just fix it.”

“You know going against Mac won’t end well,” warned Ahmed.

“So convince Jerome that he needs to work for me, and make sure Carlos is okay with that. And do it without killing them,” Toni instructed, her teeth grinding in frustration.

"How are we supposed to do that?" Ahmed eyed Toni in frustration, knowing that if there was any blowback, Toni would not be able to protect him.

"You two say you're good at making things happen. Work your damn magic!" said Toni, before hopping into her limo, which immediately pulled away from the curb.

"What do you suggest we do?" Ahmed asked Adar.

"We go to Carlos' place, wait for him to arrive, and convince him to give up Jerome. Then we go to Jerome and convince him to stay with Toni. Easy as that." Adar looked forward to using his own brand of persuasion.

"'Easy to do' is easy to say. Making it happen is going to be a lot harder," said Ahmed, thinking about the gauntlet of well-armed men they were likely to encounter at both locations.

"Good, I like hard. Let's go pay a visit to Queens," Adar said, a sardonic smile on his face.

***

Ahmed grabbed his car and drove Adar to Queens. He parked in the alley across from Carlos' place and waited for the mobster to show.

"There he is," Ahmed said, pointing as Carlos entered his high-rise apartment building.

A suave guy of medium height in his early 50s, Carlos was of Puerto Rican descent. Known as a dancing, skating and well-dressed ladies' man, Carlos ran the Latin Kings for a while, before he decided to go mainstream to gain more power and influence. Carlos didn't like the idea of women being in charge, certainly not running a family.

They should be at home watching their kids, he thought. Carlos planned to slowly pick away at Toni's territory, until he grabbed it all. He viewed the acquisition of Jerome as just the beginning of his planned expansion.

"I will follow Carlos inside, cloaked, and let you know how it goes," said Adar.

"You're going to teach me how to do that one day, right?" Ahmed quipped, hitting Adar on the arm.

"Sure, when you become an alien," said Adar, running to catch up with Carlos.

The Latino mob boss walked into his office with his bodyguard, Jesus, removed his leather sport coat and took the seat behind his desk.

"Hello, gentlemen," said Adar, appearing suddenly in front of the desk.

Carlos jumped, startled. "Where'd you come from?"

"That is not important. I'm here to ask you to tell Jerome that the deal is off," Adar said sternly, leaning toward Carlos over his desk.

"Why would I want to do that?" Carlos asked, nodding to one of his bodyguards.

The bodyguard reached for his gun. Before the weapon cleared the holster, however, Adar lunged and sliced through the man's body diagonally from shoulder to hip.

"Now that is going to leave an ugly stain on your rug," Adar said, smirking.

"You kill me, and Toni gets nothing. She'll be kicked out of the Syndicate and be worse than dead." Carlos tried to sound confident, but couldn't stop the quivering in his voice.

Adar calmly wiped the blade of his spear on the dead man's pants. "I don't want to kill you. I want to educate you." The alien grinned at Carlos.

"Wylyy, we're ready for that trip to the zoo," Adar spoke Euclidian into his UCD.

The pilot of the alien ship immediately whisked Adar and Carlos to the local zoo via transporter, to a spot just above several sleeping lions.

"How the hell did we get here?" Carlos yelped.

"Shush, you don't want to wake up the lions," Adar whispered. "They would probably become agitated, seeing you in their den like this. I will leave you here to study the animals and let Toni know that you are not interested in helping her out." Adar patted Carlos on the shoulder and smiled.

"No, wait, don't go. You can't leave me like this," Carlos pleaded, suddenly contrite.

"I am having trouble hearing you!" Adar shouted, waking up one of the lions, which trotted towards the two.

"Please get me out of here. I'll do whatever you want!" the terrified mob boss begged.

"Wylyy, take us back," said Adar into his communicator.

Instantly, Carlos and Adar were back in the mobster's office.

Adar studied Carlos for a few seconds. "Why don't you make that call to Jerome now, while I am still here? And let Toni know that you won't be interfering with her deals in the future."

Carlos looked at his hands and his surroundings, trying to figure out what had just happened.

"Do you think you can make that call now?" Adar prodded.

"Anything you say, mister. Just no more weird head trips, please," squeaked Carlos, wiping his brow.

***

"How did it go?" asked Ahmed, watching Adar slip back into the car.

"He pissed his pants."

"You're kidding," Ahmed cried, as he started the car.

"No, I am not. He called Jerome and told him that he changed his mind about the deal. Now let's go see Jerome," said Adar, punching a fist into his hand.

"You know Jerome will be waiting for us."

"I hope so. I could use the workout. Why don't you just drive to our place? I will have Wylyy transport me to Jerome's current location," Adar suggested, not eager to share the upcoming battle with Ahmed.

"And miss all the fun? I want to join you." Ahmed wondered if Adar wanted to take all the credit for himself.

"It could get bloody, and I may not be able to protect you," the alien said. He didn't want to have to protect his sidekick while he was fighting.

"I'm not a chump. Let's do this," Ahmed said, looking to insert himself back into the action.

"Fine. Pull over and park, and I will have Wylyy transport us both there."

Ahmed found a parking spot, while Adar contacted Wylyy.

After Ahmed turned off the car, Adar gave Wylyy the go ahead to transport the two of them to Jerome's office, where the defiant mobster had barricaded himself with six of his men.

When Adar and Ahmed appeared in the office, all six bodyguards reached for their guns.

Ahmed, who already had his gun out, blasted away, while Adar used his spear to hack his way across the room.

Jerome, paralyzed with fright, hid under his desk. When the fighting ended, Adar wiped the blood from his spear before putting it away. He walked over to Jerome's desk and lifted it high above Jerome's head.

"You can come out now, we won't hurt you," said Adar, tossing the desk over his head to land in a broken heap of wood behind him. Jerome pulled his .38 pistol and attempted to fire it at Adar.

Before he got off a shot, Adar kicked him into the back wall, sending the gun skidding across the floor.

"Please don't hurt me. I don't want trouble." Jerome cowered, lifting his hands and ducking his head at the same time.

"I'm not convinced you are ready to play nice," growled Adar. "Stand up for a moment. I want to see if you can fly out the window," he added, grabbing Jerome around the neck.

"Wait, Adar." Ahmed stepped forward. "Jerome, I'm Ahmed, Toni's lieutenant. Adar is Toni's enforcer. We met at the Syndicate meeting earlier today."

"I know who you two are. Mac said I didn't have to go with Toni. If you kill me, there will be a price to pay," said Jerome nervously. "Not just for you, but Toni as well."

"How about if I just cut off one of your legs," said Adar, looking at Jerome sideways. "Would that be okay?"

"No, not at all. Ahmed, do something. This guy has some real problems," objected Jerome, obviously shaken. He attempted to pull away from Adar's grip without success.

"You don't know the half of it. He wanted to eat you," Ahmed confided.

Adar revealed his sharp teeth to Jerome in a feral smile.

"He won't though. We would really like you to join us on a ride to Toni's place to let her know that you would be happy to become part of her team." Ahmed's tone was conciliatory.

"Jerome, what's going on in there?" someone shouted, banging on the door.

"Tell him that we had a slight disagreement, but everything's okay now—unless you want more of your men dead. Now open the door," Ahmed ordered. Adar released Jerome, who stumbled over to answer the door.

"Mason, put your gun away," said Jerome, opening the door. "These guys work for Toni. I'm going to go over and do the deal with her."

"What, are you crazy?" asked the henchman called Mason, looking around the office in shock. "Look at this place. You don't mean to let them get away with this do you?" he cried, trying not to look at the chopped-up and shot-up bodies of his former colleagues strewn across the room amid the broken furniture.

"Do as you're told. I'll be over at Toni's," Jerome snapped, looking defeated as he left his office.

***

That same evening, Charlie watched TV in his office while having drinks with Sharon, Sheila, Daloi and Dholi, and yelling at the screen.

"Look at that bastard," Charlie said, staring at a commercial advertising an upcoming concert featuring Kanye West with Lady Gaga at Madison Square Garden.

“What’s wrong, boss?” asked Sharon, confused by his reaction to the ad.

“That guy, that guy right there screwed me over, and I’m still pissed about it,” said Charlie, pointing at the screen and looking back at Sharon.

“How do you know Kanye?” asked Sharon, having never heard him mention Kanye before.

“Our paths crossed on occasion at parties. At one of those parties, I overheard him say that he planned a trip to the Bahamas, but wanted more privacy than the hotels there could give him. I offered up my bungalow on the island of Nassau, and in return, he promised to drop by my daughter’s sixteenth birthday party. He accepted, but guess what?” Charlie asked, pointing at Sharon.

“He didn’t drop by.”

“Exactly! No apology, no excuses, and no responses to my copious voicemails and emails,” Charlie snarled, grinding his teeth in angry frustration.

“So how should we resolve this slight to your honor? Sheila and I would be happy to give him a beat-down in a club,” suggested Sharon.

“I want more than that. I want him bitch-slapped during the damn concert!” demanded Charlie, pounding on the arm of his desk chair. He then began rocking back and forth, anger suffusing his face.

"That would be tough to pull off and not spend a year in jail, or longer," Sheila muttered, considering the idea.

"Dholi and I can do one better," boasted Daloi. "We'll *stab* that bitch in the middle of the concert." Daloi leaned over Charlie's desk with a confident look on her face.

"How the hell you going to do that and not serve major time or get killed in the process?" demanded Sharon, her voice laced with skepticism.

"We have our ways," Daloi said coyly. "When we succeed at this job, we want to be part of your inner circle and have territory assigned to us," Daloi continued, locking eyes with Charlie.

"You pull that off, and I will happily give you what you want," said Charlie, nodding his head at the disguised alien.

Daloi huddled with Dholi to discuss a possible plan. "Yes, yes, I think that will work."

"What the hell are you two giggling about?" Sharon asked, showing a bit of attitude. "You waltz in here thinking you just gonna jump past people who have been working here for years?"

"Cool your jets, Sharon, we're not trying to take your place. We just want a small slice of a very large pie. We'll be in touch, Charlie. Meanwhile, figure out what territory we are going to be getting," said Daloi, waving at Sharon and Sheila as she walked out with Dholi.

"Charlie, this is bullshit," said Sharon. "They walk in here out of nowhere and in a short period of time, you start handing them stuff like we don't exist."

The mob boss buffed his nails on the lapel of his $3,000 charcoal Armani suit and looked at Sharon for several minutes, his baleful gaze steady.

Charlie's tone was icy when he finally spoke. "They're delivering, and they don't complain. More than I can say for you two. Go do your rounds and get me my money," he spat.

***

The night of the concert, the Cheoili twins reviewed the plan to seek revenge for Charlie, while relaxing in Sonny's condo.

"Dholi, I've got everything set up for tonight," said Daloi. "I'm going to impersonate Lady Gaga while she's performing at Madison Square Garden. Kanye West is going to join her during the second part of the show. I'll replace her just before then. When the lights come up, I'll stab him in front of the cameras and dash out via one of the openings in the stage."

"Brilliant idea," said Dholi. "What can I do?"

"I need you to have a limo waiting right outside the arena on 31st Street so we can make a quick getaway. I'm going to morph several times so you may not recognize me. Just look for this ring on my right hand. As a last resort, use the transporter device to come and get me."

Daloi looked at Dholi with a bit of trepidation, knowing the plan was merely a prelude to a long con that would permit them to disappear for good.

"Don't worry, sis. I'll be there waiting for you." Dholi hugged Daloi, realizing her sibling was taking the bigger risk.

***

Jerome walked into his office to find Mason cleaning up the mess Adar and Ahmed left behind. Mason paused in his work to confront Jerome about what he felt was a bad decision.

"Jerome, doing the deal with Toni is the wrong move," he said. "You know you can't trust that bitch."

"What choice do I have? That enforcer of hers is invincible. Did you see what he did to my men? If I thought we could take him out I would consider telling Toni to shove it," Jerome said, covering his mouth in an attempt to keep himself from losing it in front of Mason.

"You know, I've seen that crazy bastard around," said Mason, tapping his lips with his index finger. "He was hanging out with that waitress, Aundria, at the Whiskey Tavern."

"Really? I'll tell you what you can do for me. You and one of the guys grab her and take her to some undisclosed location. You stay there until this situation has ended. Turn your phones off and take out the batteries. Send me an email using a new email account over a VPN once you get it set up. Besides that, don't communicate with anyone else. If you need to, let your family members know you'll be incognito for a while. I don't want to take any chances with this. You'll be the only insurance I have to stay alive."

Jerome clapped his hands together believing he'd found a solution to his predicament. *I'm going to make that maniac pay for what he did to my people. And he can forget ever seeing that bitch of his again.*

“Okay, I can do that,” said Mason. “I’m glad you’re not going to roll over for that crazy bitch.”

“Once you have her, send me an email, once every six hours. Don’t use your real name, though. I want you to be protected in case this goes south. If I don’t respond within 15 minutes, chop her up and throw her body parts in Times Square.”

Mason flashed Jerome a vindictive smile. “I would be glad to.”

“Before this is all over, that rat bastard is going to be working for me!” Jerome declared, making a fist.

***

Captain McKee placed a stakeout on Foster’s apartment to monitor who might be coming and going. Unfortunately, Foster never showed up. Daloi and Dholi came and went, though the police couldn’t determine their identities.

“Captain, our guys followed one of the women from Foster’s apartment to the Garden,” said Peters, calling McKee over the police radio. “I don’t know which one. She arrived alone. I guess she’s going to watch the concert.”

“I’ll certainly be watching it from my office. Did our guys follow her in?” McKee asked.

“Sort of,” said Peters, obvious frustration in his voice.

“What do you mean, sort of?” asked the captain, uneasily.

“She went into a bathroom and never came out. A female officer went in and couldn’t find any trace of her. You know what, though?”

"What's that?" the captain asked impatiently.

"Sharon, that woman who works for Charlie, walked out of the bathroom as big as you please. Can you imagine that?"

Is it possible she changed herself to look like Sharon? McKee mused. *Was that alien right in suggesting that the women who killed the assistant DA were aliens? Now I'm thinking crazy.*

"Let the arena security know to add Sharon to the list of people to track. Let's find out what they're doing there," ordered the captain, worried that things might get out of control.

If that alien was right that the person who stunned the crowd at Times Square could kill that many people with one blast from a weapon, we could have a catastrophe on our hands. If I bring in the FBI, it would limit my exposure, but if nothing happens after explaining this stupid story, I could be heading for early retirement. Arghh! McKee wrestled with his thoughts for a moment before eventually deciding to handle the situation himself.

***

Adar and Ahmed kicked back on the couch in their apartment, preparing to watch the concert on television. Ahmed was sipping on an IPA, while Adar bit into a large raw steak. Ahmed, a Kanye fan, couldn't wait for the show to start. Just as he got comfortable, his phone rang. "This is Ahmed."

"Hello Ahmed. This is Jerome. Is Adar with you?"

"Yes, we're just watching the Kanye concert," Ahmed affirmed, surprised to hear from Jerome.

"Would you pass him the phone?" Jerome requested impatiently.

"Sure, hold on. Adar, it's Jerome," Ahmed said, shrugging his shoulders at Adar's inquiring glance.

"Hello, Jerome. What do you want?" asked Adar, not expecting good news.

"I've got your girl, Aundria, here. If Toni isn't dead by Sunday night, I'm going to chop pretty Aundria up into little pieces and scatter her across the city." Jerome hung up.

"Arghh!" growled Adar, slamming the phone down.

"What's wrong?" asked Ahmed.

"Jerome kidnapped Aundria and wants me to kill Toni, or he is going to chop Aundria up into little pieces," Adar growled.

"What are you going to do?" Ahmed asked, fearing Adar would not take threats kindly.

"I am going to finish eating this steak and watch the concert with you and then I am going to go to Jerome's place and kill everyone there." He then bit off another chunk of his steak.

***

At Madison Square Garden, the crowds clapped and danced in rhythm with the music coming from the artists on the stage. The first half of the concert ended, leaving the crowd begging for more. After a 30-minute pause, the stage lights came back on. The crowd cheered as Lady Gaga headed to the microphone.

"Good evening, everyone. Welcome to the second part of the show," said Daloi, waving to the crowd as Lady Gaga. Moments later, another eruption of applause occurred as Kanye joined Lady Gaga on stage. "I'm proud to be standing alongside my good friend and fellow performer, Kanye West." The crowd erupted once more in cheers and applause. As the noise died down, Daloi pulled out a knife and shouted, "This is for Charlie." She then stabbed Kanye in the chest.

A collective gasp rose from the arena crowd as Daloi ran past the band and slid under the curtains and into an opening in the stage floor.

"Captain, are you seeing this?" shouted Peters into his police radio.

"Yes, I'm still watching. Have one of our men grab Lady Gaga," said McKee. "I can't imagine Lady Gaga would actually stab someone on stage like that. It must be one of those chameleon women Adar warned me about."

"There's chaos here, captain. I can't seem to reach anyone," said Peters, frustrated at the lack of response from the surveillance team.

"Just keep trying. I'll send someone to Charlie's place to pick up Sharon and Sheila, if they are there. We can ask them what they know about their impersonators and about the City Hall killing again."

***

At Adar's apartment, Ahmed stared at the TV screen for a moment, speechless.

"Adar, did you see that?" he finally gasped. "Why the hell would Lady Gaga stab Kanye West?"

"I saw it." Adar sat forward, all of his senses alert. "Her eyes looked a little funny. It had to be one of the Cheoili. Sounds like Charlie ordered a hit. Go back to the show, so I can see her face. Then show me where that place is on my device screen." Adar pulled out his UCD for Ahmed to look at.

"Position the screen near 8th Avenue and West 31st Street. Zoom in right here. That's the place!" Ahmed shouted.

Adar used his UCD to capture an image of Lady Gaga to share with Wylyy and his crew.

"Wylyy, find the woman on this screen at these coordinates and transport her to the ship now!" Adar shouted into his UCD in Euclidian.

"Okay, give me a moment to look for her. Adar, I have her!"

"Transport me to the ship now. Ahmed, they found that woman and have her on the ship. I'm going there to interrogate her," Adar said, grabbing his coat and weapons.

"What about Aundria?" asked Ahmed.

"That whole business will have to wait. Catching the Cheoili is more important," said Adar, picking up his UCD.

"Take me–" Ahmed started, but Adar cut him off.

"No!" said Adar, before disappearing to the ship. "Wylyy, did she have anything from the *Andrea* on her?" Adar asked, after arriving on the attack vessel.

"No, just this bag. Nothing interesting is in it."

"Hello, Cheoili," said Adar to Lady Gaga in Euclidian.

"I don't understand what you are saying," Lady Gaga replied in English. "Where am I? How did I get here? Who are you people?"

"Stop playing games. I saw what you did at the arena. Where's your sister?" Adar insisted, switching to English.

"Someone attacked me in my dressing room and tied me up. I don't know who took my place on stage and whatever that person did had nothing to do with me. The person obviously impersonated me. I saw her change into me right in front of my eyes. Look at me. I'm still wearing a robe," Lady Gaga said indignantly, and motioned for Adar to look closely at her.

"Your eyes look normal, but that could be a trick," said Adar, pulling out his spear. "You tell me what I want to know, or I'm going to start cutting off body parts until you do."

"Please, don't hurt me. I can pay you a lot money. I'll do anything you want, just let me go," Lady Gaga pleaded.

Adar grabbed her arm and cut off her left hand. Lady Gaga screamed and passed out, blood gushing everywhere.

"Adar, that is not a Cheoili," said Wylyy, beginning to worry about repercussions.

"I can see that, now," Adar replied in disgust.

"Should we send her into space?" Wylyy suggested.

"No, she's some famous person. Get Valera to fix her up and put her back where you found her. First, send me to McKee's office."

***

Wylyy paged Dr. Valera on the *Andrea* to take a look at Lady Gaga. He explained how the amputation happened, but she was not happy to hear about the incident. The impetuous nature of military men frequently annoyed her. She grew tired of constantly cleaning up after their mistakes and childish stunts.

"How did you guys do this?" she demanded, as she worked to reattach Lady Gaga's hand.

"We mistook her for one of the Cheoili women," said Wylyy, attempting to justify the mistake. "Adar cut off her hand, and she fainted."

"Good thing you got to me in time. A little later and she would be dead. I have better things to do than clean up after your messes. You know, you could have just pricked her finger and seen she did not have Cheoili blood," Valera observed, looking at Wylyy with disdain.

"You should be more accommodating, considering this mission is a priority for Captain Shisal," Wylyy retorted. Valera's criticism made him defensive.

"You have a point. Maybe I should buzz him and give him an update on your progress." Valera knew that the captain did not like being disturbed, especially when it was to discuss mistakes being made with an important mission.

"That won't be necessary, Valera," Wylyy said quickly, taking a more apologetic tack. "We are very appreciative of the time you are giving us."

"That's what I thought," Valera purred, looking at Wylyy expectantly. "Does that mean I can expect a trinket from your trip here?"

"Of course, Valera. Anything you would like." Wylyy gave her a big smile.

"I like gold," the doctor said, smiling back at the pilot. "Something substantial."

Valera spent more long minutes working on Lady Gaga before giving Wylyy good news.

"Okay big fella, her hand is as good as new," she reported. "She will feel a little sensitivity in it for a while though. I gave her an intoxicant, which will make her a little groggy when she comes to, and wipe her short-term memory. Just put her back where you found her, and you should be good to go."

The doctor hailed her transport tech on the *Andrea*. "Krystyy, I'm ready to return," the doctor said, before waving farewell to Wylyy and his crew, and vanishing.

***

"Are you ready to work with me?" asked Adar, swiveling around in the captain's chair to face McKee as he entered his office.

"Tell me what the hell happened at the arena, and I'll be glad to work with you," McKee returned, seemingly agitated.

"One of the aliens I told you about pretended to be Lady Gaga. She stabbed that Kanye guy and vanished. What do you know?"

"The real Lady Gaga is in one of our interrogation rooms. One of my men found her stumbling drunk backstage at the arena. She says she thought somebody cut her hand off, but she can't remember much about it. I would like to think that it's just part of her drunken state, but she has a hard time moving her hand," McKee said, mimicking the pop star by flopping his own hand around.

"Sorry about that. I mistook her for one of the aliens. She should be as good as new in a couple of days," Adar apologized, looking uncharacteristically sheepish.

"Great! Now that I have you here, let's talk about your buddy, Ahmed. I'd like you to bring him in for questioning regarding the murder at Luigi's place. I just want to hear his side of things," the police officer demanded, pointing his finger at his desk as he tried to lock gazes with Adar.

"That's not going to happen. I told you he is not responsible for that incident. I don't want him locked up for something you humans can't understand," the alien said, baring his teeth at McKee.

"Fine, I'll accept that for now. If I can get my chair back, I'd like to show you something on my computer," said the captain, deciding to pick his battles.

"Of course." Adar moved aside so McKee could slide behind his desk.

McKee punched the keyboard and the computer screen lit up. "Look at this video taken from the stadium. One of our men grabs the imposter. Now she grabs him on the arm, and he just walks away from her." McKee looked at Adar for his reaction.

Adar nodded. "The aliens I'm looking for have enzymes in their hands that act as a relaxing agent when they come in contact with a person's skin. They can then manipulate the victim as needed. So be careful about letting them touch you."

"Thanks for the tip. Notice, the woman moves into a corner, takes off her dress exposing the shorts she is wearing underneath, and now she morphs into an Asian woman. She walks down a hallway and comes out the other end as a black woman, the same one that visited me earlier this week. From there she gets into a limousine and disappears into the night. The limo driver said he dropped two women off near Sonny Foster's apartment building."

"That's all we have," McKee ended, looking up at Adar from his seat. "We are in the process of heading to Foster's place now and taking any women we find there into custody."

"Tell me where the place is and I will take care of them myself," said Adar, moving toward the door.

"No, you said we would work together on this."

"Fine. I will accompany you. I can assure you that you will not be able to apprehend them on your own," Adar ended, giving the captain a skeptical look.

Chapter 18

The Cheoili are Cornered

After the meeting with McKee, Adar once again felt on the verge of catching the Cheoili. He had agreed to join forces with the police captain, but didn't like relying on humans. Still, he felt certain that joining forces with the human authorities would improve the chances of snaring his quarry. Captain Shisal was breathing down his neck, but more than that, he feared the hit his pride would take if he let the twins slip through his fingers again.

McKee felt his own frustration. He knew he was smart and good at his job. But he now had two murder investigations that appeared to be getting the best of him. Moreover, he needed to unravel the strange circumstances surrounding the mayhem at Max's and the attack in Times Square that left a crowd of people temporarily immobilized.

The rash of murders seemed to be perpetrated by a couple of women who appeared to show up in two places at once.

Could the two series of incidents be related? Have aliens been infiltrating our society all along, and we just ignored the evidence? McKee viewed himself as being conservative and not easily seduced by flights of fancy. Still, the evidence made it clear, to most of his staff at least, that the person they recently arrested in connection with the crimes came from another planet.

McKee kicked back in his chair and started shooting rubber bands at a picture of Mike Hammer that he had hung on the wall to his right, all the while ignoring Adar. *What do you think, big guy?* McKee spun a rubber band around his index fingers for a moment, considering. Then he jumped up from his chair. "Let's go, Adar!"

"Peters, I'm leaving now for Sonny Foster's apartment with a team of officers," said McKee, when he paused at his subordinate's desk in the squad room. "Adar will be joining us as a civilian consultant. I want you to stay here to help coordinate any assistance we may need from the precinct."

"Forgive me for asking, captain. But two days ago we had this guy in custody, and he escaped. Now he's a civilian consultant–" Peters used air quotes. "Do we need to be worried about undue alien influence here?" Peters once again used air quotes.

Before McKee could respond, Adar stepped forward to explain the circumstances of his involvement.

"Excuse me Sergeant Peters, but the only alien influence is being exerted by two women, who are wreaking havoc on your city," Adar said gruffly. "They have the power to force any human to do their bidding, even your United States president. I shudder to think what would happen if they got access to the White House."

"Sergeant, these are extraordinary circumstances that call for drastic action," McKee interjected. "I assure you, I'm in complete control of my faculties and this situation. Now I expect you to remain here and assist me as needed, Sergeant."

"Will do, Captain," Peters said, nodding and returning to his paperwork.

"Wylyy, I need you to be alert and monitor me with the ship's scanners," Adar said, speaking Euclidean into his communicator. "I believe we are closing in on the Cheoili."

"What's going on, Adar?" asked McKee, noticing Adar speaking a foreign language he didn't recognize into a small, flat, gray box that fit snugly in his palm.

"I'm having my ship monitor us in case we need backup."

"I don't want an alien attack on our city," said Captain McKee, icy dread making the hairs on the back of his neck stiffen. "I only want you involved if we get overwhelmed and the safety of the city is at stake. You know our military is tracking your spaceship? If they start moving their troops into the city, it could trigger a panic that wouldn't help your efforts any."

"I'm not worried about your military tracking us, and I don't want to risk losing those escapees just because you are afraid of panicking the city. Your team doesn't have the capability to take on the two aliens without our assistance. Believe me when I say those two aliens will obliterate your city if you piss them off."

"I hear you, and want your assistance, but I'm asking for restraint," the captain insisted, as they crossed the police parking lot and climbed into an unmarked sedan.

Reluctant partners for now, McKee and Adar headed out of the parking lot, with McKee driving. The police captain turned on the car's flashing lights but not its siren. A police van full of officers, led by Officer Ming Chow, followed them closely.

'I hear you?' What does that mean? I should just kill these people and finish this job myself, Adar thought.

An awkward silence fell between the pair as the little convoy raced down the street toward Foster's place.

"Okay, we're here," said McKee, about 10 minutes later, as he parked the vehicle at the corner of Foster's building. The police van also parked a few cars back on the side of the street and eight officers piled out.

"Officer Chow, establish a perimeter around the building," McKee ordered. "No one gets in or out. I don't care what they look like. Adar and I will go up to Foster's apartment."

"Got it, Captain," replied Officer Chow.

McKee turned to the alien. "Are you ready, Adar?"

"Yes, let's go," Adar responded, checking the placement of his weapons.

McKee pulled out his service weapon as he and Adar approached Foster's apartment. He signaled that he would shoot the lock.

Adar waved him off, and then pointed at his head. He proceeded to ram the door, his skull making contact with a loud thwack that popped the lock and forced the portal wide open.

Dholi, disguised as Sheila, stood across from Adar.

"Hello, Cheoili. Where's your sister?" asked Adar, with a sneer on his face.

"Right here, Ossie!" shouted Daloi, disguised as Sharon and standing in the corner of the room. Aiming the photon gun in her hand, she blasted him with an energy charge, flinging him against the far wall. Adar's shield diffused the blow, protecting him from certain death, but not from intense pain.

"Don't even think about it," said Daloi, pointing her blaster at McKee, whose grip tightened on his gun. Dholi moved quickly to her side, and they both disappeared.

Adar then disappeared as Wylyy transferred him aboard the ship, worried about his condition. "Adar, are you okay?"

"Me?" shouted Adar. "Don't worry about me. Where are the Cheoili?" Adar looked around the ship.

"They transported themselves to the other side of the city," replied Wylyy, confused by Adar's anger.

Adar grimaced, intense frustration distorting his features. "Send me back to the apartment," he growled. "Next time grab the Cheoili first, then worry about me."

At the apartment, a baffled McKee stared around the room.

"Ming, get your men up here to search the premises," he ordered over the police radio. "Sergeant Peters, I need an update on the location of Foster's phone." McKee jumped when Adar reappeared in front of him.

"Oh, Adar, you're back." He stared at Adar in wonderment. "I would love to know how you do that."

"It would be better if we didn't discuss that," Adar said dismissively. He still looked a bit shaken from the twins' attack, but pushed through it. "According to my people, the two women are still in the city. They recently arrived in Times Square. I suspect they are on the move."

"Good. I'm having one of my people get their location now," said McKee, touching his earpiece.

"Captain, we located the phone. It appears to be in a car heading south on Seventh Avenue away from Times Square," said Peters. "Officers on the scene said they saw two women appear out of nowhere and jump into a yellow cab going in that direction."

"Have every unit in the area block off that section of the city," McKee ordered urgently. "Ming, you can have your people stand down. This place is clear. Adar, our data seems to corroborate what your people said."

"Wylyy, are you tracking what they're saying?" Adar murmured into his UCD.

"No! I don't speak their language," the alien pilot replied. "You'll have to translate for me."

"What's going on?" asked McKee.

"I'm trying to get my people to help track the car," said Adar.

"What do you mean by that?" screeched McKee. "I don't want an alien ship flying around the city. It would just cause panic."

"Be calm," said Adar impatiently. "My ship can monitor the traffic without flying around. If we spot the fugitives we can transport them to our ship without causing harm to anyone else."

"What about the cab driver?" asked the captain, still worried the aliens might do something awful.

"The driver won't be touched. If he starts talking about aliens and people vanishing, you humans will just think he is another nut."

"So you aliens do this a lot?" McKee asked, now concerned that other aliens might be roaming the Earth.

"No, at least not us," Adar said, shrugging.

The NYPD, meanwhile, blocked off Seventh Avenue and began a car-by-car search of traffic. They noticed a cab make a U-turn in front of the roadblock and drive away, and gave chase.

"Sergeant Peters, can you give me a quick update on that phone?" Officer José Gonzalez called from the roadblock.

"Gonzalez, we have the phone now going north on Seventh Avenue. How is that possible?" asked Peters, knowing that Seventh Avenue is a one-way street, going south.

"We just spotted a cab making a U-turn on Seventh Avenue. I sent some cars after it, but will continue to check cars here," reported Gonzalez.

"Okay, Gonzalez, I'll send you some additional support," replied Peters, switching frequencies on the radio to speak to the captain. "Captain, we located the phone. It appears to be in a cab heading north on Seventh Avenue against traffic."

"Have every unit in the area block off that section of the city," McKee ordered, before switching radio frequencies to order a helicopter. "Crnekovic, take the police helicopter to Seventh Avenue near West 30th Street and assist Sergeant Peters with chasing down a cab."

"Right away, Captain," replied Officer Crnekovic, pulling on the controls of the helicopter to steer it towards the action.

"Sergeant Peters, I need you to manage the search while I cover the investigation of Foster's apartment," said McKee.

"I'll take care of it, Captain!" replied Peters, eager to be in charge of the situation.

***

In Manhattan, a cab driver navigated the stream of cars around him, hoping his fare, two middle-aged people, wouldn't grow impatient with his slow progress down Seventh Avenue. The radio blared, a Bob Marley tune filling the interior of the cab: "*We're jammin', jammin', and I hope you like jammin' too.*"

"Is the music okay, you two?" asked the cabbie.

"Oh, yes," said his female passenger. "We love us some Bob Marley. I used to listen to him in high school. We would smoke doobies behind the gym and listen to his tunes on a jam box."

"Dig that. Jammin' on a jam box. Hah! And he passed so young, along with Hendrix. And now we got MJ, Bowie, George Michael, Al Jarreau and Prince all gone," said the cabbie, shaking his head.

"Yeah, that is so sad. I could use a doobie right now, to tell you the truth, Albert," the female passenger told her companion, holding her mouth as she thought about a close friend who recently died.

"Honey, I think you're saying too much there," said Albert.

"Don't worry about it. He still affects me like that, too," said the cabbie. "He's been dead over 35 years and his music is still dope. He certainly smoked plenty of it himself. Ha, ha!"

"What's that up there?" Albert asked, pointing at police cars blocking the road.

"Damn police roadblock. They won't leave me alone," said the cabbie.

"How do you know they're after you?" Albert threw a confused look at his wife, before again eyeing the scene outside the cab's front windshield.

"They're always hassling me about parking tickets, Ganga smoke, or my papers. I've been here eight years and they continue to treat me like some Syrian refugee," the cabbie groaned, slamming the vehicle into reverse. "Hold on, I'm going to make a U-turn."

The cabbie made the Uey, climbing the curb to dodge cars.

"Wait, this is a one-way street! Wow, okay, you made it," said Albert excitedly, while clutching his chest.

“Officer Moss, you and one of the other officers take squad cars and go after that cab,” Gonzalez said, pointing to a cop standing near him. “I’ll call Sergeant Peters for backup.”

“What should we do with the expired licenses we pulled over?” another officer asked.

“Tell them it’s Christmas and to fix them before they get caught again,” Gonzalez replied. “I’ll stay here in case they head back this way.”

Two police cars drove away in pursuit of the cab, now two blocks away but still in sight.

“Sergeant Peters, this is Eric Crnekovic in the police chopper. The cab is headed for the Lincoln Tunnel.”

“They cannot get to the tunnel! You hear me! I want all available cars to ram them if they have to. I don’t care if it crushes their gonads. I want that car stopped!” shouted Peters.

“Got it, sergeant.”

“You see all those cop cars after us?” The cabbie’s gaze kept returning to his rearview mirror.

“Shouldn’t we pull over?” asked the male passenger, nervously leaning forward in his seat.

“No, they’ll just hold us up for questioning, and you’ll never make it to your dinner,” said the driver, looking back at them.

“What’s that bright light?” asked Lisa, Albert’s wife.

"It's a police chopper. I told you they had it in for me," said the cabbie, hunching over the wheel and looking up at the helicopter. "The 99 percent never get a break in this country. Hold on, we'll be in the tunnel in a few seconds. Oops, change of plans."

"Look, they've turned north onto 12th Avenue," said Peters, who was monitoring the cab's progress from a screen in the squad room. "Why wasn't that turnoff blocked? All available cars, close off 12th Avenue north and all side streets." *How hard is it to keep one damn cab contained?*

"Wylyy, have you spotted the yellow vehicle?" asked Adar, still at Foster's apartment.

"There are several yellow vehicles in the vicinity.".

"It has the numbers 447 on the roof!" Adar shouted into his UCD.

"And what do those numbers look like in their language?" Wylyy queried.

"Damn you, Wylyy!"

"No, damn you, Adar. Give me some coordinates."

"It just turned north near the tunnel entrance," said Adar, attempting to calm himself.

"Oh, that one. We have a lock on it," Wylyy said, setting his tracking system to follow the vehicle.

"There should be two Cheoili in the back compartment. I want them transported out of there as soon you confirm their identity," instructed Adar.

"Hold on, let me check– There are only humans in that vehicle. No Cheoili."

"Are they carrying any of our devices?" Adar asked, feeling frustration building up in him.

"Nothing. It's clean," said Wylyy, scanning through the cab again.

"Adar, what did your people find out?" asked McKee. "Can they stop the cab?"

"They are not in that cab," replied Adar, holding his head down in deep thought.

"What do you mean? We're tracking their phone," said the captain, with a confused look on his face.

"They obviously dumped the phone in the cab to throw us off. I'm leaving," said Adar, heading towards the door of Foster's condo.

"Can we at least check the car before you go?" pleaded McKee.

"Okay, I'll wait until you can check the car," Adar said, leaning back on the wall next to the door and putting a foot up. He quickly scanned the room as he stood there, spotting a joint on top of a book in a bookcase, but nothing else out of the ordinary. He quietly grunted to himself, before focusing on McKee as he worked with his officers to stop the cab.

***

"Damn it, another roadblock!" yelled the cabbie as he looked for another escape route.

"What are you going to do?" Albert asked.

"Hold on, I'm taking another shortcut." The cabbie spun the steering wheel, and the vehicle veered sharply to the left.

"Uh-oh, this might be a hard landing," he cried, trying to regain control of the cab, but failing miserably.

"Sergeant, he just made a hard left on West 48th towards Pier 88. I don't think he's going to make the ramp," shouted one of the cops in the police helicopter. "There they go. They're not going to survive that fall."

"Peters, what's going on down there?" yelled McKee, listening in to the radio chatter.

"Adar, the car is plunging off the road," Wylyy reported via Adar's UCD. "The impact will probably kill the occupants. We're holding it in place for now. Should we let it fall?"

"Let me check," replied Adar, who looked forward to McKee's reaction. "Captain McKee, my people momentarily stopped the cab from falling to its destruction. Should we just let it drop?" He flashed McKee a sarcastic smirk.

"You really have to ask that?" an incredulous McKee retorted, staring at Adar.

"I thought you didn't like us aliens interfering in your humans' lives," Adar said mildly.

McKee held up his hands in resignation. “Please don’t let them die, okay?”

“Wylyy, set them down gently,” Adar murmured into his communicator. Turning to McKee, he continued, “It’s done. I’ll check on you in the morning. You’re on your own for now.” The alien then turned and walked away.

“It would be great if you could come by the office at 9:00 tomorrow morning,” McKee requested humbly. Adar merely waved and kept walking.

***

As the cab gently came to rest on the pier, several police cars surrounded it.

“Get out of the car with your hands up,” an officer ordered over a loudspeaker.

“Honey, we’re about to be arrested. What will we tell our friends and family?” Lisa cried.

“Whatever we tell them, it’ll be a great story, sweetheart.” Albert laughed. “I hope someone is tweeting this.”

Chapter 19

Closing in on the Cheoili

That same evening, Sgt. Peters debriefed his men after the cab chase concluded in disappointment. When the prolonged and dangerous pursuit ended, they bagged a shaken-up couple of tourists and a cab driver with a stack of traffic tickets, while their quarry, the Cheoili, eluded them again. Peters felt it more prudent to let the cabbie and his passengers go than deal with the paperwork.

"Calvin, what did your men find out?" the captain demanded, when a downtrodden Peters walked into the squad room.

"It looks like the ladies ditched the phone in a cab and disappeared." He avoided the captain's eyes to hide his humiliation and frustration.

"The people in the cab are certainly not the women we're looking for," Peters continued, squaring his shoulders and hardening his features.

"How do you know they didn't disguise themselves?" McKee persisted, hoping his team had missed some clue that would provide a new lead for his investigation.

"Unless they can change themselves into an elderly couple with valid driver's licenses, it wasn't them." Peters' misery overshadowed the hint of dry sarcasm in his voice.

"Fine, let's call it a night and I'll see you in the morning."

***

The next morning McKee sat in his office, again shooting rubber bands at his poster of Mike Hammer, wishing the fictional detective would offer some words of wisdom to make him feel better about the previous evening's fiasco. He glanced at his open door, looking for Adar and Peters to show.

It was almost 9:00 in the morning. He had already been there for two hours and had downed three cups of strong coffee from the kitchenette in the squad room. After reviewing video feeds, scanning reports and making phone calls, he had nothing. Finally, he saw Peters wave as he headed to his desk to drop off his lunch and computer bag. As the sergeant moved toward McKee's office, Adar stepped out of the elevator.

"Thanks for being prompt, gentlemen," McKee greeted them. "Have a seat, and let's look at where we are. The phone is no longer of use to us. We don't know where Daloi and Dholi are. Sharon and Sheila are clean, at least for now. Foster knows nothing. Charlie knows nothing. There is nothing in the apartment that is of any use to us. At least we know how Sharon and Sheila could be in two places at once. Adar, do your people have a way to track these aliens?"

"Only if they use their transporter recklessly," Adar admitted. "And they are too smart to do that now."

"So what are our options?" asked McKee, sounding desperate.

"Stake out Charlie's and Sonny's places and hope to get a bite," suggested Peters. "We could also check in on the other mob bosses."

"Okay, let's leave it at that and hope we get lucky. And let's connect every morning for a while, if that works for the two of you," the captain proposed, looking at Adar.

"Fine with me," said Adar.

"Me, too," echoed Peters.

***

That same morning in Charlie's office, Charlie found himself debating with Sharon and Sheila how to reward Daloi and Dholi on their achievement.

"Come on, Sharon, don't be angry," Charlie urged. "You have to admit, Daloi made a pretty impressive play. On live TV, surrounded by security. And they got away with it. So, they deserve something."

"Now what?" asked Sharon, in disbelief that Charlie fawned over the newcomers.

"I think I'll give them Jersey City," Charlie mused.

"Isn't Bobby trying to take that territory from the Russians?" objected Sheila, whose disdain for the twins was as vocal as that of her cousin.

"Those ladies seem pretty creative. I'm sure they'll figure something out." Charlie chuckled, gleeful anticipation lighting his expression.

"Charlie, I got a lady named Daloi on the line for you," said the receptionist, opening the door and poking her head into the room after a brief knock.

“Thanks Caroline, I’ll take it in here.” Charlie picked up the phone receiver.

“Daloi, you totally nailed it last night. I owe you big time.” The mob boss laughed as he praised his new henchwoman.

“Good, because we are ready to do some serious business. We have an idea we want to run by you,” said Daloi, pausing to hear Charlie’s response.

“Sure, though you know I had planned to give you Jersey City.”

“The Russians run Jersey City. I don’t want to work that hard for my money,” said Daloi, sounding dismissive. “Anyway, Dholi and I have a plan to bring in a lot of cash for you, but we need your help getting the idea off the ground.”

“You’ve piqued my interest,” replied Charlie, raising his eyebrows. “Tell me more.”

“I’d love to, but I don’t want to do it over the phone. Can you have Sharon and Sheila meet us at the Village Underground in Jersey City?” suggested Daloi. “We want to include them in the plan.”

“Sure, but why all the cloak and dagger?” asked Charlie, a little suspicious of the request.

“Because the police are after us, okay?” Daloi sounded nervous.

“Sharon and Sheila, you down with meeting the ladies at the Village Underground tonight? They say they’ve got a big deal brewing and they want to include you.” Charlie briefly placed the handset against his chest.

“Yeah, we can do that,” said Sharon, curious about Daloi’s interest in working with them.

“Sharon, I don’t trust them,” said Sheila, nudging Sharon.

Charlie paused and glared at the two ladies.

“Sheila, it will be okay,” replied Sharon. “If they cross us, we’ll take them out.” Sheila shrugged in capitulation. “We’ll do it!” said Sharon.

“Did you hear that, Daloi? It’s a go,” Charlie said, smiling.

“I heard it,” replied Daloi. “Tell them to get there around 10:00 tonight.”

“Got it. By the way, I really enjoyed watching Kanye screech last night.” Charlie chortled again.

“Glad we could take care of that minor irritation for you,” Daloi said, hanging up.

***

Daloi should have trusted her feelings about not using her phone to do business, because the police definitely listened in on everything they said. Their conversation gave the police and Adar the lead they needed to track the twins down.

Adar sat in his apartment across from Ahmed, eating a raw steak, when he received a call from Wylyy.

“Did you get all that, Adar?” asked Wylyy, who had been listening in on the conversation in Charlie’s office and patched the audio to Adar.

"Yes. This makes up for your slip up last night," said Adar grimly.

"You won't let that go, will you?" asked Wylyy, annoyed by Adar's unforgiving attitude.

"I'll let it go when I have those two in custody. I'll meet them there, and we will end this tonight." Adar growled. "I want you monitoring Charlie's and Sonny's places just in case."

"I'll be watching." Wylyy ended the transmission.

"Adar, did you find out anything new?" asked Ahmed, who eyed him from across the dining room table.

"Those two aliens I am after will be at a club in Jersey City tonight. I plan to intercept them there and bring them to justice." Adar's face was firm with conviction. "I need you to tell Captain McKee to meet me there at 9:30. And tell him to be discreet."

"Did you check in on Aundria?" Ahmed asked, hoping he could interest Adar in saving her.

"I went to Jerome's place and found it vacant. I will have to revisit the issue later. I'm certainly not going to kill Toni," Adar said, taking another bite out of his steak.

"What's with the hoodie?" asked Ahmed, having never seen Adar wear anything other than his long black coat.

"I don't want the aliens or Charlie's people to recognize me if they happen to show up," Adar said, pulling it over his head. "I'll step outside and have Wylyy transport me to the meetup."

"What do you want me to do?" Ahmed asked, hoping to get involved in the alien chase.

"After you call McKee, do what you can to find Aundria. Or at least find Jerome for me. He can't stay hidden forever. I may be gone for a while, depending on how the evening goes."

"No problem. You can always find me at the apartment or the Whiskey Tavern." Ahmed smiled.

***

Adar arrived at the Village Underground early and settled down to wait in a shadowy corner outside the club. He could hear dance music blaring from the open door, unlike the other bars he frequented. The clientele entering this venue appeared younger and dressed differently, in more flashy, fashionable clothing. McKee showed a few minutes later, and Adar met him as he climbed out of an unmarked police car.

"I have been here for a few minutes and I haven't seen or smelled them yet. What are your plans?" Adar asked McKee, as he continued to scan the parking lot.

"I'll have those two plainclothes police officers inside," McKee said, pointing to a man and woman stepping out of an unmarked car nearby and nodding to McKee and Adar. "And I'll have several more outside. My men won't engage anyone until I give the word. I'm counting on you to identify the aliens, as well as neutralize them. I'll do what I can to help you out." McKee worried about all that could go wrong with the operation.

"I appreciate you identifying your people to me. I'll let you know as soon as I see something. If I can take care of the situation quickly, I'll do that," said Adar, turning and walking towards the entrance to the club.

Adar walked into the club and took a quick look around. He was surprised to see the flashing lights, people dancing and the more flirtatious atmosphere of the crowd. He found a dark, out of the way corner where he could spot the Cheoili if they decided to show up. He sniffed the air and monitored his DNA scanner, hoping to notice Daloi and Dholi before they noticed him. He ordered a tonic water from a server and found himself tapping his hand on the table to the beat of the song, "Bad Blood," playing over the speakers. When his drink arrived, he took a sip and settled in for what could be a long wait.

Where are you two? You've been evading me long enough. I can't believe I'm missing the boredom of the ship, Adar thought. *Aundria has been the most worthwhile experience I've had since I've been here. Well, fighting those extremists in Syria was pretty rewarding, but I would probably pick Aundria over them.*

Still, as much as I like Aundria, I can't take her with me, and I can't bear to stay on this backward planet any longer than I have to. The archaic state of treatment for illness and disease on this Earth is astounding. And they make people PAY for it. Aundria would have died if I had needed to rely on these Earthlings to save her. Now she'll probably die anyway, which is her fate.

Why are people dancing? It's an odd way to get exercise and an even odder mating ritual. The music is too loud to have a conversation. Adar sat in the corner, bored and frustrated. *There we go. Finally, some action.*

Sharon and Sheila walked into the club dressed to impress, wearing short shimmering dresses with low necklines. Adar made a quick pass by them with his hoodie up and dismissed them as being human, but kept his eye on them.

“Do you see them, Sheila?” Sharon asked, taking a short stroll around the large one-room club.

“No, I don’t see them. If we have to be in this dive, we should at least have a good time,” said Sheila, smiling and doing a quick shimmy, keeping time with the beat.

“I heard that,” said Sharon. They strutted to the dance floor and spent the next half hour getting their swerve on. That’s when a strange man approached them.

“Hello, ladies. Daloi and Dholi want to meet you out back where they say it’s quieter,” said the unknown stranger.

“As soon as ‘Bitch Better Have My Money’ ends, baby,” said Sheila, dismissing the man. “I’m not walking off the dance floor with Rihanna blasting over the speakers. Daloi and Dholi better be listening to this,” she shouted to Sharon, giving her a high-five.

Once the song ended, the two women sashayed down the hall to the back of the club and out the exit door. As they stepped into the alley, they looked around for Daloi and Dholi.

“Hey, let Captain McKee know Charlie’s ladies are here and on the move, then follow me,” Adar said to an undercover cop, before following Sharon and Sheila.

The officer made a quick radio call to McKee and both undercover officers trailed Adar to the back of the club.

"Hello, Adar," said Daloi in Euclidian as she approached him, grabbed his throat and forced him against the hallway wall. Being taller than Adar, the Cheoili used her leverage to shove the Ossie off balance. She didn't realize that the hoodie tied tightly under his throat protected him from the enzymes in her fingertips. Adar grabbed her crotch and slammed her into the ceiling before tossing her down the short hallway.

Daloi's home planet of Cheoili had stronger gravity than Earth. This meant Daloi was stronger and more agile on Earth. She twisted in mid-air and grabbed a nearby door jamb to reverse her momentum and lunge back at Adar, kicking him in the chest and sending him crashing to the floor. The Ossie quickly jumped up and ran at Daloi, who bounded over him while reaching down and grabbing him by the face to sling his body to the floor, where she held him tightly between her thighs.

"You like the feel of my hands on your face? Stop resisting. Did you really think wearing a hood on your head would protect you?" Daloi said mockingly, pulling down his hood and lifting him off the floor. "Nod and let me know you're my bitch," Daloi whispered into his ear. Adar slowly nodded. "Now tell me what you did with my baby brother," Daloi demanded, slamming his face against the wall.

"He's dead and soon you will be."

"Not before you are. Your time on this planet has just come to an end," Daloi chided in a menacing tone.

The two undercover officers attempted to intercede on Adar's behalf, but Dholi appeared and stunned them with two quick blasts from her photon gun. She then dragged them into a storage room, waving off nosy patrons who came to investigate the noise with a curt smile.

“Good work, sister,” said Daloi in Cheoili, looking over at Dholi. “Now let’s get rid of this Ossie for good. Why don’t you take his weapons and get out of here. I’m going to wear his personal shield for a while, then meet you at the rendezvous point.”

“I remember the plan. See you soon, sister,” said Dholi, giving her twin a quick hug.

Dholi grabbed Adar’s weapons and walked out the front of the club and down the street to wait for Daloi.

Daloi, meanwhile, pulled Adar down the hallway behind her by his neck.

“Hello, ladies,” she said, stepping into the alley. “I hope I didn’t keep you waiting too long.”

“We kept ourselves busy,” said Sharon. “What do you have there?”

“This is the ferocious Adar who took out Luigi’s crew, and now’s he’s my little bitch,” Daloi said, patting Adar’s cheek with her free hand.

“You’ve got to show me how you do that,” said an admiring Sharon.

“I will. Right now, I need to get rid of this pest. You can come watch if you like, but stay back.”

Daloi walked down the alley toward the front of the club, dragging Adar to where the police stood waiting by their cars.

“This is for Tatan,” Daloi whispered in his ear before pulling out a gun and shooting at the cops until they returned fire, sending dozens of rounds toward her and Adar. She let Adar fall to the ground and retreated to the back of the club.

“How the hell did you survive that?” asked Sharon, in shock.

“Using this little device right here,” said Daloi. “You just attach it to your body like this. Turn it on with this switch and you are protected from things being fired at you. People can still punch you or tackle you, but other than that, you are pretty safe. I stole it from a government research center. To show you there are no hard feelings, you can have it.”

“You are totally my BFF now,” said Sharon, hugging Daloi.

“Sorry ladies, I don’t have time to go over the new project Dholi and I cooked up. Let’s get together soon. Right now, I need to run,” said Daloi, disappearing through the back door of the club, and walking out the front with a new identity. She walked down the street to where Dholi was waiting to transport her to safety.

Chapter 20

Saving Adar

Adar slowly came to. He could make out a light in his face and a blurred image hovering over him. *What is this? Have these bastards locked me up again?* "Arghh! Why am I restrained?" He struggled against metallic mesh restraints that bound his wrist, ankles and waist.

"Adar, this is Valera. You're aboard the *Andrea*. I need you to calm down. You're being restrained because I'm afraid that you will hurt yourself or others. Once you have shown me that you won't harm anyone, I will release you."

"Again! Why does this keep happening to me? Valera, I don't feel well, but I promise you, I can contain my violent tendencies," Adar growled.

Though he felt no physical pain, a wave of mental anguish over his inability to capture the Cheoili threatened to swamp his spirits. Moreover, the wily fugitives repeatedly got the drop on him, this time bringing him close to death.

Adar had killed many different species, mostly in battle, or while protecting diplomats, or as a sniper. However, investigative work to bring someone to justice wasn't his bailiwick.

"Tanya, go ahead and free him from his restraints," Valera instructed her assistant, who was a human and previously a nurse on Earth.

“Adar, you lost a great deal of fluid and you have a lot of Cheoili toxins in your system. It’s going to take a few more hours to restore your chemical balance. I suggest you just rest here for a while,” Valera said, as she bustled around the infirmary bed where the Ossie reclined.

“We will bring you some fresh meat when you are ready to eat. You need to be more careful. Sooner or later, your luck is going to run out,” she said, shooting a baleful glare in Adar’s direction.

“What happened to me?” Adar shook his head, trying to clear the lingering bits of confusion clouding his thoughts. Daloi’s attack plus the gunshots not only wounded his body but upset his mental equilibrium.

“You got shot up pretty badly by the Earthlings,” said Valera. “Wylyy noticed the transport being used, tracked you with your UCD and found you bleeding on the ground.” Valera’s expression turned somber.

“When can I get access to my UCD?” Adar asked, trying to sit up. “I need to plan my return.”

“I’ll give back your UCD in a couple of days, and you can decide what to do then.”

Valera administered a sedative to Adar before bustling away as he faded, with his thoughts turning to Aundria.

***

When he recovered, Adar returned to his apartment in Manhattan to find Ahmed relaxing with his family in front of the TV.

"Adar, so good to see you, man!" Ahmed got up from the couch and slapped Adar on the shoulder. They then moved into the kitchen where they could speak privately. "Everyone here thinks you're dead," Ahmed exclaimed.

"What's happened since I've been gone?" asked Adar, going straight to the heart of the matter.

"The police found Sharon and Sheila dead, but they've also been seen about town," said Ahmed. "The police are keeping it quiet, but I have a contact inside who told me that Captain McKee is hoping to connect with you or your people, since they think you're probably dead."

"They felt bad about shooting you up the way they did. But they're worried about dealing with the aliens without your help," Ahmed reported. "Man, how did you survive that? McKee told me how badly your body was riddled with bullets, and that you were bleeding all over the place before you disappeared. I thought you died, too," he added, a parade of emotions marching through his dark eyes.

"I was out of it for a while, but I'm fine now. It was the Cheoili who caused the shootout. I'm sure they killed Sharon and Sheila and are now posing as them." Adar wondered where they might be.

"There's a rumor that Sharon has some sort of special power that keeps her from getting shot. When the bosses add that to the time Toni supposedly killed Carl by pointing at him, they think some women are learning to be witches." Ahmed laughed, because he knew the truth.

"One of the Cheoili took my personal shield, so that has to be them. Where do you think they are?" asked Adar, who was eager to settle the score with the twins.

"I would guess at Charlie Butters' place. The police have it staked out, but they don't have probable cause to search the premises. They got burned bringing them in on murder charges twice, and both times having to let them go."

"They can't be there," Adar replied, shaking his head. "Wylyy has been monitoring Charlie's place. What about Sharon and Sheila's place?"

"They're dead, why would anyone–oh, because if the aliens stole their identities, why wouldn't they take their place as well," Ahmed exclaimed, nodding his head. "No one would think to look for them there."

"Exactly! Do you know where they live?"

"Some place in Chelsea. I'll find out real quick," Ahmed said, taking out his phone.

"We should start walking. I'll update Wylyy on the way," said Adar, standing.

"Okay, let's go." Ahmed headed for the front door. He paused in the living room and switched to Arabic. "I'll be back soon, honey," he told his wife before kissing her on the cheek.

***

Adar and Ahmed headed down the street towards Chelsea. It was a cool, overcast evening with a bit of drizzle falling. Adar ignored the rain droplets landing on his unblinking eyes. He had his focus locked on hurting Daloi and Dholi the way he had been hurt.

Ahmed tracked down the address to Sharon and Sheila's place, while Adar updated Wylyy using his UCD.

"They live in an apartment building at 25th Street and 10th Avenue," Ahmed said, feeling proud of himself.

"Good, let McKee know."

"Calling him now."

"I'll be right there. Don't make a move until I get there," Captain McKee said, after Ahmed updated him.

"I can't promise you that, Captain," said Ahmed. "You know how Adar can be. I suggest you hurry."

"Just do what you can," McKee barked, grabbing his coat and rushing out of the office.

Adar and Ahmed arrived outside the building where Sharon and Sheila had lived, and stood looking up at the apartment's windows. Ahmed headed for the entrance before Adar stopped him.

"Ahmed, wait here for a moment," said Adar. He switched to Euclidian. "Wylyy, tell me if they're in the building."

"Yes, they are in an apartment on the 11th floor. One of them is wearing your personal shield."

"Tell me if you see my weapons anywhere up there."

"Hold on. They're in a closet in a back room," Wylyy replied, a bit of glee in his voice. "I don't see their personal transporter anywhere."

"Good, we won't have to worry about them vanishing on us. Grab my weapons. I'll walk up to their location. I can't wait to see their faces when they find out I'm still alive," Adar said, letting out a grunt and pumping his fists into the air. "Monitor me, but don't do anything unless I say so. Let's go, Ahmed. They are on the 11th floor."

"So what's the plan?" Ahmed asked, following Adar into the building.

"You just watch my back and witness the takedown."

Adar broke in the door to the apartment with a quick, no-nonsense head butt, and Ahmed followed him inside closely with his gun drawn. Outside sirens could be heard approaching the building.

"Adar!" shouted Sharon and Sheila, standing up from the couch where they sat.

"Hello, ladies. Surprised to see me?" Sharon went for her gun, but Adar tackled her to the ground before she could get a shot off. She attempted to resist, but Adar knocked her unconscious. "That shield isn't much good against a punch to the face, is it?"

Sheila, meanwhile, began to reach for her gun, but stopped when she saw Ahmed already had a pistol trained on her.

"Please give me a reason to take you out," said Ahmed, a sneer curling his lip. "I don't appreciate you trying to kill my friend."

"I didn't try to kill him," said Sheila, shaking her head vehemently. "I just happened to be there when it happened."

"Whatever you say, lady. Just stay chill, and I won't have to ventilate your skull," Ahmed replied, his cold stare turning glacial.

Adar turned away from Sharon and trained his focus on Sheila.

"Look, Adar, you're making—"

Adar cold-cocked her, and slammed her against the wall.

"Adar, you're alive!" cried McKee, walking into the apartment.

"Yes, I am, no thanks to you," Adar groused, giving the police officer a cold stare.

"Look, I had no control over the situation back at the club. Once she started firing at the officers, they had to return fire. I hope you understand that?" McKee said, a plea for understanding in his voice.

Adar only shrugged.

"So what's going to happen to them?" McKee asked, pointing at the women Adar was holding.

"I'll take them back with me. They won't be troubling you or your planet anymore."

Adar made a call to Wylyy who transported Adar, the women and Ahmed to the attack ship.

Ahmed gave a nervous wave to the alien crew on the ship, who merely responded with toothy grins. “So tell me, Adar. What *are* you going to do with them?”

“They will probably be sold to a collector or a labor camp on some planet on the far end of our galaxy. They’ll spend the remainder of their sad lives in captivity, away from civilization. They’ll wish for death, but they won’t get it anytime soon. I’ll make sure of that,” Adar replied, happy to see the ordeal over.

“I guess I won’t be seeing you again.” Ahmed looked at Adar sadly.

“I can’t leave the planet yet. My captain wants me to stay here until he returns. I may spend some time in Syria and kill some bad guys. Who knows?” Adar said, feeling a little giddy.

“What about Aundria?” asked Ahmed, looking for any sign of compassion for his human girlfriend in the alien.

“It’s better if I stay away from her. My being around just places her in danger. Tell Toni to give Jerome a pass. If she agrees and Jerome knows I am gone, he may let her go.”

“If he doesn’t, I will seek retribution for you,” Ahmed promised, placing a hand on his gun.

“I appreciate that,” Adar said, grabbing Ahmed’s shoulder. “You are on your own for now. Just be the badass I know you can be. I gave McKee a story about the Cheoili influencing you to kill that guy at Luigi’s, so he should leave you alone.”

"Can I keep any of your alien gadgets?" Ahmed asked, a hopeful smile lighting his face.

"No, but you can keep the apartment until the end of the year. If the power goes off and all your electronics stop working, take your family and go underground for two days."

"Is there something you're not telling me?" Ahmed asked, suddenly very concerned.

"No, just take care of your family. Wylyy, transport him to my apartment," Adar shouted in Euclidian.

With that, Adar's mission on Earth ended. Or so he thought.

***

The Acela train sped down the track from New York toward D.C. The sun shone brightly on the countryside, and water scenes intermittently broke up views of the many small towns the train passed at high speed. The two men, riding in a train for the first time, marveled at the scenery, consisting of rural buildings, fields of grass and crops, and bodies of water.

"It's funny that we posed as twins so often and in the end twins saved us from being caught. You see them here, dragged off by Adar? They are not going to enjoy the rest of their lives. Take a look," said Dholi, tipping the screen of the personal transporter for Daloi to see.

"They behaved like evil bitches anyway," said Daloi. "Using their twins to do their dirty work while they hung out with Charlie. Giving them that expensive floral-smelling perfume was a nice touch Dholi."

"Looks like we got away scot-free. We had better stay disguised as men, just in case. I can't believe we stood so close to Adar in that club, and he didn't recognize us until you grabbed him. A little musk disguised our scent, then a little grip around his neck forced him to succumb to us like everyone else," Dholi said, taking off her sunglasses and smiling at Daloi.

"I love the idea of going to D.C., sister. I hear it's just as corrupt as New York, but it's all legal because they make the laws there." Daloi let out a sigh and pushed her head back on the cushioned seat in the first-class compartment of the train.

"We are going to spend the rest of our long lives in the lap of luxury, my dear." Dholi replaced her glasses and turned back to the window to enjoy the scenery.

"We certainly are, sugar." The two aliens exchanged a bro hug and laughed.

Part III

Washington D.C.

Chapter 21

Tracking down the Cheoili

At Mason's hideout, where Jerome was keeping Aundria under wraps, he walked in to find Aundria choking Mason.

"What the hell do you think you're doing?" Jerome shouted. Aundria lay on a bed with one arm wrapped tightly around Mason's neck. With her other arm still handcuffed to the bedpost, she used her muscular legs to grip his body around the waist. "Aundria, he's supposed to be letting you go. Why are you trying to kill him?"

"If he's here to release me, why did he pull down my pants and throw them to the floor?" Aundria demanded between grunts, as she continued to tighten her grip on the man in both places. "If you look at my face, you can see he's been punching on it. I think you would agree that I'm within my rights to snap his neck."

"I can't let you do that," said Jerome, reflexively reaching for his gun.

"Shoot her. Just shoot her," pleaded Mason.

"You pull out your gun, and I promise I'll rip his head off before you can pull the trigger," Aundria snarled, tightening her grip around Mason's neck again. "Give me a knife so I can cut off his manhood, and I'll let him go."

Mason flailed away, attempting to free himself from Aundria's stranglehold. He desperately gasped for air, while Jerome watched helplessly.

"Aundria, be reasonable. If you kill him, I'll have to kill you. And no, you can't cut off his penis."

"A finger, then," an unsmiling Aundria said.

"I'll grant you a toe, but that's it," Jerome said, looking to compromise with her.

"Deal!" barked Aundria, as Mason renewed his struggle to escape her clutches.

"You okay with that, Mason?" asked Jerome, taking a knife from his pocket.

Mason eyes bulged. His oxygen cut off, the bodyguard's face had begun to turn blue. It was all he could do to nod his consent.

"Aundria, take it easy," said Jerome, seeing Aundria stiffen at the sight of his knife. "I'm laying my knife on the bed. Now I'm going to take off his shoe and sock." Jerome moved slowly, his eyes never leaving the woman.

"Damn, your foot stinks, Mason. You could stand to lose a toe," Jerome muttered in disgust.

He proceeded to slice off the little toe on Mason's left foot with a clean motion of his razor sharp pig sticker.

Mason shrieked in pain, but Aundria loosened her hold, which allowed him to breathe again.

"Put it in his mouth!" she snapped.

Jerome did as Aundria demanded, stuffing the dirty appendage between Mason's thick, shiny lips. "Choke on it, you bastard!" she growled, releasing her grip and shoving Mason to the floor.

The bodyguard coughed and grabbed at his throat as his toe fell on the floor in front of him. He panted angrily and went for the gun at Jerome's waist.

"No, Mason, we're not going to kill her," said Jerome, pushing the injured man away.

"What about my toe! You can't let her get away with this." Mason whined between giant gulps of air. "You think she's just going to walk away and forget about being held here against her will? And how do you know that crazy guy is really gone?" Mason shouted angrily.

"Take your toe and go to emergency and see if they can sew it back on. Be happy I don't kill you myself. Raping a woman is despicable, you piece a shit. Get a girl or a hooker like normal people!"

"As far as my safety goes, Toni agreed to accept me on her team without harm and that crazy guy is no longer in her employ. If you're worried that she's lying, we can keep Aundria for a few more days until we verify that everything is back to normal," Jerome proposed.

Mason hobbled out of the room, cradling his little toe in his hands like a tiny baby. As he stepped into the hall, he glanced over his shoulder at Aundria, the menace in his stare letting her know they still had unfinished business.

“This is bullshit!” protested Aundria, twisting her arm back and forth in a futile attempt to loosen the handcuff holding her wrist. “I’m not interested in retaliation. I just wanted payback for that asshole attacking me. There’s no reason to keep me here.”

“It’s just for a couple more days until Mason calms down. I also want to verify that your boyfriend is indeed gone. You know, I could use someone with your talents on my team. You could keep your current job. Just keep your eyes and ears open for me, and I’ll pay you well for any information you pass on to me.” Jerome spoke softly to her as he offered to shake her hand in a sign of friendship.

“I’ll consider it. As a sign of good faith, could you remove this handcuff from my wrist? I promise I won’t try to get away,” Aundria said.

“Sure, but if you give the guards any trouble I’m going to have them kill you.”

“No trouble, I promise. So come over and free me,” Aundria cajoled, holding her arm up toward him.

“I’m not that gullible. I’ll stand over here with my hand on my gun, while an unarmed guard unlocks the cuff.” Jerome chuckled before moving to the doorway. “Roger, get in here and unlock her handcuff.”

“Thanks. I appreciate the trust.” Aundria flashed him a mischievous smile.

"Just prove you deserve it. Roger, if she causes any trouble just kill her and dispose of her body. And keep Mason out of here," Jerome said, with a frown.

"Will do, boss," said the beefy hunk who unlocked the handcuff.

Aundria sat up, striking a sexy pose on the bed and waved at Jerome as he and Roger stepped out. Once they disappeared, she rubbed her wrist, her thoughts swirling as she considered her predicament.

I can't believe Adar abandoned me. I guess alien lovers are no better than the men here on Earth. If I don't accept Jerome's offer, he'll probably kill me. If I accept it, that means betraying my friends. There are too many of them to kill, as if I want to risk being placed in a real prison.

As the reality of the dire Catch-22 facing her sank in, Aundria dropped her face into her hands and wept. *I hate my life. It's just a series of teasing moments. I get accepted to college only to drop out due to lack of money. I develop great physical abilities only to lose the sporting event because of the flu. My nice looks only attract assholes. I'm back in school, but broke again. What am I supposed do now? Maybe I should accept Jerome's offer. I could use the money. Why should I care about criminals offing each other? Ugh, I hate my life.*

Aundria threw her head back on a pillow and stared up at the ceiling. Taking deep breaths, she tried to calm down. Her captivity hadn't been that bad. Except for the attack by Mason, she mostly had been left alone. The bedroom where they held her was quite comfortable. It had its own bathroom, a large screen TV with cable access, and a microwave oven. Though it had no windows, it had plenty of light.

Being handcuffed to the bed most of the time was annoying, but other than a sore wrist, she wasn't harmed.

Aundria's thoughts veered toward the practical, before again turning gloomy. *I can't imagine what state my bills are in now. My rent, my cable, my utilities, my credit cards, and car note are all past due. And as long as I'm in here, I don't get paid. I guess my dream of starting my own athletic training business to help people keep in shape is out the window now. Here I am, screwed again! As always, no good deed goes unpunished.*

***

Aboard the bridge of the *Andrea,* a conversation between Captain Shisal and an agent of Central Control wasn't going well for Shisal.

"Captain Shisal, I got word from the Bertrilli group that the two Cheoili you sold them did not perform as advertised," said Burrtha, angrily. "They can't morph, their fingers do not contain any intoxicating enzymes, and they aren't the sexual vixens the customer expected. They just stand in a corner, holding each other and crying. Do you know how sexy crying is, Shisal?"

"Probably not very. But I had been assured that—" Shisal said, before Burrtha interrupted him.

"Before you start giving me your excuses, I need to add that they don't even speak Euclidian, or any other intelligible language. Their DNA is clearly not Cheoili. Are you inept, or are you just trying to pull a fast one? I have them right here, if you want to challenge me on any of my statements." Burrtha belched, a mean scowl distorting her face.

"I'm sure you are right on all accounts. However, Adar confirmed to me that the women are not only Cheoili, but are the ones that killed the people on Alpha," the captain said confidently, looking to reassure Burrtha.

"If you saw them, you would agree that they have trouble killing time, and couldn't possibly have killed a group of trained officers," Burrtha scoffed.

"I apologize for the inconvenience—"

"I don't want an apology!" Burrtha yelled, slapping a hand on her desk. "I want you to fix this. This is not about some horny alien who wants a refund. Those Cheoili have left a string of dead bodies across several planets. Your crack team of professionals has gotten nowhere in bringing them to justice." Burrtha shook her fist at the screen as spittle formed around her lips.

"We have killed one of them," Shisal offered.

"That's not good enough! First, you are going to send someone to come pick up these pathetic aliens. Second, you are going to refund the Bertrilli all of their money plus 10 percent. I'm canceling your current mission and transferring it to another ship. With your newfound free time, you are going to bring me those damn Cheoili. And I want real evidence this time!" Burrtha shouted, leaning into the screen.

"Burrtha, you're going too far. That is going to cost me tens of millions of credits," the captain complained.

"I don't think I'm going far enough. I think you should be jailed for fraud and aiding a fugitive. Until you hand over the real Cheoili, your ship is on lockdown."

She pointed at the screen as she continued. "If anyone steps a foot off your vessel without my permission, they'll be stepping into a jail cell right along with you."

Burrtha was feeling pressure from the governor and didn't mind passing that along to Shisal, with emphasis.

"I need to be able to send someone to Earth to find the Cheoili," Shisal reasoned.

"Fine, but keep it to a minimum. Burrtha out." The transmission ended abruptly with the screen in front of the captain going dark. Shisal looked around the bridge, but everyone trained their eyes on their workstations, afraid of drawing attention to themselves and incurring the captain's wrath.

"Krystyy! No one leaves the ship until further notice," Shisal snapped over the ship's intercom. "Cancel all leave and have the entire crew report to the ship, immediately. Then coordinate with Central Control to retrieve our two returned aliens."

"Aye, aye, Captain," Krystyy replied tersely.

Captain Shisal paced back and forth across the bridge, wondering if he should send a contingent of troops to Earth to track down the Cheoili, or replace Adar with a real tracker.

"Security Officer Adar!" Captain Shisal yelled into the ship's communicator.

“Yes, captain,” said Adar. “How can I help you?” The Ossie had a feeling this call wouldn’t bring good news.

“The two aliens you captured are not Cheoili!” shouted the captain.

“How is that possible?” Adar replied in disbelief.

“I don’t know and I don’t care. Krystyy will have them in a holding cell soon. Return to the ship and find out what you can from them, then get back to Earth and get me those Cheoili! Dead or alive, I need them returned whole!” Shisal ended the conversation and headed to the arena with Pheebee to watch a fight.

“Aye, aye Captain.” Beside himself with anger, Adar pounded his fists against a wall in a Syrian alley where he had just chopped up two fighters and let out a scream. *First the Cheoili get the jump on me on the prison planet. Now after several attempts on my life while on Earth, they escape yet again and fool me with a couple of mere Earthlings*.

My reputation is at stake here. I’m known as a ruthless assassin. It’s rare that an opponent can outwit me, but these Cheoili have slipped my grasp repeatedly.

***

Adar stepped into the holding area where he saw Sharon and Sheila, the two women he mistook for the Cheoili. They cowered on a bench, hugging each other tightly. They looked unsightly with their hair in disarray, their clothes tattered, and they smelled horrible. They also looked emaciated, as if they hadn't eaten well in weeks.

After spending some time on Earth, Adar felt empathy for them. "Hello, ladies."

"Adar, what are you doing here?" asked Sharon, clearly startled, sitting up on the edge of the bench.

"This is the alien ship I'm assigned to. The captain of this ship sent me to Earth to retrieve Daloi and Dholi, who are escaped alien fugitives."

"I knew there was something odd about them. So you're responsible for us being here. I guess you're an alien, too. Are you going to kill us now?" asked Sharon, hoping for an end to the nightmare.

"No, I'm not here to kill you, and I didn't mean to kidnap you. I mistook you for Daloi and Dholi who previously pretended to be you two. Someone told me that you had been killed. How is it you're still alive?" Adar asked, attempting to sound sympathetic.

"It was our twin sisters that they killed," said Sharon. "The two of us concocted a scam where we would feed kill orders to our sisters from Charlie and then dine in a restaurant while they perpetrated the crime. That way we always had an alibi. The police could not make use of the DNA they found on the scene because identical twins have the same DNA and the police couldn't explain how it got there when we could be seen somewhere else. They had no way to know that we had twins because we left no paper trail," Sharon explained, wiping tears from her eyes.

"Tell me about Daloi and Dholi," Adar asked, continuing his calm tone.

"Those two are some crazy bitches. They have a way of hypnotizing you and you lose all self-control. I believe they killed our sisters," stated Sharon, in an accusatory tone.

"Do you know where they might be?"

"No. They said they came from Chicago. But they didn't really interact with us much." Sharon looked at Sheila for verification, who silently nodded to her sister.

"So what happens to us now?" asked Sheila.

"You join the crew of this ship. I'll have someone get you fixed up and help you with indoctrination. You won't have to worry about being abused anymore," Adar reassured them.

"Why can't we go home?" pleaded Sheila.

"You're safer here on the ship. Your planet is likely to be harvested soon and you would probably be sold again to another collector or sent to a work camp. That is, if you survived the harvesting process. If you prefer to be sold to another collector, I can arrange that," Adar offered, giving them a chance to choose their destiny.

"No, we will accept your offer to be crewmembers. What about fresh clothes and a place to stay?" Sheila asked, pulling on her worn clothing.

"I need to leave now. I will have Dr. Valera come down and take care of you. Don't be afraid of her. She speaks some English and won't hurt you. A month from now, you will be excited about this adventure. Embrace this moment and relish the idea that you have the ability to create new lives for yourselves among the many planets across the galaxy in the Euclidian Alliance. I will come back and check on you later. For now, I need to go capture those escaped aliens."

Adar got up and left the room, leaving Sharon and Sheila alone in the holding area to reflect on all that he said.

Before they had an opportunity to discuss their future, Valera entered the room. Here stood another alien, larger and more menacing-looking than Adar. They had seen a Euclidian before, but seeing one when they were sober was not the same as seeing one when they were drugged and in shock. They remembered Adar's words and worked to be open to this new alien as a fellow crewmember.

"Hello, ladies. I'm Valera. I'm going to take good care of you," she said, smiling. "I know you're afraid, but I want you to know that you are not the only Earthlings that have joined our crew. When we decided to investigate your planet, we looked for some humans to abduct who wouldn't be missed, so we could learn more about your species. We got lucky and discovered an aircraft that had crashed into the ocean on its way from D.C. to the Bahamas during a storm. The craft held affiliated humans on their way to a junket. We saved them from certain death, and they joined our crew. I'm going to introduce you to some of them, so that you can see that being a crewmember here isn't as bad as you might think."

"Here they are," Valera said, gesturing toward the doorway. "Aruna, Janice, Ji, Jen and Karen," Valera said, pointing to each of the humans in turn.

"Hello." "Hi." And "whassup?" they said, in scattered greetings.

"I know this all seems scary," said a dark-haired woman whom Valera had identified as Karen. "But if you can get over being away from Earth, you are going to have an awesome time here. The things you can do on this ship are literally otherworldly," she confided in a friendly, gossipy manner.

Hearing these encouraging sentiments from a fellow human helped to assuage many of Sharon's and Sheila's fears.

"If you two ladies come with me, I will start your indoctrination. You will be happy to know that my assistant, Tanya, is from Seattle," the doctor said, smiling.

***

"Ahmed, what's new?" said Adar, walking into Toni's club in Greenwich Village. Ahmed sat at the bar, enjoying a Hendricks and tonic, while he kept one eye on Toni, who sang on stage, and the other on the crowd to ensure that no one posed a threat to the club's lively atmosphere.

"Adar, I thought I'd never see you again," exclaimed Ahmed, giving the alien a big hug.

"Enough with the hugs. You know I'm not a touchy-feely kind of guy unless I'm beating someone up," Adar protested, backing out of the embrace.

“I heard that. So what brings you back to New York? I thought you finished your business here.”

“So did I. Those Cheoili escapees pulled a fast one on me. They set up Sharon and Sheila so I would think it was them, and now they have disappeared. They’re still somewhere on this planet. Have you heard anything about Daloi or Dholi since I left?”

“No, nothing. At this point, I’d say they are probably either dead or have left town. If they had stayed around here, I would know about it,” Ahmed said, throwing his hands up.

“Where would they go? They came here from Chicago. What would be the next best choice for them?”

“I don’t know. I would guess Philly, Boston, D.C., or maybe Baltimore.”

“Put the word out. I want to know where they are. I’ll give $10,000 for any information on their whereabouts. This needs to be discreet, and I don’t want them touched,” Adar said, pointing his finger at Ahmed.

“I’ll put some feelers out and let you know what I find.”

“I’m going to check every major train and bus station from Boston to D.C. for their DNA,” Adar said, with a sense of urgency.

“What about Aundria?” Ahmed asked, wondering why he hadn’t mentioned her.

“I don’t have time for her. Focus on finding the Cheoili. They may have taken any number of forms.”

Adar appeared callous, especially toward Aundria. He allowed his anger to surface partly because of his failure to capture the Cheoili and partly to mask his feelings for Aundria. She meant more to him than he let on. But he knew that being close to people meant risking their lives. Even his relationship with Ahmed worried him.

Adar forced a quick wave to Toni as she finished up her set, and headed outside into the cool Manhattan air. He first headed to Penn Station where he examined every inch of the space and found no traces of Cheoili DNA.

From New York, Adar traveled to Newark, Philadelphia, Baltimore, and D.C. At each location, he found a trace of their DNA, but nothing conclusive. He checked Boston and found nothing. After returning to New York, he checked in with Ahmed.

***

"Hello, Adar," said Ahmed, answering the door to the alien at his apartment. "You don't look too happy. I hope you don't mind that we took over your bedroom."

"No, I expected you to do so. Any word from your sources?" asked Adar, taking a seat on the couch next to Ahmed.

"No, nothing. It's still early, though. It hasn't been 24 hours yet," Ahmed replied, hoping for more time to get an answer.

"Mr. Adar," said Ahmed's wife, breaking into their conversation, "I never got a chance to thank you for saving me and my children from certain death. I don't know how you did it, but I am so thankful." Adar only grunted and looked away.

"Honey, you're wasting your time," Ahmed told his wife in Arabic. "He does what he does and doesn't like being thanked." She nodded and went back to the bedroom and closed the door.

"Adar, it wouldn't hurt you to be pleasant on occasion," Ahmed said, stretching the corners of his mouth tight in irritation.

"I'll tell you what," said Adar. "You find Daloi and Dholi for me, and I'll give your wife a hug and a big 'you're welcome'. How about that?"

"I get the hint. I'll make some more calls." Ahmed sighed, reaching for his phone and pinging more people for clues.

"I'm going to eat a huge raw steak and then I'm going to take a nap in the coat closet. When I wake up I want to kill some people. Can you set that up for me?"

"Of course. I'll take care of it." Ahmed watched Adar walk into the kitchen and grab a steak from the refrigerator.

Ahmed studied his alien friend. *How can he be so emotionless and at the same time be so protective? Time and time again he risks his life to save others. I need to make sure he has a good time tonight, and help him find those escapees.*

Ahmed picked up his phone and dialed Toni. When she answered on the third ring, he spoke into the mouthpiece, "Ahmed here. Adar is back in town for a while and wants some action. Do you have anything for us?"

"About time. Let's not do this on the phone. Bring him by the club around 9:30. I'll have something for him," Toni replied, ending the call.

Ahmed made a few more phone calls, then left the apartment to follow up on a tip.

***

At a hotel in Washington, D.C. a senator was looking to make a deal that would help with his re-election.

"Sen. Rivera, that is going to be nearly impossible to deliver on," said Director Langston Lewis, attempting to steer the senator toward a more reasonable request. "They are very wealthy women and quite famous. They like their privacy. Getting them to be your private playthings is unlikely. You'd be better off trying to get the First Lady to do it."

Lewis ran the JW Marriott Hotel across from the White House. He had experience dealing with powerful people and catering to their whims, and he surprised himself at times with the desires he had been able to fulfill. He'd also learned over the years when to say no.

Lewis had achieved too much to end up in jail or the morgue. In this particular case, he felt compelled to accept the challenge.

Rivera sat across the desk from Lewis, wearing his blue pinstripe suit with the congressional pin on his lapel. The hotel director wore an even nicer blue suit. His office was appointed with fine art and gifts from foreign dignitaries who were happy to show their appreciation for Langston's assistance and discretion.

"Langston, my benefactor has promised to place his company's new automotive plant in my state and support my re-election bid. I've got progressives crawling up my ass, and I need this favor to squash them, but good. The performers will get $5 million cash when they show up to spend two hours entertaining him in the nude. No singing, no bumping and grinding, just tasteful conversation. He promises that the idea of sex won't even be brought up. It's against his religion, you know."

"Of course, but nudity is okay? And do I get my standard 10 percent finder's fee?" Langston asked, raising his eyebrows at the senator.

"No, you'll get 2 percent, and I'm sure you'll be happy to get it," the senator challenged, knowing it was still a good deal.

"I'll see what I can do, but no promises," Lewis replied, standing up and walking to the other side of his desk.

"They're already in town for their concert this weekend. How hard can it be?" The senator was a formerly good man who had been corrupted by the system. Being a senator meant promising to campaign for money. Not just for himself, but for others in his party. If you asked enough people for money, eventually you started owing favors. He didn't want to become that person, but the system sucked him in. Now he faced the largest possible contribution of his career, and that meant giving his all to secure it.

"Langston, if you can't pull this off for me, I may have to take my business elsewhere," the senator threatened with a smile. He stood to meet the director's gaze.

"Sen. Rivera, you can count on me to make this happen. I would hate to see you go to a competitor." Langston held out his hand, while urging the senator toward the door with another hand under his elbow.

"I believe you, Langston. Get back to me as soon as you can. I'd like to have some good news when I meet with my benefactor tonight," the senator said, dismissing the hotel manager with a nod and walking away.

Rivera, who served on several powerful subcommittees on Capitol Hill, trusted Lewis, but he didn't like to place all his faith in one person with so much at stake.

Thus, he decided to contact a few other people to hedge his bets. Those contacts made inquiries, which soon reached the ears of Daloi and Dholi. The aliens had settled in a comfortable spot on a quiet street in the Woodley Park neighborhood of D.C.

***

"This man must be nuts," Pers Olsen told Daloi and Dholi who sat on a couch in his den, enjoying a toke in front of the fireplace. "He wants Rihanna and Beyoncé to be the special guests of some hotshot for the evening." Olsen laughed as he coughed out some smoke.

"Why is that so strange?" asked Daloi.

"Because the guy wants them to be naked the whole time. I've been able to pull together some exotic trysts for the ambassador, but this guy is off his rocker. Even for $5 million he will have a hard time getting them to agree to do something so vulgar."

Olsen had been assigned the position of personal bodyguard for the Danish ambassador to the United States. Except for the time that a Danish newspaper published an image of Mohammed, Danes had not made anyone's hit list. As a result, Olsen's job was easy and gave him plenty of free time to get into trouble, while the diplomatic immunity that he wore like a personal shield protected him.

"Call the man back and tell him you can do the deal," replied Daloi, who lit up like a Christmas tree at the thought of getting her hands on all that cash.

"You can't be serious. How am I supposed to make that happen?" asked Pers, looking at Daloi in confusion.

"Let us worry about that." Daloi smiled as Dholi gave her a knowing glance. Dholi knew her sister well and just how she planned to pull off the stunt.

"That's not good enough. I need confirmation before I can commit to something so outlandish."

"Okay, give us until tomorrow afternoon to set this up," Daloi said reassuringly, while rubbing his thigh.

Daloi and Dholi retired to the room they shared in Olsen's house and hatched their plan. Impersonating Rihanna and Beyoncé would not be an easy task. They would be taking the place of two very famous entertainers, who have looks, mannerisms, and ways of speaking that are very well known to their fans. They also would have to answer the odd question about the entertainers' pasts.

***

Later that evening, Adar and Ahmed left the NYC apartment and headed over to Toni's place.

"Hello, Toni." Adar hailed the club owner as he strolled into the Blue Note with Ahmed. "I hear you have some work for me."

Toni concluded her conversation with the bartender and strolled over to the pair.

"Great to see you back on the block," said Toni, extending her slim, manicured fingers. "I'd give you a hug, but I'm afraid you'd kill me." She laughed, only half joking.

"Toni, I'm not that bad. I'm just focused," Adar said, trying to sound less threatening. "I have a lot on my mind these days. A good assignment could help me relieve some stress, though."

"I think I have something that will make us both happy," Toni caroled, a sly smile painting her lips. "Since you left, I've been holed up here avoiding assassination attempts from Mason, one of Jerome's lieutenants. Jerome called me for a truce, but Mason didn't go for it. Jerome still has Aundria, but as far as I know, he hasn't hurt her. I need you to take out Mason and his crew. I suspect Jerome will come around if Mason is out of the way. You have my permission to give any of them who want to join me instead a free pass. Just send them my way," Toni said, lighting a cigarette.

"I will happily take care of that for you." Keen anticipation lit Adar's strange features.

"Feel free to launch a rescue attempt of Aundria, once you're done."

"That won't be my priority," Adar said, feigning disinterest. Adar fought against his feelings for Aundria, fearing she was distracting him from his mission. Still, staying involved with the mob gave him a greater chance of finding the Cheoili.

"Fine, suit yourself," Toni replied, lifting an eyebrow at the alien's apparent coldness.

Ahmed spoke up. "Toni, I've got a proposal for you, if you're interested. The GFE Crew wants to join your team. Their pimp has been slapping them around and taking all their money. They like the way you run your operation and want to know if you would give them a good deal." Ahmed rubbed his hands together.

"Oh, I'm definitely interested. We can house them here once I move back to Harry's old place," said Toni. "Way to take initiative, Ahmed! You'll do well here." Toni praised her new lieutenant, while tapping ashes from a cigarette into an ashtray.

"Adar, let's go take care of Mason and the pimp. Once we are done, I may have some news for you about the twins." The corners of Ahmed's mouth lifted in a smirk.

"Okay, now you're getting me excited. Let's go."

***

"Pers, this is Daloi. We're at the Verizon Center. I need you to come here, to entrance 12B, as soon as you can. The guard will have your name on the access list. Ask him for directions to Beyoncé's rehearsal area."

"I'll be right there," Pers replied, quietly throwing a fist in the air.

***

Olsen approached the stage where Beyoncé could be heard rehearsing and stood next to Daloi just as she finished a set:

Say my name, say my name
You actin' kinda shady
Ain't callin' me baby
Baby say my name

"Okay, guys, let's take five," said Beyoncé, noticing Olsen's arrival. "Daloi, is this your contact?"

"Yes, this is Pers Olsen."

"Okay, let's go to my dressing room and talk over your deal," said Beyoncé without acknowledging Olsen.

Unbeknownst to the bodyguard, Daloi and Dholi had used their powers of persuasion to convince Beyoncé to meet with Olsen.

"Everyone have a seat and let's quickly go over this so I can get back on stage," said the superstar.

"You don't mind if I sit next to you and hold your hand, do you?" asked Dholi, taking Beyoncé's hand into hers. "I just love your nails."

"Go ahead, knock yourself out. I spoke with Rihanna earlier and she is down with participating in this little soiree of yours, but it's going to cost you $5 million for each of us, payable in cash when we show up. No press, no recordings, no guests, and no mention of this ever happening. No exceptions," Beyoncé stated, a no-nonsense, focused expression on her face.

"There will be two men involved in the event," said Olsen. "I suppose they will have at least one servant there."

"No servants! You need to work out the logistics before we get there," Beyoncé insisted.

"We'll make it work. Lewis, the director of the JW Marriott, will escort you to the private suite on the top floor of the hotel. That end of the hall, around the suite, will be completely blocked off."

"Good. I'll be bringing a security guard along as well."

"Is it okay if Olsen acts as your security guard?" asked Dholi. "He runs security for the Danish Embassy and can ensure discretion."

"That works for me," said Beyoncé. "See you tomorrow. And one more thing. We'll be wearing G-strings. They don't get to stare at or touch our coochies."

"Understood," said Olsen, walking out.

***

Adar and Ahmed waited until dark before making the sixteen-block trek to Mason's place to take care of business.

"I'll sneak up and take care of the guards at the door and in the entryway," said Adar. "You watch my back."

"I got you covered, Adar," said Ahmed, screwing a silencer onto the nose of his 9mm Beretta.

Adar eyed the weapon with curiosity. "What's that for?"

"You don't want Mason to hear us coming, do you?" replied Ahmed, slamming a fresh magazine into the gun.

"Doesn't matter to me. Either way he is going to die tonight."

Adar approached the entrance to Mason's building, a plush high-rise complete with a doorman at the front entrance. Using his spear, he chopped his way through the guards, while the doorman hid on the floor behind the reception desk.

Ahmed quickly shot other guards as they jumped out of their vehicles to join the fray.

Nodding at Ahmed, Adar moved into the building, fighting his way to the elevator with Ahmed at his back, a trail of dead bodies in their wake. He pushed the button for the penthouse. Ahmed endured agonizing moments until the elevator doors opened.

"Since I've got my personal shield on, I'll go out first," said Adar.

"I'll be right behind you, buddy," said Ahmed, bravely concealing the trepidation that he felt.

The doors opened and Adar ran into the corridor amid a hail of gunfire. He proceeded to slice his way through the gunmen, directing the barrage of bullets his way, while Ahmed, crouching low, shot his way out of the elevator in an attempt to keep up with Adar. Once they cleared the hallway, the duo rounded the corner and began to clear the floor, room by room.

Adar sprinted down a hallway to the left, while Ahmed went right. Ahmed ducked into one office where he shot two of Mason's men, but not before one of them drilled him with a .38

slug to the chest. As Ahmed lay bleeding to death, a door at the rear of the office opened to reveal the distorted face of Mason cowering behind one of his guards.

"Ahmed, you little traitor," growled Mason. "You picked that bitch and that psychotic midget over me! I thought we had a deal. How did you think your betrayal would play out?"

"I'm thinking, with you dead," Ahmed retorted. "You smell that aroma of cinnamon in the air?"

"What's that supposed to mean? You want to bake me cookies?" Mason laughed.

With a *whack* and a *thud,* Mason's guard's head fell to the floor and rolled past him as Adar came into view.

"Oh shit," cried Mason.

"Oh shit is right," said Ahmed, panting as he tried to keep pressure on his wound. "My boy is about to slice you into some little cookies."

"I'm unarmed!" Mason shouted at Adar, dropping his gun to the floor. "And remember, I still have your woman."

"You think I care about that?" Adar grabbed Mason by the back of his shirt and flung him to the far side of the office. "Are you going to be okay, Ahmed?"

"I'm not sure. Do what you need to do," the injured man replied, grimacing in pain.

"Look," pleaded Mason, "I got money, I got connections. I'll give you anything you want. Just don't kill me."

"All I want from you is your head," said Adar, before proceeding to separate Mason's head from his body with surgical precision.

"You could have asked him where Aundria is being held before you killed him," Ahmed remarked.

"Oh, yeah. You know where Jerome lives, right?" Adar asked.

"Some house on Long Island, but he hasn't been there since they kidnapped Aundria," Ahmed gasped, clearly fading.

"That is not a problem. Let's get you fixed up and pay the house a visit."

Adar sent Ahmed to the attack ship, knowing Valera would attend his wounds. Adar, meanwhile, took some thin cable and strung it through the heads of the men he and Ahmed had killed and transported his creation back to the ship. Next, he checked on Ahmed.

"Are you better?" asked Adar, rubbing his friend on the chest.

"Yes, but I'm never going to get used to these strange aliens you hang out with. They tried to shove a probe up my ass," Ahmed said, grabbing the back of his pants.

"What did you expect? You humans are always accusing us of wanting to do it."

"What do you want to do next?" Ahmed interjected.

"We need to drop my present off at Jerome's house," said Adar, showing Ahmed his string of skulls. "Do you know where he lives?"

"That is just disgusting." Ahmed turned away to keep from becoming nauseated. "He has a house somewhere on Long Island. I'll get his address from Toni. Then we can go out there."

Adar addressed the attack ship's transporter tech in Euclidian. "Rookeley, transport us to some secluded spot on Long Island."

The tech engaged the transporter and sent Adar and Ahmed to a wooded area on Long Island where Ahmed phoned Toni to get Mason's address. Wylyy transported them to outside of the house and Adar placed his odd piece of artwork between two trees on the front lawn, along with a sign that read, "Release my woman, or your family is next."

"Now what?" asked an exhilarated Adar as they strolled away.

"Can Wylyy take us back to the city?" Ahmed asked. "I want him to drop us off on the Upper East Side."

"Sure, let me ping him."

In a few moments the duo found themselves walking through a little known part of the Upper East Side.

"The pimp's place is right there on the corner," said Ahmed. "The front door is always open. It's normally just the pimp and two bodyguards in the place."

"Good. Let's go in and extricate the annoyance," Adar said, pounding his fists together.

When the duo entered the bordello, they saw that it had been decorated with Persian rugs, comfy leather furniture and gaudy light fixtures. The pimp, in the middle of a pep talk with his women, looked annoyed at the interruption.

"What the hell do you two want?" he shouted at the two intruders.

"You have a piece of lint on your coat," said Adar. "Let me get that for you." The alien pulled out his short sword and sliced the pimp in half.

Adar looked at the two guards angrily. "You can join Toni's team or join your pimp, your choice." Slowly, he stalked toward the two men, blood still dripping from the tip of his spear.

"We'd be happy to join Toni's team. We endured unspeakable horrors working for that asshole," one of the guards said, holding his hands up to surrender.

"Great. Drag his body parts out back and go report to Toni. Ahmed, let her know they're coming," said Adar, wiping the spear on the pimp's pants.

Ahmed made the call and then turned to address the women. "Ladies, you now work for Toni. She's going to take lots better care of you than that asshole."

"Thanks a lot," said a slender woman in a blue nightie, walking up and kissing Ahmed on the cheek. "Would you like to stay for a while, so we can express our gratitude?" she asked, her smile inviting as she licked her lips.

"Unfortunately, we have some other things to take care of, ladies. Maybe next time. Adar, let's move," Ahmed urged. "I think you want to hear the news I have for you."

***

Adar and Ahmed left the bordello, satisfied with what they had accomplished. The evening air cooled the perspiration on their skin from the altercation inside. Adar felt relaxed and ready to focus on finding the Cheoili.

"You did a good thing for me tonight, Ahmed," Adar said, patting the Syrian immigrant on the back.

Ahmed returned the alien's smile. "Trust me, the good news is yet to come."

Chapter 22

End Game

Adar and Ahmed continued their walk south through Manhattan, quietly taking in the sights on the way back to the apartment. Adar enjoyed basking in the glow of the evening's events, but he anxiously wanted to hear Ahmed's news.

"So what's the news you have for me?" Adar prodded.

"While we were finishing up back there, I got a text about the twins," Ahmed replied, light dancing in his dark eyes.

"What do you mean?" said Adar, pausing on the sidewalk.

"One of my contacts in D.C. told me about an incident he witnessed while he sat in his car waiting for a client in the garage of some fancy hotel, which was hosting a diplomatic event. This famous actor comes out of the elevator with two gorgeous women. Some groupie attacks the actor and one of the women pulled out some kind of weapon that she used to disintegrate the groupie. My contact saw the whole thing while sitting in his SUV waiting for the ambassador he was escorting to return. He freaked out, but never told anyone."

Ahmed marveled at the change that came over Adar as he reported the possible sighting. The alien stiffened, becoming hyper-alert as his nostrils flared and his stare intensified.

“That has to be them,” Adar said, punching his hand into his fist.

“I agree. I figure we can catch the train in the morning and check out the story then,” Ahmed suggested.

“No, we’re leaving now. Do you know where to find them?” Adar asked, his impatience evident.

“I believe so. The text I received was the actor’s name, Mads Mikkelsen. He played in that first Bond movie with Daniel Craig,” Ahmed said, forgetting that Adar was not educated in Earth’s popular culture.

“Why is that important?”

“Call Wylyy up and let’s get going. I’ll tell you on the way.” Ahmed felt that he was finally carrying his own weight in the relationship and was eager to help Adar connect the dots.

***

Based on the tip and Ahmed’s analysis, the duo investigated the Danish ambassador’s home and office. While they didn’t find the twins, they did find traces of their DNA.

“Ahmed, I need to find those two aliens,” Adar said, becoming more and more anxious as the night wore on.

“Let me call my contact again to see if he knows anything else,” suggested Ahmed.

After a brief call, Ahmed reported to Adar. “My contact says he’s seen the twins, but he doesn’t know where they live. He’s going to ask around and call me in the morning.”

"Why are we always one step away?" Adar groaned. "Let's stay aboard the attack ship until morning. I don't want to risk being seen and scaring off the twins."

"Sure, we can do that," replied Ahmed, not truly comfortable with the plan.

***

The next evening, in a suite at the JW Marriott, Sen. Rivera stared out a window while his two business partners sat on a couch in the presidential suite, waiting impatiently for the guests of honor. A brief knock at the door and Daloi and Dholi, in the guise of Beyoncé and Rihanna, entered the suite, escorted by the hotel director and Pers Olsen.

The duo looked around at an elaborate spread of food, drugs, flowers, and wine, including a magnum of champagne chilling in a bowl of ice. Prince's *Raspberry Beret* played softly over the stereo.

Watching from the far end of the suite, Byron Owens, CEO of American Car Group, and Kim Mon Pote, CEO of Korean Motors, stood like the gentlemen they were raised to be. Beyoncé and Rihanna waved at the beaming Rivera and two men from the doorway. The imposters wisely decided not to approach the men until the initial business had been concluded.

The two men awkwardly waved back at the women before returning to their seats on the couch, excitement and delight animating their florid faces. Owens wasn't so much interested in spending $5 million to see naked women, even famous naked women. However, doing a deal to build a new automotive plant in the United States that he would get to run really revved his engine.

Kim was a different story. Growing up an impoverished kid on a small farm in central South Korea, he started from nothing. His parents moved to Seoul and sent him to school to become an engineer. This set him on the path to becoming an international corporate mogul. An avid fan of American urban music, Kim idolized certain musicians, including his favorite entertainers, Beyoncé and Rihanna.

Now, having them as his guests for the evening was a dream come true. He saw having them naked as an unexpected but welcome bonus, even if they insisted on wearing G-strings.

"Hello, Beyoncé and Rihanna. I'm Sen. Rivera. I helped to set up this event. Here are two bags with $5 million each," the senator said, holding the bags up for the women.

"Hello, senator. Once the money is counted and safely stored away we'll greet your guests properly, as promised," said Daloi, impersonating Beyoncé, ignoring the bags. "Pers, would you do the honors?" she requested, pointing to the bags.

"Certainly, Beyoncé," Olsen replied, stepping forward to count the money.

"Senator, it's nice to meet you, but you're going to have to leave. Our deal involves the two gentlemen on the couch, not you," Beyoncé said, smiling politely.

"Not a problem. I wouldn't dare to intrude. Since I did set this whole thing up, what are the chances of getting a political endorsement from you two for my campaign?" the ever-opportunistic Rivera asked, brushing his tie down.

"Never going to happen," said Beyoncé firmly, offering him her trademark smile.

"Not in a million years," echoed Rihanna, raising her eyebrows and turning away.

"Understood. Director Lewis, I'll wait for you in your office," the senator said as he left the room.

***

Hanging up the phone, Ahmed shouted an exciting "Yes!"

"Tell me you have good news," Adar insisted.

"A set of twins is hanging out with the Danish security guy, which makes sense. He doesn't know where the guy lives, but he will be visiting the JW Marriott this evening to do some security work for the director. I figure we could follow him after he gets there and see what we find."

"Sounds like a longshot, but I'll take what I can get," said Adar, attempting to sound hopeful.

***

Olsen finished the count and took the bags down to the hotel's front entrance where two armored vehicles waited for Beyoncé and Rihanna. Accepting the bags from Olsen, the drivers called the entertainers to say they had taken custody of the cash. The phone call cued Beyoncé and Rihanna to engage their guests.

"Okay, fellas, looks like we've got ourselves a party," said Beyoncé, walking toward the couch. "Should we start with a bit of 'lemonade'?"

"I would love to see the style of lingerie you're hiding under your sexy clothes," said Owens. Kim only laughed shyly.

"Hold on to your britches, gentlemen," said Rihanna. "No stripping until our guard gets back and the director leaves."

"Could you come a little closer so I can at least smell your sexy bodies?" asked Kim, rubbing his hands together in anticipation.

Beyoncé grabbed Rihanna's arm and started sniffing the air. "Something's not right," said Beyoncé, putting her hand in her purse.

"What's wrong? You're scaring me," said Rihanna, or Dholi in disguise as she scanned the room nervously.

"The Ossie's here," said Beyoncé, pulling a blaster from her purse. Rhianna followed suit, taking a defensive stance.

"Drop your weapons, ladies. We know who you are," said Ahmed, entering the suite from a door in the back, holding a pistol.

"Just shoot!" yelled Beyoncé. The two began shooting at Ahmed and then fired shots randomly around the room, hoping to hit Adar. They missed Ahmed, but killed Owens and the director, who had frozen with shock once the gunfire erupted.

Adar materialized and walked out from behind a decorative table covered in flowers.

"What's going on here?" demanded Kim, lunging for the floor.

Adar got a shot off, stunning Dholi, who used her body to block Daloi from getting hit. Daloi fired at Adar, but missed him and disintegrated the flowers behind him. Daloi ran out of the front door and down the hall.

"Thanks for your help," Adar said sarcastically to Ahmed, who was peeking around the corner at him.

"I thought you had everything under control," said Ahmed, re-entering the room.

"Tie this one up while I grab the other one. Don't let her touch you," Adar warned, running out of the room.

Adar ran out the door and down the hall after Daloi, who minutes earlier had scrambled down the stairs and disappeared onto another floor.

Ahmed used the pair of handcuffs he brought with him to restrain Dholi's hands and grabbed a cord from one of the room's curtains to bind her legs and tied it to the handcuffs at her back. He grabbed her bag and ran out the door to find Adar.

Adar followed Daloi's scent out the front door of the hotel and down the street toward the White House.

"Mom, look, it's Beyoncé," said a little girl, pointing at Daloi as she ran by.

"Wow, she must be making another music video," replied the mother. "Probably a sequel to *Lemonade*."

Daloi easily cleared the White House fence and ran across the lawn. Two secret service agents ran after her, while speaking rapidly into handheld radios. Adar cloaked, jumped the fence, and joined the chase. Overtaking the two agents, he shoved them to the ground to prevent them from shooting Daloi and causing another incident he would have to explain.

Daloi cleared the other side of the White House lawn, hopped the fence and crossed the street, hiding behind the Red Cross building. She knew that at any moment Adar would come running around the corner, giving her the opportunity to finally kill him.

Anticipating an ambush, Adar ran to the back of the building from the opposite direction. He stealthily advanced on Daloi and when he drew close, he took a swing at her head. She saw his shadow and ducked, suffering only a graze to her temple.

Adar followed through with his other fist, knocking her blaster from her hand to the ground. Daloi countered by kicking Adar into the dumpster by the building. While the Ossie tried to shake off the blow, Daloi grabbed him by the throat, spun him around and slammed him into the wall.

"Don't fight it, you little bastard," she growled in Euclidian, digging her fingernail into him below his right eye, then punched him in the face. "I'm going to carve you up and watch you bleed out slowly, until there's no more life left in you."

She then threw his UCD, spear, and blaster into the dumpster before returning to slice his abdomen with her sharp fingernails and punch his face with her fists.

"That's it, watch your toys go into the trash, Ossie," Daloi mocked him. "The last thing you'll see is me ripping your insides out and then throwing your corpse into that dumpster with the other trash," she boasted, squeezing his face. "I'm going to make you pay for killing my brother."

Moments later, two loud gunshots interrupted Daloi's tirade and the Cheoili fugitive fell to the pavement.

"I don't know what she said, but it didn't sound good," Ahmed said, gulping air by the lungful to catch his breath after running down the hotel stairs and across the street in search of his alien partner. "You know you're not supposed to let them touch you, right?" Ahmed said, his gaze moving to Adar and then back to Daloi.

Adar eyed Ahmed from where he had fallen when Daloi's fingers released him, looking annoyed. Badly injured, he could barely speak. "I wanted to keep her alive," he rasped.

"Hey, I wasn't about to take her on in hand-to-hand combat," Ahmed retorted. "And look, she's still breathing. More importantly, how do I fix you up?"

When Adar pointed at the dumpster, Ahmed asked, "You want something to eat?"

"My device," the alien whispered.

"Okay, let me look for it," sighed Ahmed, eyeing the dumpster with distaste before he climbed inside to retrieve Adar's belongings. Climbing out a few minutes later, he found himself surrounded by policemen.

"Drop whatever you're carrying and get on your knees," said one cop.

"No problem, officer. Please don't shoot me. Adar, it's your mother," said Ahmed, sliding the UCD to the alien.

"Wylyy!" shouted Adar, tapping on his device.

"His mother is named Wylyy?" the cop asked skeptically. "Nobody move and stop talking on that phone."

"We're not going anywhere. He just wants to let his mother know he's not doing well."

"He can tell her later, if he lives," said the officer, snatching the device from Adar.

Suddenly, Wylyy materialized, stunning everyone witnessing the scene. Wylyy's crew locked onto Ahmed, Daloi, and Adar and transferred the three to the ship along with Adar's gear. Onboard, the crew stabilized Adar, who immediately inquired about Dholi.

"She's gone," replied Wylyy, who scanned for Dholi in the hotel suite.

"I'll change into an Earth costume and go down with your friend to search for her," Wylyy told Adar in Euclidian. He motioned toward Ahmed, pointing upward with one finger. Ahmed nodded and braced himself. He knew what would come next.

***

Dholi regained consciousness, lying face down on the floor of the suite, still impersonating Rihanna. She looked around the room and decided on a plan. "Excuse me, sir, could you roll me over? My belt is pushing into my belly," Dholi said, pouting.

“What the hell happened here?” asked Kim, still cowering on the floor in front of the couch. He crawled over to Dholi’s side.

“Just a couple of guys trying to steal your money,” replied Dholi innocently.

“Okay, I’ll roll you on your side, but I can’t let you go. Why did they tie you up like this?” asked Kim, surprised that they would leave her tied on the floor the way they did.

“As you noticed, those aren’t policemen. They’re probably going to kidnap me once they get your money. Thanks for rolling me over. That feels much better. Could you rub my hands? They’re feeling a bit numb. That’s it. Now hold them tight. Doesn’t that feel good?” Dholi smiled, knowing she had him.

“Yes, it does,” Kim said, enjoying the feeling of Dholi’s hands.

“Good, now untie me,” Dholi ordered.

“Right away, Rihanna,” Kim said, fumbling with the cord around her ankles.

“Thank you,” said Dholi, stretching her legs. “I can’t believe they did that to me. Now go back to the couch, pull down your pants, and sit quietly until I get back.”

Dholi slipped her cuffed hands under her feet to position them in front of her, then headed for the door.

“What happened to you?” asked Pers, walking into the suite.

“Pers, I’m so glad to see you. Some crazy guy got the jump on us,” said Dholi, holding Pers’ face.

"What is Mr. Kim doing?" Pers asked, looking over at Kim with his pants down.

"He's just waiting patiently for the police to arrive. Do you have a handcuff key?" Dholi asked, with a needy voice.

"Yes, I do," Pers replied, feeling his pockets for a key.

"Would you be a sweetie and unlock these for me?" Dholi asked, holding her wrists up to him.

"Of course, just a minute. There you go." Pers unlocked the handcuffs and removed them from Dholi's wrists.

"Thank you, that feels much better," said Dholi, rubbing her wrists. "Give me your gun."

"Here you go." Pers handed her his gun.

"Thanks. Now go join Mr. Kim, and sit quietly on the couch with your pants down. I'm going to go save my sister." Dholi ran down the hallway away from the suite, took the elevator to the ground floor, and headed for her car to retrieve her personal transporter. She used the device to try to find her sister.

Ahmed and Wylyy were transported to the alcove at the side entrance to the hotel.

"I'll search inside while you check for her in the car," said Ahmed. Wylyy gave Ahmed a confused look. Ahmed used steering and pointing gestures to help Wylyy understand what he meant, then ran into the hotel lobby while Wylyy went to investigate the cars.

Dholi spotted Wylyy coming and ordered the driver to speed away. Wylyy noticed the car departing and blew out the front tires. Dholi ran from the vehicle, firing at Wylyy with her gun. His shield protected him from her bullets. As she dodged around the corner of the hotel, she collided with Ahmed's fist, which knocked her unconscious.

The Euclidian pilot returned to his ship with Dholi and Ahmed. Restraining Dholi, he seated her next to Daloi and went to check on Adar.

"Adar, are you doing okay?" Wylyy asked in Euclidian.

"Yes, I'm fine. I'm just tired of getting banged up by those damn Cheoili."

"We got them!" Ahmed blurted, interrupting Wylyy. Adar merely smiled at Ahmed.

"What should I do with those two?" Wylyy asked, pointing at Daloi and Dholi who huddled together on the floor of his ship.

"Send them directly to Valera to verify their identity. I don't want any more surprises. And have her update the captain with the results," requested Adar, still struggling to recover from his altercation with Daloi.

"Of course," said Wylyy. "I'll let you know what happens. Ask your friend if he would like an anal probe before he leaves." Wylyy looked at Ahmed and poked his finger in his fist.

"What's he talking about?" asked Ahmed. "There ain't going to be no anal probing going on up in here."

"He just said goodbye and good luck." Adar laughed, sitting up in the cot where he was recovering.

"Sure he did. Where to now?"

"How about the Whiskey Tavern?" Adar suggested, wanting to celebrate his success.

"You want to see if she's there, don't you?" Ahmed asked slyly.

"If she's not, I'm going to need to find more people to kill," Adar replied, his face alight with a feral grin.

***

Adar and Ahmed walked into the Whiskey Tavern and found Aundria sitting at the bar like a patron, having a drink. Jerome had taken Adar's message to heart and thought it more prudent to let Aundria go than risk having his entire family killed. With Mason dead, he had no reason to hide. The deal with Toni was still intact, and he counted on it to keep Adar from killing him.

When she heard the sounds of more people entering the tavern, Aundria tilted her head back to see the door. Catching sight of Adar, she swiveled around on her barstool.

"ADAR, I can't believe you have the nerve to show up here," Aundria said, feigning anger. She hopped off the stool and walked over to face him.

"You're on your own, buddy. I want none of this." Ahmed slipped away and grabbed a seat at the far end of the bar.

"Greetings, Aundria. I missed you," Adar said timidly. "I would have come sooner, but I had a job to finish."

"So you left me to rot in a basement with those jerks. You had time to chop off a dozen heads, but no time to come find me."

Adar stood facing her, speechless.

"Yeah, I heard about your handiwork." She gripped her waist with both hands. "With all your technology, you could've found me like that!" Aundria snapped the fingers of her right hand for emphasis before returning it to her side in her defiant stance, and lifted her chin to challenge Adar with a killer stare.

"Look–" Adar tried to explain.

"No, you look." Aundria cut the alien off, slapping him hard across the face. "I'm not some slut for you to have fun with in your free time."

She paused in mid-tirade as she noticed the impassive expression on Adar's face. "You didn't even feel that, did you?" Aundria asked in amazement.

"You're free because of me. And I came back for you," Adar said, still trying unsuccessfully to explain. He looked her up and down, wondering again if he could take her with him.

"So how long before you're gone again?"

"Hold on. I need to take this call," said Adar, holding up a hand in front of Aundria while answering his UCD in Euclidian. "I appreciate that, captain. It's good to hear that you regained control of the mission, but I can't go with you. I need to stay here for a while. Yes. Goodbye."

"I can't believe you just dissed me so you could take an intergalactic phone call. Are you talking to your other woman, possibly your wife back home?" Aundria asked, raising her voice.

"No, no to both of those. I had to let my captain know my plans. The ship is preparing to embark on a mission, and I let him know I'm going to stay here with you, as long as you like," Adar said softly, hoping to calm her down. "If I have to leave in the future, I'll take you with me. In the meantime, Ahmed is moving back to his apartment, which makes room for you in mine, if you're interested in staying with me."

"Oh, you are such a liar," said Aundria, punching him in the chest and knocking him to the floor as the patrons looked on in astonishment.

"It's okay, everyone," Steve said, reassuring the customers. "They always behave that way. It's their way of reconnecting after a long absence."

"Why did you do that?" Adar asked. His eyes flashed at Aundria as he rubbed his chest and started to pant.

"What are you going to do about it?" She placed two fingers in her drink on the bar and flicked the liquid at Adar's face.

"Now you're going to get it," he barked, jumping up from the floor, grabbing Aundria, and throwing her over his shoulder in a fireman's carry. Gripping her thighs tightly, he headed toward the bar's office in the back.

"Just remember who's on top," Aundria grumbled, before hitting Adar in the back and lifting her head to look behind her at the bartender. “Steve, we’re going to need your office for a while.”

“Don’t you two dare tear my place up!” shouted Steve.

“Put it on my tab,” said Adar.

The End

Acknowledgements

First, I would like to thank Morgan Gendel for giving me the idea for writing this book and assisting me with its initial development. I deeply appreciate the time he devoted to the kickoff of the project.

Second, I would like to thank Rose Ragsdale for taking my early draft and helping me turn it into a much more digestible manuscript.

Thanks to Caroline Crnekovic, Chris Bennett, Ming Chow, Sheri Fisher and Valeria Stallman for reviewing my early content. A big thanks to my beta readers Ava Mortier and Kelly G. Harris.

Thanks to Verlene Kelsey-McKee for jumping in at the last minute to proofread my final draft.

Special thanks to Christie Golden and Wil Harris who gave me advice along the way.

I want to thank my good friends Carrie Culley, Euan Grant, Kristi Berry and Ron McKee for their continued inspiration.

A big thanks to my family, friends, and colleagues for their endless support and encouragement as I wrote this book.

Last, but certainly not least, I want to thank my lovely wife Renée who has always been wonderfully supportive of my writing.

www.ingramcontent.com/pod-product-compliance
Lightning Source LLC
Chambersburg PA
CBHW060614310726
48982CB00003B/554

* 9 7 8 0 9 8 8 6 4 3 5 3 6 *